Reapers of the Wind

Reapers of the Wind

A Novel of Argentina

by

Diana Mills

Doubleday Canada Limited, Toronto

First published in Canada 1989 by
Doubleday Canada Limited by arrangement with
SEVERN HOUSE PUBLISHERS LTD, London.
Simultaneously published in the U.S.A. and
Great Britain 1989 by Severn House.

Canadian Cataloguing in Publication Data

Mills, Diana
    Reapers of the wind
ISBN 0–385–25205–6
I. Title
PR6063.I466R42 1989   823′.914   C88–095230–X

Published in Canada by
Doubleday Canada Limited
105 Bond Street
Toronto, Ontario
M5B 1Y3

Printed and bound in Great Britain
at the University Printing House, Oxford

To My Daughters
With Love

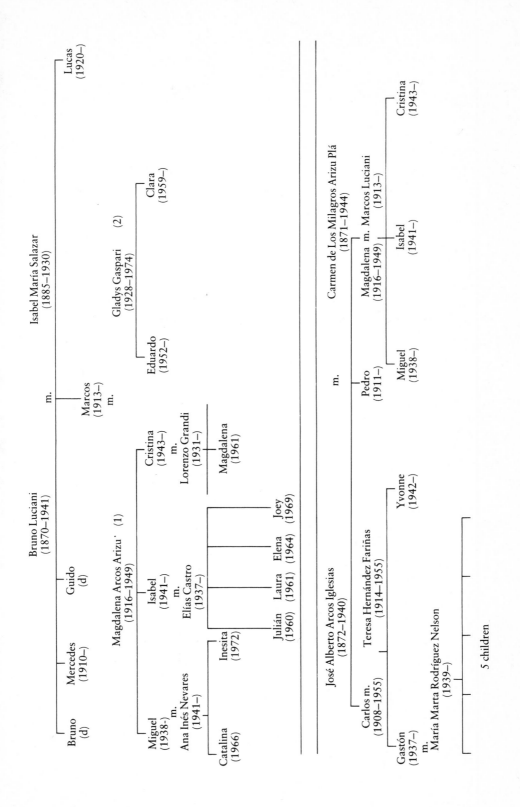

BOLIVIA

PARAGUAY

BRAZIL

ARGENTINA

URUGUAY

BUENOS
AIRES

RÍO DE LA PLATA

LA
CATALINA

EL
REMANSO

CHILE

LOS TOROS

MAR DEL PLATA

ATLANTIC OCEAN

LAKE
DISTRICT

N

W — E

S

AUTHOR'S NOTE

There is an old legend that when Mandinga the Devil saw Paradise he decided to go one better and created Argentina: a masterpiece of Nature.

It is a land of exotic rainforests rooted in rich, red soil and snow-headed mountains that nearly touch the sun. A land of stark moonscapes and long, windswept beaches. Dark, brooding forests, emerald lakes and amber streams. A land of desert and swamp and crystal blue ice-fields — but above all it is the land of the pampa.

That endless, solitary ocean of grass melting into the horizon under a cloudless sky.

Old Mandinga knew what he was doing.

Of the country's approximately thirty million inhabitants, nearly twelve million live in and around the federal capital of Buenos Aires on the banks of the Río de la Plata.

The inhabitants of Buenos Aires are called *porteños,* which means port-dwellers. They are an arrogant, witty and extremely clever lot. It is their unshakable conviction that Argentina begins and ends within the city limits. During the early years of Argentine history the gulf between capital city and provinces was often marked by bloody rivalry; today politics substitutes for bloodshed, but the gulf is still there.

Argentine politics is one of the Devil's favourite pastimes. It has always been a bitter tug-of-war between civilian and military governments, with the man in the street invariably getting the rough end of the rope. Today Argentina is still trying to come to terms with itself. Humiliation over the Falklands conflict, economic bankruptcy and chronic inflation, fierce political rivalries and restless generals — all make for a potentially explosive situation.

The outcome is anyone's guess and the Devil's secret.

This book is not a political novel: it is the story of a family caught up in the turmoil of turbulent years. The characters and incidents — with the exception of the historical ones — are fictitious.

The memories of the land are my own.

Diana Mills – England 1988

PART I

1951

'For they have sown the wind and they shall reap the whirlwind; it hath no stalk, the bud shall yield no meal . . .

(Hosea 8:7)

CHAPTER ONE

I

So this was Argentina.

Angela Morgan gazed out of the car window at the vast expanse of grassland rippling under a clear autumn sky.

'Well, what do you think of the wild pampa, angel?' asked her husband.

'There's quite a bit of it,' she replied uncertainly.

Jimmy Morgan laughed. His right hand left the steering wheel a moment to pat her thigh.

'Nothing like dear old England, eh?'

Certainly nothing like dear old England. She had expected to find more space, but not even in her wildest dreams did Angela imagine there would be so much. The pampa seemed to run on forever; over five hundred miles of it since they had left Buenos Aires yesterday and still no sign of their destination. Her eyes followed the dusty road as it snaked ahead of them and disappeared over the horizon. *O to be in England* . . . No, that wasn't fair. She was in Argentina now and this was her new life. No need to panic because everything felt so strange. It took time to get used to a new life and a new husband; time to get used to so much space.

Angela clung to the seat as the car jolted over a series of potholes. So much space was indecent. It made her feel naked and too damned vulnerable.

Near Buenos Aires the landscape had been more compact and much greener — a closely knit pattern of farms and fields and herds of grazing cattle. Villages flashed by at irregular intervals. Squat mudbrick houses daubed with plaster, dusty streets, plane trees straggling in ragged borders. A pink stucco church. Blue and white petrol pumps under corrugated zinc roofs. Walls splashed with political slogans. *Viva Perón*! Children fished on a river bank, dark-haired women gossiped over their shopping baskets. A milk cart drawn by a sway-backed roan clattered along the road, oblivious to the oncoming car.

Pleasant, fertile countryside. There had been nothing in it to prepare her for the immensity of what lay ahead.

Further west the land opened up and became drier. There were few houses, the distance between villages dragged on endlessly. The poetry of the landscape harped on one monotonous theme. Cattle and grass, grass and sky, sky and cattle. The sun set in a flood of saffron and scarlet, a startled partridge whirred across the road.

Jimmy stopped the car and they sat for a long time listening to night's unearthly silence fill the shadows. He put his arm around Angela and kissed her. High above the pampa, stars spangled the darkness like diamonds.

'Happy, angel?'

'Are you?'

'Yes,' he whispered against her lips. 'Oh God, yes! My wonderful, wonderful angel.'

They kissed again. 'When do we eat, Mr Morgan?' murmured Angela. 'I'm getting hungry.'

Jimmy nibbled her ear. 'Sugar angel.' He nibbled a bit more and then laughed. 'Tell you the truth, so am I. We'll save the hot stuff for later. The next town's about twenty miles away. A one-horse dump called Williams, but the hotel's pretty decent.' He gave her ear one final, eager nibble before starting up the car. 'A couple of steaks, a bottle of wine and a cuddle in bed – how's that for Paradise, old girl?'

Angela laughed. 'It sounds heavenly.'

They were going to be very happy together. She mustn't panic. One had to give happiness time.

II

Their night in Williams turned out to be anything but heavenly. The hotel bed was hard, the bathroom urgently needed steel wool and carbolic, the drinking water looked dubious. Even the steaks were tough. Jimmy took it all in his stride and joked boisterously with the landlord. Angela huddled on the edge of the mattress and tried not to think about the cockroaches she had seen running along the floor.

Perhaps Aunt Win had been right after all.

4

Dear, blustery Aunt Win who was not really an aunt but her mother's best friend and the only remaining link with the happy days of Willow Hill. Her hearty voice formed an uneasy background to Angela's thoughts as she lay awake in the hard bed while Jimmy, satisfied by his cuddle, snored gently.

'Are you sure you know what you're doing?'

Darkness echoed the memory of Angela's confident reply. 'I'm marrying Jimmy Morgan and going back to Argentina with him. What's wrong with that?'

'You've only known the man three weeks.'

'Three weeks or three thousand years — does it really matter how long you know someone? Jimmy's all right. You mustn't worry about me. Please.'

Aunt Win had brushed cigarette ash off her broad, tweed-encased bosom. 'Mustn't worry's no use, my girl. I'm all you have left in the world and I do worry — even if you are old enough to know your own mind. I'm not saying Jimmy Morgan's not a pleasant chap and Lord knows a ranch in Argentina must be a good business. It's just that . . .' the prominent blue eyes had studied Angela shrewdly for a very uncomfortable moment. 'What about Anthony? You two have been seeing each other for quite some time now. I rather thought you would get married one of these days.'

It had been impossible to explain to Aunt Win, who always saw things so sensibly. Angela stirred uneasily on the uneven mattress and wondered if the scrabbling noise in the corner was a rat. Perhaps she could not even explain to herself what had happened. Life with Anthony in a cottage near Cambridge had seemed to be an acceptable alternative to loneliness — until Jimmy Morgan had come along.

Stocky, exuberant Jimmy, with his sun-bleached hair and ruddy tan; his booming laughter and the twinkling glint of mischief in his blue eyes; his fascinating tales about life on the pampa.

Scholarly, pale-skinned Anthony Hobson had fared badly by comparison.

Angela punched down a lump in her pillow. Aunt Win had disapproved of comparisons, but it was too late for disapproval. Certainly too late to make her understand about England or Angela's sense of bleakness and dissatisfaction. Her parents were dead. The childhood sweetheart she had married was dead. The old familiar way of life was dead. One of these days blustery, sensible Aunt Win would die as well. She didn't want to wait for that day to arrive – not even in a rose-covered cottage on the Cam.

A new life in an exotic, unknown land – that was what Angela ached for with intense, constant hunger. She desperately needed a new beginning. How could she possibly have resisted Jimmy Morgan's stammered marriage proposal, characteristically delivered in the midst of a traffic jam in Piccadilly Circus?

'The pampa's a great place, angel. I'd like you to come out there with me. M-married, you know. How about it?'

She had said 'Yes!' as Jimmy plunged them both into a suicidal space between two buses. When they reached the opposite side of the street she had said 'Yes!' again and he had kissed her until they were both breathless. In the noisy, whirling madness of Piccadilly Circus their laughter and exhilaration had filled the future with rainbows.

III

They breakfasted at five a.m. on strong black coffee, freshly baked bread and a shot of peach brandy that nearly stripped Angela's throat. By seven o'clock unromantic Williams lay far behind, but the landscape remained unchanged.

Angela sighed. More grass. More sky. An occasional thicket of trees with strange-sounding names. Jimmy pronounced them for her. '*Chañar.*'

'Chan-yaar,' repeated Angela dutifully.

He laughed. 'Try *Algarrobo*. That's a carob tree.'

'All-gah-raw-bow.'

Jimmy shook his head. '*Algarrobo*,' he corrected, rolling his r's impressively. Angela gave up. A sudden treacherous surge of homesickness for England's familiar hedgerows and neatly chequered countryside swept over her in a wave of almost physical pain.

Jimmy grinned. 'Everything okay, angel?'

'Yes, of course.' Did that sound too abrupt? She took hold of his hand and gave it a guilty squeeze. 'How much longer before we reach your friend's ranch?'

6

He indicated a large, twisted carob tree further down the road. 'La Catalina starts there. The house isn't far off.'

'I don't see anything.'

'Twenty minutes and we'll be there.' They drove a few more miles in silence before Jimmy added, 'You're sure you don't mind spending Easter weekend with Marcos and his family?'

Jimmy and Marcos Luciani had been friends for many years. It was Marcos, he told Angela, who had given him a helping hand when he decided to buy a small ranch near La Catalina. Easter weekends with the Luciani family were a highlight of Jimmy's calendar; he looked forward to them with the same eager anticipation of a child waiting for Christmas.

'The Lucianis are like my second family,' he explained. 'Fantastic people. I can hardly wait for you to meet them.'

The Angela who had laughingly accepted Jimmy's proposal in the middle of Piccadilly Circus would have been thrilled at the prospect of meeting Jimmy's friends. The Angela who lay awake doubting in a flea-bitten hotel room longed to take refuge in her own home. She needed to establish familiarity with her new surroundings and work out a routine that would help recover certainty. Strangers - and foreigners to boot - were the last thing she wanted to face. They probably didn't speak English and her guidebook Spanish couldn't possibly cope with the situation. On the other hand Jimmy seemed so eager she didn't have the heart to disappoint him.

'Your friends sound like great fun,' she replied and wondered if that sounded too anxious to please.

The carob tree slipped behind as the road veered sharply left and dipped to cross a dry stream. A distant windmill flashed aluminium blades in the sunshine, a reaper moved steadily through a cornfield. A herd of cattle raised white faces to watch the car drive past and Angela smiled at their startled curiosity.

'Which side of the road is La Catalina?' she asked.

Jimmy made a sweeping movement with his arm. 'Both sides as far as you can see and then some. Best land in the province. It's got everything. Good water, good soil, good pasture - hell, Marcos could even make stones sprout if he planted them!' He swerved the car to avoid a clump of russet tumbleweed that had encroached on the road. 'Marcos has a thing about La Catalina, you know. Not just pride of ownership. He's literally in love with this place. It's his lifeblood, his soul – you might say even his god. Every tree, every blade of grass, every goddamned steer means as much to him as his own children do. The man doesn't have a heart, he's got twenty-four thousand acres of ranchland thumping in his chest. I'm not too sure he doesn't have earth instead of blood running through his veins as well.'

Another windmill appeared. The grassland on the right side of the road gave way to sorghum; on the left a double row of eucalyptus trees formed the long, curving border of a thickly wooded park. The car turned left and stopped before a large white gate with LA CATALINA painted on it in bold black letters. An elaborate L enclosed in a circle hung above the gate, suspended by chains from two white posts. Both the device and the chains were made from wrought-iron – solid, imposing reminders that beyond them lay the core of the cattleman's kingdom. Angela began to panic again. At various points during the past few days Jimmy had explained the Luciani family set-up, but for the life of her she couldn't remember what he had said.

'Help!' She clutched at his arm. 'What's your friend Marcos's wife's name?'

'Magdalena, but she died a couple of years ago. Didn't I tell you? She used to do a lot of riding in Buenos Aires – show jumping, that sort of thing. Her horse bolted on the way back to the stable one morning and threw her on to the cobblestones. Gave her a terrific knock on the head. She died without regaining consciousness. Marcos was here at the ranch when it happened. He was devastated. Terrible tragedy . . . I did tell you, angel! Remember?'

'I can't remember, Jimmy! All these names and people are so confusing.'

He laughed. 'Relax, it's not that bad. Marcos Luciani owns this place and lives here most of the time. His older sister Mercedes has been keeping house and looking after the kids since the wife died. Three kids: a boy and two girls. They live in BA with Mercedes during school term and come out for the holidays. Old Mercedes is a good sort – a very proper spinster and inclined to fuss, but she means well. Then,' Jimmy produced a suitably lecherous leer, 'there's Marcos's younger brother Lucas. He's pure poison. I won't let you near him. Now, Magdalena's family . . .'

'Stop!' groaned Angela. 'This is worse than a Russian novel. I'm going to need a printed cast of characters to get all these people straight.'

Jimmy patted her on the back. 'Buck up, old girl. I'll spare you the gory details, but Magdalena's family is very much in the picture. Blood and money are a hell of a lot thicker than water in this clan.'

He fidgeted with the car keys, his eyes fixed on the L above the gate. No M at Los Alamos. Not much of a gate, either. What would Angela think of Los Alamos after this? A piddling sandlot after the Garden of Eden. Maybe she would hate it. Maybe he wouldn't be able to make her understand that eight thousand acres of stubborn earth meant as much to him as La Catalina meant to Marcos. Jimmy sighed. He had had to fight for Los Alamos every inch of the way.

'Look, angel . . .' His voice grated anxiously. 'Don't expect Los Alamos to be another La Catalina, old girl. It isn't – not by a long shot.' He tried to make a joke of comparisons. 'This place is five-star deluxe with all the trimmings. We're not even in the cheap guidebooks. No, I'm serious,' as she laughed. 'The house at Los Alamos has lousy plumbing and we use paraffin lamps. The roof leaks in winter.' He took hold of her hand and frowned uneasily at the plain gold wedding band on her fourth finger. 'Maybe you should have stayed with my parents in Buenos Aires until I had a chance to fix everything for you.'

'For better or worse includes bad plumbing and leaky roofs,' replied Angela lightly. 'I didn't want to stay in Buenos Aires until you fixed up everything for me.'

'You're not sorry it's Mad Jimmy Morgan in the wilds of the pampa instead of a respectable, pipe-smoking professor in dear old England?'

Angela kissed him. 'Don't be silly.'

He grinned and went to open the gate.

A sudden gust of wind shook the eucalyptus trees, turning their blue-grey leaves to the sun. Angela caught her breath. In the morning's clear luminous light every detail stood stencilled against a cobalt blue sky: the swaying branches, the leaves shining like silver, the long sweeping line of sun-drenched fields melting into the horizon. She was very quiet as the car entered the park beyond the gate. Pine and eucalyptus formed an incongruous forest on either side of the drive, crowded cheek by jowl with clumps of dark hemlock and feathery pepper trees. Somewhere in the heart of the forest a dove murmured wistfully; otherwise the park was still. Even the sound of the car seemed muted. Sunlight sifted shimmering dust-streams through the trees and pooled amber shadows in the thick grass; the air coming through the open window smelled of resin and burning leaves. Angela's heart began to beat with a strangely urgent sense of excitement.

'There it is,' said Jimmy as they drove out from the trees and circled a smooth green lawn. 'There's La Catalina.'

She saw a large, sprawling ranch house set among acacias and salmon-coloured oleanders. The white stucco walls were spotless, the red tiles on the roof gleamed in the sunshine. Tubs of geraniums splashed vivid patches of scarlet and mauve along the wide veranda; hanging baskets of curling ferns swayed gently in the breeze. Half a dozen deck chairs were scattered in a haphazard circle on the lawn. Angela noted with amusement that one of them had been heaped with a jumbled assortment of polo sticks, croquet mallets, dolls and a huge tortoise-shell cat. She smiled faintly at the wrought-iron L anchored proudly on the wall above the front door. The cattleman's castle looked solid and enduring; a comfortable stronghold, capable of weathering the fiercest of storms.

It was uncanny, she reflected, how at first sight a stranger's home could inspire such a warm, almost magical sensation of welcome.

CHAPTER TWO

I

La Catalina had been awake since dawn.

In the field marked number nineteen on the map in Marcos Luciani's study half a dozen sweating, shouting horsemen urged a herd of Black Angus steers towards the cattle pens a quarter of a mile down the road.

'*Vamos, negrito!*'

Their cries were swallowed up in clouds of dust. A burly, moustached rider thrust his horse into the middle of the herd and slapped a few rumps with his short, flat-tongued whip. The steers rolled their eyes and jostled forward, bellowing dismally. The man blew out his lips with a curious put-putting sound to encourage them on.

'Watch out!'

The warning crackled sharply as a large steer bolted for a nearby thicket; a moment later a small girl on a sturdy bay galloped after it. The girl shrilled in hoarse imitation the men's cries and whirled her whip around her head.

'*Hui! Vamos, negrito!*'

The steer snorted and veered to the right, the bay swerved to cut it off. Two more riders appeared through the brush, blocking escape. The steer doubled back and collided with the bay. It lowed in protest as the girl's whip thumped across its back. Another hard thump. The rebel surrendered with a final, outraged bellow and trotted meekly back to join the rest of the herd.

'Lucky for us someone's got sharp eyes,' grinned one of the riders.

His companion chuckled. 'She's a Luciani all right. A chip off the old block – ain't that right, *niña* Isabel?'

Isabel's dark eyes sparkled. The men never called her brother Miguel a chip off the old block – even if he was thirteen and Papa's only son. Miguel showed little interest in La Catalina and even less in following his father's footsteps. Whenever

11

Isabel reminded him how lucky he was to be a cattleman's son he shrugged off his luck and jeered.

'Who wants to spend his life rotting on this stupid ranch?'

Isabel found Miguel's indifference difficult to understand. La Catalina was an enchanted world and its large, rambling, white ranch house the only place worth living in. She much preferred it to the family townhouse at Barranco Rosales in Buenos Aires, which Miss Nelly the governess claimed was one of the finest in the city.

'And I've seen many in my time,' she would affirm in her dry, precise voice. 'Your father's house is as fine as any gentleman's place in England.'

Twenty years in Argentina had not blunted Miss Nelly's memories, but her descriptions of English life sounded unbelievably tame to Isabel. On the other hand, even life at Barranco Rosales was dull when compared with her beloved La Catalina. Nothing but school and lessons succeeding each other in a monotonous chain that grown-ups for some reason insisted on calling education.

Barranco Rosales was rosewood and porcelain and the musty smell of *pot pourri* clinging to damask curtains, but La Catalina was rawhide and pampa grass and the unbridled song of the wind.

In Barranco Rosales the nursery was decorated with flowered wallpaper, the bedspreads were quilted satin. Miss Nelly reigned supreme and made life very difficult with her English ideas on routine and tidiness. At La Catalina there was no nursery and Miss Nelly's ideas fought a losing battle. Rough woollen blankets covered the beds, the brass bedsteads creaked, the bedside rug was a wildcat complete with bared fangs and green glass eyes. On cold winter mornings the pot-bellied stove in the corner of the bedroom gave off a cosy orange glow; in the summer the breeze blowing through the open windows smelled of freshly mown grass and oleanders.

Very early on Sunday mornings Isabel and her younger sister Cristina would pad along to their father's room and curl up under the soft, furry rug on his bed while he told them the story of Grandfather Bruno and La Catalina.

At the turn of the century Bruno Luciani left his native Italy and sailed to Argentina – one of the many thousands of immigrants drawn to the New World in the hope of making their fortune. His father Antonio, who owned a pottery factory near Venice, took it for granted that Bruno would enter the family business. Bruno – a strapping, dark-eyed twenty-year-old – had other ideas. A friend of his who emigrated to Argentina wrote back enthusiastically about the country's unlimited opportunities. Bruno read and re-read the letter until he knew it by heart. The next day he announced that he wanted to travel to Argentina, where fortunes could be had for the asking. The potter's wheel, he added scornfully, was not for him.

Antonio Luciani turned purple and threatened to kill his son if he took one step beyond the front door. Bruno waited until midnight. Then, with his mother's tearful farewell sighing in his ears and her life-savings wrapped up in a bright blue kerchief, he fled to Genoa. Two weeks later he boarded the *Amerigo Vespucci*, bound for Buenos Aires.

He never saw or heard from his family again.

In Buenos Aires Bruno found a job as a dock worker. The hours were long, the wages miserly and the work backbreaking, but he was determined to stick it out until he saved up enough to buy a plot of land. The struggle lasted for nearly a year before an English cattleman named William Bryce crossed his path.

A dockside brawl, a knife, and Bruno's shout of warning brought them together. Bryce owed his life to that shout; when it was all over he sized up the young Italian and offered him a job on his ranch. He never regretted his decision. Four years later, having neither wife nor children to succeed him, William Bryce made Bruno Luciani his sole heir.

'And then a horse called Sancho kicked *el inglés* in the head and he died,' Isabel would invariably interrupt at this point. 'And Grandfather married Grandmother Isabel. Her father was Don Basualdo Salazar and his ranch used to be the other side of the lake where we go duck hunting. It's ours now because Grandmother was Don Basualdo's only child. He died when Aunt Mercedes was born. Rosario says that's 1910 because she came to work for Grandmother then. Aunt Mercedes is almost as old as Rosario, isn't she?'

Marcos laughed. 'Your aunt's only a few years older than I am, *ñatita* – and Rosario could be my grandmother.'

Isabel and Cristina both shook their heads. 'Oh, no! Aunt Mercedes is *old*. She has grey hair and wrinkles.'

'Mama's family's been Argentine longer than us,' chirped

Cristina. 'Much, much longer. Miguel says they poured boiling oil on the English during the Invasions.'

'Eighteen-six to eighteen-seven,' chanted Isabel with all the aplomb of a world-weary scholar. 'We learned that at school. All about the gauchos and the brave women of Buenos Aires and the glorious twelfth of August.'

Cristina plucked at a clump of tawny fur. 'I wish Mama hadn't gone to Heaven with the angels. She could tell us about the viceroys.'

There was an awkward silence.

'I wish she hadn't gone to Heaven too,' said Marcos in a curiously empty voice. 'I miss Mama very much.'

The girls nestled against him. Mama was already beginning to fade into distant memory in spite of missing her. A beautiful, somewhat remote woman who preferred Barranco Rosales to La Catalina . . .

II

Isabel shaded her eyes against the sun and studied the cattle pen. 'There's Papa!' She pointed excitedly to a battered green pickup truck parked in the shade of a carob tree. 'He's arrived before us!'

The riders started after the herd. 'Those steers'll give trouble when we fence them,' they called over their shoulders. 'You stay out of the way, *niña.*'

She kicked the bay into a gallop and raced down the road, shrilling gleefully: '*Hui, negrito!*'

No time to waste if there was trouble to be tackled. Isabel stood up in her stirrups and lifted her face to the sun. The world was green and gold and blue and wonderful. It belonged to her and she could make it do whatever she wanted.

At ten she could make the world go on forever.

III

Marcos Luciani leaned against the cattle pen's high wooden railing and reached for a cigarette – his sixth since breakfast.

14

He was a tall, dark-haired man in his late thirties, broad-shouldered and with a determined set to his strong, arrogant features. As he struck a match to the cigarette his eyes studied the approaching herd of cattle, but his thoughts were not on beef and uncertain market prices. He was thinking about his son.

Thirteen-year-old Miguel was not living up to his father's expectations; he was, in fact, an increasingly irritating source of trouble. Last year he had been suspended twice from school. This school year was only a few weeks old and there had already been one note of warning from the headmaster. Marcos decided to put Miguel to work on La Catalina during the Easter holiday. There was nothing like sweat and tired muscles to knock sense into rebellious heads; besides, it was time the boy started taking an active interest in the land of his heritage. Miguel didn't want to sweat on the ranch; he wanted to go camping. He began to butter up his aunt. Mercedes, who had a soft spot for her handsome young nephew, capitulated at once.

'The boy's been studying so hard,' she explained when Marcos demanded to know why Miguel had not come out to La Catalina with the rest of the family. 'He's run down. A change of air will do him good.'

'He can get all the change of air he needs out here!' retorted Miguel's irate father. 'When I was his age I worked my goddamned ass off with the rest of the ranch hands *and* I studied as well.'

Mercedes eyed her brother with a patient smile. 'That was all very well for you, but Miguel's different.'

'What the hell's different about him? He's my son!'

'You don't understand that boy. He needs to be handled tactfully, not bullied. I know he's naughty some times,' as Marcos opened his mouth to interrupt, 'but it's just his high spirits. You were a handful at his age, you know. I remember how poor Papa used to complain. Like the time the parish priest came to tea and you nailed his cassock to the floor.'

'Oh, for God's sake!' snorted Marcos in disgust. 'I was only seven. Besides, that doesn't have anything to do with Miguel.'

'It most certainly does,' countered Mercedes triumphantly. 'He's your son.'

The arrival of the herd broke into Marcos's thoughts. His dark eyes narrowed appraisingly as he watched the steers crowd into the pen. Fine, healthy cattle. La Catalina never let him down.

He caught sight of Isabel and grinned. Her small tanned face was streaked with dirt, her blouse stuck to her back; her hoarse cries could hardly be heard above the din. She flapped her reins and waved. Marcos waved back, enjoying her happiness.

Pablo Losa, the ranch manager, came up. 'Isabel's a real *gauchita*, Don Marcos,' he remarked. His brown eyes twinkled as he watched girl and horse charge a stubborn steer. 'Too bad she's not a boy. Miguel can't handle cattle half as well.'

Marcos grunted and started towards the weighing shed on the far side of the pen. The less said about Miguel right now the better.

Isabel tied her horse to a tree and ran after him. 'Wait for me, Papa!' She clambered on to the shed's narrow platform and peered over the siding at a steer being prodded on to the scales. The animal kicked the wooden slats; it rolled frightened eyes and lunged at the gate barring escape. Isabel clapped her hands excitedly.

'I can hold him!' She leaned over and grabbed the steer's tail. '*Quieto, negrito.*'

The steer let out an indignant bellow and a thin brown stream exploded from under its uplifted tail, spattering Isabel's face.

'Hey, *ñatita*! What are you doing to my cattle?' called out Marcos as the men on the platform laughed. He wiped her face clean with his handkerchief. 'Keep out of mischief, Bela. We've got work to do.'

'I want to help.' She hugged Marcos and rubbed her cheek against the soft checked material of his shirt.

'Please, Papa – let me help.'

It was very difficult to resist Isabel's sparkling eyes or her coaxing smile. She was by far his favourite. The only one of his three children who shared his love for La Catalina. The only one who understood his passion for the land. Even Magdalena had never really understood him. Land for her was merely a means to wealth and social position; she viewed his passionate attachment to La Catalina as an eccentric, even neurotic fixation. Maybe it was – so what? The ranch was the foundation of his dreams and the wellspring of his strength. Marcos smiled down at the only one of his blood to understand.

'You can help us later, when the steers have calmed down,' he said, kissing the tip of Isabel's nose.

16

She hugged him again and sat back on her heels. A cluster of gnats buzzed lazily overhead, a horse whinnied softly in the shade. The morning smelled of cattle and warm, fresh earth. The men's voices flowed above her with a low, steady drone. Isabel closed her eyes and hummed happily to herself. The world was a wonderful place.

IV

Halfway through the morning a pale blue Ford pulled up under the carob tree and a stocky man with sun-bleached hair jumped out.

'Looks like Don Jimmy,' remarked Pablo Losa.

A woman alighted from the car and stood shading her eyes against the morning's brightness; after a moment she said something and the man laughed. He pointed towards the shed and urged her along, still laughing and gesticulating with his right hand.

Marcos grinned as he hurried over to greet them. It was Jimmy Morgan, all right. The woman must be his wife. His grin broadened as he recalled Jimmy's only letter from England where he had gone on a business trip. The letter was short on business and long on some woman named Angela. His enthusiastic praises of her had covered six pages.

She's made a new man out of me! Reformed the old bachelor . . . Tamed el loco Morgan . . . Mad Jimmy Morgan's no more, amigo . . . this woman's an angel! Wait until you meet her . . .

In 1944 Jimmy Morgan resigned from a comfortable job with the family firm in Buenos Aires and bought a small ranch just north of La Catalina. The ranch's previous owner had committed suicide after going bankrupt; his heirs were anxious to sell for whatever price they could get. Jimmy's father counselled against the venture, but he might just as well have saved his breath. Anglo-Argentine society, with its staid conventions and stubborn adherence to outmoded ways, was not Jimmy Morgan's idea of living. He needed fresh air to clear out the cobwebs and a challenge to whet his brain, he told his exasperated parents.

'I don't give a damn about your Hurlingham Club or your Saturday afternoon cricket or God Save the King! I was born in Argentina and Argentina suits me. Los Alamos is my little plot of God's earth and by God I'm going to put it back on its feet!'

So Jimmy Morgan went 'native' and the Anglos clucked their tongues on Hurlingham's well-manicured lawns. He laughed at their clucking and settled down to make good his promise. By 1951 Los Alamos was back on its feet, but the Morgans never forgave him for mocking their sacred cows.

Marcos, who knew all about sacred cows and sympathized with Jimmy, found it surprising that he should have married an Englishwoman. Not that he begrudged him his choice of wife. It was good to see *el loco* Morgan happy, but he couldn't help wondering whether the 'angel' would share her husband's enthusiasm for the land.

The two men met by the watering trough and embraced latino fashion, with much laughter and thumping of backs. The 'angel' hovered uncertainly in the background. Marcos studied her curiously. She was quite tall and slender – certainly a decided change from Jimmy's usual taste in women. An interesting rather than a pretty face, framed by a thick flaxen bob. High brow and cheekbones, large eyes fringed with dark lashes, a generous mouth. She wore no makeup and very little jewellery; her gabardine skirt was well cut, her jumper an unusual shade of lavender blue. He noticed that the jumper matched her eyes.

'Here she is!' boomed Jimmy. 'Angela, my love – meet Marcos Luciani. One of the finest chaps I know. Even Father likes him. Marcos . . .' He thrust the woman forward with a proud, possessive gesture. 'This is Angela.'

They shook hands and smiled politely at each other.

'Welcome to La Catalina,' said Marcos in heavily accented English. 'Please forgive how badly I speak English. I learned it in school, but I have forgotten much already.'

Angela laughed. 'It's certainly better than my Spanish. I spent two weeks in Seville last year and now Jimmy tells me the words are all wrong.'

'A matter of propriety, my sweet,' chuckled Jimmy. 'The Spanish use words you just cannot say in Argentina and vice versa. Never mind, you'll sort it all out soon enough.'

Isabel raced up, her dark braids flying. '*Tío* Jimmy!' She flung her arms around Morgan's neck. 'Papa said you were coming tomorrow. Miguel and Cousin Gastón went camping down south . . .'

She broke off and studied Angela with dark, appraising eyes.

Jimmy laughed. 'Show Angela how well you speak English, Isabel. Don't want to put Miss Nelly to shame, eh?'

Isabel pulled a face and planted a dutiful kiss on Angela's cheek. 'Hello.'

'Hello, Isabel.'

The dark, appraising eyes continued to scrutinize; after a moment Isabel grinned. 'Would you like to see my horse?'

'Yes, of course I would.'

'He's called Emir. Papa broke him in for me last year. Papa's horse is Sandokán. He won't let anyone ride him except Papa. My brother tried to and Sandokán threw him. Can you ride?'

Angela smiled faintly at the memory of Aunt Win's horses and her boisterous riding lessons on summer holidays. It all seemed so very long ago.

'I rode in England,' she replied. 'A friend of my mother's owned a stable. When I was your age I used to go there for school holidays. Riding's a bit different out here, isn't it? You'll have to show me.'

The two men watched them walk towards Emir, who was dozing in the shade of a carob tree. Jimmy stubbed at the ground with the tip of his boot. The silence suddenly became awkward.

'You don't mind that we came a day early, do you?' he asked finally. 'We arrived in BA on Sunday and spent two days with my parents. Sheer hell, old boy. They started on Angela the minute we walked in the front door. All about what a dreary backwater Los Alamos is and how brave of her to come out here. How we must buy a flat in BA so she can go down when things get rough. Father did his pink gin, Colonel Blimp bit and mother spouted on about the book club, the garden club, the bridge club – God, what a bloody rotten performance! They plagued Angela with questions about her family and the war. She lost her folks in the Blitz and her first husband at Dunkirk, you know. Nasty business. And she did a stint of nursing out in Burma – doesn't want to talk about it.'

'No,' agreed Marcos, 'I don't imagine she would.'

Jimmy shrugged impatiently. 'Daresay my parents are pissed off because we left before breakfast yesterday, but what the hell. I'd had enough. We spent the morning touring BA and then

19

headed out here. By the way, Mercedes gave us coffee when we arrived. She and Angela got along like a house on fire.' He held out his hand as Angela returned with Isabel from patting the unresponsive Emir. 'Come over here, angel.'

Isabel giggled. 'Why do you call her angel?'

'Because she is an angel,' said Jimmy, nibbling Angela's ear. 'My sugar angel. Mmm . . . I could eat her up!'

Angela blushed furiously. 'Jimmy!' She saw Marcos give him an ironic look and felt even more embarrassed. Jimmy's sugar angel act was a bit too much, especially in front of people she had never met before. What on earth would Marcos Luciani think? She darted him a quick, guarded glance. From Jimmy's description she had imagined a large, beefy type with a bushy moustache and swarthy skin. There was nothing beefy or bushy about this man. He was, as the nurses out in Burma used to say, a bloody handsome rouser. Clean shaven and very tanned, with a pair of the darkest eyes she had ever seen. They were looking at her now. Angela's skin prickled and she coloured slightly. An attractive man like Marcos Luciani could turn rocks on with that look.

'Carlos and his family are coming for Easter this year,' said Marcos. 'They're driving up from Los Toros today.'

Jimmy grinned. 'So it's full house, eh? Marcos's brother-in-law and his wife are Carlos and Teresa Arcos Arizu,' he explained to Angela. Double-barrelled name and very Old Guard – aren't they, Marcos? They own a fancy spread three hundred miles southeast of here. Acres of landscaped parkland and a house built like a ruddy French chateau.'

Isabel tugged impatiently at his free hand. 'Come and watch me weigh cattle, *tío* Jimmy. Losa says I do it much better than Miguel. Did you bring me anything from England?'

She dragged him off. There was a brief, uneasy pause. Angela turned to watch a couple of steers butting heads beside the railing and found Marcos studying her. His expression was a mixture of male approval and something else she found difficult to read.

'Do you like Argentina?' he asked.

His voice was deeper than Jimmy's, with a slight drawl to it that did things to Angela's insides. Her heart began to beat again with the same urgent excitement she had felt in the park.

'Yes,' she replied. 'It's a very beautiful country.'

'You do not have like this in England?'

In England there had been the house in Willow Hill. Ivy-covered brick, a flowering almond in the corner of the walled garden, the roses that were her mother's pride and joy. It had taken less than a minute to blitz Willow Hill.

'No,' she said with a trace of bitterness that surprised Marcos. 'There's nothing like this in England.'

They began to walk slowly towards the shed. Each was acutely aware of the other's presence; neither of them knew what to say. Disconnected thoughts passed through Angela's mind. The dark green shirt and baggy grey *bombachas* stuffed into black leather boots that Marcos wore suited him. He had strong, lean hands. No wedding ring. He spoke reasonably fluent English – there was no reason why they shouldn't talk to each other. She tried to think of an intelligent question to ask about the ranch. It was stupid to be tongue-tied just because the man had so much sex-appeal. She was thirty-two years old, she had been around handsome men before. Angela cleared her throat. She could feel Marcos's eyes on her – dark, magnetic eyes compelling her to look at him. She did and he smiled.

'The house of Jimmy's is an old railway station,' he said. 'You know? It is not far from La Catalina. Forty-five minutes if the road is dry, thirty if Jimmy drives. He is *loco* – crazy how he drives.'

'Along with everyone else, it seems,' observed Angela wryly. 'The traffic in Buenos Aires was a nightmare.'

He laughed. 'All people in Argentina want to be big racing drivers. If you need anything for Los Alamos you must ask us. Mercedes will help you. If you need anything from Buenos Aires, tell her. She returns Tuesday with the children.'

'You're very kind. Thank you.'

'It is my pleasure.'

Marcos continued to stare. He had been prepared to like Angela because she was Jimmy's wife – he had not been prepared to like her so much. Everything about her attracted him. He was fascinated by her blue eyes, the clear sound of her voice, the generous curve of her mouth. Her lips were soft and full; he wanted to kiss them. He wanted to hold Angela in his arms and feel her warm body pressed against his own. His wanting passed from thought to sudden, urgent desire; its intensity shook him. He was certainly not immune to the charms of an attractive woman, but no woman had ever caused such an impact on him so quickly. If

21

Angela had not been Jimmy's wife he wouldn't have wasted any time. She *was* Jimmy's wife, Marcos reminded himself. It wasn't going to be easy remembering that one essential detail.

V

Before she met Marcos Luciani, Angela's impression of Argentina had been a jumbled succession of confusing images.

As soon as their ship left England Jimmy had plotted the journey on a map and earnestly launched into detailed explanations about the land of the pampa. All very interesting, but he might just as well have been describing the moon.

Angela's first glimpse of South America had been Brazil, with its palm-fringed beaches and jungle-covered mountains shrouded in early morning mist. When the ship docked at Río de Janeiro they went ashore and spent several hours exploring an exotic, effervescent city steeped to its rooftops in tropical flowers and African culture. Fantastic, bizarre, spellbinding. A land of primeval forests and dark, earth-blooded magic.

A disturbing land, she told herself uneasily and wondered if it was a taste of what lay ahead.

Somewhere around latitude thirty-five south of Brazil they left the Atlantic and entered the Río de la Plata estuary — a vast expanse of tawny water separating Argentina from the Republic of Uruguay.

'The Spanish name for this river means river of silver,' said Jimmy, 'but the water's silver only when the sun shines against it at a certain angle and even then you have to stretch poetic licence. Treacherous little pond. Gentle as a kitten one minute, screeching like a banshee the next. July and August are the worst months. That's midwinter, when the gales whip in from the southeast.' He pointed to the hazy outline of a large city sprawled against the horizon. 'Buenos Aires gets the full brunt. Cold, damp, floods — I wouldn't live in this town for tuppence, but several million masochists do.'

Buenos Aires's European atmosphere astonished Angela.

The beautiful parks and wide, tree-lined avenues could belong to Madrid or Paris or Rome. One shopped at Harrods, sipped an apéritif at a sidewalk café in the elegant Recoleta district and dressed in the latest fashion. There was a pre-war Old World charm to the city which she found unsettling, as though by some freak time warp the clock had moved back a couple of decades to the days before the roof fell in on the civilized world.

Even her in-laws seemed incongruously un-Argentine, though they had lived in Argentina for nearly forty years.

'You mustn't bury Angela in the camp, James. There's nothing for a woman to do out there, no English people for miles around.'

Camp, Angela quickly learned, was the Anglo-Argentine word for countryside – a lazy transliteration of the Spanish *campo*. The Morgan's conversation bristled with similar words, borrowed from a language they seemed to have no interest in speaking properly. It infuriated Jimmy to hear his brothers' ungrammatical Spanish and their habit of referring to England as 'home'.

'Neither one of them's ever been near the place!' he exploded in the safety of his parents' guest room. 'They're trying to keep up some ridiculous colonial myth – damn it, this country wasn't even a British colony!'

'The British settled here, didn't they?' asked Angela.

'They tried to take it twice – once in eighteen-six and then in eighteen-seven. The viceroyalty of the Río de la Plata was part of the Spanish empire and England thought she could do with a good toehold in Spain's belly. The local inhabitants thought differently. They may have been ready to revolt against the Motherland, but they didn't fancy *los ingleses* in exchange. Both expeditions failed. The survivors eventually drifted inland, intermarried with the locals, settled down – that's why you see so many British names around. Of course there were British out here before then, trading in cattle and whatever else they could lay their hands on. Used to be the place to send younger sons to learn all about farming.' He settled back against the pillows and yawned. 'In the last century Argentina looked to Britain for its economy and France for its culture. We're still hamstrung by the ghosts of those ties. Hard for us to find a national identity. Before eighteen-sixty the country was mostly mestizo, Spanish or Italian; then immigration boomed and the melting pot's still churning us around. Spanish, Italian, British, French, German, Russian – you name it, you're bound to find it in some remote corner of the country. Even Sikhs.'

'I thought there would be Indians. Somehow that's what you think of in South America,' said Angela. 'Like the Mexicans.'

Jimmy shook his head. 'Nothing like that down here. This country has the most homogenous white population in South America. What Indians there were got wiped out in the desert campaigns at the end of the last century – or most of them did. The ones you'll find these days live in the Andes region, along the frontier with Chile and Bolivia. Or in Chaco or Formosa. Those are the large provinces bordering on Paraguay in the north. Wild places. Savannas and swamps and jungle. People keep tame snakes as watchdogs up there, you know.'

Angela grimaced. 'Don't care for snakes, thank you.'

'Have to watch out for them on the ranch. There's a nasty little number they call the *coral* and another one with a cross-like marking on its head. Deadly. And poisonous spiders, of course – a large, hairy one the locals call *peluda*.' He laughed at the expression on Angela's face and kissed her. 'You'll love it, angel. Better than the Japanese in Burma any day.'

Even as they drove across mile after mile of monotonous pampa the concept of Argentina as home did not sink in.

VI

The impact came quite suddenly as Angela stood on the platform of the weighing shed at La Catalina.

She saw Marcos Luciani outlined against the vast sweep of land and sky. She heard his voice shouting an order to one of the men. She sensed his restless, almost ruthless vitality. A thought flashed through her mind. *This is the way it should be. This is where I belong.* Marcos glanced around at her and Angela looked quickly away.

She would have to be careful of thoughts like that. She would have to be very careful of Marcos Luciani.

CHAPTER THREE

I

In La Catalina's spacious living-room eight-year-old Cristina Luciani was giving her aunt some practical advice about flower arrangements.

'Why're you putting that there?' she asked critically as Mercedes set a vase of yellow roses on a table beside a deep leather armchair. 'That's Papa's chair. He'll knock it over with his elbow. He always does.'

'The vase looks nice here, Cristina.'

'Papa says it's a damned nuisance.'

Mercedes's eyebrows shot up. Marcos should know better than to use such language in front of the children. 'Don't repeat what your father says. It's not nice.'

'Then why does he say it?' demanded Cristina. She hopped up and down in front of the large brick fireplace. 'Rosario says the codfish you bought for lunch tomorrow's as tough as nails. She's been soaking it forever, she says. Why do we have to have codfish tomorrow?'

'Because tomorrow's Good Friday. We always eat codfish on Good Friday.'

Cristina pulled a face. 'Well, I hate it,' she retorted defiantly and went off in search of an apple.

Mercedes mopped a few spots of water from the table and glanced around. Despite heavy beams and dark panelling the living-room looked very cheerful in the morning sunlight. She only wished Marcos would let her cover the floor with persian rugs instead of cowhides. The new sofa in front of the fireplace was definitely an improvement; its vivid red-and-yellow pattern, repeated in the curtains at the windows, added a much needed touch of colour. Marcos hadn't said anything about the sofa, but he had stubbornly refused to re-upholster the other furniture. The smooth shiny leather, worn over the years to a rich tobacco brown, was as much a part of La Catalina as were the

25

old-fashioned bookcases crammed with dog-eared paperbacks and a deluxe edition of the gaucho epic *Martin Fierro* bound in black-and-white cowhide. A huge photograph of a grand champion bull hung over the fireplace, rows of other champions and grand champions covered the walls. Several colourful landscapes broke the monotony of cattle dripping rosettes, but the main theme remained the same. Every single one depicted a view of La Catalina and even Magdalena had despaired of getting Marcos to change them.

Mercedes darted an anxious glance at a closed door on the far side of the living-room. Beyond it lay the ranch manager's office, with its battered roll-top desk and unwieldy typewriter holding pride of place under an impressive display of charts, maps and more rows of prize-winning cattle. She would have liked to put some flowers on the bookshelf under the full-length portrait of her father that hung above the manager's desk, but the office, like Marcos's study and the gun-room at the other end of the house, was strictly a masculine stronghold. Feminine frills and flowers were unthinkable, and the women of the household were admitted on sufferance.

The large, airy dining-room, reached through double doors from the living-room, was a compromise between Marcos's passion for La Catalina and the determination of the women in his family to have their way. The windows gave on to a wide black-and-white tiled patio filled with flowering plants in gaily painted tubs and hanging baskets. Inside the dining-room landscapes of the ranch grudgingly shared wall space with several of Gualberti's famous floral paintings and a graceful *Madonna of the Candles* by a little-known Venetian artist. The furniture might be dark and heavy, but the curtains were a soft mossy green and the huge bowl of Murano glass on the sideboard was permanently filled with an artificial flower arrangement that was one of Mercedes's more ambitious creations.

The living-room clock chimed ten. More than half the morning had already gone by; there was still so much to do. Mercedes ticked off details in her mind as she hurried off to the bedrooms. A bowl of fruit in Carlos and Teresa's room. A box of chocolates for Jimmy and Angela. She hoped Angela would be happy with Jimmy. He needed a nice wife. Mercedes gave a dissatisfied little cluck. She must remember to get out extra blankets for the guests arriving tomorrow. It was really quite surprising of Marcos to

26

invite a business acquaintance for Easter. Granted they must have things to discuss, but even so . . . Her mind passed on to more important matters. Easter eggs for the children. Light the candle in front of the Virgin's statue on Pedro's beside table. It was so comforting to have a priest in the family, and Magdalena's brother Pedro was very much a man of God.

God was very much a part of Mercedes's life.

At eighteen, much to her father's disgust, she had fallen in love with a penniless young medical student. Bruno Luciani promptly forbade the match, told Mercedes the student only wanted her inheritance and kept her safely at La Catalina until the storm blew over. It did so in a few weeks. The discouraged suitor backed away from such formidable opposition and consoled himself with less ambitious prospects. Brokenhearted, Mercedes turned to embroidery and religion.

Had her mother lived longer both distractions might have soon faded into proper perspective, but by then Isabel Luciani was too ill to be of any comfort to her daughter. Mercedes, left to her own devices, continued to embroider neat bunches of rosebuds and pray. She nursed her mother through the last two years of illness. When Isabel died there was ten-year-old Lucas to look after and her father's house to run. Convinced by now that spinsterhood was God's plan for her and she must accept it with patient resignation, Mercedes settled into a routine that was to become the pattern of her life.

Bruno Luciani died in 1941 after years of ill health; by then Mercedes was in her early thirties. Given the right clothes and make-up she might have been an attractive woman, but it was too late for experimenting with illusions. She took a back seat to her elegant, sophisticated sister-in-law and continued to lead a prim, uneventful existence as Señorita Mercedes; if she had any bitter thoughts about her fate, she never allowed them to surface.

Magdalena's sudden death eight years later gave Mercedes a new mission in life. She took up the reins of Marcos's shattered household and poured her frustrated heart into the task. She loved his children as she would have loved her own and dedicated herself to him with passionate devotion. Her cup overflowed with happiness. She was needed again; surely that could only be further proof of God's infinite wisdom and will.

It never occurred to her that Marcos might not view God's will in quite the same light.

27

II

The original ranch house had consisted of a long one-storey building set in the middle of an untidy park. Over the years Bruno Luciani had added two wings around a black-and-white tiled patio, improved the plumbing and put in a power plant. His wife Isabel had seen to the gardens, orchard and the building of a small chapel. The park remained untouched. Eucalyptus, pines, acacias – even an occasional jacaranda tree – grew in chaotic confusion beside grey-green tamarisks, pepper trees and an endless variety of unidentified shrubs. Magdalena had once laughingly dubbed the park a botanist's nightmare, but Marcos stubbornly refused to prune a single twig.

Mercedes hurried out of the north wing that housed the family bedrooms and crossed the patio to the kitchen. Domestic details continued to run through her mind. As she entered the kitchen she heard a car door slam; a dog began to bark furiously in the backyard. Old Rosario the cook looked up from the mound of steaks she was trimming for lunch.

'That ain't Don Marcos already, is it?' she asked.

'Oh, no,' replied Mercedes. 'It's too early yet.' Her thin fingers fidgeted with the slender gold crucifix around her neck. 'About Sunday, Rosario . . .'

'I'm seeing to things.'

The cook's tone implied that there was no need for Mercedes to fuss about Sunday. Rosario had been with the family nearly fifty years; she knew what had to be done. Her carving knife sliced cleanly through the meat stacked on the large kitchen table.

'Rosita says you're taking her back to the city,' she remarked sourly. 'That girl's no good as a maid.'

Mercedes sighed. 'We're shorthanded at Barranco Rosales and it's so difficult to find anyone. Girls only seem to want to work in a factory these days.'

Rosario grunted. 'Turns their head, the city does. All they can think about is painting their nails and running after men.' She paused to jab a poker at the wood in the stove and added another log. 'Been to the city once in my life with your mother,

28

may the saints rests her soul! Never again – and I'll be sixty-seven next August.'

'You don't look a day over forty,' quipped a man's voice from the doorway.

Mercedes frowned as Lucas Luciani strolled into the kitchen. No one had expected him this Easter; his presence invariably meant trouble. She wondered nervously what form the trouble would take this time.

'Killing the fatted calf?' Lucas cocked a quizzical eyebrow at the steaks and grinned. 'Who're we feeding?'

'The family,' replied Mercedes stiffly. 'Pedro's coming as well. His students at the seminary are on holiday.'

'Pharisees and a holy boy – God, what an Easter!' He helped himself to a large chunk of bread, then a wedge of cheese and stuffed them both into his mouth. 'There's some luggage in my room.'

'Jimmy Morgan and his wife are spending the weekend. We weren't expecting you. You'll have to sleep in the annex with Losa and the accountant.'

Lucas's pale, handsome face twitched. 'So Morgan's found himself a wife, eh? What's she like?'

'A very nice young woman.' The accent on 'nice' was unmistakable. 'You could have at least told us you were coming.'

'Thought I'd surprise old Marcos.'

Mercedes opened her mouth to point out that Marcos would hardly be pleased by the surprise, but then she remembered Rosario. Servants were servants, no matter how long they had been with the family. One must keep up appearances. Lucas noticed the hesitation and grinned.

'Don't look so disapproving, woman – you're wrinkled enough as it is. Who's the *chinita* sweeping the veranda?'

'Rosita,' said Rosario tartly. 'Leave that cheese alone, Señor Lucas. It's for lunch.'

He jerked his hand away. 'Looks like hell in that uniform, but she's got nice legs.'

'Are you staying long?' asked Mercedes in a voice that clearly hoped he would announce his departure within the next five minutes, if not sooner.

'Long enough to give you heartburn,' drawled the prodigal and sauntered out, letting the screen door slam behind him.

29

III

When they returned from weighing cattle Isabel insisted on touring the grounds with Angela; as they reached the swings in the orchard Cristina and a thin, ugly girl with inquisitive grey eyes appeared. Isabel grandly introduced Angela as though she were a personal possession.

'Jimmy married her in England and they're going to live at Los Alamos. I let her pat my horse and we're going riding this afternoon and she doesn't know anything about ranches, but she's nice. I like her.'

'Does she speak Spanish?' asked the ugly girl.

'*Un poco*,' said Angela, feeling ridiculously shy under their dispassionate inspection. She smiled and added with painstaking care, '*Me gusta La Catalina mucho* . . . I like La Catalina very much.'

Cristina's small, golden face brightened. 'I'm Cristina and this is Cousin Yvonne,' she said. 'Her father's Mama's brother Carlos, and they've just arrived and we've been putting thistles in Miss Nelly's bed. Miss Nelly's English, but she's not like you. You're all right. Miss Nelly has false teeth and her bones stick out.'

'Come on,' said Isabel, seizing Angela by the hand, 'let's go see the beehives.'

They ran down the path, chattering and laughing in a breathless mixture of Spanish and English that took all of Angela's concentration to follow. She didn't mind. The magic of their carefree world reached out to touch her with warm, glowing happiness. It felt good to be alive.

IV

The sound of their laughter reached Jimmy and Marcos as they strolled through the park. Jimmy grinned happily.

'Angela loves children,' he said. 'Wants to have at least three.' His grin broadened. 'Still can't believe I'm married, old boy!

30

What do you think of her?'

'You're a fortunate man.'

'Didn't think she'd marry me, you know. There was another chap in the running. Solid English type – you know the kind.'

Marcos's smile did not reach his eyes. 'I sent your message to Los Alamos. Your cook Tiburcia's up in arms, says the only part of the house fit to live in is the kitchen – and even that flooded while you were away.'

Jimmy chuckled. 'Angela won't mind. She's a great girl, she'll fix things up.' He stretched lazily, pleased with himself and with the world. 'Angela can handle an old battleaxe like Tiburcia.'

Marcos stared at the house standing in bright sunshine beyond the trees. 'You may have a bit more than Tiburcia to handle,' he remarked after a minute. 'I hear the Widow's back in Laguna Grande with a three-month-old child. There's a rumour you have something to do with it.'

Jimmy tugged at his ear and looked embarrassed.

'Is it your child?' insisted Marcos.

'How should I know? The Widow likes having a good time. Anyway, that's all in the past. I'm a reformed man, *amigo*. The Widow was just a bit of fun.' He laughed at the disapproving expression on Marcos's face. 'Oh, shit – don't look at me like that! You've had more than your fair share of a good tumble.'

'Not with whores.'

Down in the complex of living quarters, corrals and barns known as the Bajo a brass bell summoned the ranch hands to the midday meal. Marcos glanced at his watch and started across the lawn. Typical of Jimmy to dismiss the Widow so glibly, he reflected. *El loco* Morgan had enjoyed his whoring game and to hell with the consequences. Now he was enjoying a new game called marriage. What about his other games – the drinking and the gambling? Where did they fit in? Jimmy worked hard; the trouble was he played hard as well – and not always in the best of company. It was all right if a man had plenty of money and no responsibilities, but Jimmy Morgan was not wealthy. As for responsibility – Marcos's jaw tightened. Jimmy's responsibility was a charming, very desirable wife who deserved nothing but the best. Angela. He couldn't get her out of his mind. He didn't want to. He wanted to know everything about her: her thoughts, her feelings, how she made love . . . he wanted to make love to Angela. *Jimmy's wife.*

31

El loco Morgan strolled along, wrapped up in his own thoughts. He could handle the Widow; chances were the child wasn't his to begin with. Anyway, Angela would never find out about it. There was no need to worry. His spirits soared as he began to think about Angela and their life together at Los Alamos. Glorious. There was no need to worry at all.

V

As they reached the veranda Pedro Arcos Arizu waved from the depths of a deck chair. 'I've been hearing all about Miguel's latest scrape from Mercedes. Getting to be a handful, isn't he?'

'You're his godfather,' retorted Marcos. 'Maybe you can knock some sense into him.'

The priest laughed. He was a large man with thinning dark hair and a pleasant face; his eyes twinkled humorously behind horn-rimmed glasses. He had known Marcos Luciani for a long time.

'I've been trying to knock some sense into your sister first,' he said. 'Tactfully, of course.' The humorous twinkle deepened as he turned to Jimmy. 'Congratulations. I hear you've married a charming *gringa*.'

'So Morgan's put his head into the noose,' drawled Lucas, coming along the veranda. 'I can hardly wait to meet the little woman.'

Marcos scowled. 'What are you doing here? I thought you were in Brazil with that whey-faced friend of yours.'

'Brazil's off.'

'What the hell do you want this time?'

Lucas lowered himself with insolent grace into a wicker chair and propped up his feet on the iron railing. Shapely, almond-eyed Rosita brought out a tray of drinks and set it down with a clatter on the nearby table. She darted a coy look at the men, twitched up her skirt a few inches and flounced off. Lucas grinned.

'Why should I want anything?' he hedged. 'Thought I'd spend Easter with my loving family, that's all.'

Marcos splashed vermouth into a glass, dropped in a couple of ice cubes and added a generous squirt of soda.

'Whatever you've come for, you won't get it,' he said curtly and went into the house.

VI

Grey-eyed Carlos Arcos Arizu was very tall and distinguished looking; his English was as formal as his manner. At lunch he told Angela he had visited England several times on agricultural missions in the thirties, adding that he greatly admired her country's courage during the war.

'The English do not compromise freedom,' he said, with a pointed look at Marcos. 'They believe unity makes strength.'

Marcos pretended not to hear him.

'Thank God we were spared the war!' sighed Mercedes, crossing herself. 'So many dead, such a tragedy!'

Carlos's wife Teresa ignored the war and began to ask Angela about London fashions. She was a striking woman in her mid-thirties – too pale and thin for beauty, but pallor and thinness gave a dramatic edge to her features. Lustrous, curling coal-black hair and large dark eyes enhanced the effect, creating a medieval aura that cried out for the sumptuousness of brocades and velvets. Her hands were beautifully manicured, her mauve silk shirt was perfectly tailored. Even her high, well-bred voice conformed to elegance. Not the type of woman one could chat with in the fish queue, decided Angela. Not the type of woman who would queue up for fish in the first place. She wondered what Marcos's wife had been like. Probably very beautiful and sophisticated. They must have been happy together. He looked as though he would know how to make a woman happy. There was tenderness as well as passion in those dark eyes . . . Angela coloured faintly and turned away from her host's eyes. Stupid to flutter just because he kept on staring at her. Even more stupid to want to look at him again. She must not look at him. That sort of game was dangerous. She had no intention of playing it. She must not look at Marcos Luciani.

'A penny for your thoughts,' murmured Jimmy, surreptitiously squeezing her knee under the table.

Angela gave a guilty start and stared at the steak on her plate. There was enough meat to feed two people. Before that there had been a generous portion of ravioli smothered in grated cheese, and several glasses of very good, very strong red wine.

33

'Do people always eat like this in Argentina?' she asked.

He laughed. 'Why not? The food's there to enjoy. Have some more wine, angel, and don't worry about it. You're not in England anymore, remember?'

The conversation flowing around them sounded very melo-dramatic. Marcos and Carlos seemed to be arguing. Their heated exchanges were frequently punctuated by Pedro's priestly bass and the women's exclamations. Lucas sneered. The discussion, explained Jimmy to Angela in an undertone, was a standing argu-ment about Argentina's political situation and the government of General Perón, who had been in power for five years. Neither Marcos nor Carlos supported the government – but while Carlos made no bones about his opposition, Marcos was more pragmatic. He saw no point risking prison or exile by openly opposing Perón. There were ways to avoid the government's ruinous policies and strong-arm tactics; he was determined to make the best of every loophole available.

'How did Perón come to power in the first place?' asked Angela curiously.

'On the backs of the *descamisados*,' replied Jimmy. 'That means the "shirtless ones". Perón's a shrewd bastard. In 1943 he was chief of staff in the war ministry – just one more colonel with his eye on the Casa Rosada. That's the big pink government house in downtown Buenos Aires. Squatting in it seems to be every tinplate hero's dream, but Perón was smarter than most. He knew tanks weren't enough to keep him in power. There was a lot of labour unrest at the time. He jockeyed his way into the ministry of labour and began to woo the trade unions. The next general to reach the Casa Rosada made him vice-president. Some of Perón's fellow officers didn't like his ambitions and removed him in October, 1945. A week later he was reinstated after the *descamisados* went on the rampage and the trade unions called for a general strike. He became president four months later. The man's got charisma, no doubt about that. He also has the military under his thumb, which is rule number one for anyone crazy enough to govern this country.'

'Wasn't there any way of preventing him from coming to power?'

Jimmy shrugged. 'The only way would have been for the upper class to get its act together, but men like Marcos and Carlos aren't politicians. Politics has always been an intellectual pastime for them – probably because to a large extent they've always had things their way. They didn't really believe in the writing on the wall until it was too late. Perón was elected by popular majority.' He took a sip of wine and grinned wryly. 'Then there's his wife Evita. The woman used to be an actress of sorts. She intrigued her way into Perón's bed and built up her own power base. She's an attractive, ambitious bitch and tough as nails. The masses adore her. They think she's Cinderella and the fairy godmother all rolled into one. There's not much one can do to destroy that kind of myth and the upper class knows it.'

Upper-class frustration crackled in Carlos's voice. 'I had lunch at the Jockey Club the other day,' he told Marcos in rapid Spanish. 'Someone said you disagree with blackballing Perón.'

'I said I thought it was asking for trouble.'

'Trouble!' An exasperated snort of contempt underlined the word. 'We do not want that son of a bitch in the Jockey Club!'

'Carlos, not in front of the children!' protested Teresa, with an anxious eye on the girls at the far end of the table.

'What's "son of a bitch"?' asked Cristina, while Isabel and Yvonne giggled.

'Angela, this is Argentine dessert,' said Mercedes in a loud voice as a maid appeared with a large silver platter. '*Panqueques de dulce de leche*. How do you say? Pancakes with . . .' She appealed to Jimmy in a rapid Spanish. 'Tell her what *dulce de leche* is.'

'Ambrosia.' He smacked his lips. 'Can't live without it.'

'*Dulce de leche*,' explained Teresa in carefully enunciated English, 'is the milk and sugar boiled. You stir it all the time with the spoon for many hours to make it thick. It must be brown like this, you understand?'

Mercedes smiled hopefully. 'You like? I teach you so you make *dulce de leche* for Jimmy.'

The pancakes turned out to be delicious crêpes: wafer-thin, filled with a creamy, caramel-like confection and glazed on top with burnt sugar. Angela pushed away a sudden guilty memory of post-war queues and food rationing. This was Argentina, land of plenty. She must not forget that.

Carlos took several impatient mouthfuls of dessert and glared at the maid. When she left the dining-room he picked up where he had left off, this time more indignantly than before.

'Perón a member of the Jockey Club? It's unthinkable!'

'A national scandal,' jeered Lucas. 'Our hoary heroes must be writhing in their graves.'

'The Jockey's board of directors traditionally invites the country's president to become a member,' replied Marcos, ignoring Lucas. 'Perón's president of Argentina whether we like it or not, Carlos.'

'We've got to draw the line! The only way to survive this government is for everyone to stand united – and that means all of us!'

'The Jockey Club is the most exclusive set-up in the country,' Jimmy told Angela. 'Not that I'm a member. It's pedigree and pesos that get you in – mammoth amounts of both. The board of directors blackballed a proposal to invite Perón to join.'

'If the Jockey's directors had any sense they would have made the invitation and left it up to Perón whether to accept or not,' said Marcos. 'This way they've played into his hands. For God's sake,' as Carlos started to interrupt, 'we've made enough mistakes! We can't afford any more.'

'Hear, hear!' applauded Jimmy, momentarily forgetting to translate. 'If I were Perón and the Jockey Club blackballed me, I'd burn the place to the ground.'

'He wouldn't dare!' Carlos pounded his fist on the table. 'Perón would not *dare* touch the Jockey Club!'

Pedro saw Angela's bewildered look and observed wryly in English, 'Politics spoils digestion.' His eyes twinkled at her. 'It is our – how do I say it? Our national sin. In England there is not so much talk of politics, eh?'

'Who else is coming for the weekend, Marcos?' asked Teresa, eager to change the subject.

'The usual bigwigs from Laguna Grande for the *asado* on Sunday.' He smiled at Angela and switched back to English for her benefit, but she thought he looked on edge. 'You know *asado*?'

'*Asado* means a barbecue,' translated Jimmy. 'We'll gorge on beef fresh off the hoof and sausages and black pudding and offal – maybe even a few *chivitos*. That's kid to your sweet Saxon ears, angel. La Catalina's famous for its barbecued kid.'

The maid glided in with a tray of coffee and set it down in front of Mercedes. A pungent smell of herbal tea floated up from one of the cups.

'By the way,' said Marcos, 'we've got two more guests coming tomorrow.' He dropped a couple of sugar lumps into his coffee

36

and began to stir it with a slow, deliberate motion. 'I've invited Juan Gaspari and his sister for Easter.'

'Juan Gaspari?' Carlos stared at him in astonishment. 'You mean your government contact? You've invited him to La Catalina?'

'That's right.'

'The man's a Peronist!' exclaimed Teresa.

'A useful one. We have some business to discuss. In case you didn't know,' added Marcos shortly as Carlos began to protest, 'the Peronists recently set up a Party branch in Laguna Grande. The bastard in charge is a former slaughterhouse boss named Artemio Mendes. He's been stirring up trouble among the ranch hands and I won't stand for it. I pay Gaspari to keep men like Mendes muzzled. That's one of the reasons why he's coming to La Catalina this weekend.'

'But why invite him to La Catalina?' insisted Teresa. 'Couldn't you discuss your business in Laguna Grande? You know how Carlos and I feel about the Peronists!'

Marcos impatiently snapped a lighter at his cigarette. 'I'm sorry if you're upset,' he said. 'It just happens that certain government contacts are very important to me; unfortunately I have to throw them a social sop every now and then.' He smiled apologetically at Angela and continued in English, 'Our politics is boring for you.'

Angela made a determined effort to remain detached. 'Not if Jimmy's translation is anything to go by,' she laughed, reaching for her husband's hand. 'I find it all quite fascinating.'

Jimmy stifled a yawn. 'Don't know about the rest of you, but I could do with a siesta.' He winked at her. 'Come on, angel. Let's leave the country's future to the experts. We've got better things to do.'

VII

No one lingered long over coffee after Jimmy and Angela left the dining-room. Only the girls protested at having to sleep a siesta; the grown-ups were glad to get away. The prospect of spending two days with a Peronist under his brother-in-law's roof had given Carlos acute indigestion. He tossed about on the bed in the main guest room and complained that Marcos had lost all sense of proportion. Teresa agreed.

'I remember how he used to upset poor Magdalena,' she added. 'Will you ever forget the time he invited one of those unbearable characters to Barranco Rosales for dinner – it was Gaspari, wasn't it?'

Carlos groaned. 'Yes.'

'I don't think I've ever seen Magdalena so angry. It was their wedding anniversary and she had arranged such a lovely dinner party. Marcos refused to cancel Gaspari's invitation. What a fiasco!' Teresa slipped into a pale blue silk négligé and walked over to the dressing table. 'Magdalena told me she and Marcos had a terrible quarrel about it afterwards. He can be so unbelievably pigheaded.' She began to brush her dark, lustrous hair. 'Isn't Angela a charming woman? I never expected Jimmy Morgan to have such good taste.'

'I only hope Marcos knows what he's doing,' muttered Carlos sourly. 'My stomach's killing me. Did we bring any bicarbonate of soda?'

VIII

Jimmy turned down the fur rug on the bed in Lucas's room. 'Old Marcos really dropped a bombshell,' he chuckled. 'This Gaspari chap's a crafty character. Short and pugdy, with an egg-shaped head and black hair slicked back under at least four inches of grease.'

Angela yawned. The room was warm in spite of a breeze blowing through the open window. Too much lunch and too much wine had made her head ache. There were too many new impressions to sort out, but she didn't want to think about them right now. The bed felt like heaven. She snuggled down in the sheets and closed her eyes. A couple of hours' sleep was what she needed to put things back into perspective.

My sugar angel, thought Jimmy. I'm going to eat her up. He kicked his underpants across the room and struck a pose in front of the full-length mirror on the wardrobe door. His reflection mimed approval; behind it lay the bed. He could see Angela's flaxen hair spread across the pillow and the shape of her breasts under the sheet. Gorgeous. If he angled the mirror properly they could watch themselves making love. Get some hot excitement going. He grinned at the most important part of his reflection. It was rearing up and raring to go. Jimmy gave himself a few congratulatory pats.

'Hey, angel,' he said. 'Sexy stuff, eh? Look at the treat I've got for you.'

Angela pretended to be asleep. He threw back the sheets. She was wearing only her bra and panties; that excited him more than if she had been naked. He squatted down by the bed and began to kiss her thighs; when she protested, he laughed.

'Wake up, gorgeous. I've been dying all morning to do this.' The blonde triangle between her legs drew him like a magnet. He pulled down her panties and teased it with his fingers. 'Come on, angel. Let's heat up.'

Angela stirred uncomfortably. She didn't want to be excited and she didn't want to make love. 'Jimmy, no.' It was no good. He had a hundred fingers and a dozen tongues; a hard, thrusting penis. Uncomfortable. She began to panic. He wriggled down to the end of the bed, clutching her on top of him. 'Look in the mirror, angel. Look at us jiggling.' Jiggle, up and down. Their naked bodies sweated and jiggled and pumped in the mirror; jiggled and pumped and sweated on the bed. Hot, sticky discomfort. Contorted like belly dancers at the foot of Lucas's bed. Jimmy and the mirror competed for excitement.

'Come on, angel!' he gasped. 'That's good hot stuff, that's *good*!'

The jiggling slackened to a standstill, the bodies in the mirror stopped moving. Angela opened her eyes. Jimmy's backside appeared incongruously reflected against rumpled sheets and pillows; her own legs were spread like disjointed members underneath him. She gave an involuntary shudder of disgust. The sheets were wet.

'Did you like it?' asked Jimmy. 'Did you like doing it that way?'

Copulation, not lovemaking. Steamy, sweaty intercourse, complete with her own fake orgasm. She answered 'Yes' because Jimmy sounded so earnest, like a little boy begging for approval. He scratched lazily and yawned.

'So did I. You screw great guns, old girl.'

You don't make love, you screw great guns. At the beginning of their relationship it had excited her because of comparisons.

Anthony Hobson had been so damned unimaginative, Jimmy was so exotic. The sexy gilt on the gingerbread. Angela stared at the curtains blowing in the breeze. Why the hell did she feel like crying? So she hadn't enjoyed Jimmy's lovemaking this time – that didn't mean the end of the world. She was tired. The rush and excitement of the past few months had caught up with her. A new country, unfamiliar customs, her inability to speak the language properly – it all added up. Once she found her bearings everything would be all right again. Jimmy loved her; she would do her damnedest to make a success of their marriage. She would screw great guns and forget about making love. One had to give these things time.

IX

After lunch Marcos went into his study at the end of a short passage off the living-room. He had a number of matters to see to; he found it very difficult to concentrate on any of them. His thoughts kept returning to Angela. She was intelligent as well as attractive. A woman of character. He liked that. Empty-headed females bored him; he wanted more from a woman than just sexual pleasure. He wanted Angela . . . Marcos made an effort to pull his thoughts together.

He had a less enjoyable but far more serious problem to consider.

He frowned at the letter on his desk. It had been written by Artemio Mendes and it was brief. The local Party branch was planning to build a hospital on the outskirts of Laguna Grande; it wanted La Catalina to make a donation. Marcos glanced at the sum Mendes demanded and laughed, but there was little mirth in the sound. The hospital would never get past a bombastic groundbreaking ceremony and most of the funds would end up in the Party's coffer. The rest would probably line Artemio Mendes's grubby pockets.

His eyes strayed to the crooked signature scrawled at the bottom of the page.

Six months ago Artemio Mendes had been sent to the town of Laguna Grande by Perón's political strategists. His mission was to inject new enthusiasm into a disappointingly lukewarm area.

Mendes's ambitions, however, aimed higher than a mere cattle town; he wanted to be governor of the province. His political drum was agrarian reform and he beat on it with alarming gusto. The land belonged to the people. The idle, bloodsucking oligarchs who squatted on thousands of acres and stuffed their bellies must be hanged from the lamp-posts. If he was successful in the next election, bellowed Artemio Mendes, ranches like La Catalina would be carved up and distributed among the people.

Marcos swept the letter angrily aside. His hand knocked over the photograph of Magdalena on his desk; her smiling, golden-haired elegance mocked him as he righted the silver frame. Magdalena wouldn't have approved of Juan Gaspari at La Catalina. She had always bitterly condemned what she called Marcos's betrayal of his principles; try as he might, he had never been able to make her understand that these days survival came first. With men like Artemio Mendes breathing down his neck the question of principles was purely academic.

Mendes's threats struck at the root of something far more important than the loss of twenty-four thousand acres. La Catalina was Marcos's entire life; without the ranch that life would have no purpose. Worse still, there would be nothing to pass on to the coming generations. His children and his children's children would have no surety for the future. The continuity which was vital for stability and order would be broken; the breakdown would destroy the values to which he was deeply committed. Agrarian reform be damned. La Catalina was Marcos Luciani's kingdom and his family's only safeguard against the disintegration of its heritage. He would fight to protect kingdom and heritage by every available means.

He would sell his soul to the Devil before he let Artemio Mendes or anyone else lay a hand on La Catalina.

CHAPTER FOUR

I

Juan Gaspari might not look like the Devil, but at the moment he made a useful substitute. On his way into Laguna Grande the next morning Marcos told himself that a greengrocer's son was just the kind of galling humour the Devil would enjoy. Even more galling was his own need of the greengrocer's son for survival.

For once the train was on time.

Gaspari – dapper in grey pinstripes, black hair slicked carefully over incipient baldness – stood on the platform surrounded by a battery of new suitcases. A woman in her twenties and a chubby, plain-looking girl Isabel's age hovered nearby. The woman looked uncomfortable and out of place in a tight-fitting electric-blue suit made of cheap material. A small white hat perched unsteadily on a head of tightly crimped yellow curls. Her white shoes were too high, and she clutched a large blue handbag with a rhinestone clasp. The girl, dressed in shapeless brown wool trousers and a bilious green jumper, chewed on stubby fingernails and looked miserable.

'*Amigo* Marcos, good to see you!' Gaspari rushed forward and energetically pumped his host's hand. 'You're looking splendid! The *campo* agrees with you, eh? How're things?'

'Hello, Gaspari.' Marcos glanced inquiringly at the woman.

'Gladys!' Short, plump white hands waved a commanding gesture. 'Come over here and meet Marcos Luciani. My sister, Gladys Gómez. And this,' dragging the girl forward, 'is her daughter Claudia.'

'How do you do,' murmured Gladys.

Marcos shook hands with a woman surprisingly pretty in spite of her inappropriate clothing. She had small, regular features and a well-shaped figure that would probably be shapeless by the time she reached middle-age, uncertain hazel eyes, a bow-shaped mouth carefully painted dark red. The mouth quivered nervously.

Marcos smiled politely. 'Did you have a good journey, Señora Gómez?'

'Excellent!' boomed Gaspari. He mopped his brow with an orange bandana and darted a quick look around the platform. 'First-class service on the train. Staff knows me well, of course. Treated us like royalty – eh, Gladys?'

Gladys nodded, her uncertain eyes still on Marcos Luciani. He was not at all what she had expected.

II

Gladys Gaspari's ambition was to make a good marriage.

A good marriage meant money, social position and security. At eighteen she married Teófilo Gómez, who owned the iron-monger's shop four doors away from her father's greengrocery. Gómez, a childless widower in his mid-fifties, was reputed to have a considerable amount of money in the bank and Gladys congratulated herself on her good luck. It didn't matter that he snored or left his false teeth in a glass by the bed – or even that he retold the same joke every evening after supper. Teófilo Gómez was a rich man and she was his wife. In their lower middle class neighbourhood that made her a person of considerable importance.

Claudia was born nine months to the day after the wedding. Two weeks later her proud father, one of Quilmes Football Club's more exuberant fans, collapsed at a match and Gladys became a widow.

Her husband's wealth proved to be non-existent. Humiliated by the unkind change in social fortunes, she sold his business to pay off bad debts and returned with baby Claudia to her parent's shop.

'The next time,' stormed Gladys bitterly, 'I'll marry *real* money!'

Real money proved difficult to find, and the next ten years of Gladys's life passed uneventfully between lettuce crates and sacks of potatoes.

Juan Gaspari was a born opportunist who thrived on the political game. His sister's politics were purely sentimental.

Gladys idolized Evita, whose spectacular rise from rags to riches mirrored her own ambitious dreams. She had no interest in Eva Perón's manoeuvrings for power and even less in policies or political platforms. All that mattered was the dazzling, golden-headed Cinderella herself – what she wore, her fabulous jewels, her elaborate hairstyles, what social functions she attended.

By a stroke of luck Gladys happened to be on the fringe of one of those social functions.

At the time she was working as a salesgirl at Harrods. Her counter stood near the entrance to the store's restaurant and when she wasn't busy Gladys enjoyed watching the parade of well-dressed, wealthy people passing through the restaurant's swinging doors. On this particular afternoon there seemed to be more activity than usual. Elegant women in furs and jewels streamed past, spotless waiters bustled nervously back and forth, a stout man in uniform barked orders. Gladys nudged the salesgirl beside her.

'What's going on?'

'Big society tea. Evita's coming.' The girl eased her left foot out of its tight-fitting shoe and groaned. 'Saint Sophronia – my corns are killing me! I bet that old bag in mink over there doesn't know what it's like to stand on her feet all day.'

Gladys ignored her companion's corns and edged towards the far end of the counter facing the lifts. Her eyes widened as the doors of the middle lift rolled back with a clatter and a galaxy of important-faced men marched out. Gladys caught a tantalizing glimpse of a dazzling blonde head and the unmistakable sparkle of diamonds. She stood on tiptoe, ogling eagerly. The galaxy swarmed past the counter, a woman laughed, the blonde head and diamonds disappeared through the swinging doors.

'Some of us have all the luck!' muttered the salesgirl, easing off her other shoe. 'Used to listen to Evita in the days when she was on radio. A lousy actress, but she knew where she was headed, all right.'

'You don't like her?'

The salesgirl shrugged sloping shoulders. 'Makes no difference to me, dearie. Some of us is born with all the luck, that's what I'm saying. If the woman gets away with it, why not?'

Gladys was about to reply when the door of the restaurant opened and a tall, grey-haired woman wrapped in persian lamb swept through. Another woman followed – and then another.

One by one, without a word, the well-born, wealthy women of Buenos Aires turned their backs on Eva Perón and walked out of the restaurant.

Their official guest of honour was left sitting alone.

Evita, not one to take such a deliberated snub lying down, would strike back where it hurt most. She set up her own Eva Perón Foundation, which by presidential decree controlled all public charities. The society women, who had administered Argentina's charity institutions for generations as part of their inherent right, fumed in fury – but could do nothing about it. Evita took sweet revenge and ran the foundation as her own fief. Over the years it became one of the most lucrative rackets in the country.

Gladys, an outraged eyewitness to her idol's humiliation, immediately joined the local women's branch of the Peronist Party. Her parents disapproved of politics and said so in no uncertain terms. She took offense and defiantly placed a photograph of Evita between the gilt-framed pictures of the Virgin Mary and the Sacred Heart of Jesus on her bedside table.

At night, as she lay listening to the traffic rumbling down the cobblestone street or pipes gurgling dismally behind her bed, Gladys Gómez imagined herself sweeping along in a mink coat and diamonds, escorted by an as-yet nebulous but nonetheless gallant Prince Charming.

Her brother's announcement that she had been invited to spend Easter weekend at an oligarch's ranch stunned Gladys. She vaguely knew that Juan had dealings with some wealthy businessmen, but that world was too far removed from reality. It existed only in her dreams and in her more down-to-earth moments Gladys knew that dreams seldom, if ever, came true. She could only stare at Juan and splutter in astonishment.

'He's invited *me*? But wh-why?'

Gaspari repressed an impatient sigh. 'Because I am very friendly with Marcos Luciani. We do a lot of business together.'

He refrained from adding that the invitation had been his own suggestion – or that Marcos Luciani's reply was limited to an indifferent, 'Bring your sister along if you want to.' Juan Gaspari had his own reasons for thrusting Gladys into the limelight. She was still young, attractive and reasonably intelligent. A valuable asset. He saw no point in keeping valuable assets hidden under lettuce crates when there was a wealthy widower around — especially when the man belonged to the landowning class.

Bring them both together and Juan Gaspari could be guaranteed lifelong protection on all sides.

Gladys's Peronist friends in the blue stucco building that served as the neighbourhood Party headquarters approved of the invitation. This was the perfect opportunity to infiltrate enemy ranks and report back on the rot festering within. Gladys must collect as much information as possible and take note of any weakness that could be exploited for Evita's glorious cause. One oligarch was much the same as another. If the decay behind the Luciani façade was exposed, then all the others would fall as well.

'Who knows?' crowed Juanita Sánchez, self-styled leader of the branch's militant faction and one of Gladys's close friends. 'When Evita hears of this maybe she'll award you with a gold medal.'

Juan gave Gladys money to buy clothes for herself and for Claudia. She took the day off and went shopping with Juanita. They spent hours trying on dresses and discussing the details of Gladys's wardrobe — especially what she would wear in the evening. Juanita favoured scarlet satin with sequins, but Gladys had her eye on a strapless white tulle number because it vaguely resembled Evita's gown in the photograph by her bedside. The white tulle won in the end, but to please Juanita she bought a spray of artificial scarlet carnations for the bodice.

Finally, in a gesture that defied her parents' moralizing views on the subject, Gladys Gómez dyed her brown hair a bold, brazen blonde.

III

Probably nothing unsettles a woman more than to discover that her clothes are unsuitable for the occasion. The moment Gladys stepped out of the car at La Catalina she knew she was ridiculously overdressed.

Mercedes wore a grey jumper and pleated skirt, the other women wore trousers. Teresa's dark colouring was highlighted by yellow cashmere and an ivory-coloured scarf. The scarf was thick Italian silk and had cost more than Gladys's shoes and handbag together. She eyed the ivory silk in awe and wondered uneasily if her stocking seams were straight. Nothing looked worse than crooked stocking seams.

Angela, being English, she dismissed as negligible.

Gladys distrusted the English. Together with the Americans and the Germans they were foreigners – *gringos* who had strange customs and did not believe in God. This thin, pale-haired woman with blue eyes and unpainted lips was a typically insipid *gringa*, not worth more than a passing nod. Gladys nodded briefly and turned her back.

The snub compensated slightly for her own discomfort.

IV

Claudia Gómez had not wanted to come to La Catalina.

She was a shy, unprepossessing girl, painfully tongue-tied among strangers and frightened of her luxurious surroundings. She tried to cling to her mother, but the grown-ups, intent on sorting out their own social hurdles, thrust her on to the other children with the usual adult rite of dismissal.

'Go play nicely together, girls.'

The children trudged dutifully off with Claudia in tow. A few formalities were exchanged under the fig trees in the kitchen yard.

'What's your name?'

'Claudia María Celestina Gómez.'

Cristina giggled. 'Gómez what?'

'Nothing,' replied Claudia, looking bewildered. 'Just Gómez.'

'We're Luciani Arcos,' said Isabel importantly. 'And Yvonne's Arcos Hernández.'

'Oh.' Claudia stubbed at the ground with her new white shoe.

'What school do you go to?' asked Yvonne.

'It used to be called Escuela Rivadavia de Quilmes, but now it's called Escuela Eva Perón.'

'You mean a state school?' chorused Isabel and Yvonne in astonishment.

'I've never met anyone who went to a state school!' exclaimed Cristina. She peered at Claudia as though studying some

47

outlandish, neolithic insect. 'Do you wear those stupid white uniforms with a silly blue bow tied round you neck?'

Claudia blushed.

'We go to the Convent of the Holy Assumption and wear kilts,' announced Isabel. 'My brother Miguel and Yvonne's brother Gastón go to San Gregorio. They're the best schools in Buenos Aires.'

Formalities ended.

The girls decided to ride out to the indian burial ground in the south field and see if they could surprise the Devil, who was said to return every Good Friday looking for his lost soul.

Cristina asked Claudia if she knew how to ride. There was a pause.

'Yes,' lied Claudia.

'You can ride old Pampa. He goes like a snail.'

They started off for the Bajo. Isabel and Yvonne ran ahead; Claudia lagged behind, her heart thudding uneasily at the thought of mounting snail-like old Pampa. Cristina, still awed by the presence of a state pupil in their midst, trotted beside her in wide-eyed fascination. A large brindled greyhound bounded through the trees and jumped up to lick Claudia's face. She shrank back, then scuttled forward with a startled bleat as a turkey gobbled indignantly at her heels. Cristina howled with laughter.

'They won't hurt you, silly!'

Yvonne and Isabel came racing back. 'Pardo's caught a puma!' they shouted. 'A large one! He's skinning it down by the barn.'

The girls ran across the dusty yard to where a short, grizzled ranch hand whetted a long knife against a flat stone. A wildcat was tied spreadeagle on an upright wooden frame behind him. The man grinned.

'Come to see the skinning, eh? Caught this kitten up in the *monte* – the wood in number thirteen. It's been killing goats. You don't want to go riding that way for a few days.'

'Why not?' demanded Isabel.

Pardo sauntered over to the animal on the frame and eyed its belly thoughtfully. 'There's more than one cat prowling, *niña*.' He traced a vertical line the length of the fur with his thick index finger. 'Here, out of the way!' as the girls crowded around. 'Don't want you all dirty with blood.'

'Do you think it's the Devil?' whispered Cristina.

Yvonne touched a large front paw. 'Can I have a claw?'

'What for?' asked Isabel.

'Good luck. Our cook says puma claws are the best thing against the Evil Eye. She has three hanging around her neck on a piece of black string.'

Pardo laughed as he eased the frame down. 'Not this one, *niña*. Don Marcos says I can sell it in Laguna Grande. There's a man who buys them for the foreign folk in Buenos Aires. They like the claws. I'm going after the other cat this afternoon.'

Claudia stared at the puma. Such a beautiful animal – a stiff, tan coat, the tail tipped with dark brown. It looked so helpless spread out on the frame. Her heart began to beat very fast as Pardo worked his knife carefully into the pale fur on the underbelly. The blade hesitated for a moment, then slit cleanly to open a good-sized gash. Dark blood spurted into a bucket; after a moment Pardo reached into the gash and began to pull out a warm, steaming mass of intestine.

Claudia gulped. Her palms grew moist, her stomach gave a sickening lurch. She retched violently and began to cry while the girls stared at her in scornful disgust.

A weak stomach was even more degrading than wearing a state school uniform.

CHAPTER FIVE

I

Teresa Arcos Arizu practised the subtle art of social snubbing with consummate skill.

Her manners were perfect. Nothing she said or did could be pinpointed as blatant discourtesy towards her brother-in-law's unwelcome guests, but only a complete fool would fail to detect the undercurrents. Gladys might be sentimental, she might lack social sophistication – but she was no fool. She was determined to meet the challenge with flying colours and counter with weapons of her own. Her determination had nothing to do with striking a blow for the glory of Evita. It obeyed a deep-rooted and very human need to be respected as an individual in her own right.

Gladys's only concession was to remove her hat. Further than that she refused to budge. Her clothes had cost money and she saw no reason to be ashamed of them. She doggedly refused Mercedes's offer of a pair of walking shoes and toured the grounds in her white heels. Angela and Mercedes accompanied her, but it was not a comfortable stroll. Gladys spoke no English and Mercedes, badly flustered by the entire situation, made a poor interpreter. Angela's two weeks of textbook Spanish in Seville were definitely unable to cope; after a few feeble attempts she left Gladys and Mercedes to their own devices and walked along enjoying the sunshine.

By the time they reached the olive grove surrounding La Catalina's private chapel conversation had come to a virtual standstill.

II

The morning dragged on.

Mercedes, who always fasted on Good Friday, retired to the chapel before lunch to pray for divine intervention in her brother's affairs. Not that Marcos was doing anything wrong, she assured God earnestly. He just seemed to have lost all sense of proportion by inviting Juan Gaspari's sister . . . the rosary beads clicked feverishly.

'Terribly ordinary, poor thing,' sighed Mercedes between Hail Marys. 'You can tell she's not used to moving in good circles. I must say Marcos is very polite to her and she acts very grateful . . .'

The Hail Marys faltered, cut short by a sudden, chilling thought.

III

Teresa presided over lunch against a richly hued background of floral paintings and landscapes of La Catalina. She was devastatingly civil to Gladys.

'Do you like the theatre?'

Gladys tore her eyes away from a gleaming collection of silver *maté* gourds on the massive sideboard and looked uncomfortable. Her shrill voice grated nervously. She had never been to the theatre. Teresa smiled.

'How silly of me to ask,' she said. 'Tell us about – where is it you live? Quilmes? Do you know,' with the air of someone discussing a place on the moon, 'I've never been there.'

Gladys looked even more uncomfortable. She did not want to talk about Quilmes. Teresa, implacable, tried again.

'You do go to the cinema, don't you?'

Gladys went to the cinema. Her favourite actress was Lola Pasiones. She had seen her latest film five times.

Teresa raised her eyebrows in an eloquent gesture. 'Lola Pasiones?' Her laughter rippled. 'Oh – a local actress. How interesting. I'm afraid we never go to Argentine films. They're so fourth-rate.'

'I like them,' replied Gladys boldly, but Teresa was already on to another subject – this time an intricate description of the nuptial mass for the marriage of her brother's eldest daughter.

'It was a magnificent ceremony at the Basilica of the Blessed Sacrament,' she said. 'Quite the most fashionable church in town. Sofía looked like a dream! Chez Georgette made her wedding gown. Ivory satin and alençon lace embroidered with pearls — absolutely superb! The veil belonged to her husband's great-grandmother.' Teresa's high, well-bred voice caught slightly. 'Magdalena would have enjoyed Sofía's wedding so much, Marcos!'

'I'm sure she would have,' he replied — a shade dryly, Angela thought.

Teresa trained her dark, brilliant gaze on Gladys again. 'Chez Georgette is the only decent place in Buenos Aires for wedding gowns. Well worth the expense. You've heard of Georgette, haven't you?'

The barb was there, concealed behind a polite smile, but this time Gladys proved equal to the challenge.

'Oh, yes.' She smiled back at Teresa. 'Georgette makes evening gowns for Evita.'

Conversation veered quickly into safer channels.

IV

In the afternoon Carlos and Teresa took the girls riding down to the lake. Claudia, whose horsemanship was limited to occasional pony rides at the zoo, found herself mounted on sleepy-eyed Pampa. She sat stiffly on her *recado* — the typical gaucho saddle piled high with sheepskins — her feet glued to the stirrups and her hands wrapped in the horse's mane. Isabel and the others grinned and charged off down the road at a reckless gallop, followed by Carlos on a wild-eyed chestnut. Teresa heard Claudia's stifled bleat of terror as Pampa neighed restlessly.

'Don't you know how to ride?' she asked.

The girl's chubby face flushed and her eyes filled with embarrassed tears. She shook her head. 'N-not very well, señora.'

Teresa sighed. Gladys Gómez was one thing, but a frightened

child was quite another. She leaned over and gently unclenched Claudia's small hands from Pampa's mane.

'Hold the reins in your left, like this.' She arranged the reins and pushed at Claudia's knees. 'Grip here and put just the tip of your foot in the stirrup. Sit well into the saddle and ride with the horse . . . That's right,' as Pampa ambled patiently forward. 'Don't be afraid. We'll go slowly.'

They left the corral along a wide track shaded by carob trees; after a while the trees thinned out and the track entered broken country – scrub and yellow-flowered goat's beard and tall, thorny *espinillo* thickets. Long plumes of pampa grass swayed like creamy streamers in the wind. A black-and-white *tero* bird planed overhead, croaking its harsh, repetitive cry. Claudia took a cautious breath and relaxed slightly. Riding was not such a terrifying adventure after all.

'Would you like to go a little faster, Claudia?' asked Teresa.

She nodded shyly. 'Please, señora.'

The horses broke into a slow trot. The road wound through high grass, climbed a low rise and dipped to the shores of a marshy lake. Carlos and the girls had already arrived and were searching for arrowheads. Isabel waved excitedly to Claudia.

'You're so slow!' she called. 'Hurry up! Come and see what we've found.'

Half a dozen triangular flints and a few shards of broken pottery. The girls squatted on the ground and tried to fit the pottery together while Carlos told them stories about the Indian campaigns. A small yellow lizard wriggled through the dust and slipped under a clump of grass, a hawk-like *carancho* wheeled above the trees. The lake's muddy waters made a gentle, lapping sound against the shore.

Teresa stretched out in the sun. The afternoon was so quiet and peaceful one could almost forget the Gasparis – or at least push them aside with the rest of life's insignificant nuisances. She closed her eyes and began to think about Marcos. Not a happy man. The strain of being alone was beginning to tell on him. He needed to remarry and settle down with a charming, intelligent woman. Granted Mercedes kept house competently enough – but a sister was definitely not a wife.

'I must get him interested in Aurora Grandi,' murmured Teresa and drifted off to sleep.

V

Mercedes cornered Pedro in the living-room after lunch for some priestly advice about Marcos. Pedro told her Marcos was old enough to take care of himself and countered with a few home truths about the upbringing of young Miguel. He was still at it when Jimmy and Angela strolled in after their siesta. They left hastily and went for a walk through the park; by the time they returned Mercedes had disappeared and Pedro was snoring peacefully in the far corner.

Jimmy grinned. 'Must be a bit of a busman's holiday for a priest when the family bends his ear. What do you think of Gaspari and Co?'

'He's dreadful, but I feel sorry for Gladys,' replied Angela. 'She's so far out of her depth and trying hard not to let it show.'

'Like something out of a soap opera, isn't she? Still, I wouldn't be surprised if our Gladys didn't have a trick or two up her electric blue sleeves.'

'What do you mean?'

'Haven't you seen her making sheep's eyes at old Marcos? Fair panting for him is the woman.'

Angela prodded at a log on the hearth. Yesterday's hopes of regaining her perspective had vanished the minute she saw Marcos again. Last night they had all gone *vizcacha* hunting. It was quite an adventure to drive back and forth across the dark fields, picking out the *vizcacha* holes with the headlights of the car. Marcos and Carlos had shot four of the rodents, Lucas nearly shot himself in the foot. Angela had tripped over a root and Marcos had caught hold of her. His hands were warm and strong; the pressure of his fingers against her arm sparked off a shock wave of emotions that left her weak-kneed and shaking. He had held her for a few seconds longer than necessary – or perhaps her imagination was working overtime. How stupid to get so excited just because Marcos had touched her. She was as bad as pathetic little Gladys, making sheep's eyes and panting for a man she could not have.

'You're imagining things, Jimmy,' said Angela after a moment's silence.

54

'Care to bet, angel? I'd say that blonde from a bottle knows a good thing when she sees it.'

'But he couldn't possibly be interested in her!'

The words jerked out sharply. She avoided looking at Jimmy and continued to prod at the log as though prodding at the snake in her heart.

Jimmy shrugged. 'You never can tell with Marcos.' He darted a quick glance at the sleeping Pedro and kissed her. 'Know what I'm in the mood for?' His kisses grew insistent. 'Let's go outside.'

Angela squirmed. The gilt on the gingerbread was beginning to wear thin. She didn't feel like any of Jimmy's exuberance right now.

'It's almost tea-time,' she pointed out.

'Not for another half hour. Come on, gorgeous.' He gave her a hard squeeze. 'You need a breath of fresh air.'

Mercedes was cutting flowers in the garden. She smiled at them and called out, 'Are you going for a walk?' Jimmy waved. The garden path swerved left and wandered through a maze of overgrown hedge. They came to the thickest part and he pushed Angela into it.

'Jimmy, behave yourself!'

'Don't be so prim,' he said thickly. 'No one'll see us . . . just a quickie, angel . . .'

She had never experienced anything so embarrassing in her life. Jimmy was in a hurry. He pulled down his zipper and went for her trousers. They slithered down around her ankles; her panties stopped somewhere below her knees. Their bodies came together in an uncomfortable, grotesque half-crouch, working frantically for a quick climax in the bushes. Dogs coupled more gracefully. The back of Angela's legs began to ache. God, I wish he'd get it over with! she thought. What if someone finds us like this? Mercedes or Teresa – or the children. Or Marcos. God – not Marcos! Voices sounded on the far side of the hedge. 'Someone's coming!' hissed Angela wildly. 'For heaven's sake, Jimmy . . .' He backed her into a narrow space between the prickly branches; his whispers burst in short, jerking gasps. The voices passed within a few yards of their hideout – Carlos and Teresa returning from their ride with the children. Angela's cheeks burned with mortification; she felt cheap and degraded.

'Close shave,' chuckled Jimmy, straightening up. He tore off some leaves and began to scrub his hands; his blue eyes glowed. 'I liked that.' Boyish enthusiasm for a quickie in the thicket.

Jimmy was her husband, Angela reminded herself. An intelligent, good-natured man. If he behaved like an oversexed goat at times – well, she'd have to learn how to handle that. Once they were settled in their own house he would calm down. There was no need to panic. Certainly there was no need for the snake in her heart to think the things it was thinking.

VI

Marcos Luciani's men respected him because he ran La Catalina from the saddle and not from a desk in Buenos Aires. Their relationship was a clearly defined one in which each man knew his place and what was expected of him. It would never occur to Marcos to ignore a request for advice or help from his men or their families; by the same token it would not occur to them to withhold their work or loyalty. Within the increasingly chaotic realignment of Argentina's political and social boundaries, La Catalina constituted a small, well-structured unit, self-sufficient and secure in itself.

Artemio Mendes brayed to the skies that it was a shameful example of feudalism and exploitation of the masses.

The majority of the men on La Catalina had little time or interest in Artemio Mendes and his politics. They worked hard from sunrise to sunset; Mendes's claim that work must be restricted to eight hours a day was laughable and just went to prove that city men didn't know what they were talking about.

'Mendes ain't a city man,' interrupted El Rubio, a newcomer to La Catalina. 'He's a *paisano* – a country man like the rest of us. He knows the land and if he says unions is right for us, they must be!'

'You try telling Don Marcos you're only going to work eight hours,' grunted Pardo, the puma skinner. 'He don't hold with them trade unions – and he knows the land like he knows his own two hands.'

El Rubio's thin, sallow face darkened. 'The law's the law. If the *patrones* don't hold with the law we strike!'

56

There was a short silence. Some of the older men edged away; others eyed El Rubio uneasily, uncertain in their own minds. He continued to hold forth on Artemio Mendes and the rights of the exploited masses for another five minutes before Pablo Losa appeared.

VII

Losa had heard most of the discussion, but said nothing at the time. Later, catching Marcos in his study with Juan Gaspari, the ranch manager repeated El Rubio's remarks, adding that he wouldn't be surprised if the man had been planted by Mendes himself. Marcos frowned.

'How long has he been on La Catalina?'

'Since last winter.'

'Pay his wages and tell him to get off the ranch. I don't want trouble with the men.'

'You must give the man notice,' pointed out Gaspari. 'And dismissal pay – plus a valid reason for dismissing him.'

A vein bulged dangerously above Marcos's right temple. 'You don't think I have a valid reason?'

'Not politically, you don't.' Gaspari flashed a toothy grin. '*Vamos, amigo*! You're no fool. Fire this El Rubio who shoots his mouth off and you play right into Artemio Mendes's hands. Even Losa here can see that.'

Pablo Losa looked unhappy. 'He's right, Don Marcos.'

He was trapped and all three of them knew it. Marcos tapped the desk with his pencil and glared at Gaspari with hard, angry eyes. The little man shrugged.

'Make the full donation for the hospital and I will tell Artemio Mendes to keep his jackal quiet,' he said. 'Talks of strikes and political action are not necessary on La Catalina. That man's an ass if he doesn't know it.'

The pencil broke.

'All right,' said Marcos in a strangled voice. 'Just tell Artemio Mendes to keep away from my land!'

CHAPTER SIX

I

Laguna Grande lay thirty miles east of La Catalina – a bustling, middle-sized town built around a large central square dominated by the church at one end and the police station at the other. Between these outposts of divine and earthly justice were ranged a hotel, a petrol station, a chemist, an assortment of shops, and finally the blue-and-white stucco building which housed Laguna Grande's Peronist headquarters.

A straggling row of lime trees bordered the square; the lime trees continued along the dusty streets that branched off in a haphazard grid dotted with mud-brick houses and tiny gardens. The north end of the town was taken up by the railway station, stockyards, and a large bronze bust of Perón strategically placed in front of the entrance to the station's only platform. Half a mile east of Laguna Grande stood an imposing three-storey convent school, surrounded by a high brick wall. The primary school, much more modest in scope, was located on one of the back streets between the butcher and the undertaker.

Artemio Mendes and his wife lived in a small pink house with green shutters behind the Party headquarters. The swarthy, bull-necked politician had just woken from his siesta when Juan Gaspari arrived with Gladys. He shuffled out to meet them in his carpet slippers, a gourd of steaming *maté* tea in one hand, a kettle in the other. Gaspari introduced Gladys and announced she had come to visit Norma while he and Artemio 'talked'. Mendes's bushy black eyebrows bristled.

'Trouble?'

'Not at all. Just wanted to exchange a few impressions with you, *amigo*.'

Mendes grunted and waved Gladys towards a room crowded with stuffed furniture and bric-à-brac.

58

'Make yourself at home, *compañera*,' he said, using the familiar form of address so popular among the Peronists. 'The wife'll be along in a minute.'

He ushered Gaspari into another, smaller room and closed the door. A round table covered with a yellow-and-blue checked cloth stood squarely under a bright red hanging lamp. Four chairs with straw seats were placed at angles around the table; Gaspari selected the sturdiest one and sat down gingerly. Mendes poured boiling water into the gourd and held it out to him.

'What's up?'

'That was a steep donation you asked Luciani for. He kicked like hell.'

'He can afford it.'

Gaspari sucked *maté* through a metal straw. One had to tread very carefully with Artemio Mendes. He was bull-necked, bull-brained bull-tempered -- and had no idea how to handle men like Marcos Luciani. What was worse, he wouldn't be told. Gaspari sighed. Men like Mendes might be indispensable to the Party, but they made life very trying.

'Luciani'll pay this time,' he said, 'but it took some doing, *compañero*. My advice is to treat him gently in the future. Coax the man along . . .'

'You don't know the first thing about these bastards!' exploded Artemio Mendes. 'The whip and the boot's all they understand. I've got Luciani pegged. I'll handle him my way.'

Juan Gaspari sighed again. He had a feeling it was going to be a difficult 'exchange of impressions'.

II

In the sitting-room Gladys perched on a bright green settee and listened to Norma complain about the difficulties of getting local women interested in politics.

'Stone-age mentalities, that's what they've got! All they think about is their brats, their men's stomachs, and the price of bread!' Norma lit a cigarette and blew indignant smoke rings at the ceiling. 'Try to tell them about the rights of working women, the Party cause, the liberation of the masses – they haven't a clue what you're talking about! Nothing like our people back in the city.'

Gladys agreed somewhat timidly that the people in the city seemed more interested in politics. Norma blew another impatient smoke ring and droned on.

'I said to Artemio the other day, I said, "It's for Evita and the general that we're fighting, *compañero*! Don't lose heart, we're in the cause together!"'

Gladys glanced at a coloured photograph of Evita and the general hanging on the wall above her hostess's auburn head.

'Personal gift, that was,' said Norma, following her gaze. She held out a plate of pasties bursting with quince jam. 'Have one of these. They're Artemio's favourites. Now,' licking her fingers and brushing a sprinkle of sugar off her ample bosom, 'what're the oligarchs out at La Catalina like?'

A cautious grimace. 'Like you'd expect.'

'That Luciani – he's a bloodsucker, all right! Works the men to the bone, drives them like slaves. I've got a cousin working on the ranch, you know. The tales that poor boy has to tell! Orgies and all sorts of goings-on. Luciani's drunk all the time. El Rubio – that's my cousin – says he's so drunk at times he can hardly sit on his horse.'

'I haven't noticed any of that,' said Gladys warily. 'They seem quiet enough.'

'Don't you let quiet fool you!' Norma bit into another pasty. 'There's an *asado* at the place on Sunday, right? We're not going, of course. The other bootlickers in this one-horse town are, but not us. Artemio won't break bread with a man who exploits the poor. He's got his principles, he has.'

A thick red line of quince jam dribbled down her chin and Gladys looked away. She had known women like Norma Mendes all her life; some of them were her close friends. There was no reason for her to feel uncomfortable, but she did. The small, smoky sitting-room made her head ache. Norma's shrill, staccato voice stabbed her ears. Gladys pressed the palms of her hands together and tried not to yawn. She wondered if it were true that Marcos Luciani drank and did all those other things. She hoped not. He was attractive, he had money. Real money. He was unattached.

'Oh, well – the day'll come when we'll string the likes of Luciani from the lamp-posts,' predicted Norma cheerfully. 'Have another pasty and let's hear some gossip from Buenos Aires.'

III

Back at La Catalina Lucas was busy with plans of his own.

His main problem this Easter was money – quite a large sum of it. Useless to cadge from Marcos, who would only lecture about living within one's monthly allowance. It was all very well for Marcos to talk – he spent his life covered in dust and roughing it. For a young man-about-town who needed a new suit for practically every occasion and dined at the luxurious Plaza Hotel at least three times a week the pittance eked out in a monthly allowance was laughable.

Wine, women and gambling were expensive pursuits. Lucas had an inordinate weakness for all three.

He put his ear to the door of the study and listened carefully. He had seen Marcos leave the house with Jimmy and Angela after tea, but it was best to make sure anyway. After a moment he tried the door. It opened a crack; Lucas held his breath, then pushed the crack wider and slipped through.

The coast was clear.

He crossed over quickly to the desk and tried the drawers. Locked. Lucas cursed and searched in his pockets for a piece of wire. Handy little gadget. Many years ago a maid in Barranco Rosales had taught him how to pick locks and he had never forgotten. He studied the drawers again, decided the upper right-hand one looked promising, and slipped the wire into the lock. As he worked it on to the catch he kept his eyes trained on the photograph of Magdalena on the desk. Beautiful bitch. He wouldn't have minded going to bed with her; he had even tried one night when they were alone in Barranco Rosales . . . The catch clicked and Lucas grinned. He wondered if Magdalena had ever told Marcos about that incident.

The drawer slid easily open but contained no cash. It would have to be the chequebook, then. He pulled out the nearest one, saw that it belonged to Marcos's personal account, and laughed.

'Easier than stealing sweets from the blind.'

Lucas turned to one of the last cheques, settled himself in the chair and practised a few strokes on a sheet of paper. Perhaps a few thousand more than he needed, just to tide him over until next month. Marcos owed it to him. Criminal of the man to expect his brother to live on nothing.

'As if I were some blasted *peón*!'

The pen scratched uneasily over the paper. Lucas knew Marcos's signature by heart, but it was best to make sure. That was more like it. He thrust the tip of his tongue between his teeth and applied himself to the cheque.

Three seconds later Marcos walked into the study.

He reached the desk in two strides and grabbed a fistful of Lucas's brown silk shirtfront. 'What the hell do you think you're doing?'

'Nothing! Let go!'

'Nothing?' Marcos snatched up the half-written cheque. 'You call forgery *nothing*? You stupid son of a bitch, how did you open that drawer?'

Lucas's gaze slid past him to Angela, frozen in the doorway. He licked his lips. 'It was open.'

The blow struck him across the mouth and drew blood. He reeled, cursing. Another blow followed. Lucas lunged out blindly and barked his shins on the desk. Marcos slammed him against the wall.

'What did you want that money for?' he rasped.

Less than two inches separated their faces. Large beads of sweat glistened on Lucas's brow: his breath rattled, thick and sour with fear. He moved his lips, but no sound came.

'*What did you want it for?*'

'I l-lost at . . . at c-cards.'

'How much?'

Lucas named a sum. Marcos flung him off and returned to the desk. He wrote a cheque for half the amount and held it out.

'This comes out of your allowance next month,' he snapped.

'What the hell am I supposed to live on?'

'Try working for a change. Listen, you crook,' as Lucas continued to protest, 'I'm not throwing you off La Catalina today because it's Good Friday and we have guests in the house. You'll leave on Monday. Two more days of your filthy face is all I can stomach. Now get out!'

Lucas went.

IV

Marcos threw the chequebook into the drawer, slammed the drawer shut and locked it. His face was hard. After a moment he said, 'I'm sorry. I lost my temper. Lucas is foolish.'

That, thought Angela wryly, is the understatement of the year.

She glanced curiously around the study. It was severe to the point of austerity. White walls, unadorned except for the map of La Catalina behind a large, uncluttered desk. Dark bookshelves stacked with what appeared to be books on farming and cattle management. A black-and-white hide on the floor. The only colour came from the expanse of lawn and park beyond the open window.

'You were going to show me a map of the ranch,' she said.

'Yes, of course.'

He began to describe the map, but his mind was obviously elsewhere. When he finished speaking there was a long, uncertain silence.

'Doesn't Lucas work?' asked Angela, just to say something.

Marcos shrugged. 'What does he know to do? Nothing. My father spoiled Lucas because he is the baby. We are very rich now, my father said. There is no need for Lucas to work.'

'Not very practical. How does he live?'

'I make him an allowance. It is never enough.'

'Can't you cut his allowance so he'll be forced to take a job?'

'He will steal or worse — maybe even go to prison.' Marcos took a pack of cigarettes from his shirt pocket and offered her one. 'Lucas is my brother. I cannot allow that.'

Their hands touched as he held out a match. Angela swallowed. There went her emotions again. Shivers, weak knees, heart pounding — the whole bloody lot. There was a low leather sofa under the window and she moved towards it, needing suddenly to sit down. The handsome rouser was too handsome and too much of a rouser. A lethal combination of male self-confidence and charm. No quickie in the thicket for this man. She should never have shown so much interest in the ranch or asked to see the map in his study. He was far too dangerous. You had to watch out for latinos. They knew how to make a woman feel all woman just by looking at her. The way he was looking at her now.

Damn Jimmy! He should have had better sense than to leave her alone with Marcos Luciani.

'My father used to call men like Lucas pudding-maggots,' said Angela unsteadily. 'They grow fat on the fruits of other men's work and rot everything they touch.'

His dark eyes continued to search her face. 'Your father was a wise man.'

She began to tell him about her parents. Not just who they were or what they did, but long-treasured details of family life she had never spoken of even to Jimmy. Old, familiar memories she kept stubbornly buried in the rubble of Willow Hill. Brought to light in the black-and-white austerity of Marcos's study they sounded strangely unreal, as though they had not really happened to her but to another Angela. A light-hearted, innocent stranger who had wept over Keats's poetry, adored her parents and married Harry Redfield in the old Saxon church on the village green.

Laughing, blue-eyed Harry, who had dreamt of making a fortune in Australia and died at Dunkirk six weeks after the wedding.

For months afterwards she had lain awake praying for a bomb to take her life as well.

'Silly of me, really. We needed the living to fight the war, not the dead. I went into nursing and ended up with a mobile field hospital in Burma. Two years of it. Hell most of the time, but we did manage a few laughs in between.'

'You have much courage,' remarked Marcos quietly.

Angela grimaced. 'One does one's job. When I returned home after the war I discovered that people in England felt they were the only ones who had done any fighting. Life had changed as well. People's attitudes, their unwillingness to work . . . I don't know. Maybe it was me, but somehow it no longer seemed like the England I had grown up in. I felt like a stranger in my own land. When Jimmy asked me to marry him last January – well, to be perfectly honest it seemed like a miracle. A chance to escape and start all over again.'

She had not meant to say that. She would never have said it if Marcos had not been looking at her. He sat close to her on the sofa, his right arm stretched along the back. Less than an inch separated his hand from her shoulder. She could hear the ticking of his watch. Stupid how such a commonplace sound aroused her. The ticking of Marcos's watch and a faint fragrance of eau de cologne. Nothing cloying or effeminate – just a hint of lavender that stirred sensations which were definitely not decorous. Every womanly inch of her prickled. She could feel the warmth of his body. The prickling grew worse. The tension between them was agony. Her heart fluttered in her throat. She ran her tongue over her lips to moisten them; his eyes followed its movement hungrily.

'We had better get back,' said Angela.

Marcos's eyes lingered on the generous curve of her lips; even without looking he was aware of every other part of her body. She had firm, well-shaped breasts. The nipples showed hard under her blouse; it was all he could do to keep himself from reaching out to caress them. The blue flannel trousers she wore fitted like a glove. His hands itched to stroke the warm skin underneath. Her lips smiled at him and his mouth burned to kiss them. She was like a fever in his blood. He had to touch her. He couldn't help himself. His hand moved towards her cheek.

'Angela . . .'

'We really must get back to the others,' she insisted uneasily. 'Jimmy will be wondering what took us so long.'

His hand checked in mid-air. Angela was Jimmy's wife. He must try not to forget that. Marcos drew a deep breath. 'Yes.' The word dropped impatiently, damning Jimmy and the world. 'We must get back to the others.'

For the rest of the weekend they went through the motions of their respective roles as Jimmy's wife and Jimmy's friend, but the ghost of that unfinished caress lay between them.

CHAPTER SEVEN

I

Years later Angela found herself smiling when she recalled that first Easter weekend and the bewildering days of Los Alamos which followed. At the time her sense of humour was trapped in a whirlpool of conflicting emotions and flatly refused to cooperate.

The weekend itself passed without any major disaster. Even Gladys's white tulle gown, ludicrous though it might be in such a setting, caused no more than a startled ripple of laughter quickly stifled. The artificial courtesy which followed was, if anything, more embarrassing, but Gladys stubbornly continued to defy ridicule.

Even then we underestimated her, reflected Angela. Secure in our own arrogance we took her for a fool.

Strange how quickly that particular weekend blended into memory – parts of it more distinct than others, parts of it indelibly etched into her mind with bittersweet sharpness.

Easter Sunday Mass, for instance.

The candlelit interior of Laguna Grande's pink stucco church, the gaily painted plaster saints. The unfamiliar liturgy and shrilly enthusiastic choir of schoolgirls backed by a wheezing organ, the reverently silent congregation – all added surprising poignancy to a morning whose ancient symbolism lay buried in the rubble of Angela's childhood.

The first day of the week cometh Mary Magdalene early, when it was yet dark . . .

Beside her on the hard wooden pew Mercedes's thin fingers worked doggedly through the ivory beads of a rosary; beyond Mercedes stretched a row of women's heads veiled in short black mantillas and bowed in prayer. Their devotion moved Angela deeply. She began to pray herself, groping awkwardly for half-forgotten words from the happy days of Willow Hill.

. . . give us this day our daily bread and forgive us . . .

Something broke her concentration. She turned her head and saw Marcos standing by a column at the back of the church. A shaft of light from a side window streamed across his face, stripping it of shadows; in the brightness every feature lay exposed as though sculpted in relief by a remorseless hand. The eyes alone seemed alive, dark and hungry, staring at her and demanding recognition.

. . . our trespasses . . .

The words faltered and came to a halt. Prayer at such a time seemed like blasphemy.

II

Memory of the afternoon's *asado* came in flashes of sight and sound. A long trestle table under the trees in the Bajo; faces and names, voices and laughter. Two large, smouldering fires; the ranch hands grouped along tables on the far side. Dark-eyed women, their black hair neatly braided, bustled energetically to and fro. Isabel ran up with a thick sausage on a chunk of bread.

'Here's your *chorizo*, Angela. Can I have some of your wine, please?'

Wine. Fillets of beef, whole kids, mounds of short ribs and flank steaks roasting over hot coals. Sizzling rows of sausages. Black pudding, kidneys and sweetbreads. Wine again. Trays of Rosario's feather-light meat pasties seasoned with cumin seed and bursting with green olives. Demijohns of red wine, baskets of crisp bread, huge bowls of green salad. Jimmy's voice, slightly thickened with wine.

'Enjoying yourself, angel? Here, have some more beef.'

A relentless sun beat down on the dusty yard; the air reeked of smoke and grilled meat. Jimmy began to tease Pedro about his polo-playing. The priest grinned good-naturedly and several of the other men joined in the fun. Angela's head throbbed. She longed for a glass of water, for cool green grass, for silence. It was not fair to blame Jimmy for her frayed nerves, of course. He knew these people and felt at home with them. Their language, their jokes, their laughter were part of his world.

Part of my world now – for better or worse.

A guilty feeling of disloyalty prompted Angela to make the effort and match Jimmy's mood, but her eyes kept straying to the end of the table where Marcos sat talking to a grizzled man in uniform. He looked up, caught the glance and smiled at her; before she could stop herself Angela smiled back.

The sudden intimacy of that brief, seemingly innocent gesture nearly undid what little composure she had left.

III

Lucas was the first to leave on Monday. He stormed off after breakfast, having failed to cadge any more money. With the exception of the maid Rosita, whom he had cornered in the garden shed for a lusty half hour on Saturday afternoon, everyone was glad to see him go.

Jimmy and Angela followed shortly afterwards.

They headed north along the narrow, winding road that would soon become so familiar; what seemed now a featureless sea of grass would reveal its hidden details one by one until every inch of the way was printed in Angela's heart. The solitary clump of carob trees that marked La Catalina's northern corner, the abandoned farm house eight miles further on, the unexpectedly steep rise as the road swung east and snaked across a dry lake bed, the railroad crossing and stockyards five miles before the turn-off. Forty-five minutes if the road was dry, Marcos had said. Thirty if Jimmy drives.

The road was as dry as a bone, but *el loco* Morgan was enjoying his honeymoon and it took forty.

IV

The house at Los Alamos stood in the middle of a dusty yard, surrounded by listless poplars and a few straggling acacias.

At the turn of the century it had enjoyed a brief blaze of glory as the private railway station of an eccentric Russian count who won eight thousand acres of land at roulette and built his own track so he could survey his property in comfort. Seven years later an outraged neighbour had surprised his wife cuddling with the count in the Russian's private train and shot them both dead on the spot; when the local scandal-dust settled Los Alamos was put up for sale.

'Has a bit of an unlucky name around these parts,' laughed Jimmy as he negotiated a narrow bend. 'Folks are superstitious. They horn their fingers and cross themselves whenever one mentions the old Russian. Don't pay any attention to it. I haven't seen a ghost or its shadow in the seven years I've lived here.'

The car drew up before a low, faded red building with a zinc roof. A ramshackle porch ran the length of the front. Several beds of dispirited flowers were scattered at random around the house, but any attempt to resemble a garden had long since been undermined by sturdy ranks of weeds and thistles. A black dog scratched industriously among roses that were all stalk; other dogs of varying sizes and colours emerged from under the porch steps and sniffed at Angela's ankles as she got out of the car.

A large, shapeless woman dressed in black waited in the yard; a cadaverous man with a drooping moustache hovered behind her. They looked as though they had been painted into position against the backdrop of the house – heads erect, eyes impassive, the woman's hands folded across an ample stomach, the man's shoulders hunched under a worn leather jacket. As they came forward Angela saw he only had one arm.

'Welcome back, Don Jimmy.' The woman studied Angela through startlingly pale, heavy-lidded eyes, obviously gauging the challenge to her authority. 'I've lit the fire in the big room to take off the chill.'

Jimmy drew Angela forward into the gaze of those wary eyes and smiled somewhat sheepishly. 'This is the Señora Angela, Tiburcia. My wife.'

The woman wiped her hands on a faded blue apron; a thin wedding band gleamed between folds of swarthy skin. The eyes continued to scrutinize Don Jimmy's wife as though she were some strange, unwelcome worm.

'*Cómo está usted?*' said Angela with painstaking care and a smile, but the dour face did not change expression.

'We've been having trouble up at the stream, Don Jimmy,' said the man. 'That Remigio Juárez, he's blocked the sluice gate to draw off water for his tobacco field. We fixed it, but he's dug a canal further down. You'd better go see for yourself. Juárez don't pay no attention to me.'

'There's my morning shot to hell.' Jimmy unloaded the cases and tossed Angela a bunch of keys. 'Here, angel. Tiburcia'll show you around. Tell her to give you lunch. I'll be back sometime in the afternoon.'

'But . . .'

'Juárez and I have a long-standing battle over that stream.' He got back into the car and beckoned to the man. 'Come on, Saúl. Let's see what the old fool has to say about it this time.' They drove off in a cloud of dust, leaving Angela and poker-faced Tiburcia staring at each other.

V

Tiburcia took several hours to thaw. She showed Angela around the house, pointing out different details in laconic monosyllables as though expecting each word to be challenged; somewhat to her surprise no challenge was forthcoming.

Bedroom, bathroom, Jimmy's office. A narrow passage painted blue; a second bathroom dominated by an old-fashioned tin tub; a spare bedroom and an empty room that overlooked a grape arbour. Back down the passage and into the front room. A green door set between large windows gave directly on to the porch, which faced south; the west wall was taken up by a red-and-white tiled fireplace, the opposite one was cluttered with wooden filing cabinets. Old magazines, dog-eared westerns, and a mouldy collection of the *Encyclopaedia Britannica* crowded on a makeshift bookshelf against the remaining wall. Angela prodded at a low sofa covered in shabby brown cotton.

'You could do with something flowered and a good restuffing.'

She looked up at a sudden sound and saw Tiburcia watching like a hawk.

They went through a wide door half concealed by the filing cabinets and down a short flight of steps into the kitchen. Wood-burning stove, blue dresser decorated with red hearts and white flowers, a rectangular table covered with pink oilcloth and three chairs painted bright orange. A battered icebox had been thrust uncomfortably into a corner next to a chipped enamel sink. Tiburcia took a deep breath, planted herself squarely in front of the stove and fixed Angela with a flinted eye.

'*Mi cocina*,' she announced. My kitchen.

Angela knew enough Spanish to catch the emphasis on *my*. In a sudden flash of inspiration she smiled and indicated the gleaming row of pots and pans ranged along the dresser.

'*Tu cocina*.'

Your kitchen. *Your* told the defiant cook all she wanted to know and her face relaxed visibly. Don Jimmy's pale-headed wife might not be so bad after all; certainly she didn't give herself airs the way his mother did. Tiburcia detested Cora Morgan. A thin, sharp-nosed *gringa* who never missed an opportunity to meddle and complain; a sour-face who took little pains to conceal her dislike for her son's way of life.

'*Gringa bruja*, that's what she is,' Tiburcia would mutter in disgust after one of the Morgans' rare visits. 'A witch and there's no telling me she ain't.'

Señora Angela was another matter. Too thin and pale like all *gringas*, but nothing Los Alamos's food and sunshine couldn't remedy. She had the makings of a good wife and as for Don Jimmy himself . . . Tiburcia plunked a steaming cup of coffee down on the table and motioned for Angela to sit down.

A blind man could see Don Jimmy was crazy about her. As long as she didn't meddle and gave him healthy children everything would be all right.

VI

Jimmy returned at four o'clock with a plump turkey Remigio Juárez had reluctantly handed over as a peace-offering. He found Angela perched on a rickety stepladder in the front room; she grinned happily and waved at the two front windows.

'Brick-red curtains, I think. And we must have blinds. How can you live without them?'

'Never thought about it.' His eyes swept the room incredulously. 'Where the hell are my filing cabinets? What's that table doing in the corner there?'

71

Angela came down gingerly off the stepladder. 'One of the men helped me move the files into the empty room. I want that corner for our dining-room.'

'I've always eaten in the kitchen.'

'We're going to have a proper dining-room.' She ran her fingers through her thick, flaxen hair with an impatient gesture. 'There's so much to do! I want to go into Laguna Grande tomorrow and look for material to make curtains and covers for the chairs. The sofa has to be re-stuffed. I can do it if you find me some wool – you know, scraps and things. There's an old sewing machine in the spare bedroom I can use . . .'

Her voice ran on, listening details.

When Jimmy had casually assured Marcos that Angela could cope with everything he had not given much thought to what form that coping would take – except possibly for a vague notion of magic wands or a snap of her very capable fingers. To hear her now enthusiastically discussing measurements and materials and curtains as though embarked on a major operation sounded ominous. The house had suited him as it was for seven years; all he needed was his angel to grace it with her fair presence and make him happy. Precise, technical discussions about redecoration smacked of feminine warfare, which he found decidedly alarming. Somewhat taken aback by this unsuspected sidelight to his angel Jimmy pulled a face and hedged.

'We'll send off to Buenos Aires for what you need. My mother probably knows some places – or we can ask Mercedes. I'll get one of the women to do your sewing when the time comes.'

'I'll do my own sewing, thank you,' retorted Angela firmly. There's no need to bother your mother or Mercedes. I'm sure I'll find what I need in Laguna Grande.'

'But no one buys – damn it all, Angela! Laguna's a hole in the wall. Only the locals buy things like material there.'

'Aren't we local?'

'Yes. No. I mean – oh, hell! You know what I mean.'

'I'm afraid I don't.'

'Angela . . .'

'I don't want silks or satins, Jimmy. I want good, strong rustic stuff that can stand up to sun and wind and dust or whatever else there is out here. Don't tell me people in Laguna Grande don't have curtains or don't cover their furniture.'

The general was marshalling her forces. Jimmy laughed ruefully and tried another tack.

'How're you going to get into Laguna tomorrow?'

'Drive, of course. Oh, for heaven's sake!' as he started to protest. 'I'm not a hot-house lily! After driving jeeps through Burma I certainly think I can handle the roads in Argentina!'

'Mercedes is returning tomorrow. Tell me what you need and I'll ring in a while and ask her to send it from Buenos Aires.'

'Jimmy, it's our home!'

Our home contained a half-desperate urgency that puzzled him. He stared at Angela for a moment, then kissed her.

'Do whatever you want with the bloody place, angel. Let's have tea.'

VII

In the weeks that followed Angela sanded floors, scrubbed walls, splashed on coat after coat of paint; Tiburcia, having recovered from the initial shock of seeing the señora on her knees scraping at old varnish with a broken knife, recruited one of her eleven granddaughters to help. The girl, named Dominga, threw herself into her task with an enthusiasm that delighted and encouraged Angela. Her fondest recollections of those early days at Los Alamos were bound up in the warm smell of fresh paint, the sound of Dominga's humming, the slap of Tiburcia's shapeless feet as she shuffled in with the inevitable kettle and gourd for a few rounds of strong, bitter *maté*.

The ranch hands shook their heads in amazement when they heard that Don Jimmy's wife worked on her knees like an ordinary woman, but they decided it must be the way of the *gringos*. You couldn't hold it against her. The woman had a pleasant word for everyone, tried her best to speak Spanish and did not despise local customs. One-armed Saúl, Tiburcia's husband and foreman of the ranch, told how the *gringa* had taken to brewing Don Jimmy's *maté* in the morning before breakfast and even drank it herself.

'Hot and strong without sugar,' he added approvingly. 'Don Jimmy, he nearly split his sides the first time she tasted *maté*.

73

Coughed like her lungs was bursting and burnt her lips on the metal straw, but now she draws it like an old hand.'

They soon learned the *gringa* had other talents as well.

One morning shortly after Jimmy and Saúl left for a cattle auction a newly sharpened axe sliced through a ranch hand's leg, leaving a thick flap of his calf dangling by a thread. Tiburcia brought the news.

'It's young Benito Cifuentes,' she said, rolling her eyes. 'Never seen so much blood! And the *patrón* ain't here – what'll we do, Señora Angela?'

Señora Angela wasted no time. She bound the flap of flesh into place as firmly as possible with clean rags and put Cifuentes into the back of the car; then she ordered a quesy-looking Dominga to sit with him and pack ice around the bandages. The drive to the surgery in Laguna Grande nearly broke Jimmy's own record and caused a stir among the local townspeople, but Benito Cifuentes's leg was saved.

Small, spare Dr Feldman, who ran the surgery, raised his eyebrows when he saw Angela's handiwork. 'Quick thinking, señora.'

'I was a nurse in the war,' explained Angela in her best Spanish.

Jacobo Feldman stared at her over his glasses. 'In that case you will help with the operation. My nurse is not here and I must sew up this mess quickly.'

News that *el loco* Morgan's wife had helped stitch Benito Cifuentes's leg spread like wildfire. In the Mendes's over-crowded sitting room Norma listened to Feldman's nurse complain that the *gringa* had done her out of what by rights was her job.

'Because I wasn't there, says the doctor! All I had was a headache. I can't work with a headache, but I'd have been there if he really needed me!' the woman spluttered indignantly. 'It's all a plot, *compañera*. That *gringa*'s been planted by the Americans to swindle us out of our work! Yankee imperialism, that's what it is – and the doctor's in with 'em. He's a Jew, isn't he?'

Norma, scenting political fervour to rival her own, made discouraging sounds. 'The doctor's a good man who's sympathetic to the cause, Lola. Besides, the *gringa*'s English and I hear she was a nurse in the war. Stands to reason she'd help if asked. Goes to show there's some decency in her, even if she did marry that bastard Morgan.'

Lola shook a synthetically blonde head. 'There must be something because this happened while I was absent from surgery. If I had been there they wouldn't have dared!'

Not even Norma Mendes could shake the nurse's muddled convictions on that point.

VIII

One incident two months after her arrival stood out very clearly in Angela's memory.

She had driven into Laguna Grande with Tiburcia's weekly shopping list and measurements for curtains in the spare room. The mornings were much colder now; this particular one was raw and overcast. As she parked in front of La Federala, the general shop on the main square, she noticed a group of men lounging near the blue-and-white Party headquarters in the next block. They did not appear to be locals, but beyond a cursory glance she went about her business and gave them little thought.

La Federala was crowded and Angela had to wait some time. While the owner was adding up her purchases a blast of martial music crashed across the morning and rattled the shop windows. Don Tito looked up from his column of figures and scowled.

'Don't know what they think they're doing, making all that racket,' he grunted. 'Leave us working folk in peace, that's what I say. All this politicking – we don't need none of it.'

Two months dealing with Tiburcia had considerably improved Angela's Spanish. She agreed that the noise was deafening and paid the bill. Don Tito looked at her uneasily as she gathered up her purchases.

'I wouldn't go outside just yet, señora,' he warned. 'That's a rough bunch out there and they're looking for trouble. You shouldn't have come in today.'

'Oh, I'll be all right,' laughed Angela and walked out into a blustering, icy wind.

It whipped through the lime trees around the square, rattling branches and raising thick swirls of dust. A large crowd had gathered round a platform in front of the Party headquarters; they were chanting and clapping to the strident strains blaring from the loudspeaker. Uneasy clusters of bystanders hovered on the fringes of the crowd. Angela recognized Dr Feldman and waved. He came over and shook her hand.

'Have you come to watch the rally, señora?'

'Is that what all this noise is about?' She pointed to a large, bull-necked man fiddling with a microphone on the platform. 'A rally for what?'

Feldman twisted a neat, sardonic little grin. 'Artemio Mendes is officially launching his campaign for governor today. Quite a celebration. I see he's brought in followers from outside Laguna as well.'

'Do you think he will be elected governor?' asked Angela.

The doctor shrugged. 'Maybe. It makes little difference to me – but I imagine the local cattlemen won't be pleased if he is.' Out of the corner of his eye he saw someone entering the surgery and sighed. 'Ah, well, I must get back to work. Give my regards to Don Jimmy, señora – and don't linger in Laguna today. There may be trouble.'

Artemio Mendes bellowed at the crowd and waved his fist in the air. The bystanders muttered nervously. The crowd around the platform roared. Angela got into the car and started the engine. It stalled. She tried again. Through the rear-view mirror she saw another crowd of men and women marching into the square from the opposite end. They advanced ten abreast and five deep, waving placards and banners. Her heart thudded with sudden fright and she pumped frantically on the accelerator.

The newcomers fanned out and began to shout at the bystanders. Angela caught sight of swarthy, grimacing faces and clenched fists. A buxom, auburn-haired woman screeched and Artemio Mendes brayed in reply. The music boomed and crashed above the wind. High over the square Perón and Evita conferred a pasteboard blessing on Artemio Mendes's dreams of glory.

Angela pushed the starter button. The car stalled again and her insides lurched.

God, get me out of here!

Someone wrenched open the car door and seized her by the arm. It was Marcos.

'Why are you here?' he demanded. 'Where is Jimmy?'

This was not the charming host who had played havoc with her emotions during Easter; the Marcos Luciani who stood staring down at her with blazing eyes was an alarmingly grim, forceful man of action. She had not seen much of him since that disturbing

76

weekend. The few times they met he had been on edge, but she never thought he could get as rattled as this. His voice crackled as he repeated the question.

'Where is Jimmy, Angela?'

She stammered. 'At the ranch. I came into town to do some shopping.'

'Today!' He cursed under his breath. 'What is the trouble with your car?'

Fists drummed on a nearby truck, drowning out her reply. Marcos grabbed the shopping bags from the back seat and motioned to her angrily.

'Get out! I will take you to Los Alamos. *Vamos!*'

She needed no urging. The truck owner ran out of the hotel, shouting and brandishing a crowbar; the crowd drummed harder on his truck and jeered. Marcos pushed Angela through the bystanders. Someone recognized him and yelled his name; Artemio Mendes raised meatpacker's fists above his head and bellowed into the microphone.

'Bloodsucking oligarchs!'

'Run!' ordered Marcos as the crowd in the square took up the cry.

They dodged a group of Mendes's loyal followers and veered off down a side street. A few hopeful diehards gave chase. Marcos's car was parked near the corner. He thrust Angela inside and jumped in after her. A stone hit the boot. Marcos switched on the engine. Several more stones flew through the air. He slammed down the accelerator and the car roared off in a cloud of dust. The diehards laughed. The next time they would catch the bloodsucking oligarch. They would string him up from the highest lamp-post in the square.

IX

Angela sat huddled in a daze.

Her mind whirled with screaming voices, blaring music and the rocking speed of the car as they raced through the maze of lanes and narrow, twisting tracks that formed Laguna Grande's back streets. The main road west was blocked by a crowd of women wrapping Perón's statue in blue-and-white bunting and flowers.

Marcos swerved sharply east, circled the convent, bumped over the railway crossing and picked up a parallel road heading west again. He drove at breakneck speed, his face hard, his knuckles white around the steering wheel. Angela closed her eyes. To be rescued from a mob in order to be jolted to death in the middle of the pampa was the last straw. She began to feel sick and wondered if it was safe to stop for a moment.

'Why did Jimmy let you come to Laguna?' demanded Marcos impatiently. 'He knew about the rally today. It was crazy for you to come.'

'Please,' said Angela in a very small voice. 'Please stop the car.'

He pulled over to the roadside, opened the glove compartment and took out a silver flask.

'Drink some *caña*. It will help the nerves.'

The *caña* proved to be raw, burning brandy. Angela took a few hasty gulps and shuddered; when he replaced the flask she saw the cold, dark barrel of a gun.

'Why did Jimmy let you come?'

'I don't know!' snapped Angela, suddenly irritated by his insistence. 'Maybe he forgot all about the damn rally!'

She caught her breath because her stomach lurched again; after a moment her teeth began to chatter. She tried to make them stop, but they continued to click like castanets. Angela closed her eyes. The next thing she knew the car was moving and Marcos had his arm around her. It was the most natural thing in the world to lean against him and feel the steadying strength of his arm. Once again a deep sense of belonging swept over her, but this time she did not turn away.

They drove like that for some time without speaking. The sky hung in low, leaden billows, swollen by the wind; when the car stopped again Angela heard the wind whistling eerily down the telegraph wires along the road.

'Are you feeling better?' asked Marcos.

She nodded, caught up in her belonging and his nearness. The car enclosed them both within a separate universe far removed from time and space. A purely physical world, warm and sensual and intimate, although there was no contact between them other than the weight of her head on Marcos's arm. If only I could stay like this forever, thought Angela. If I touch him, I'll feel his heart. If I look at him . . . She stirred and turned her head. Their eyes met.

'How very lovely you are,' he whispered.

Their kiss filled the universe. They felt nothing but the warmth of their mouths, the texture of their lips, the eagerness of their tongues flowing into each other. Fullness of flesh and form. Sweet warmth, sweet moisture, the exquisite sweetness of their desire. Their lips flamed white heat, their bodies took fire. Angela moaned softly. Marcos found the hollow of her throat. Their lips came together again, his hands searched for her breasts. Full and sweet. He wanted to stroke them, kiss them, taste their sweetness. He wanted to enter her, become part of her, love her to exhaustion . . . *Jimmy's wife.*

He drew away abruptly, chilled by those two damning words. His hands fumbled blindly for a cigarette and lit it. The harsh, acrid smoke shattered their isolation and brought dimensions into unwelcome perspective.

'I am Jimmy's friend,' said Marcos hoarsely. 'It is very difficult for me.'

I'm Jimmy's wife, thought Angela unsteadily. It's a hell of a lot more difficult for me. She began to rearrange her windbreaker, trying to act as though a heavy petting session with her husband's friend was a casual occurrence.

Marcos leaned over and brushed a flaxen strand from her forehead. His smile and the look in his eyes made nonchalance next to impossible.

'It is very difficult for me,' he repeated. 'I am in love with you, Angela.'

Angela's stomach did a somersault and landed in her throat. Oh, my God! she thought in horror. I'm going to be sick.

'Marcos, please . . .'

'No, listen to me. If I say I love you it is not because we have been kissing and I speak foolish things to amuse myself. What I say . . .' He frowned at the top of her head, struggling for the right words in a language that seemed inadequate. 'I speak from the heart. I like women, to amuse myself with them – why not? I am a man. But love – that is different. I am in love with you. At Easter I knew it. Since then I try to keep away, but I have business with Jimmy. I cannot say to him I will not do business because I love your wife. It is very difficult. Do you understand?'

Angela kept her eyes fixed on the bleak expanse of pampa stretching on either side of the road. She mustn't think. Thoughts led to comparisons and comparisons were unfair. It wasn't

Jimmy's fault that she had met the right man at the wrong time. That right now all she wanted for that man to keep on kissing her without explanations or justifications of friendship and love.

A rose-covered cottage on the Cam would have been far less complicated. Certainly more in keeping with her conscience. Damn her conscience. Damn Marcos. Damn the world.

She dared herself to look at him and immediately wished she hadn't. His half guilty, half pleading smile was too disarming. His voice matched it.

'You are not angry with me, *gringuita?*'

'No. It 's just that . . .' Her stomach churned uneasily. 'I'm tired, Marcos. Please take me home.'

He stopped the car again before the turn-off for Los Alamos, but this time the reason had nothing to do with love. When they reached the ranch Angela stumbled up the porch steps and was promptly sick again.

A week later she announced to Jimmy that in eight months' time, give or take a few days at either end, he would become a father.

CHAPTER EIGHT

I

Barranco Rosales was a secluded cobblestone street in one of Buenos Aires's most exclusive residential quarters. It was a short street: three blocks lined with jacaranda trees, discreetly wedged between an avenue and a park at the top of a steep slope which in colonial times had overlooked the river. With the exception of a small Benedictine abbey at one end, the buildings were all private homes; the Luciani house and gardens occupied more than half of the middle block and were jokingly referred to by their neighbours as 'the palazzo'.

An architect with a passion for Italian Renaissance had originally built the house for himself. His passion and imagination had combined to create a graceful, four-storey villa set in terraced gardens and screened from curious eyes by high railings covered with ivy; beyond the heavy gate a short gravel driveway led to the front entrance flanked by stately magnolias and ornamental shrubs.

The architect died in 1914 without ever having occupied his dream house; in 1915 Bruno Luciani bought it for a song. Until then his main interest had been La Catalina, but now he set about turning the 'palazzo' into a showplace. He employed a master carpenter from Venice to carve the heavy dark beams in the library and a Florentine artist to decorate the ceiling in the drawing-room. A Neapolitan landscaped the grounds, a monocled Russian emigré advised on the furnishings. Shrewdly aware that wealth alone was of little social value, Bruno also embarked on a crash course in culture. His tall, arrogant figure became a well-known sight at auctions. He took a keen interest in ivory and jade, read innumerable books on arts and antiques, attended concerts and in due course made a name for himself as something of a connoisseur in society circles.

His wife Isabel thought Barranco Rosales pretentious, but she loved Bruno too much to spoil his enjoyment by complaining.

Privately she yearned for the early, simpler days of La Catalina when their fortune was still a dream; publicly she accompanied her husband in his cultural pursuits and humoured them with a half-indulgent smile.

Two of Isabel's five children died in their first year; of the remaining three only Marcos shared her understanding and love for the land. He took after *her* family, the Salazars, she would boast proudly when Bruno was not around. Solid, salt-of-the earth cattlemen with little time for frills and frippery. Marcos finished agricultural college at twenty-two; by the time he was twenty-six he had already married Magdalena and virtually ran La Catalina on his own. He cared as little as his mother did for Barranco Rosales, but Magdalena adored the elegant 'palazzo' and during her lifetime had spared no effort to improve on her father-in-law's ambitions.

II

Young Miguel Luciani, just turned fourteen, was in his father's bad books again. He shuffled from foot to foot in Barranco Rosales's large panelled library and stared at a painting of a robust XVI century Madonna. His father stood in front of a massive ebony desk, arms crossed and mouth compressed in a hard, disapproving line. Miguel shifted his gaze from the Madonna's earthy smile to the thick persian rug underfoot. The sound of his sisters' laughter echoed from beyond the wrought-iron and glass door that led to the winter garden. Lucky kids. He had been romping with them through tropical flowers and potted palms when his father summoned him to the library. Miguel slanted a resentful glance at the towering figure of parental authority armoured in dark grey flannel and swallowed.

'Well?' demanded Marcos severely. 'What have you got to say for yourself?'

'I d-don't know, Papa.'

'You don't know.' Marcos shook a letter from the headmaster of San Gregorio school at him. 'You were caught smoking and playing cards during the lunch-break, and you still have the crust to tell me you don't know!'

Miguel transferred his gaze to the stern portrait of Bruno Luciani behind the desk. No one would have found out about the card game if the maths teacher hadn't been a snoop. Silly old fart. He should have been eating lunch, not prowling around the empty classrooms. What was wrong with a couple of cigs and a game of cards anyway? Miguel stared miserably at the rows of heavy leatherbound volumes lining the library walls. Ten to one the others would get off easy. Ten to one their fathers weren't like Papa. Ten to one they didn't nag their sons to death about being responsible. Miguel didn't want to be responsible. He wanted to enjoy life.

'Boys of your age don't smoke and they don't play cards,' Marcos reminded him in a dry, clipped voice. 'They pay attention to their studies. In future I expect you to do the same. The school's suspending you for a week; during that time you will not leave this house. I've instructed your aunt to cut your pocket money by half for the remainder of the year. Don't try to sweet-talk her into giving you any more,' he added, catching a hopeful glint in Miguel's dark eyes, 'because there'll be hell to pay if she does. The holiday with your friend Pierre next summer is cancelled as well. I've already spoken to his parents.'

'My holiday's c-cancelled?' Miguel's voice squeaked in anguish. He had boasted to all his classmates how the son of a French count had invited him to spend the summer at the count's fabulous seaside villa. 'But – but Papa, please . . .'

'It's your own fault. Maybe you'll think twice before joining in another game of cards.' Marcos tossed the headmaster's letter on the desk. 'I'm warning you, Miguel. One more notice like this and you'll find yourself roughing it with the *peones* on La Catalina. Now go to your room and stay there. You're not having any supper tonight.'

Miguel left the library with ill grace. No supper and he was starving. His stomach growled rebelliously. Papa had meant that last bit about roughing it with the *peones* on La Catalina. That was the way grandfather had brought him up. Miles and miles from nowhere, stuck among *chañar* and stinking cattle. God, what a rotten life! Miguel climbed the long, curving stairway past Flemish and Italian masterpieces and trudged dejectedly towards his bedroom. Half an allowance was as bad as none at all. Aunt Mercedes wouldn't cough up any extra money this time, either. He pulled a face as he passed his father's study. Papa had really laid it on thick, summoning him into the library like that. Trust the old man to make a mountain out of a molehill.

'He probably thinks I'm impressed,' sneered Miguel. 'Awed by family portraits and trophies and all that crap.'

He slammed his bedroom door and threw himself on the bed. A mammoth painting of St Sebastian stuck with arrows stared gloomily down from its place above the headboard. Miguel sighed. He fished a drawing pad and pencil out of his bedside table drawer and started to doodle. He had a fiendish talent for caricature. St Sebastian began to take shape. Heavy, angry lines produced an arrogant nose, a gaping mouth, a pair of sunken eyes. A travesty of martyrdom dressed in cattleman's clothes. The arrows bristled like daggers.

'Why the hell can't Papa leave me alone?' muttered Miguel. 'I don't want to be a rancher. I want to have fun.'

III

Marcos watched the winter rain pelting against the drawing-room window. He hated the drawing-room. Its polished, contrived elegance stifled him. There was too much velvet, too much white-and-gold, too many priceless antiques. He didn't care for the library either – probably because the library had been his father's inner sanctum. A room where Bruno Luciani laid down the law. Perhaps that was why he had summoned Miguel into the library instead of his own study on the second floor. Apart from the family dining-room in the lower regions of the house, his study was the only other place where Marcos felt comfortable at Barranco Rosales. It was his intimate, personal refuge. He could withdraw there at any time and no one would disturb him. He had not wanted to lay down the law to Miguel in his own sanctuary.

How much attention had Miguel paid to his lecture? Probably not much. He was at an age when boys resent authority and discipline. They were rebels. A man didn't love his son the less for that. He taught his son discipline

84

and held up authority. He made him understand and respect the values of heritage. Bruno Luciani had taught his son that lesson at a much earlier age than fourteen. Marcos frowned at the rainsoaked garden outside. He loved his children. He tried to be a good father to them. He wanted them to have the best in life.

In the silk-walled antechamber that housed Bruno Luciani's jade collection a miniature clock whirred twice and chimed six. It had been chiming six ever since Marcos could remember. The real time was half past four. He wished he were back at La Catalina. He wished he were with Angela. He leaned his forehead against the window and began to torment himself with memories of her. Five minutes later his daughters burst into the drawing-room.

'It's almost tea-time, Papa!' sang out Cristina, making for the grand piano at the other end. 'Aunt Mercedes says there's chocolate cake and strawberry tarts. Do you want to hear the piece I'm learning?'

She plunked herself down and methodically began to hammer out elementary Schumann. Isabel took hold of her father's hand.

'Why are you so sad, Papa?'

'I'm not sad, *ñatita*.'

'Yes, you are. Your eyes look sad.' She threw her arms around him and hugged with all her might. 'Do you miss Mama?'

Marcos smiled faintly. 'Yes, I miss her.'

'Miss Nelly says you should get married again,' announced Cristina, banging a few enthusiastic chords. 'I heard her say so to the cook.' She pursed her lips in a droll imitation of the governess's stilted Spanish. 'Such a shame for Señor Marcos to be on his own. He's a nice gentleman . . .'

'Well, he's not getting married!' interrupted Isabel fiercely, her arms still circling Marcos's waist. 'He's not on his own 'cause he's got us and anyway I'm going to take care of him, aren't I, Papa?'

They began to squabble cheerfully about taking care of Papa. Marcos listened with half an ear. He was badly shaken. For the first time since Magdalena's death loneliness hit him with bitter, empty anguish. The shock only served to deepen his pain and longing for Angela.

IV

Mercedes thought Marcos looked poorly, but put it down to the political situation. Men always worried about politics more than was good for them. She remembered how her father ranted during the political troubles in the late twenties and what a time she had calming him down. The hours she had spent praying for his health. Bruno Luciani had been openly scathing of her prayers, but Mercedes had persisted – and included a battery of digestive teas in his diet as a means of lending God a helping hand.

Marcos, unfortunately, was another matter.

If only he would rant, she could cope. Men's explosions of anger were solid, tangible things; what frustrated her were his long silences and the dark, abstracted way he looked at her whenever she addressed him.

He's working himself up to an ulcer or worse, Mercedes diagnosed as she studied her brother's unresponsive face across the dinner table. He's barely touched his food. Perhaps he should see a doctor.

Out loud she said cheerfully, 'We'll be fourteen tomorrow night. Teresa rang to say that Aurora Grandi's brother is coming – the one who paints such strange pictures. Can't say I care for him, but Aurora's quite a pleasant woman. Don't you think so?'

He gave her another distant look, but did not reply.

'I thought we would all have cocktails here before going on to the Jockey Club for dinner,' continued Mercedes, doggedly determined to break through his silence. 'It's hard to believe it's Teresa's thirty-seventh birthday.' She patted a few grey hairs into place and added with a wistful little sigh, 'I remember when I was thirty-seven.'

It was a candid, intimate admission that called for gallantry. Marcos ignored the hint and pushed away his plate. If only he could have avoided tomorrow's dinner party – but Teresa had cleverly arranged matters so that he could not refuse without offending her, and Mercedes had clinched them by inviting everyone for cocktails before dinner. Women's dreams, women's schemes. He wondered with mounting irritation if they had both schemed to pair him and Aurora Grandi together. The irritation edged his voice.

'Ring the bell, Mercedes.'

A studiously solemn butler supervised the removal of the dinner plates. Rosita, imported from La Catalina and looking self-conscious in her black uniform and white lace apron, brushed breadcrumbs on to a small silver dish. The butler brought in a chocolate soufflé. Mercedes beamed. A rich sweet was just the thing to pamper a man's temper.

'How nice to have the Morgans join us tomorrow,' she commented, scooping a generous fluffy mound on to her plate. 'Angela's such a charming person – very *simpática*. She sent me a lovely note thanking us for the crystal goblets we gave them as a wedding present.'

Something so painful in its intensity that it startled Mercedes flickered briefly through Marcos's eyes.

'Jimmy's a fortunate man,' he said flatly.

'Angela will have quite a steadying effect on him and now that there's a baby on the way . . .' Mercedes broke off to stare accusingly at her brother's empty plate. 'Aren't you having any?'

Politics were definitely ruining Marcos's health, she informed God that night and added several fervent pleas to the Virgin Mary to intercede for his well-being.

V

Teresa sat on a white brocade sofa and studied the flower arrangement on a table by the drawing-room window. Pink carnations, a few hopeful sprigs of asparagus fern, a pale pink porcelain vase. Hopeless. Magdalena always kept an ornate silver bowl filled with red and white roses on that table; against the royal blue curtains the arrangement provided a cleverly contrived Gallic touch. More pink carnations on the piano as well. Pathetic. That corner needed something bold, exotic, even flamboyant. Birds-of-paradise and orchids or even double chrysanthemums – bronze and gold with a few white ones to heighten the effect. Poor Mercedes. She tried so hard, but the atmosphere lacked something.

Teresa sipped her cocktail thoughtfully.

Opulence. That was it. The luxuriously sensual aura created by a combination of colour and texture and fragrance that only a woman with artistic sensitivity could achieve. Her dark eyes lingered on a tall, auburn-haired woman talking to Marcos at the far end of the room. Aurora Grandi had artistic sensitivity. All the Grandis were artists – little money for the children after old Enzo drank away his fortune, but they made up for it with a phenomenal amount of culture and artistic talent. Fabio painted, young Lorenzo was a concert pianist, Aurora . . . Teresa smiled to herself. Aurora would make the perfect wife for Marcos.

'My beautiful, enigmatic Mona Lisa – how I long to paint you!' murmured a man's voice and she glanced up to see Fabio Grandi looking down at her with a crooked little smile that might have had any meaning or none at all.

'If you painted me as the Mona Lisa you would probably give me a breast for a head and cover it with eyes,' retorted Teresa. 'Your latest exhibition's scandalous.'

He laughed and fitted a cigarette into a long amber holder. 'If I painted you it would be à la Van Eyck – austere, virginal, and eminently desirable. Naked, of course. May I paint you naked?'

'You may not paint me at all.'

'Are those Don Carlos's orders?'

She cocked a finely pencilled eyebrow in a gesture that both irked and excited him. 'Mine. I have no intention of becoming another one of your mockeries.'

'It would not be a mockery, I assure you.' When Teresa did not reply Fabio turned to survey the rest of the room. 'Now there is a charming Mona Lisa – no, a Saxon Edith.' He waved his cigarette in the direction of Angela. 'The Swan Neck who bartered for Harold's corpse and came away empty-handed. That woman over there has an empty-handed look about her in spite of the smiles.'

'You're quite observant tonight,' remarked Teresa dryly.

'The fair Saxons have always fascinated me, my dear. *Chiaroscuro*: a perfect balance to my passionate Italian temperament, don't you think?'

Teresa's lip curled. 'I would advise you to keep your Italian temperament under control around Jimmy Morgan,' she said.

'He doesn't strike me as being the cuckold type you're so obviously used to.'

'Morgan looks like a peasant.'

Teresa rose from the sofa and walked off without bothering to reply.

'Fabio's been snubbed,' Aurora Grandi remarked to Marcos with a slightly embarrassed laugh. 'He's not cutting any ice with Teresa tonight.'

Politely, because it was expected of him: 'How are Fabio's paintings doing these days?'

'He's struck a gold mine. He turns rich, bored women into surrealist erotica and charges the earth. I'm afraid it's my fault he's here. He's been at loose ends lately and it seemed a good opportunity to keep him out of mischief. When Teresa mentioned she was a man short for dinner I suggested bringing him along.' Aurora made a small, appealing gesture. 'You don't mind, do you?'

'Of course not.'

There was an empty pause, made more awkward by the fact that everyone else had gathered at the other end of the drawing-room. The isolation annoyed Marcos because he felt it must be deliberate – a devilishly female strategy worked out between Teresa and Mercedes to publicize a relationship which did not exist. He had no particular feelings about Aurora Grandi except that physically and intellectually there was too much of her.

Out of the corner of his eye he could see Angela's fair head gleaming in the lamplight. He turned slightly so that he could watch her without appearing too obvious. Feast on her for his own secret dreams.

Jimmy's wife.

She wore a rose-coloured maternity dress made of some soft, flowing material. He thought how well the colour suited her, how it contrasted with her flaxen hair and light golden tan. In the safe upstairs there were a pair of sapphire and diamond earrings which had belonged to his mother. He wished he could give them to her. The large, square-cut ring and the necklace that were part of the set as well. He wished he could give Angela everything he owned.

He wished he had given her the child she carried.

'Have you read Pierre Gotha's latest book?' asked Aurora brightly. 'It's an excellent analysis of existentialism.'

She launched into an animated discussion of Gotha. Marcos had little time for reading books and even less interest in intellectual movements, but he forced himself to appear interested. Existentialism was followed by politics, politics by a request for advice on a business venture, business by a ruthless critique of Fabio's latest work. Aurora was a brilliant conversationalist; her large, rather prominent hazel eyes glowed, her big hands with their glittering garland of rings gesticulated expansively. She used her intellect as a weapon and used it well, but a careful observer might note that she used it in despair.

Marcos listened, replied to questions, agreed or disagreed. Smiled and laughed in all the right places. When the party broke up he helped Aurora on with her coat, escorted her out to his car, continued to smile and listen all during the ride to the Jockey Club in the centre of town.

Courtesy and charm: he wore them like a hairshirt all evening.

VI

Los Alamos was only one in the variety of worlds which, when viewed as a whole, form the complex pattern of Argentina.

There was the world of Jimmy's parents: red-brick house, white shutters, neat flower beds. A tidy world, carefully ordered to reflect the distant memory of England.

A day's journey separated that world from Los Alamos; an hour's drive through Buenos Aires's busy streets and avenues led to the sophisticated elegance of Barranco Rosales. Between these three worlds lay another one which had once contained Angela and Marcos, but tonight seemed unbelievably remote and even unreal.

Angela had not seen him since the day of the rally. Her first three months of pregnancy had been difficult; when she finally began to feel like a human being again, Jimmy reported that Marcos was shuttling like a madman between La Catalina and Buenos Aires.

'I've never seen him so much on edge. Mind you, I don't say there isn't cause for worry. He's got truckers threatening not to move his cattle and problems with the old couple who work La Catalina's cheese plant — hell, it's no joke, but even so he's

90

driving himself too hard.' Jimmy leaned back in his easy chair and puffed thoughtfully on his cigar. 'The irony is that Artemio Mendes keeps his head low these days. There's a rumour that Laguna's bigwigs aren't too keen on his rabble-rousing. Old Marcos has everything out of perspective.'

Angela accepted Teresa's dinner invitation with mixed feelings. It would be exciting to meet new people and dine at the famous Jockey Club, but how the hell was she going to handle Marcos? They had almost committed adultery in his car; they certainly would have if he hadn't suddenly got cold feet and backed off. Or was it really a question of cold feet? Had he meant everything he said – and if so, what was she supposed to do about it? Angela did some soul-searching. Her behaviour in the car had been stupid, to say the least. Marcos knew how to turn a woman on and she had foolishly let him try. Very foolishly. Her marriage was important; she wanted it to succeed. Certainly it was not worth jeopardizing for the sake of a handsome latino's hot kisses. If Marcos Luciani made another pass at her, she would very calmly and politely put him in his place.

Much to her relief Marcos acted as though nothing had happened between them. He clapped Jimmy on the back and teased him about the baby; his brief peck on Angela's cheek would not even have offended a nun. He spent the rest of the cocktail party talking to a tall, intense woman who never took her eyes off him. Teresa, stunning in écru lace and sapphires, told Angela the woman was Aurora Grandi and added with a conspiratorial laugh, 'I think they will announce their engagement soon.'

So that was that. Angela decided to be sensible and enjoy herself. She was doing very well until Marcos came face to face with her on the landing as they were leaving the house. The anguish in his eyes went right through her; what made it worse was that they were alone. She stammered a compliment about the house and followed it with a few inane remarks about the weather.

Marcos did not reply. They stood gazing at each other for several seconds longer before he murmured, 'I cannot forget you, Angela.' He glanced quickly over his shoulder, brushed her mouth with his lips and hurried down the stairs to the entrance.

Angela watched him go. It was no use pretending any more. No use searching her soul for excuses. She was falling in love with Marcos Luciani. It was as simple as that.

VII

On the way down from Los Alamos Jimmy had described the Jockey Club as grand. It was very grand – a large, imposing building on Florida Street, one of Buenos Aires's main shopping thoroughfares. Marble steps, uniformed porters, thick carpeting on the floors; the rich, mellow fragrance of well-worn leather; panelled walls, priceless paintings, the sober hum of male voices behind heavy doors. A world of tradition, wealth and indispensable social connections.

A smiling head-waiter ushered them to a table in a secluded area of the dining-room. Carlos had evidently lavished considerable care on the details for his wife's birthday party. A magnificent display of roses, gardenias, and tiny green orchids cascaded from Bohemian crystal along the centre of the table. Each guest's name was printed on place cards embossed with the Arcos Arizu monogram and perched on the backs of tiny silver dolphins. A green leather box tooled in gold rested between the folds of Teresa's napkin. Inside, sparkling proudly on pale green velvet, sat a flawless diamond and emerald ring.

The women gasped in admiration.

'The emerald was part of my mother's dowry,' said Carlos. 'It was my great-grandfather's gift to his bride the morning after their wedding.' He slipped the ring on Teresa's finger and raised her hand to his lips. 'They loved each other very much.'

In another man both speech and gesture might have seemed ostentatious, even pretentious. Not in Carlos. He conferred on them a dignity and tenderness that brought a sudden lump to Angela's throat. She felt Marcos's eyes on her; it took all her willpower not to return that look.

Angela's dinner partner was a handsome, reddish-blond horsebreeder named Alfredo Rodríguez Nelson; like everyone else at the table he spoke to her in surprisingly fluent English. Over the caviar he said, 'Call me Freddy,' and proceeded to be obnoxiously gallant.

A clear sherried consommé followed the caviar. Carlos and Freddy began to discuss horses; Fabio Grandi studied Angela through small, impertinent eyes. She wished he would look somewhere else. He waved his long, spatulate fingers and said in affected English, 'You must let me paint you, my dear. Van Eyck to perfection – so austere, so virginal. So eminently desirable.' Angela smiled politely and glanced down the table to where a heated political argument was threatening to monopolize the conversation. Marcos was watching her. She began to fiddle with her bread. His eyes were dark magnets.

'Have you found a flat in Buenos Aires yet, Angela?' asked one of the women.

'I haven't looked for one,' she replied.

The woman laughed. 'But you can't bury yourself in the wilds of the pampa! There's no social life at all.'

'The end of the world,' agreed Fabio Grandi with a shrill little cackle. 'Just imagine it, my dear,' he said to Angela. 'A life without education, culture, fashion – so provincial! A peasant's existence.'

'I like the *campo*,' said Angela defensively.

Fabio waved his fingers. 'You still find it quaint, I imagine. Just wait a few more months, my dear. Believe me, the *campo* is worse than hell. Certainly not as amusing.'

'I'm sure you must have first-hand knowledge,' she retorted and ignored him the rest of the evening.

Two waiters in impeccable white jackets deftly changed plates for the main course. Teresa touched Marcos's arm.

'You haven't been down to Los Toros for a long time,' she said with a reproachful little laugh. 'We've made a number of changes in the garden and put in another tennis court.'

'I've been very busy,' he replied somewhat shortly. 'Besides, I'm not much of a tennis player.'

Her voice lifted. 'Don't be silly! You need a rest. Why don't you and Aurora come down next weekend? It would be just the four of us.'

It was not the most subtle of invitations. Marcos heard Aurora Grandi's half-eager, half-embarrassed laugh and fought down a rising wave of anger.

'I'm returning to La Catalina the day after tomorrow,' he said. Then, realizing how abrupt that sounded, forced a smile. 'Thanks just the same, Teresa. Some other time perhaps.'

Only a very insensitive woman could ignore the irritation behind that smile. Aurora flushed, annoyed with both Teresa and herself for having taken Marcos's interest for granted. At thirty-six and still unmarried she could ill afford to throw away her chances; any reminder would be found in the mirror on her dressing table. Men like Marcos Luciani must be charmed, not bullied, into marriage. She took a sip of wine to steady panic and launched frantically into a brilliant account of the Colón Theatre's latest staging of *Aida*. Across the table Mercedes glanced at her watch and stifled a yawn. Freddy Rodríguez Nelson moved closer to Angela.

'What do you do with yourself all day?' he murmured, smoothing down his moustache. 'Los Alamos must be a very boring place for such a charming young woman.'

Angela edged away and sketched a chilly smile. 'Not at all. You'd be amazed how much I enjoy making a home for my husband.'

She forced herself to sound convincing. A home for her husband was the only weapon she had against Marcos. It was her only talisman against the treacherous magic of falling in love.

CHAPTER NINE

I

Artemio Mendes's political campaign was flagging. With elections two months away he still had not been able to drum up much support outside Laguna Grande — and even there his efforts were being hampered by jittery moderates like the mayor, Eustaquio Flores. Flores might swear on his children's heads that he was a loyal Peronist, but Mendes suspected him of secretly supporting the landowners. Always cautioning against a head-on confrontation, always trying to lick their boots. He was as bad as Juan Gaspari: political parasites who kowtowed to God and the Devil alike in order to secure a place for themselves in Heaven and in Hell.

Artemio Mendes knew you could only have it one way.

He also knew that his problem was one of influence. The governor of the province was a former trade union boss who claimed to be on a first-name basis with everyone, including Evita.

'That doesn't mean anything,' snorted Norma Mendes scornfully. 'I've heard say that Evita doesn't like him. He won't get re-elected without her backing, don't worry.'

Artemio looked doubtful. 'I know the señora has the last word, *compañera*, but I don't trust González. He's so crafty he'll see his way to getting round her.'

'No one gets around Evita!' protested Norma.

'Maybe — but I still don't trust him.'

Influence could be challenged with promises, provided one contacted the right people. Artemio had friends among certain militant sectors of the Party, some of whom owed him favours. Clearly the time had come to call his debts.

As further incentive and to boost his own self-esteem he decided to ignore Eustaquio Flores's pleas for moderation and stage a show of strength.

II

During the two weeks that followed Marcos's return to La Catalina there was an outbreak of serious trouble in the Laguna Grande area.

Some cattlemen were unable to find transportation for their herds, others had their farm equipment sabotaged. One rancher's barns were burned down by unidentified arsonists. Tadeo Ortíz, whose ranch, La Juana, lay ten miles southwest of Laguna Grande, complained bitterly to Marcos about labour problems when they met at the stockyards during an auction. One of La Juana's ranch-hands had taken off on Friday night and returned drunk the following Tuesday; when Ortíz docked his wages the man threatened to report him to the local Peronist headquarters.

'Can't think what this country's coming to,' added the rancher in disgust. 'It's got so I'd even take a shot at Artemio Mendes if I thought it would do any good.'

'It won't,' replied Marcos grimly. 'Get rid of him and someone else'll fill his shoes before the bastard's cold.'

Tadeo Ortíz ran his fingers through thick grey hair and sighed. 'Peronism's rotting this country to the core, that's the trouble. Worse thing is there's no getting rid of it. I tell you, *amigo* – Peronism's the curse of this land and it's here to stay.'

Marcos's own troubles began in earnest when he closed down La Catalina's small cheese-making plant.

Old Doña Tránsito and her husband had worked the plant for thirty years. Their original arrangement with Bruno Luciani had been a simple one: they provided him with cheese, he provided them with a roof and the opportunity of making a few pesos on the side. There was no signed contract. Marcos had allowed the arrangement to continue for old time's sake, but Artemio Mendes told Doña Tránsito and her husband that they were being exploited.

'You should be protected by industrial regulations,' he said. 'Tell Luciani he has to sign a formal contract or you'll denounce him for breaking the law.'

Marcos refused to become involved with industrial regulations; his lawyer warned him that if he didn't sign a contract he might find himself in very serious trouble.

'Not even your man Gaspari will get you out of it,' concluded the lawyer dryly.

That was the end of the cheese-making plant. Doña Tránsito and her husband protested indignantly.

'I'm sorry,' said Marcos when they confronted him. 'If it were up to me I'd keep the plant open, but with these new laws it's out of the question. You'll be paid adequate compensation for loss of tenancy.'

Doña Tránsito and her husband were stunned. El Rubio, the wily ranch-hand who acted as Mendes's mouthpiece, had assured them there was nothing to worry about. The *patrón* would sign a contract because it was his duty.

'What's more,' he had added, 'there's great changes coming, *compañeros*. When Artemio's governor, ranches like La Catalina'll belong to the people. You'll own the cheese-plant and a herd and anything else you want.'

All Doña Tránsito and her husband wanted was the security they had known for thirty years. Now they were left with nothing. They complained to Mendes, who immediately made political capital out of their woes.

His wife Norma held a public collection for 'these poor, starving victims, driven ruthlessly out into the cold with nothing but the clothes on their backs!' and managed to collect fifty-six pesos. Doña Tránsito was embarrassed.

'There ain't no need,' she protested proudly. 'We've got enough clothes. Don Marcos says we can stay for three months while we look for another place. He's even offered to help with the mortgage for a small farm.'

'You've been treated like dogs!' cried Norma. 'Shameful! Evita will hear of this outrage, *compañera*! She'll weep over it like I do!' The ample bosom heaved as twenty pesos were thrust into Doña Tránsito's gnarled hand. 'This is for you.'

The old woman's shrewd eyes studied the money. 'There was more than that,' she said after a moment. 'You counted fifty-six pesos.'

'The rest is your donation to the cause,' retorted Norma firmly. 'We're fighting a battle, *compañera*. Every bit counts.'

That evening Artemio Mendes organized a rally in front of the church. Father Antonio, Laguna Grande's elderly priest, complained that the noise disturbed his catechism class. Mendes held his ground.

'God protects the poor, father!' he boomed. 'Doña Tránsito and her husband are destitute now, thanks to Luciani's greed! I want God and everyone to hear their story!'

The priest observed mildly that God would undoubtedly prefer to hear both sides of the story. He was a kindly man who did not believe in mixing religion with politics. As the strident strains of the 'Peronist March' crackled through the cold evening air, Father Antonio reflected with a sinking heart that his beliefs belonged to a rapidly disappearing world.

III

After an unseasonably dry winter it was raining at La Catalina. Heavy gusts of wind whipped across the park, tossing the trees like beggars' arms against a leaden sky. Down in the Bajo rain drummed a steady tattoo on zinc roofs and turned the cattle pens into muddy swamps.

In one of the barns El Rubio was busy explaining to the ranch hands about Doña Tránsito and her husband. About exploitation of the poor by men like the *patrón* and the need for decisive action.

'What kind of action?' asked someone curiously.

El Rubio shook his fist. 'A strike!' he bellowed. 'The victims of greed need our support!'

'Stop talking crap, man,' growled the ranch-hand named Pardo. 'That old couple's troubles ain't got nothing to do with us. If Don Marcos wants to get rid of them, that's his business. He's the boss.'

One of the younger men argued that El Rubio had a point. El Rubio seized on this support to expand on the need for action. Pardo listened for a few more minutes, then slipped out of the barn and made his way up to the big house. Marcos and Pablo Losa were having lunch. They looked around in surprise as the ranch-hand appeared in the doorway of the dining-room.

'What's the matter?' asked Marcos.

'El Rubio's making trouble, *patrón*,' replied Pardo anxiously. 'Talking about going on strike because of the cheese plant. He's trying to keep us from taking the herd to the stockyards in Laguna this afternoon.'

'Is anyone paying attention to him?' demanded Losa.

Pardo shrugged. 'Five or six of the younger lads. The rest of us don't want nothing to do with it.'

Marcos pushed back his chair with a violent oath and strode out of the house.

IV

El Rubio continued to harangue the men in the barn. His thick voice echoed harshly across the empty yard, punctuated by the clatter of rain on zinc. It was criminal to work for a man who exploited them the way Luciani did, brayed the voice. Look at Doña Tránsito and her husband. Thirty years working like slaves and now they were being thrown off La Catalina like dogs.

'That herd of steers out there'll make men like Luciani fat while we starve!' roared El Rubio. 'Let him move it if he wants to sell his beef! There's not a man among us who'll betray the poor!'

The few feeble cheers he raised were quickly stifled as Marcos appeared in the open doorway. The ranch-hands drew back and watched uneasily to see what would happen. The *patrón* was half a head taller than El Rubio and just as muscular. Strength for strength, they were equally matched. An expectant silence filled the barn.

'You're fired,' Marcos told El Rubio sharply. 'Losa'll pay you a month's wages. I want you off La Catalina in half an hour.'

The ranch-hand leered. 'You can't fire me. I ain't done nothing.'

'You've been inciting my men to strike. I won't have politics on my ranch. Half an hour — and I don't want to see you around La Catalina again.'

El Rubio licked his lips. Accusing the *patrón* of social injustice behind his back was one thing; repeating that accusation to his face was quite another.

'Anyone who wants to join El Rubio gets his wages and half an hour to leave La Catalina,' snapped Marcos.

No one spoke. He turned on his heel and strode out; he was halfway across the yard when Pablo Losa shouted.

'Behind you! Watch out!'

He whirled as El Rubio whipped out a knife and raced after him. Marcos threw up his left arm; the blade slashed through his sleeve and opened a long, crooked gash. El Rubio cursed and struck again. Marcos jumped aside; the knife missed him by inches. He grabbed the ranch-hand's wrist and twisted it hard with a rough, upward motion. The knife flew beyond reach. El Rubio spat an obscenity and jerked free. They began to circle each other step by step, arms extended, muscles tensed to spring. Inch by inch around a slippery circle, their eyes locked in hatred. El Rubio crouched and feinted. Marcos continued to circle; blood seeped through the tear in his sleeve and ran down his left hand. The wind drove hard, stinging needles of rain across the yard. El Rubio feinted again. He swayed from side to side and lunged. Marcos's right fist whipped a savage blow across his face. The ranch-hand reeled. The fist crashed again. His arms flailed wildly and he collapsed headlong in the mud.

Pablo Losa ran up, visibly shaken. 'Holy Christ, that was close! Let me see your arm.' He took out his handkerchief and bound it tightly around the gash. 'Féldman should put a couple of stitches in this. It's deep.'

Marcos winced. He was pale and breathing hard. 'All right. Later. Have Pardo saddle my horse. I'll ride herd with the men down to the stockyards.' He took another deep breath; he felt cold and sick to his stomach. 'Pay El Rubio what he's owed and drive him into town, Pablo. I want to make sure he leaves the ranch without causing any more trouble.'

'I'll drop the son of a bitch in the deepest cesspool I can find,' grinned Losa. 'Do you want me to report this to Captain Cordero at the police station?'

'There's nothing Cordero can do,' replied Marcos grimly and returned to the house, cradling his injured arm.

He had never struck one of his men before. Until today his word alone had always been strong enough to maintain order on La Catalina. Marcos poured himself a stiff brandy and stood sipping it in front of the fireplace. He did not trust himself to sit down. The brandy steadied his queasy stomach, but he still felt

100

cold. The gash on his forearm was not serious, but the memory of how it happened left a bitter taste in his mouth. It was as though La Catalina's own tightly woven fabric of order and stability had been torn: the vital fabric which he had received intact from his father and must pass on intact to the heirs of his blood. Marcos frowned at the flames flickering on the hearth. By challenging his authority, El Rubio had attacked La Catalina. He had thwarted that attack this time, but there would be others. He held no illusions on that score. As he sipped his brandy he wondered uneasily where the next attacks would come from and what would be necessary to defend himself from them.

V

El Rubio dripped blood and mud in the middle of Mendes's kitchen.

'Luciani tried to knife me in the back,' he said, spitting the words through a pulpy space where a front tooth should have been. 'He went for me while I was talking to the *compañeros*. He tried to knife me and two of his henchmen beat me up.'

Artemio Mendes poured a stream of boiling water into his *maté* gourd and took a long, noisy sip. 'Any witnesses to that, *compañero?*'

'Plenty, but they won't talk. That filthy bloodsucker's got 'em sewed up tight.'

'You been paid?'

'A miserable month. I forced him to.'

There was a short silence as Mendes sucked thoughtfully on the metal straw. 'Some of my pals from Buenos Aires are in town,' he said finally. 'I want you to tell them what you've just told me.' He added some more water to the gourd and handed it to El Rubio. 'The local cattlemen's association meets tomorrow afternoon.'

The hot metal straw scalded El Rubio's swollen lip. 'So what?' he grunted painfully.

Artemio Mendes bared his teeth. 'It's time to teach pigs like Luciani a lesson.'

CHAPTER TEN

I

Angela had become very friendly with Tadeo Ortíz's wife, Julia, a dark, rangy woman in her early thirties. Ten years ago Julia had run away from an engagement arranged by her socialite family to marry Tadeo, a widower fifteen years older than herself.

'A provincial cattleman to boot,' she chuckled. 'Father still refuses to have anything to do with me, but it was the best decision I ever made.'

On the afternoon of the cattlemen's association meeting the two women drove into Laguna Grande together to do some shopping.

'We'll meet Nena Gabán at the Hotel Estrella for tea afterwards,' said Julia when she picked up Angela in her car. 'Her husband Roberto owns El Ombú about twelve miles northwest of Laguna. They're absolute dears, both of them. Very old-fashioned and kind – the sort of people who are always ready to help others. Everyone around here thinks the world of them.'

Angela had been looking forward to her outing. The past two weeks had been trying in more ways than one. To begin with there had been a row with Jimmy's parents the day after Teresa's birthday party. John and Cora Morgan were well-meaning, but tactless. They told Jimmy he should buy a house near their place. It was much more sensible for Angela and the baby to live in Buenos Aires. Los Alamos was far too primitive. Jimmy had disagreed violently. His parents had insisted. No one had bothered to ask Angela what she thought.

Back at Los Alamos there was Marcos. He had come over a number of times during the past fortnight to discuss the situation in Laguna Grande with Jimmy; he generally stayed longer than necessary. Every time his car drove into the yard Angela's heart stopped. She caught herself listening for his arrival or waiting for the telephone to ring. The days when he didn't come she was irritable; the days when he did she walked on clouds. It was not just that Marcos attracted her physically. She liked him as a person. He had strength of character and determination; he conveyed a tremendous sense of security. He was, she thought, a man one could lean on and trust. The good looks and the charm were superficial assets; what lay beneath them was intelligent, dependable and warm-hearted. It was damnable. They got on so well together. If only they didn't, then perhaps she wouldn't feel so desperate about falling in love with him.

Falling in love with Marcos Luciani was totally out of touch with reality, Angela told herself. She was Jimmy's wife, she carried Jimmy's child. That was reality. She must keep her feet firmly planted on the ground. An afternoon with nice, sensible women who loved their husbands was just the tonic she needed – but Julia Ortíz did not know that.

'Did you hear about the fight at La Catalina yesterday?' she asked as they drove towards Laguna Grande.

Angela nodded. She could not bear to think what might have happened if, as Jimmy said, Pablo Losa had not shouted in time.

Julia rolled down the window and a gust of rain-scented wind blew through the car. 'Marcos isn't his usual self these days,' she remarked after a moment. 'He should get married again. A man needs a wife to look after him and keep him happy.'

'I expect he'll find someone,' replied Angela, trying not to think about tall, intense Aurora Grandi.

They drove on for a few minutes in silence.

'When Marcos told us Jimmy had married an Englishwoman we didn't know what to expect,' Julia said suddenly. 'I was afraid you might be unbearably *gringa* like Cora Morgan – or that you would think Buenos Aires is the beginning and the end of everything. I'm glad you're not like that. You do like it out here, don't you?'

'Oh, yes. I love it.'

'You're not homesick for England?'

Angela shook her head. 'I've only been here six months but, well, Argentina's very much my home now. In a way I feel as though I've lived here all my life. It's a sense of belonging to the land, if you know what I mean.'

'Marcos should marry someone like you,' grinned Julia.

So Angela's secret heart kept whispering. 'I should imagine Marcos knows what he wants,' she said somewhat dryly and changed the subject.

II

The Hotel Estrella was a two-storey yellow stucco building on the west side of Laguna Grande's main square. Its panelled lobby was crammed with faded plush furniture and yellowed photographs; the front lounge boasted a couple of dilapidated leather sofas and dingy net curtains.

From her place on one of the sofas Angela had a clear view of the street and part of the main square. On this bleak, windy Tuesday afternoon the town hummed with more than its usual activity. Men strolled up and down the streets or gathered in clusters on the corners; there were more men lounging near the building next door where the cattlemen's association was meeting. A car with a loudspeaker attached to the roof began to circle the square. There was a blaring, metallic fanfare and then a woman's voice thrilled over the loudspeaker, '*Viva Perón!*' Artemio Mendes, announced the voice, was the best choice for governor. Julia rolled her eyes.

'Heaven forbid,' she commented wryly.

A waiter in wrinkled black trousers and a dirty white jacket thumped down a tray on the table between the sofas: muddy tea, limp sandwiches, stony scones.

'To think that this hotel used to be a decent place,' said white-haired Nena Gabán indignantly as soon as the man left. She jumped as another blast of music blared over the loudspeaker circling the square. 'I'm so sick of these Peronists! They're ruining the country!' Her voice quavered. 'All this trouble – it's making Roberto ill.'

'Hush, Nena,' warned Julia, with an anxious glance at the door.

The older woman's hands shook as she poured out the tea. 'It's disgraceful,' she said in a lower voice. 'Why doesn't somebody do something about these scoundrels!'

At the meeting next door Roberto Gabán had just asked the same question.

104

'I've been in Laguna Grande for forty years and I've never had so many problems,' he complained bitterly. 'Not even in the twenties. It's time we did something about Mendes!'

The question was, what could they do? The cattlemen began a heated discussion. Tadeo Ortíz was about to suggest that a delegation should visit the governor when the door opened and El Rubio, surrounded by a dozen of Mendes's pals from Buenos Aires, burst into the room. Ortíz stopped in mid-sentence.

'What the hell are you doing in here?' he demanded angrily. 'This is a private meeting!'

'Fuck your meeting!' hissed El Rubio through the gap in his front teeth. 'We're going to teach you bloodsuckers a lesson!'

Ortíz turned crimson. 'Get out of here!'

The intruders laughed. They advanced into the room, kicking tables and overturning chairs. Someone shouted, 'Throw them out!' Roberto Gabán rose to his feet. He pointed imperiously at the door; his neat white moustache bristled.

'You will leave at once!' he ordered.

A thick-necked *porteño* leered. 'Shut up, you old prick!'

Fighting broke out near the door. The *porteño* shouted something. Roberto Gabán said 'Scoundrel!' very loudly and caught hold of his arm. The *porteño* pulled a gun. El Rubio saw it and grinned. He had a gun too. It was better than a knife. Safer than using his fists against the *patrón*. He aimed his gun at the tall, dark-haired man rushing to Roberto Gabán's rescue and pulled the trigger.

III

Nena Gabán was pouring out the second round of muddy tea when they heard shouting outside. The women froze; after a moment Julia set down her cup very deliberately and pushed aside a corner of the shabby net curtain.

'I can't make out where . . .' She broke off, frowning. 'It sounds like next door, but that blasted music makes it difficult to hear.'

'Holy Virgin!' breathed Nena and crossed herself. 'Is it next door, Julia?'

Men ran past the hotel window; some shouted and jeered,

others looked startled. Angela saw Captain Cordero come out of the police station, followed by a lanky subordinate. The windows rattled as a truck rumbled by. Like tumbrils, she thought. Like bloody tumbrils.

'Jesus, have mercy on us!' Nena's face was ashen. '*Where is it?*'

The shouts grew louder. Men's harsh, angry voices rose above the music braying from the loudspeakers. Angela thought she heard shots and glanced at Julia in alarm. Several more shots, very clearly this time. Men raced from the building next door. She saw them scattering across the street.

'It's nothing,' said Julia in an unnaturally even voice. 'A car backfiring. Don't worry, Nena.'

But Nena Gabán had already rushed from the hotel.

Laguna Grande milled excitedly around the entrance to the building next door. Dogs barked, children wailed, a horse tied to a hitching post neighed nervously. Angela caught sight of Nena's small, white-haired figure struggling to press through the crowd and felt her heart sink. She pushed after her, but a man with a red-and-white poncho slung over his shoulder put out his hand.

'Don't go in there, señora!'

'Get the priest!' yelled a voice from the doorway.

'Keep the women back!' someone shouted. 'Señora – don't go inside the building!'

Angela wrenched away from the strong, calloused hand and charged across the threshold. The afternoon, which had been chilly, seemed unbearably warm and clammy now – or perhaps it was fear that stuck to her forehead in glistening little drops and ran shivering fingers along her spine. She jostled past grim men crowding the hallway. The close, heavy air reeked of leather and sweat and another frighteningly familiar smell that raised unwelcome ghosts from the jungles of war.

The child, sensing her sudden terror, kicked hard.

In a large room to the left of the hall a woman screamed a name and began to sob. Angela pushed past the men blocking the entrance. There were dark red stains on the floor and walls. She stared at them, too stunned to grasp their meaning. Someone took her by the shoulders and spoke; still in a daze she looked up and saw Jimmy.

He looks like an old man, Angela thought dully. Grey. Ugly. His hands are shaking . . . She touched one and was startled to find it icy cold.

'Let's get away from here, angel,' he said unsteadily. 'There's nothing we can do.'

The woman screamed again. Angela tore her glance away from Jimmy's face and saw Nena Gabán clutching wildly at a motionless body on the floor.

'Roberto.' Jimmy moistened his lips, forcing out words that even now sounded too preposterous to be true. 'Shot through the head. Others shot as well . . . For God's sake, Angela! Don't go over there! It's . . . horrible.'

She thrust him impatiently aside. 'I must go to her.'

Even with help it was a struggle to lift Nena away from her husband's body. She screamed and fought like a mad woman, pleading with God to help her . . . to kill her as well . . . to bring back Roberto . . . Twice she broke away and hurled herself on top of him; twice they hauled her up, dripping blood and tears. It was an exhausting, heartbreaking scene; only when Father Antonio appeared and spoke to her did Nena subside enough to be placed on a chair. Jacobo Feldman, kneeling beside one of the men wounded in the shooting, looked around at Angela.

'You should not be here in your condition, señora.'

'Did you expect me to stay away?'

He shrugged. 'There is a sedative in my bag that will keep Señora Gabán calm until I can see to her. Please administer it. Then come and help me. My nurse, as usual, is indisposed.'

Someone brought Angela a glass of water. Outside in the hallway Captain Cordero's gruff country voice asked questions; inside the room Father Antonio recited sorrowful prayers for the dead. A thin, sandy-haired man Angela vaguely remembered from the Easter weekend at La Catalina helped her hold Nena still, but even then it took another struggle to get the sedative down.

'Señora – over here, please!' ordered Jacobo Feldman. He pointed to the wounded man's blood-soaked shirt. 'A bullet is lodged in the shoulder. Hold him steady while I cut this away and see how much damage has been done.'

The man groaned. Angela looked down and saw Marcos.

IV

That night, over a double whisky, Jimmy told Angela about the shooting.

'Poor old Roberto didn't stand a chance. The bastards shot him point-blank. They were all armed . . . bullets flying all over the place . . . I saw Marcos go down. He – he was trying to help R-Roberto . . .' Jimmy passed a shaking hand over his face. 'Jesus! It was like some goddamned wild west film.'

'The police will catch the men who did it, won't they?'

'Cordero'll go through the motions, but ten to one nothing'll come of it.' He sat staring for a long time at the fire before reaching for her hand. 'You're a wonder, old girl. Feldman say he doesn't know what he would have done without you. That nurse of his is an ass.'

Angela managed a pale smile. 'She recovered from her headache as soon as she heard I was helping him. Nearly tore the dressing out of my hands. Quite silly, really.'

A train whistle's eerie warning floated through the darkness outside and faded into silence. Jimmy glanced at the clock on the mantelpiece.

'Nearly midnight.' He stretched out a leg to kick the logs on the hearth. 'Damned lucky for old Marcos the bastard who shot him didn't have a better aim.'

There was no need to tell her. She had seen Marcos's wound; she had staunched the blood. She had held him while Jacobo Feldman extracted the bullet. It was a bloody business and very painful. Angela had been through the war. She was used to dealing with pain. Such a relatively minor operation should not have upset her, but it did. Her lips trembled.

'Oh, God!' she whispered. 'Oh, God!'

Jimmy's arm went around her. 'Let's not think about it, angel. Everything's all right now.'

Everything was not all right. The memory of Marcos's ashen face and the blood welling up through the hole in his shoulder would not go away. She buried her head against Jimmy and began to cry, but even that was not all right because she couldn't tell him the reason for her tears.

V

Officially the shooting was blamed on unidentified hooligans whose main intention had been robbery. The local newspaper printed a brief account of the incident on the last page and devoted the front page to Artemio Mendes's election campaign. The national newspapers ignored Laguna Grande's troubles altogether.

The mayor of Laguna Grande paid his respects to the bereaved family, but the formality smacked of embarrassment. Captain Cordero interviewed the four men wounded in the shooting and entered their account in his report. Then he drove aimlessly around the countryside for several hours. Not finding any clues, he closed the case with a statement that those responsible for the trouble had fled across the provincial border. Technically, they were now beyond his jurisdiction.

His duty done, the captain went home to bed.

VI

Roberto Gabán's funeral was held on Thursday morning in a church packed with local cattlemen and farmers. Outside, the sky hung dark and heavy with storm; inside, the candles threw flickering half shadows against more darkness and made death into a tangible, living presence.

Cold, cold Death, thou dreary king . . .

The half-forgotten lines slipped through Angela's mind and were lost in sadness.

Jimmy and Tadeo Ortíz were among the pall-bearers. Jimmy looked ludicrously young and vulnerable in his dark suit and shock of sun-bleached hair; as he put his shoulder to the coffin Angela felt her throat tighten. *Cold death* . . . She turned away with a shudder and found Marcos beside her.

'I want to thank you,' he said. 'Feldman told me how much you helped with my operation the other day.' His voice dragged wearily. 'I am taking the evening train to Buenos Aires. Is there anything you would like me to bring back for you?'

Angela glanced at his left arm strapped tightly to his chest. 'Are you well enough to travel? It was a nasty wound . . .'

'This morning I learned that the truckers and the railroad refuse to load my cattle. Spare parts of machinery that were ordered months ago have not arrived. Another order has been blocked.' Marcos uttered a short, bitter laugh. 'My problems cannot wait for my shoulder to heal.'

There were dark circles under his eyes and he had nicked his chin in several places shaving that morning. Her heart went out to him with a sudden rush of tenderness.

'Will you be able to do anything?' she asked gently.

'I must.'

There was a stubborn determination in those two words that made Angela smile. The world was caving in, but the cattleman would not let it bury his kingdom. She remembered something Jimmy had once said about Marcos and La Catalina. *It's his lifeblood, his soul – you might even say his god.* She thought she was beginning to understand this man's passion for his land. Perhaps that was why she said now, 'You love your ranch very much.'

'Yes,' replied Marcos. 'I love my ranch very much and Roberto Gabán was my friend. He taught me many things – not only about ranching, but about dignity and justice and courage. He was a good person.' His voice faltered. 'I have never killed a man, but I think I would kill the man who shot Roberto. When I woke up after the operation that was my first thought. The second was to remember your face.'

Angela's eyes filled with sudden tears. She turned her head quickly, but not before Marcos had seen them.

'What is it?' he asked. 'Why are you crying?'

The words slipped out before she could stop them. 'I've been so worried about you. So – frightened.' The last word was barely a whisper.

'You were frightened for me, *gringuita*?' When she did not reply Marcos bent his head and said in a low voice, 'When I

110

return from Buenos Aires we must talk, Angela.'

She panicked. 'No, please! You don't understand.'

'You don't understand that I love you,' he said and taking her by the arm moved into the crowd of mourners filing down the aisle.

VII

After the funeral Jimmy told Angela he would be returning to La Catalina with Marcos and Tadeo Ortíz for what he wryly termed a 'council of war'.

'Why doesn't Julia spend the day at Los Alamos with you?' he suggested. 'I'll bring Tadeo back for supper and we'll play a few hands of bridge afterwards. God knows we all need the distraction.'

He kissed her and went off to his car where the others were already waiting. As he crossed the dusty street a woman clutching a scrawny, dark-haired baby suddenly stepped out from the crowd of curious bystanders under the lime trees and called to him.

'*Loco* . . .'

Her voice had a peculiar, honey-toned lilt Jimmy remembered only too well. Last year that voice had drawn him to her like a magnet. Not once but again and again, driven by a frantic craving . . . He backed away from the woman with her cheap flowered dress pulled taut over large breasts and her husky, honeyed whine. Under its ruddy tan his face was pale.

'Why don't you come no more to see me?' She thrust the baby at him. 'I don't have money. I wrote you for some. Why didn't you bring any?'

Three letters, painstakingly penned in a childish, ill-formed hand. Jimmy thrust the woman roughly aside and hurried on without looking back. The letters were ashes now, but there would be more. He'd stake his life on that. She might even come out to Los Alamos and tackle Angela . . . He fetched up sharply against the car, his mouth dry with sudden apprehension.

Not Angela. She must never know.

VIII

Marcos stared bleakly out of the train window.

He wished he and Jimmy weren't such close friends. If they had nothing to do with each other, life would be much simpler. He liked Jimmy, his friend; he resented Jimmy, Angela's husband. That resentment was getting in the way of their friendship. Angela was too much of a woman for *el Loco* Morgan. He wanted to give her all the things Jimmy could not give her. All the things she deserved. Happiness and security and love. So much love. There was nothing he could do about it now, but after the baby was born . . . Marcos winced as the carriage jolted over the tracks. When he returned from Buenos Aires he was going to talk to Angela. He wanted to know exactly how she felt. He thought she was in love with him, but he wanted to be sure. It was a serious matter.

His shoulder gave a sharp twinge. Marcos fumbled for the bottle of painkillers Feldman had given him, shook out two and swallowed them dry. They helped, but not much. He leaned his head back against the seat and closed his eyes. Better think about something else. The train wheels clattered relentlessly through the night. After a while he began to remember Roberto Gabán.

112

CHAPTER ELEVEN

I

Juan Gaspari stood in the room over his father's shop and glared through the window at the street below. Six months since the weekend at La Catalina and still no sign of Marcos Luciani showing any interest in Gladys. It was all her fault, of course. If only she had tried harder, flirted with him, displayed some interest in the ranch. She had just as much class as any of those snotty-nosed society women; what she lacked was the gumption to put it across.

'Stupid cow,' muttered Gaspari as his sister's high-pitched voice floated up from the shop below. 'Serve her a prize catch like Luciani on a silver platter and she throws away her chances without even trying. That's gratitude for you!'

He broke off with a sudden grunt as a taxi rattled along the cobblestones and screeched to a halt outside the shop. Gaspari narrowed his eyes against the September sunshine; a moment later he raced down the narrow stairs and cornered Gladys as she was about to enter the kitchen.

'Luciani's outside! This is your chance,' he hissed. 'If he asks for me I've gone out. I may be back this evening. You don't know anything.'

Gladys stared at him blankly. 'Luciani? *Here*?'

'Getting out of a taxi. I'm leaving by the back door now. Remember — you don't know where I've gone.'

'But . . .'

'You want to spend the rest of your life weighing sacks of potatoes?' He shook her impatiently. 'Do as I tell you! Go on — get inside there and see what he wants!'

She started to say something, but he shoved her towards the entrance and was gone.

The greengrocer's shop boasted a faded striped awning and a white sign with VERDULERÍA NÁPOLI painted on it in uneven green letters. A limp display of vegetables sprawled haphazardly

113

on the pavement; inside, the place was cramped, dark, and smelled of old drains. An elderly man sawing through a large orange pumpkin glanced up as Marcos hesitated in the doorway.

'Are you looking for something, señor?'

'I'm looking for Gaspari.'

The old man's eyebrows shot up in astonishment. He set aside the saw, wiped his hands on an apron that had seen better days, and limped around the counter. His voice was thin and querulous.

'I'm Gaspari.'

'It's all right, Father. I'll see to this.' Gladys came quickly through the entrance, then stopped dead at the sight of Marcos Luciani rumpled and unshaven, his left arm strapped in a sling. 'You've had an accident?'

He managed a pale smile. 'Is your brother home, Señora Gómez?'

'Juan's gone out.'

'He was here a moment ago,' grumbled her father.

'He's gone out. He – he had to see someone.'

'Always going off to see someone.' Gaspari senior picked up his saw and began to file away glumly on the pumpkin. 'Never stays put long enough to do an honest day's work.'

Marcos frowned. He had spent a sleepless night on a noisy, crowded train. On an impulse, instead of going straight home he had taken a taxi all the way across Buenos Aires to Gaspari's address in Quilmes – more than a good half hour's drive made endless because the taxi driver, who didn't know the southern suburbs, lost his way. It was now half-past ten. His head ached, his shoulder and arm throbbed white-hot needles, the inside of his mouth felt like sawdust. He moistened his lips and asked in a voice that did not sound like his own, 'When will your brother return?'

'I don't know. Late.' Gladys stared at the tiny drops beading his forehead. 'You should have rung up before coming.'

'The telephones in the station didn't work.'

'Are you all right?'

The floor slipped from under Marcos's feet. He groped for support and felt himself being propelled briskly between sacks of potatoes into a large kitchen. A stout, grey-haired woman stirring a pot on the stove turned her head in astonishment.

'Give me some brandy, Mother,' said Gladys. 'The señor isn't feeling well.'

'I'm all right,' he protested feebly and found himself sitting on a chair at the kitchen table.

'He's a friend of Juan,' said the old man from the doorway. 'Where's Juan gone to? Always going somewhere. I heard him . . .'

'Get back to the shop, Father!' ordered Gladys sharply. She wiped a glass, poured in a generous amount of brandy and handed it to Marcos. 'Drink this. You look feverish.'

Her bright yellow curls had been pushed back and secured in place by two small red combs. The dark blue skirt and brown jumper she wore could hardly have been less flattering, yet even so they failed to disguise the fact that Juan Gaspari's sister was a surprisingly pretty woman. Marcos sipped his brandy and wondered idly why she had not married.

The stout woman bustled around the table, her eyes bright with curiosity. 'Would the señor like some coffee? It won't take a minute to boil – or a *mate* perhaps?'

He drained his glass and stood up, feeling uncomfortably lightheaded. 'No, thanks. Tell Gaspari to ring me as soon as he returns. It's urgent.'

'I'll tell him,' said Gladys shortly and led the way out to the waiting taxi.

II

When she returned, the Gasparis fired a barrage of curious questions. Gladys flushed with annoyance. The man was Marcos Luciani and he wanted to talk to Juan; that was all she knew.

'Luciani? Isn't that where Juan took you and Claudia for Easter?' asked her mother. 'Claudia says it was a big place. She didn't have a very good time.'

'Nonsense,' retorted Gladys. 'She loved every minute of it.'

Celestina Gaspari gave the kettle she was drying an energetic rub. 'That's not what the child told me. I always thought it silly

115

of you to take her in the first place. They're not the sort of people Claudia's used to.'

'Upper-class people,' agreed her husband in his thin, plaintive tenor. 'I could tell the minute I laid eyes on the man. Walked into the shop like he owned the world. What's Juan up to carrying on with people like that?'

'It's all this politicking, that's what it is,' snapped Celestina. 'It's given Juan fancy ideas. He used to be a good boy before all this politicking.'

Gladys turned on the tap and began to scrub potatoes. Marcos Luciani had been forced to accept help on her terms and in her world. The brief memory of his helplessness gave her a bitter little stab of satisfaction.

III

The return from Quilmes to Barranco Rosales took nearly two hours. Buenos Aires's narrow downtown streets were congested with midday traffic and a rally in support of Evita near the Ministry of Labour. The taxi driver swerved to avoid a tram, shook his fist at the passengers, backed down a two-way street and inched through a crawling mass of pedestrians with his large hand firmly glued to the horn.

'They ought to rip open this city right down to the river,' he growled as they turned at last on to a wide avenue where traffic flowed more freely. 'This is just the place!' He made a sweeping motion with his right hand. 'Rip out the 9 de Julio. Better still . . .' The hand came off the steering wheel and gestured obscenely at a lorry driver. 'Move the federal capital away from Buenos Aires altogether! Take the government offices and shove the whole mess out!'

'Where to?' asked Marcos curiously.

'Drop 'em in the sea, eh?' The man spat out of the window. 'Mar del Plata – that's where the capital ought to be. You know the place, señor?'

'Nice city.'

'Pearl of the Atlantic, that city is! Good climate, peaceful – only two hundred and fifty miles from this hell-hole.' He fished a pack of cigarettes off the dashboard and offered one. 'My brother-in-law's got a little place down in Mar del Plata. The wife and I go down there for holidays – have a dip in the sea and a shot at the roulette wheel.'

'Ever win anything?'

The taxi driver brayed. 'Would I be driving this tinpot if I had? Not on your life! I'd be scratching my belly in the sun all day long.'

He rambled on cheerfully as Marcos stared out of the window and watched Buenos Aires slip by. The *ombú* trees in Recoleta Park spread dark, glossy canopies over sloping lawns; children sailed boats on the ponds next to the art museum and stiffly starched nannies pushed prams along shady pavements. The spring light was pale blue and unbelievably clear, tinged with the faintest hint of summer heat; flower vendors splashed brilliant colours on the street corners and the river was dotted with sailboats tacking in the breeze.

After the noise and close, concentrated bustle of downtown the northern part of the city seemed like another world.

Broad, tree-lined Avenida del Libertador General San Martín flowed past elegant blocks of flats, stately townhouses and embassies; curved around the imposing white marble monument to Spain; swept on through Palermo's parks and gardens, past the polo grounds and the racecourse. Marcos closed his eyes as the taxi turned up the steep slope towards Barranco Rosales. The jacaranda trees were not in bloom yet; they blossomed later in the spring, carpeting the streets with lavender tears.

He rested his head against the seat and dreamt briefly of Angela running towards him through a lavender cloud.

IV

His arrival halfway through lunch created a minor upheaval in the house's orderly routine, already badly shaken by news of the shooting. They had expected him on the morning train, Mercedes cried. She had called the ranch twice already, but Pablo Losa was not very helpful. She had been worried sick . . . The thin voice trembled.

'The least you could have done was advise us you'd be coming late. We thought . . . an accident . . .'

'I'm going to lie down,' Marcos broke in. 'Wake me up when Gaspari rings.'

'I really don't think you should be disturbed.'

'For God's sake, don't argue!' he snapped and somehow made it up the stairs to his bedroom.

Trust Mercedes to blossom in a crisis. As Marcos crawled into bed he heard her issuing earnest instructions to the cook over the house telephone; two minutes later she was on to the family doctor.

Lucas poked his head around the door. 'How about letting me have a couple of thousand before you pop off? I've got a sure winner in the third race on Sunday.'

Mercedes stormed into the bedroom, her eyes blazing. 'Leave your brother alone!' She thrust Lucas out and closed the door, then swept around drawing the curtains and straightening clothes. When she had rattled and straightened and fussed enough she stood by the bed and placed a trembling hand on Marcos's forehead.

He opened his eyes, startled by her touch. 'What's the matter?'

'Oh, my dear!' Mercedes fumbled for a handkerchief. 'If anything had happened to you . . . I couldn't bear it!' She traced a wavering sign of the cross over him. 'To think you might have been . . . Holy Mother, I couldn't bear it!'

'Go to hell, woman,' muttered Marcos impatiently and closed his eyes again.

He dozed fitfully all afternoon. Sounds came and went like restless waves: an occasional car driving past the house, children's voices, the whine of a knifegrinder's whetstone. Downstairs a clock chimed the half hour. The drawn curtains shut in the room with heavy silken shrouds and stirred up memories of Magdalena. The flowery fragrance of her scent still lingered in the air, troubling his dreams. Angela ran through jacaranda blossoms – only this Angela held a glass in her hand and said in Gladys's voice, 'Have another brandy, it won't kill you.' Over and over again, like some ridiculous jingle rattling through his thoughts at triple speed . . . Marcos opened his eyes with a start and saw Isabel peering around the door.

'Can I come in, Papa?'

He held out his hand and she scuttled on to the bed with a jump that made him wince.

'Does it hurt?' asked Isabel anxiously.

He shifted against the pillows and put his good arm around her. 'Not too much. What's the matter?' as she gulped.

'Aunt Mercedes said you were shot and . . . oh, Papa!' Hot tears splashed on to his cheek. 'I'm f-frightened!'

'There's nothing to be frightened about, Bela,' Marcos said gently.

'B-but I heard Aunt Mercedes tell Miss Nelly a m-man died. She s-said the men who hurt you killed him. Why, Papa?'

His arm tightened around her. 'Because they were bad men.'

'I don't want there to be bad men,' she sobbed. 'I don't want them to hurt you.'

'No one's going to hurt me,' said Marcos. 'I'm all right. Hush, girl – you're soaking me through.'

She gulped again and wrapped her small fingers around his hand. 'C-can I go back to La Catalina with you? Please?'

The wistfulness in her voice touched Marcos deeply. She's so close to my heart, he thought. So much like me in every way. He felt a brief stab of disappointment that Miguel had not come up to his room. He would have liked to have talked to him about Roberto Gabán and the things that had happened. It would have been an opportunity for them to grow closer; an opportunity to teach his son the values he had learned from his friend. If only his son had come up to see him . . . Marcos stroked Isabel's dark head.

'You can come out to La Catalina the day after school finishes,' he promised. 'It's only two more months, *ñatita*.'

'But we're going to Los Toros with Gastón and Yvonne until Christmas.'

'Let Miguel and Cristina go. You come with me to La Catalina. Just the two of us.'

'And Aunt Mercedes?'

Marcos grinned. 'We'll find her a boyfriend.'

Isabel giggled through her tears. 'She's too old.'

'Then we'll keep her in a case downstairs with the jade collection.'

They both laughed at the thought of Mercedes squatting like a jade Buddha behind glass doors. Isabel snuggled closer and rubbed her head against her father's chin.

'When I grow up I'm going to live on La Catalina and take care of you,' she said. 'Cristina wants to play the piano and be famous, but I'm going to live on La Catalina.'

He smiled, but did not reply.

'Jimmy rang and I talked to Angela,' said Isabel after a moment. 'She says I can help her take care of the baby this summer. I like Angela. Can I sing to you?'

'If you want to.'

She began to drone softly in a cheerful tuneless monotone that plumbed the depths of pain and dulled its edges until nothing was left but a vague, empty ache; after a time the ache disappeared as well and Marcos drifted into an uneventful sleep.

V

Juan Gaspari appeared the following afternoon with a large basket of blue hydrangeas for Mercedes.

'Fresh from the Tigre,' he said, referring to the river delta northeast of Buenos Aires. 'Straight from the Party's island resort. Another basket like this was sent to Evita.'

Mercedes curled her lip at the hydrangeas. 'You really shouldn't have bothered.'

'Please, Señorita Mercedes – no bother at all.' Gaspari rubbed his hands briskly together. 'Well, now – how's Marcos? My sister got the fright of her life when she saw him yesterday morning. Says he could hardly stand on his feet.'

'Your sister?' Mercedes's thin eyebrows climbed several disapproving inches. 'I didn't know . . . He saw your sister?'

'Nearly fainted while he was with her, Gladys tells me. She took care of him.'

'I see.' There was a frigid pause. 'I'm afraid my brother is resting, on doctor's orders. He is not to be disturbed. If you care to ring on Monday . . .'

'Gaspari, come up here,' called Marcos's voice sharply. He glared at Mercedes from the top of the stairs. 'Send the butler to my study with some coffee.'

She flushed. 'You shouldn't be walking around! The doctor said . . . Marcos!'

'I don't want to be disturbed for the next couple of hours,' he snapped and strode off, followed by a grinning Gaspari. A moment later the study door slammed shut behind them, raising a solid barrier against Mercedes's indignation.

VI

Gaspari darted a curious eye around the study: solid oak panelling, deep leather chairs, a Persian carpet that must have cost a fortune. His previous visits to Barranco Rosales had been purely social ones, relegated to the sumptuous formality of drawing-room and dining-room, with a brief, surreptitious peek into the library. The fact that he was summoned upstairs and that his summons sparked a minor crisis told him quite a bit about the coming interview. Uneasiness, uncertainty, perhaps even fear . . . Gaspari's round hazel eyes gleamed with satisfaction.

'My sister sends her regards,' he said affably. 'She is very concerned for your health.'

Gladys's concern did not cut much ice. His host toyed with a silver-and-onyx paperknife and frowned darkly at an invisible point on the desk. Gaspari tried again.

'Unfortunately I had to travel to the provinces yesterday. An important errand, you understand.' His toothy smile implied a bit of political skulduggery they would both be familiar with. 'I returned a few hours ago to find your message. You have problems, *amigo?*'

A discreet knock at the door brought the butler with a tray of coffee. Gaspari helped himself generously to sugar, waited until the man had left, and took an unerring stab in the dark.

'Artemio Mendes is up to his tricks again, eh?'

'You might say that,' said Marcos shortly and repeated everything that had happened during the last week, including the fight with El Rubio. 'I told you to keep Mendes and his dogs off La Catalina. I pay you good money to obey my orders, Gaspari.'

A plump right hand rose and fell with a gesture which could have meant anything. Juan Gaspari knew all about Mendes. The man was a pain in the neck, but if he played his cards right the pain could turn into a very profitable little venture.

'Artemio Mendes is a very influential man in the province,' he began after a careful pause. 'He has contacts among certain elements in the Party.' Again the hand rose and fell. 'There are miracles which not even Juan Gaspari can perform, Marcos. If Artemio Mendes is elected governor it will mean trouble for

121

you, yes. Most certainly he will do everything in his power to seize your land.'

Marcos's face hardened. 'Votes can be bought. We've all agreed to that in Laguna if the worst comes to the worst.'

'It would cost a fortune, *amigo* – and you would still not be certain of success. The man who sits in the governor's chair today will not sit there after November. Evita dislikes him. He will be "promoted" down south – preferably Tierra del Fuego.' Gaspari sipped his coffee slowly. 'Do you want to know the truth? Artemio Mendes will be the next governor of the province. Not my choice of a man, but I have no say in the matter.'

There was a very long silence. Marcos stared dully at a large photograph of La Catalina under the glass top on his desk. It had been taken four years ago and showed the full spread of the park in the background. A herd of Black Angus steers grazed hock-deep in grass to the left of the picture; to the right the children on horseback waved happily at the camera. His throat tightened. Four years ago Gaspari had been no more than a name to him. A man to contact if there were difficulties with imports or spare parts or bank loans. A useful clown.

'Even I have difficulties,' said the useful clown softly. 'You tell me about the problems with moving your cattle, the orders for machinery that are blocked and I say to myself, "Juan, here is my good friend Marcos asking for help and what have I to offer him? Nothing but more problems." Sad, *amigo*, but true. My contact in the ministry has been transferred to another department and I don't know the new man in his place. It is a very delicate operation, you understand.'

Marcos looked up from the photograph. 'You're paid to handle delicate operations.'

Gaspari flung out his hands. 'You saw my father's shop. It's old and damp – the old man has rheumatism badly these days. He shouldn't be working. I'd help, but I'm a very busy man. Gladys, now – she gives a hand, but her life isn't easy either. Gómez left her without two pesos to rub together and there's the child. You yourself know what children cost to clothe and feed! Of course, Gladys has an important position in our local Party headquarters now . . . Did I tell you Evita commended her two months ago? During a tea for Party workers at the presidential weekend residence in Olivos. I have a picture somewhere . . .' He searched through a pigskin notecase and pulled out a blurred newspaper photograph of Gladys shaking hands with Evita. 'She received a medal with Evita's head on it and an autographed picture — not bad, eh? Evita's personal commendation. That's something to be valued these days. *Si, señor* — with Artemio Mendes in the governor's chair a personal commendation from Evita should be worth its weight in gold.'

Marcos pushed back his chair with a violent movement and crossed over to the window. The study gave on to the garden; from where he stood he could see Isabel and Cristina skipping near the rosebeds. They looked up and began to make funny faces at him. Their carefree laughter floated across the lawn, mocking the bitterness in his heart. He felt sick and drained and unbelievably weary, unable to see his way past one chilling thought. His shoulder began to throb, driving the message home with each stab of pain.

The trouble with El Rubio and the shooting were merely a foretaste of what lay ahead if Artemio Mendes succeeded in getting his way.

'Bring your sister to dinner tomorrow night,' said Marcos without turning around. 'Nothing formal, just a family meal.'

No further words were necessary, but Juan Gaspari found something to say just the same.

'Come to think of it, I've just remembered the name of the new man in the ministry. It's Isidoro Sánchez. His sister Juanita is Gladys's best friend.'

CHAPTER TWELVE

I

After Gaspari left, Marcos went for a walk. He had to get away. The house suffocated him; even the sound of laughter in the garden jarred his nerves. He turned into the small church belonging to the abbey at the end of the street. It was cool, peaceful and empty. Thank God for that. He sat on a wooden pew in the candlelit darkness and tried to collect his thoughts. He was cornered and Gaspari had offered him a way out. The useful clown knew he was desperate. Alone he stood no chance of saving La Catalina when Mendes became governor. If he accepted Gaspari's offer, he would at least be protected by close political connections. Marcos leaned against the pew in front and rested his face on his arm.

He did not want to marry Gladys Gómez.

Marriage meant a lifetime commitment to his wife and the children she gave him: an unshakable commitment to the rules of family and heritage dictated by responsibility. He had made that commitment once to Magdalena out of love; he would commit himself this very instant to Angela out of even greater love if it were within his power to do so. A lifetime with Angela was far too short. A lifetime with a woman like Gladys Gómez could only be eternal hell. He had nothing in common with her; she didn't even interest him physically. The thought of having to make love to her because that was part of his commitment filled Marcos with disgust.

He raised his head and stared at the crucifix on the altar with bitter eyes. His children deserved a better woman than Gladys Gómez to take their mother's place. He felt he would betray them.

He was ashamed of that betrayal, but facts were facts. La Catalina did not only represent his whole life — it was his children's future. If he refused Gaspari's offer, he would jeopardize that future. He did not have the moral right to do

124

so. The question of how much longer Perón might continue in power did not arise. Look at old Franco in Spain. He had been ruling the country for twelve years and there was no sign of change. Dictators like Perón and Franco could only be removed by acts of God, and He did not appear to be in any hurry. In the meantime La Catalina was in danger.

Marcos buried his head again. There was only one way he could save La Catalina. He tried to pray for strength, but all he could think of was Angela.

II

Gladys did not want to go to Barranco Rosales. The memory of her Easter weekend at La Catalina still rankled; it was a Cinderella dream turned sour and she did not welcome a possible repetition. Juan, however, insisted. Marcos Luciani was grateful for her help, he said. It would be rude not to accept the invitation.

'We can't afford to be rude, *hermanita*. A man like Luciani has to be treated with kid gloves,' Gaspari added with a grin. 'Don't be a fool, Gladys. This is your big chance.'

Maybe. She was silent all during the train ride from Quilmes into Buenos Aires, but when the taxi drew up in front of the heavy iron gates and she caught sight of the house looming among the trees at the end of the drive her heart skipped a beat. A tall, poker-faced butler opened the front door, a maid in stiffly starched black took their coats and disappeared noiselessly into dark caverns smelling vaguely of sandalwood and roses. The butler escorted them through a maze of rooms shaded in mellow light, down a marble staircase and into the family living-room. The Lucianis came forward, their restrained smiles and polite phrases a blueprint for social ritual. Another maid appeared, this time with a tray of cocktails. Gladys hesitated, then took a glass of sherry and glanced surreptitiously around.

So this was how the rich lived.

Deep, comfortable furniture upholstered in fawn-coloured velvet and a carpet so thick it felt like walking on clouds. The curtains at the windows were heavy silk, the pillows scattered on the sofa and chairs added brilliant touches of scarlet and

125

green and bright metallic blue. Elegance, softness, luxury. Her gaze rested on a group of pure white porcelain figurines on the mantel above the fireplace. *The Four Seasons at Play* – long, freely flowing lines and graceful curves wrought with the artistic simplicity of a master's hand.

'Do you like them?' asked Mercedes, who had been watching her closely.

Gladys blushed, embarrassed at having been caught staring. 'They're pretty.'

Mercedes's eyebrows climbed a fraction of an inch and she pursed her lips. *Pretty* was hardly the word for what one art expert had enthusiastically dubbed 'the most perfect creation of this century'. She darted a glance at where Marcos and Gaspari stood talking by the window.

'My brother gave his wife those figurines on her last birthday,' she said, lowering her voice slightly. 'He loved her very much, you know. It was a perfect marriage.' The thin, well-bred voice tightened. 'Even after two years he hasn't forgotten Magdalena.'

If there was a warning in the tone Gladys chose to ignore it. Luxury and comfort were already weaving their spell; she settled back into her armchair with a little smile of satisfaction and decided to enjoy the evening.

Gaspari saw the smile and decided he had misjudged his sister after all. Encouraged, he entered wholeheartedly into the spirit of the game, playing the jovial, simple-natured young man. Small talk rolled glibly off his tongue; during dinner he related several amusing anecdotes about life in Quilmes, his parents – even the vagaries of local politics. Gladys crumbled her breadsticks and looked uneasy, but Juan's conversation provoked no scornful reactions; after a while, fortified by a third glass of wine, she gathered up courage and contributed several entertaining stories of her own.

On the whole the evening went off very well – too well, Mercedes informed God as she prepared for bed. Gaspari's sister was quite an attractive woman and Marcos had eyed her more than once during dinner. He had even gone as far as addressing her by her first name towards the end of the evening. Heaven only knew why he had invited them, unless he felt duty-bound to Gaspari and the sister had manoeuvred her way into the picture as well.

Mercedes knelt on the small, velvet prie-dieu that had belonged to Grandmother Salazar and began to flick a rosary automatically through her fingers. It was perfectly clear that Gladys Gómez had designs on Marcos, and it was equally clear that the poor man was quite taken by her. All men were the same. A pretty woman only had to flutter her eyes . . . Mercedes launched into a fervent stream of Hail Marys while her own eyes filled with tears.

She would fight for her brother tooth and nail, but some deeply primitive woman's instinct warned that the battle was as good as lost.

III

On Tuesday Marcos invited Gladys out to tea.

His invitation raised eyebrows at Verdulería Nápoli, but she stubbornly ignored them. The Cinderella dream began again, this time with hopeful vengeance. Gladys studied the reflection of her bedroom in the cracked mirror above the chest of drawers that was all she had salvaged from Teófilo Gómez's bankruptcy. Cramped. Chilly. Stains of damp on the walls and ceiling. The bed she shared with Claudia sagged in the middle, the floor buckled, the air smelled of stale cooking. Strange how she had never noticed these things before – or at least not as consciously as she noticed them now.

Gladys jabbed a comb savagely into her short yellow curls. Her brief glimpse of Barranco Rosales had aroused a greedy hunger for thick carpets, velvet armchairs and a house filled with the fragrance of hothouse flowers.

Sour cabbages and rotting potatoes. Enough was enough was enough.

'You know what Luciani's after!' snorted Juanita when she heard about the invitation. 'A man like him wipes his feet on women and throws them away after he's through. I wouldn't go if I were you.'

Gladys bristled. 'I can handle him, don't worry!'

All the same she felt slightly apprehensive about their meeting. Gaspari senior protested because he would be alone in the shop most of the day, but Juan pressed a wad of banknotes into her hand and told her not to pay any attention to the old man's grumblings.

'Go buy yourself something really smart to wear,' he ordered. 'Luciani likes well-dressed women.'

It occurred briefly to Gladys as she hurried down Quilmes's main street that her brother could spend more of his mysterious income on their parents, but the thought was a fleeting one.

'They've lived their life,' she muttered outside the window of Casa Elisa dress shop. 'I certainly don't plan to spend the rest of my days rotting among old drains and sour cabbages!'

This time she chose a tight-fitting beige suit with brown velvet lapels, almost identical to one Evita had worn at a recent public appearance. With a coquettish froth of veils and violets atop her yellow curls, a frilly white blouse, and more violets pinned to the collar her reflection in Casa Elisa's full-length mirror breathed a happy sigh of admiration, but apprehension continued to sow butterflies in the pit of her stomach.

They had arranged to meet at five o'clock by the Florida Street entrance to Harrods and have tea in the restaurant on the third floor.

Gladys left the house at two o'clock to give herself enough time in case trains were running late or the bus got stuck in Buenos Aires's chaotic traffic. She arrived at three and spent the next two hours pacing nervously up and down in front of the store windows. Apprehension played unfair tricks on memory. Had Marcos said five o'clock? Was it the Florida entrance? Since Harrods occupied most of the block there were three other entrances as well. Gladys made the tour, her heart in her mouth. Maybe it wasn't Harrods at all. The telephone connection had been poor, she might have misunderstood him . . . She set off around the block again, sick with uncertainty. By now the violets were limp, her left heel was blistered, her hands felt clammy inside their white cotton gloves.

Which entrance was it?

She returned to Florida and suddenly Marcos stepped out from the crowd strolling down the street. Gladys's heart did a somersault under the frilly blouse.

'You look charming,' he said and pressed her hand with automatic gallantry.

128

They sat at a small table in a secluded corner of the restaurant. An eight-piece orchestra played waltzes on a stage flanked by potted palms. Over the cakes and sandwiches Gladys talked about Teófilo Gómez. Marcos listened attentively, asked the right questions, smiled on cue. He kept his dark eyes on her as though every word was the most important one he had ever heard. Her cheeks glowed and she began to speak a little faster, laughing breathlessly to cover up her nervousness. The crowd ebbed and flowed around them; it might have sprouted pink cauliflowers and rhumbaed on the roof for all Gladys cared. Her eyes were riveted on Marcos. Impeccably tailored. Gold cufflinks, gold tie-clip, dark patterned silk tie. A watch like the one she had seen in a shop across the street. It must cost . . . Cinderella caught her breath and reached for a chocolate éclair.

Quilmes seemed very far away.

Anonymity in Buenos Aires is virtually impossible at any time of day. As they stepped out of the lift on the ground floor Marcos saw Teresa and Aurora Grandi standing by the perfume counter. He attempted to steer clear, but Teresa's voice hailed him above the hum of afternoon shoppers — high and bright, ringing with unmistakable delight.

'Marcos, what a surprise! I thought you had returned to La Catalina.' Her hand touched his injured shoulder with a light, careless gesture. 'How are you?'

'Mending, thanks.' He continued to grip Gladys by the elbow. 'Hello, Aurora.'

She returned the greeting eagerly. There was an awkward pause.

'You remember Gladys Gómez, don't you?' asked Marcos, thrusting her forward. 'You met at Easter.'

His smile had a sardonic little twist to it that irked Teresa. She nodded coolly and turned her dark, brilliant gaze back on her brother-in-law. 'How long are you staying in town?'

'Until I wind up a business deal.'

'You must come home to a party next Wednesday. Aurora's brother Lorenzo is back from Europe and I've arranged for him to give us a piano recital after dinner. Do you remember Magdalena's friend Malpieri, the conductor? And the critic from *Música* . . . Do come, Marcos! It'll be a lovely evening. Lorenzo's a brilliant young musician.'

He smiled vaguely at Aurora. 'The Grandis all seem to be very gifted.'

'Only my brothers.' Her large, well-manicured hands gesticulated expressively, showing off their clusters of rings. 'Lorenzo's been in Paris for two years on a musical scholarship. He played for Rubenstein, you know. I'd like you to hear him. He's hoping to put some concerts together, but in the meantime . . .' Again the same gesture, accompanied by a deprecating little laugh. 'He'll have to give lessons, I'm afraid.'

'Cristina's quite a little pianist for her age,' broke in Teresa. 'Don't frown, Marcos! The child does have talent. It's a shame not to have her taught properly. Lorenzo would be just the person.'

'I don't know about that.'

'Of course you do! Come and listen to him on Wednesday. Nine o'clock,' laughed Teresa and moved off with Aurora trailing in her wake.

'Would you care to hear young Lorenzo murder the keyboard?' murmured Marcos, staring after them.

Gladys looked uncomfortable. 'I wasn't invited.'

He turned to her, a curious expression on his face. 'My sister-in-law has appalling manners at times – but you will have noticed that already, I imagine.'

An instinctive timing for opportunity made Gladys hold her tongue. She smiled up into his eyes and said with a light-hearted laugh, 'Not at all,' as though Teresa's rudeness were too negligible to be taken into account.

It was the first of many tactics in a game she would play time and again during the years to come.

IV

On Wednesday a phone call, on Thursday a stroll through Palermo, on Friday tea again – this time in the slightly shabby elegance of the old-fashioned Confitería Paris. Gladys did most of the talking, while Marcos listened and went through the motions of appearing interested in the problems of Gaspari senior's rheumatism and Claudia's tonsils.

He did not dare think about Angela, even when he was alone.

Gladys's friends took a dim view of the oligarch Luciani's attentions, especially since they prevented her from attending to her duties at branch headquarters. When she missed a speech by an influential leader of the metalworkers' union several of the more outspoken Party members even went as far as accusing her of disloyalty – a charge both Gladys and Juanita Sánchez stoutly denied.

'It's the best way of studying corruption, from within, *compañeras*!' shrilled Juanita as one particularly vociferous woman moved that *Compañera* Gómez be publicly reprimanded. 'What none of you realize is Gladys's spirit of sacrifice! Instead of remaining with her friends she's forced to spend hours with the enemy, walking among them like a martyr among lions! Evita is proud of her, *compañeras*!' Juanita's voice carried sharply above shouts of 'Long Live Evita!' and rounds of furious applause. 'Our Gladys does us proud and let no decent Peronist doubt that!'

All the same she advised Gladys to forego her spying on Saturday and attend a mass rally for Evita in the industrial suburb of Lanús.

Gladys agreed with mixed feelings. Jolting along in the back of the truck with the rest of her crowd she sang and cheered lustily, caught up in the fervour of the moment. It was a glorious day – blue and clear, with cotton-puff clouds scudding overhead and a warm breeze that filled the banners on the trucks like blue-and-white sails. The factory smokestacks stood clearly etched against the sky; the low, flat-roofed houses and orange trees lining the cobblestone streets looked as though they had been painted into the picture with bright, happy colours. Like a child's storybook, thought Gladys, and felt a sudden rush of love for them and for the crowds of smiling people strolling along in the warm spring sunshine.

'Long live Evita, our captain!' sang Juanita at the top of her voice and a rousing chorus of women sang with her.

The rally took place in the central square of Lanús. Evita was scheduled to address the crowd at three o'clock after inaugurating a day centre for working mothers. A stand had been erected at one end of the square under a long white banner with the ubiquitous slogan *Perón Cumple, Evita Dignifica* painted in large blue letters. The stand was draped in blue-and-white bunting, with political posters hung at regular intervals and a gigantic photograph of Evita in the middle. Loudspeakers blared

131

the 'Peronist March', the crowd shuffled excitedly. Half-past two. Excitement mounted. At twenty-five to three a shrill wail of sirens echoed in the distance; as the sirens drew closer people at the back of the crowd began to cheer.

'E-vi-ta! E-vi-ta! E-vi-ta!'

The motorcade swept through Lanús's narrow streets and screeched to a halt in front of the day centre. The chant and cheers rose in volume. Juanita and Gladys joined hands and swayed enthusiastically to the rhythm.

'E-vi-ta! E-vi-ta!'

At exactly three o'clock Eva Perón stepped on to the stand, raised her arms to embrace the crowd, and began to speak in the strong, husky voice they loved so well.

'*Compañeras!* . . .'

Halfway through Evita's speech Gladys's attention turned disloyal and began to wander. The sun beat down on the square, the crowd sweltered in its heat. She began to think about Marcos. He had taken the children to a friend's ranch for the weekend. A polo match and an *asado* – perhaps it might even be warm enough to go swimming. Gladys mopped her face. Claudia would have enjoyed a swim. It must be very lonely for her playing in the back yard of Verdulería Nápoli among broken vegetable crates. She did not make friends easily. What sort of a future did Claudia have in Quilmes? What future did she herself have? The crowd burst into frantic screams of 'Evita!' and Gladys joined in automatically.

Her thoughts were still on the future.

V

On Monday it rained buckets and Quilmes flooded. Gladys spent most of the day mopping up water. Her father grumbled about his rheumatism and Claudia caught a bad cold that went to her chest. A rancid smell of dampness seeped into the kitchen. The telephone was ominously silent.

Juan came around in the evening and quarrelled with his parents. Gladys decided that anything was preferable to a damp, smelling madhouse and went for a walk in the rain; when she returned her mother flounced out of the kitchen.

132

'That man rang for you. Juan's friend.'

Gladys's heart stopped. 'Did he say he'd ring back?'

'Couldn't hear. It was a bad connection.' Celestina Gaspari eyed her daughter speculatively. 'Is there anything going on between you two?'

'What are you talking about?'

'You know what.'

Gladys flushed. 'Of course not!'

'You watch out for men like that. They like to have their bit of fun and it's the woman who's left to pick up the broken pieces. You're a respectable widow and you've got a little girl to think about.'

'*Por Dios*, Mother! I'm not a child!'

'You're my daughter,' said Celestina crisply. 'I brought you and your brother up decent. Not that it's done Juan any good, the way he carries on. And all that money – where's he get it from? Never spends a peso more than he can help here at home, but I've seen the wads of banknotes he carries around. That man Luciani – he's rich, isn't he?'

'Yes, he's very rich!'

'Well, don't you have nothing to do with him. Rich is rich and poor is poor. We're poor, honest folk. Your father's spent his life making a decent living for us and he's never cheated anyone – which is more than you can say about most people these days. You leave the rich men to find their fancy pieces elsewhere.'

'I'm sick of being poor!' screamed Gladys and fled to her room in a flood of angry tears.

Next morning the most expensive florist in Buenos Aires delivered four dozen red and yellow roses to Verdulería Nápoli. Celestina spluttered in astonishment when she saw them.

'There must be some mistake!'

'There's no mistake,' retorted Gladys, reading the card. 'They're from Marcos. He's asked me to dinner tonight.'

'*Marcos?*' Her mother's eyebrows bristled. 'Who's Marcos?'

Gladys swept up the roses and stalked out of the kitchen without bothering to reply.

At eight o'clock that evening the Luciani chauffeur rang the bell at Verdulería Nápoli. It gave Gladys a great deal of malicious pleasure to see half the neighbourhood gaping at the sleek black car parked in front of the shop. She sailed out, her bright yellow head held high.

'Where's Gladys Gómez going to?'

It was none of their damned business.

Claudia, peering from the upstairs window, made a small face at the car. Grandmother and Grandfather disapproved. Their disgruntled mutterings droned steadily in the background. She could not understand why they thought it was wrong for Mother to have dinner with Señor Luciani. After all, he had invited them to his ranch and even though Claudia had not enjoyed herself she liked to see her mother have a good time. When Gladys was happy she didn't snap or scold or quarrel with everyone.

'I wish mother was happy all the time,' sighed Claudia wistfully.

VI

Gladys peered curiously out of the window as the car glided through streets congested with late rush-hour traffic. Somehow the world looked very different now, crowded and noisy, peopled by anxious puppets jostling mechanically to and fro. It began to rain again. The sky sluiced the city with streams of water and sent the puppets scurrying frantically for shelter. Someone – she could not distinguish whether man or woman – darted in front of the car, swerved to avoid another one, and chased after a bus packed to the roof. The car braked gently, then gathered up speed as though the interruption were of no consequence.

The world outside was commonplace and uncomfortable.

The world inside was bliss. Except for the steady purr of the engine everything was quiet; the heavens might deluge until Doomsday, but not a single drop of rain would touch the car's warm luxurious interior. A remote, privileged world, safely bolstered against the commonplace one by gleaming chrome and maroon leather that smelled of French scent and Turkish tobacco.

Gladys leaned back against the seat with a small, dissatisfied sigh. Politics notwithstanding, she would give anything to be a part of privilege and comfort.

They drew up under the Plaza's columned portico. Marble steps, glittering chandeliers, a carpeted lobby walled with mirrors and elegant showcases. As a dour, uniformed personage led

Gladys down a winding flight of stairs to the bar she tried not to stare at the scarves and handbags on display. Exploitation of the masses and not worth a true Peronist's glance — but an alligator handbag in the middle case made her mouth water with envy.

The uniformed personage deposited Gladys on the threshold of a large room decorated with hunting prints, and disappeared. She hovered anxiously, ill-at-ease and disconcerted to find herself once again in alien territory. The well-dressed women sitting at the tables all reminded her of Teresa Arcos Arizu. Not one of them cast more than a casual glance in her direction, but even their indifference took on a sinister meaning. Perhaps they were already talking about her, their sleek heads bent forward as they gossiped and sneered. Gladys bit her lip uncertainly and glanced around. No sign of Marcos. A tall, reddish-blond man standing at the bar strolled over, drink in hand.

'Hello,' he drawled. 'Looking for someone?'

His drawl contained more than a hint of male arrogance which she found offensive. Her colour rose. 'It's all right, thank you.'

The man laughed. 'We can't let a pretty girl stand all alone, can we?' His blue eyes inspected her approvingly. 'Come and have a drink while you're waiting.'

'I'm quite all right,' said Gladys loudly. A couple seated at a nearby table looked around and grinned. 'I-I'm waiting for somebody.'

'Stood you up, eh? All the more reason to have a drink with me. Come on,' as she pulled away from his large, freckled hand. 'I won't bite. You're a pretty little doll, you know. I like blondes.'

'Then find yourself one that's unattached,' said Marcos's voice sharply behind them. 'The señora is with me.'

Gladys flushed, embarrassed to tears, but the man merely laughed again, clapped Marcos on the back, and wandered off to try his luck with a willowy redhead at the other end of the room.

Marcos took Gladys's arm. 'Picking up women is Freddy's hobby. Let's go in to dinner.'

The Grill at the Plaza turned out to be yet another privileged world of comfort. Dark beams, blue-and-white tiled walls, gleaming cutlery and sparkling glassware, flowers on the tables, spotless linen. A smiling headwaiter handed Gladys a large leather-bound menu with at least eight pages of dishes she had never heard of before. To make matters worse the names were in French. She struggled frantically to make sense out of *Canard à l'Orange, Tournedos Edouard VII, Ris de Veau Richelieu* . . . Gladys peered over the edge of the menu to find Marcos studying her. He seemed amused by something.

'Do you like oysters?' he asked.

In for a penny, in for a pound. 'Yes, of course I do.'

Half a dozen oysters in their shell, served on a bed of cracked ice. A bottle of Chilean white wine. Gladys eyed the oysters warily and took a sip of wine for inspiration. Very dry, very chilled, very worldly. She took a second sip and prodded at an oyster with a small, two-pronged fork. The oyster sliped back on to its shell with a rebellious plop! and quivered defiantly as the fork prodded again. This time she got the oyster into her mouth where it squiggled between her teeth and refused to be chewed. Gladys gagged and the oyster slid down her gullet like a piece of thick salty slime.

'Have some bread,' grinned Marcos and held out a plate with thin buttered slices. 'What have you been doing since I last saw you?'

Disloyalty raised its treacherous head again as the rally at Lanús was firmly pushed into the background.

'Nothing much.' Gladys chased after another oyster. 'Claudia has a cold.'

They discussed Claudia's cold and Marcos's children, Gaspari senior's rheumatism, Claudia's school. After roast beef that melted like butter in the mouth and a bottle of claret Gladys found herself telling Marcos about Evita's commendation; she made quite an amusing story out of it, but his only comment was to indicate the dessert trolley.

'Would you like something sweet?'

Meringues filled with strawberries and whipped cream. Gladys sank her teeth blissfully into the crunchy white shell. Too delicious for words. It was a glorious, enchanted evening. On an impulse she reached across the table and touched Marcos's hand.

'Thank you.'

He looked startled. 'Thank you? For what?'

'For everything. You've been very kind and I . . .' Something in his expression made Gladys withdraw her hand quickly. She gave a nervous little laugh. 'Dear me, I feel like Cinderella!'

His reply was cut short by the appearance of Fabio Grandi, drunk and in a truculent mood. A jealous husband had ruined his latest masterpiece, he informed them loudly. The man had actually had the audacity to burst into the studio and drag his wife out during a sitting.

'After throwing a pot of Carnelian thirty-three at the canvas,' spluttered the painter. 'Ruined it — absolutely ruined it! The man's a savage! An immoral philistine!' He slumped down on an empty chair without being invited and waved his cigarette holder at the rest of the diners. 'Look at them! Vandals!'

'You're sure to find another model,' remarked Marcos dryly.

'Not like this one! Sheer perfection, old boy! Pure Van Eyck. Vir-virginal, austere . . .' Fabio hiccoughed and stared at Gladys. 'My God, it's a Georges Klack! Perfect — even the crumbs clinging to the lower lip. No, don't spoil it,' as she blushed furiously and tried to wipe away the offending particles. 'Such a splendid little touch of kitsch. What's your name, blondie?'

Gladys stammered it uncertainly and he laughed.

'Splendid! Even the name's pure corn. Tell me . . .' He leaned over and wiggled his fingers at her. 'Is this philistine bringing you to hear little Lorenzo tickle the ivories tomorrow night?'

'Yes,' broke in Marcos curtly and signalled to the waiter. 'If you want a table, Grandi, this one's free. We're just leaving.'

The painter leered. 'Enjoy yourself, old boy.'

VII

The car slipped away from the Plaza and headed north along the tree-lined avenue bordering the riverfront. Marcos pressed a button and a glass partition enclosed the back seat in a world of warm, silent motion. He stared glumly out of the window. Buenos Aires lay flat against the darkness — angular lines and squares of light arranged in haphazard rows along the outline of a cartoon city. A scale-model metropolis constructed by black-humoured gods. Rage and frustration rose in his throat.

'About tomorrow night,' he said out loud. 'I do want you to come with me to Teresa's dinner party, Gladys.'

She sat rigidly upright in the corner, her hands clasped around a ridiculous little white handbag. *Commonplace. Tasteless. Stupid.* Marcos gripped the leather box in his jacket pocket and repeated his request.

'I want you to come to Teresa's tomorrow night.'

Gladys fumbled with her handbag. 'She didn't invite me.'

'I'm inviting you.'

A thin, watery moon slid briefly between the clouds and retreated into darkness.

'Will you marry me, Gladys?'

'M-marry you?'

He gritted his teeth and forced a smile. He even took hold of her hand.

'Why not? You're a very attractive woman. I . . . you must know what I feel by now.'

Her hand struggled briefly in response to its own rules and then sank submissively in his grasp.

'I d-don't know what to say,' murmured Gladys, deliberately dragging the words. 'I mean . . . it's so sudden.'

'What's sudden about it?'

She adopted the breathless, half-toned whisper that used to tantalize Teófilo Gómez.

'We've only known each other a week.'

'It doesn't take me a week to know what I want,' said Marcos impatiently. He drew out the box and opened it; a large diamond solitaire sparkled on black velvet. 'I want to marry you as soon as possible.'

Gladys drew in her breath sharply, then advanced a trembling hand. The ring slipped on to her finger as easily as the slipper had fitted Cinderella.

CHAPTER THIRTEEN

I

On Wednesdays Mercedes did volunteer work at the Italian Hospital. This particular morning when Marcos asked her into his study after breakfast she protested anxiously.

'Sister Marta is very particular about punctuality. Can't it wait until lunchtime?'

'I have something to tell you,' he said. 'It won't take long.'

Something to tell you sounded ominous. Mercedes perched on the edge of a chair and fidgeted with the buttons on her pink volunteer's uniform. Marcos stood at the window with his back to her. The clock on the desk ticked seconds off time with uneasy precision. Downstairs in the kitchen a woman laughed.

'I'm getting married,' Marcos said without turning around.

Mercedes's fingers froze. After a moment she made her lips move, but the words that came did not sound like her voice at all.

'M-married?' A button dropped to the carpet and gleamed at her like a small, malevolent eye. 'But . . . but *why*?'

He grimaced bitterly at the garden below. 'Why does a man marry, Mercedes? I want a wife.'

'But I . . . Who are you marrying?'

'Juan Gaspari's sister.'

She gripped the edge of the desk, the colour draining from her face. 'You *can't*!'

The shoulders hunched against the window did not move.

'Marcos, you've gone mad! Have you really looked at her — the way she dresses, the way she talks? And her brother? He's a . . . how could you possibly want to marry such a common woman!'

Still no reply.

'Marry someone if you must, but for God's sake think of your position! Think of the children! Don't think of me — I don't count, but at least think of the children!'

'Don't be ridiculous,' he said harshly.

'Marcos, *please*! Dear Holy Virgin, what has come over you? To even think of marrying a woman like . . . If you won't consider us,' she cried, half rising against the desk, 'at least remember Magdalena!'

'Magdalena's dead.'

'How can you be so disrespectful of her memory, Marcos! How can you even dream of that woman taking her place! My God, you've gone mad! She's tricked you – can't you see that? Can't you understand she's after your money? How can you be so blind?'

He swung around, his face livid. '*Shut up*!'

Mercedes stared, too shocked to reply. Marcos strode over to the desk, snatched a cigarette from the silver monogrammed box that had been an anniversary present, and jammed it between his lips. The fingers fumbling with his lighter were all thumbs.

'I'm sorry,' he said thickly after a moment. 'I didn't mean to shout at you.'

Mercedes's thin fingers pressed white marks against the glass desk top. 'You're not serious about Gaspari's sister. For God's sake, Marcos – tell me you're not serious!'

'I'm marrying Gladys as soon as everything can be arranged.'

'But why *her*?'

His jaw tightened. 'I have my reasons, Mercedes.'

Her knees gave way and she sat down abruptly. 'I see.' Then, fighting to keep her voice steady, 'I shall leave, of course.'

'Leave? What the hell are you talking about?'

Her eyes brimmed with tears. 'You'll want me to leave Barranco Rosales. I understand. I'll find a f-flat in town. Something small, easy to run . . .'

Mercedes's voice broke. Everything she loved would be taken from her when Marcos married Gaspari's sister. Years of devotion and sacrifice no longer counted; they were not strong enough to safeguard a brother from a scheming woman's wiles. No one needed her anymore. She would have to live in a flat, the children would forget her – children forgot so easily. They would go about their own lives while she grew old alone . . . Mercedes drew a low, shuddering sob and felt Marcos's arm go around her.

'This is your home,' he said unsteadily. 'There's no question of your leaving.'

The rough tweed of his jacket scratched her face. She sobbed again, torn by his nearness and the ghost of his coming marriage.

'I c-can't stay on. Not if you're married.'

'What's that got to do with it? You lived here when I was married to Magdalena.'

Muffled. 'That was . . . d-different.'

There was a short silence before Marcos said dully, 'I need you here, Mercedes. It won't be easy for any of us. The children . . . We need you.'

Anger was gone, leaving his face drawn and unhappy. Mercedes dabbed at her eyes with a crumpled handkerchief. She did not want to remain in Barranco Rosales a second longer than necessary if Gladys Gómez was going to live there; on the other hand she could not bring herself to leave Marcos. Not with that expression on his face. Something was very wrong. She stood up and took his head firmly between her hands, forcing him to look at her.

'Tell me the truth,' she ordered. 'Why are you marrying Gaspari's sister?'

His glance strayed to the photograph of La Catalina and the children. It was a bleak, unguarded look that confessed in silence what he could not bring himself to say to her in words. She would never understand and he was too weary, too frustrated in his own pride to try and explain. Mercedes touched his cheek, her eyes suddenly very hard and bright.

'I hate that woman,' she said fiercely. 'I shall hate her to my dying day!'

II

Marcos made a point of having tea with the children whenever he was at Barranco Rosales.

It was a pleasant domestic ritual which he thoroughly enjoyed. There was little formality when the children invaded the family dining-room. Their laughter and squabbles added a light-hearted touch to the elaborately carved furniture, the majolica plates on the sideboard, the tapestries on the walls. An eighteenth century Japanese print hung opposite the sideboard. Fine black brushstrokes cut stark lines of motion across a neutral background – a stallion in full gallop. It had been a Christmas present from Magdalena . . . Her slender, patrician ghost stared at Marcos from the lines of motion, one eyebrow raised in a hauntingly familiar gesture of disdain.

'What's the matter, Papa?' asked Isabel through a mouthful of bread and jam. 'Does your shoulder hurt?'

He turned quickly from the print and smiled at her. 'I'm all right, *ñatita*.'

'Gastón says he'll teach me to play tennis this summer at Los Toros,' chirped Cristina importantly. 'I'm going to have much more fun than Isabel.'

'Papa and I'll have much more fun than you.' Isabel ran around the table and hugged Marcos. 'We're going to ride and herd cattle and swim in the lake and do everything together.'

He had forgotten about that. 'I'm afraid there's been a change of plans this summer,' he said uncomfortably. 'Do you remember Claudia Gómez?'

'Porky,' chorused the girls with an outrageous whoop of laughter. 'She goes to a state school.'

Marcos cleared his throat, embarrassed. 'Yes. Well, I . . . I've been seeing quite a bit of her mother lately . . . I . . . We . . .' The words stuck.

Three pairs of eyes stared at him. No one spoke.

'I'm going to marry her,' he rushed on, shaken by their silence. 'At the end of October. We'll all be going to La Catalina together.'

Isabel's eyes filled with tears. 'But you said it was just the two of us! You promised!'

He reached up to stroke her head. 'I'm sorry, *ñatita*.'

'I don't want you to get married!' Two bright red spots flamed in her cheeks. 'I want to go to La Catalina with you, like you promised!'

'Isabel, listen . . .'

'Claudia's stupid! Her mother's stupid! Stupid stupid stupid! I hate them!' she shouted and rushed sobbing from the room.

Cristina eyed her father as though inspecting some exotic creature from outer space. 'Are you *really* going to marry Claudia's mother?'

'Yes.'

'Do you love her like you loved Mama?'

'No, not like I loved Mama.'

'Then why are you getting married?' demanded Miguel, turning beet-red as his voice shot up half an octave. 'We don't need another mother! We've got Aunt Mercedes.'

Beyond the swinging doors that led to the yellow-tiled scullery the cook's voice rose and fell in an exasperated monotone.

'Just because I'm getting married again doesn't mean things will change or that I don't love you, children,' said Marcos somewhat testily. 'Claudia's mother is a very nice woman and she's fond of you.'

'But Aunt Mercedes . . .'

'Will continue to live with us. Nothing is going to change.'

Tea continued in doubtful silence. Afterwards Marcos went in search of Isabel. She was huddled on the sofa in his study, hugging a moth-eaten teddy bear and sobbing as though her heart would break; when he touched her shoulder she pulled away. Marcos let a moment go by and tried again.

'Bela, listen to me. Please.'

The teddy bear glared at him with crooked, accusing eyes. Someone knocked on the door; he opened it impatiently and found Miss Nelly on the threshold. The governess sniffed.

'I don't know what's come over that child, Mr Marcos! I tried to stop her . . . Isabel, come out of your father's study at once!'

Mercedes appeared in the background. 'What on earth is going on? I never heard such a racket.'

'Isabel's having a tantrum,' clucked Miss Nelly crisply.

'Isabel, dear – tell Aunt Mercedes . . .'

'She's a very wilful girl . . .'

'Isabel, please stop crying . . .'

Point and counterpoint in shrill syncopation. Marcos shut the study door against them and went back to the sofa. The teddy bear had fallen to the floor; he propped it awkwardly against the lamp on his desk and sat down. Outside the door Mercedes and Miss Nelly continued to syncopate. He slipped his hand under Isabel's chin and turned her face towards him. It was flushed and swollen, the eyes swimming like dark pools of misery under long, curling lashes. Marcos brushed away a few damp strands of hair stuck to her forehead.

'I'm sorry if I've made you unhappy, *ñatita*,' he said gently. 'I love you very much.'

She gulped. 'Then wh-why are you getting married?'

'Because I need a wife to take care of me.'

'I'll take care of you!'

He managed a faint smile. 'It's not the same thing. Now don't start again,' as she began to wail. 'When you grow up and get married you'll understand.'

'I don't want to get married!'

Marcos fished a handkerchief from his pocket and handed it to her. 'You will someday and so will Cristina. And Miguel. It's only natural, Bela. It's only natural for me to want to marry again.'

Isabel blew her nose. 'But she's awful! And Claudia's awful! Why can't you marry someone like Angela?'

He laughed, but the sound was harsh and painful as though laughter hurt. 'There's only one Angela, *ñatita*, and she's married to Jimmy.'

III

Mercedes rang Teresa, who made no bones about her indignation. On Wednesday evening she received Gladys with an icy smile and barely acknowledged her brother-in-law's presence. Marcos defied the snub and paraded his fiancée like a prize peacock among the startled guests. It mattered little to him whether Teresa or society was outraged. He had already burnt his boats and if he was to sink in flames he would do so in style.

He needed no help in handling his own damnation.

Gossip threatened to overshadow Lorenzo Grandi's recital by drowning out the love pangs of Chopin and Liszt. Gladys was the only one who paid close attention to his playing. She recognized one of the melodies from a favourite soap opera and applauded enthusiastically even before his last arpeggio rippled away. Lorenzo responded with an impassioned rendering of the 'Revolutionary Etude'. He was an ambitious, intense and very gifted young musician. He also needed money. The simpering blonde hanging on to every note looked as though she might have quite a bit to throw away. He hammered out patriotic fervour in tempestuous minor chords and tossed his handsome profile with one eye on the blonde.

Chopin had never begged so hard for recognition.

Aurora Grandi managed to put on a brave face all evening, but behind her brilliant smile and witty conversation burned a secret hell. Why, she thought miserably, did Marcos want to marry that preposterous woman? What could he possibly find attractive in her? She was a common cow. Look at her stupid smile. Aurora darted a hungry glance at Marcos. Ever since Teresa's birthday party she had been tormenting herself with dreams about him. Imagining his kisses. His naked body. Both their naked bodies lying together . . . She excused herself and fled to the powder room. Her flushed face mocked her from the mirror. Marcos did not want Aurora Grandi, he wanted a common cow.

Carlos cornered Marcos in the library before dinner and demanded an explanation.

'If this is your idea of a joke,' he added indignantly, 'I can tell you right now it's an insult!'

Marcos stared at the drink in his hand. He owed Carlos the truth, but he could not look him in the eye.

'It's no joke,' he said. 'I'm getting married for protection. There's every indication that Artemio Mendes will be our next governor and if that happens, I'll lose La Catalina. If you were in my shoes you'd understand!' he cried as Carlos started to speak. 'You don't know what the past weeks have been like! When Mendes is governor it'll be a thousand times worse. I'll be damned if I'm going to stand by and let those fucking vultures lay their claws on La Catalina without doing anything to stop them! If marrying the clown's sister is the only way — oh, Christ!' he rasped and turned to the window.

'Are you sure it's the only way?' asked Carlos after a short silence.

Marcos stared down at the traffic in the street. 'Mendes is going to be governor,' he said dully. 'Gaspari is as sure of that as he is of the nose on his goddamned face. There's no way we can buy enough votes to influence the election. I don't have any choice, Carlos. I have to marry Gladys or risk losing my ranch.'

After the guests had gone Carlos repeated that conversation to Teresa. She stared at him in outraged astonishment.

'But he's absolutely mad, Carlos!'

'He's trapped. I was afraid something like this would happen. You can't make deals with the Peronists and expect to keep out of their clutches.'

145

Teresa's dark eyes flashed. 'I've never been so humiliated! For Marcos to bring that woman here – and Aurora! What about her? How do you think she feels about all this?'

'I haven't the faintest idea. Is she supposed to feel anything?'

'Well, of course she is! Everybody expected them to announce their engagement before the end of the year!'

Carlos sat down on the edge of the bed and began to untie his shoes. He doubted very much that Marcos had ever given Aurora Grandi serious thought, but there was no point arguing about it with Teresa. He liked and respected his brother-in-law, in spite of their different approach to politics. If circumstances had forced Marcos to take such a desperate step, then matters must be very serious indeed.

'It's an absolute scandal!' snapped Teresa, smoothing cold cream over her face. 'I certainly hope Marcos doesn't expect me to receive that woman in the future!'

'That woman,' her husband reminded her, 'will be his wife.'

'To think of her in Magdalena's place – it's unbelievable!'

'We can't cut them off, Teresa. We have too many family interests in common. It galls me to hell, but there's nothing to be done except pray the brother doesn't wriggle his way into the picture. Not that I believe he'd get very far, but you never can tell. These Peronists are sly worms.' He stared at the rug, a shoe dangling from his lean forefinger. 'Mind you, I don't agree with what Marcos has done – but I can see why he did it.'

'How can you? She's a greengrocer's daughter!'

'With handy political connections,' added Carlos wryly and went into the bathroom.

IV

Gladys floated on clouds, oblivious to everything but her dream come true. Marcos bought her clothes and jewellery. They lunched at the Yacht Club. He bought her a fur coat. She remembered the alligator handbag in the showcase at the Plaza; he bought that as well and a pair of brown pigskin gloves so soft they felt like velvet. On the day following the dinner party at Teresa's he announced they would be married on 21 October.

'A small church ceremony after the registry office. We'll have your parents to lunch at Barranco Rosales and take an evening flight to Brazil for our honeymoon. I want to be back at La Catalina by the first of November. Spring's a busy time of year on the ranch.'

Juan Gaspari appeared to be the only person delighted by his sister's good fortune. He kissed her enthusiastically several times, told her she looked as beautiful as Evita, and rang Marcos to congratulate him. The curt acknowledgement on the other end of the line made him chuckle. With Gladys firmly established in Buenos Aires's upper crust, life would be a bed of roses.

The elder Gasparis took a far less optimistic view of their future son-in-law.

'Marrying out of one's class brings nothing but headaches,' warned Celestina. 'And what's Claudia going to do in that fancy nun's school you'll be sending her to? No one ever made a silk purse out of a sow's ear. The child'll be miserable among people she doesn't like or understand. You mark my words!'

'Don't be silly,' retorted Gladys. 'We are going to be very happy – aren't we Claudia?'

The plain chubby face looked dubious. 'I guess so.'

'We won't ever get to see her now,' wheezed Gaspari senior. 'Why can't you marry some nice man from the neighbourhood, eh? The butcher down the street – he's a fine chap. Owns his shop, too. Never been married.'

Celestina took up the chant. 'He doesn't gamble, doesn't drink, doesn't carry on with women. He'd make a good husband, Gladys.'

She shrugged off the butcher. 'So will Marcos Luciani – and he's rich.'

Her parents grumbled that money wasn't everything, but she pretended not to hear.

The crowd at Quilmes Party headquarters received the news in consternation. Juanita Sánchez made an heroic speech about Gladys's supreme sacrifice, but even that fell flat after ten minutes. Most people felt that *Compañera* Gómez had, if not betrayed them outright, at least overstepped the bounds of duty.

Marcos was not interested in social or political qualms. Two days later he returned to La Catalina; on the Sunday evening he went to have supper with Jimmy and Angela.

V

The old Russian count would not have recognized his railway station.

Brick-red curtains at the windows picked up the lamplight's mellow reflections and threw the gaily printed fabric on the furniture into bold relief. There was a terracotta bowl of flowers on the table by the door and a graceful arrangement of pampa grass in a large copper urn near the hearth. The hides on the floor were new, the floor itself gleamed with polish. A hunting print hung over the fireplace – a gift of nostalgia from the Morgans. Angela sat on the sofa stitching white rabbits on to a baby's blanket. The snip of her scissors and the crackle of the logs on the hearth were the only sounds to be heard.

Marcos put down his coffee cup. He had been waiting for Angela to say something ever since Jimmy had left the room a few minutes ago, but she continued to stitch and snip in silence. It was a chilly silence, tinged with disapproval. She had been like that ever since he told them he was going to marry Gladys Gómez; the chill and her disapproval were beginning to get on his nerves.

'Are you angry with me?' he asked.

'Why should I be angry?'

'You look it.'

Angela studied him for a moment, her eyes very blue and cool; the lamplight tangled in her hair and turned it to silver. She was angry and disappointed and bewildered. All three edged her voice.

'I don't understand you, that's all.'

'There's nothing to understand. I told you. I'm marrying Gaspari's sister because of La Catalina. I can't afford not to.'

'Is that the only reason?'

'Of course!' When she did not reply he added impatiently, 'Why else would I marry a woman like Gladys Gómez?'

One rabbit was completed. Angela snipped a few threads. Marcos had solved his problems with a cold-hearted, calculated marriage. He was a pragmatic man. She pinned another rabbit to the blanket. Perhaps it was just as well. Good riddance to her secret, guilty dreams. *Adiós* to falling in love. She began to thread her needle again.

Marcos lowered his voice. 'I am in love with you, Angela. You know that already. This other thing – it has nothing to do with love. Nothing at all.'

'Not very nice for Gladys, is it?' Angela observed dryly as she jabbed the needle into a new rabbit's foot.

He moved over to the sofa and took hold of her hand. 'Look at me.' Her eyes flickered up and down again. He leaned forward and began to murmur gently. His tension flowed through the fingers pressing her skin. They burned.

'I've never loved any other woman as completely or as madly as I love you. Never.' His breath touched her cheek; it burned like his fingers. 'I can't stop thinking about you. You're a fever . . . no, much more than that. One can be cured of fever. I'll never be cured of you. I want to give you everything I have, everything I am . . .' the words echoed hoarsely in her ear. '*I want you so badly, Angela!*'

His touch and voice stirred a response no amount of disapproval could control. Just for a moment Angela forgot about Jimmy in the kitchen, forgot about the baby, forgot about everything but her love for Marcos. She turned to look at him with wide, helpless eyes; her heart pounded wildly in her throat. If he kisses me . . . The baby, as though outraged, kicked her hard inside, jolting Angela back to reality. She drew back from danger in alarm.

'Marcos, please!' Her eyes darted uneasily towards the kitchen door. 'Please stop it.'

His fingers stroked her wrist. 'Why?'

'Because it's wrong, that's why!'

'Because you are Jimmy's wife and I will marry Gladys? Does that offend your very proper English conscience?' His breath burned her cheek again. 'You haven't forgotten that day in the car, have you?'

There were sounds on the far side of the kitchen door. Angela struggled frantically to break away from Marcos's grasp.

'Jimmy's coming!' she hissed. 'Let me go!'

'You haven't forgotten.' His hand gripped hard. 'Tell me the truth: are you very much in love with Jimmy?'

'Yes, I am! Now for God's sake, let me go!'

She could not meet his eyes. Marcos grinned wryly.

'You make a very bad liar, *gringuita*.' He caressed the palm of her hand with his lips and tongue for a moment before moving away. 'Shall I tell you about young Lorenzo Grandi's performance?'

When Jimmy returned he found their guest standing in front of the fire, describing the antics of long-haired Lorenzo at the keyboard. It was just as well Marcos's lips had left no visible imprints, reflected Angela with a guilty smile at her husband. The memory of his kiss seared her palm like fire.

VI

As Marcos was about to leave Jimmy climbed into the car beside him and lit a cigarette.

'Let me off at the gate,' he said. 'I want a word with you.' He smoked for a few minutes in silence before speaking again. 'Do you remember the Widow?' He took several anxious puffs. 'There's a child.'

'I warned you about that at Easter.'

Jimmy stared through the windscreen at the dark outline of land silhouetted against the starless sky. 'She claims it's mine. She's written for money, stopped me in the street, written again. I didn't reply.'

A startled cavy scuttled across the path of the headlights and vanished into a clump of tumbleweed at the side of the road.

'Father Antonio cornered me in Laguna today,' continued Jimmy after a short silence. 'He wants the Widow to have the child baptized, but she told him she won't unless I recognize it. There's a bitch for you. The priest's having nightmares about innocent little souls roasting in Hell. He practically begged me to say the brat's mine.'

'Is it?'

'Morgan ears and Morgan chin – including the cleft. I went around to see. That goddamned little bastard looks like me when I was his age. Just like my parents' picture of me hanging over their bed.'

Marcos burst out laughing.

'Christ, it's not funny!' cried Jimmy, exasperated. 'The Widow's threatening to tell Angela if I don't recognize the brat. She wants money as well.'

There was a long, curiously empty silence.

'Angela wouldn't understand,' said Jimmy.

'It happened before you met her.'

'That doesn't make any difference. She . . . I don't want her mixed up in this sort of thing.'

'No,' agreed Marcos with a touch of asperity. 'You're a fool, Morgan. If you had to screw the local whore you should have at least taken precautions.'

Jimmy lit another cigarette and flicked the match impatiently out of the window. 'I should have done a lot of things. Maybe I should never have married Angela. Maybe it was a mistake.'

The car swerved sharply. 'A *mistake*?'

'I just wonder if she's really happy with me out here, old boy. Sometimes she looks unsettled and . . . I don't know. As though she has something on her mind.'

'If you want my advice,' said Marcos after another silence, 'find yourself a couple of reliable fools to be godparents and tell Father Antonio you'll agree if the baptism is kept secret. The old man's a good sort as priests go – he doesn't want a scandal any more than you do. Give the Widow enough money to keep her quiet and think up a good story to tell your wife if the woman appears on your doorstep anyway.' He slowed down as the gate loomed up in the darkness. 'I'll see you at the stockyards tomorrow.'

Jimmy opened the door and paused. 'Will you be a reliable fool?'

'And stand as godfather to your bastard?'

'I can't trust anyone else.'

Somewhere out in the darkness an owl hooted.

'All right,' said Marcos reluctantly. 'Get the priest to find a godmother. Maybe one of the nuns at the convent would do it.' He jingled the car keys impatiently. 'Open the gate, *loco*. I want to go home.'

As the car moved forward Jimmy poked his head through the window. 'Not a bad-looking little bastard, you know,' he

151

grinned. 'I've done myself proud, old boy. Bloody, ball-busting proud.'

VII

The wedding was strictly a family affair, but Angela and Jimmy were invited because, as Mercedes told them, the Lucianis definitely counted them as 'family'. The only outsider was Juanita Sánchez, who tagged along as one of Gladys's witnesses.

'Her other witness is Gaspari. He wouldn't miss a chance like this to be in the limelight,' added Mercedes acidly. 'Fortunately the Sánchez woman has to get back to her factory shift and won't be able to stay for the wedding breakfast.'

Gladys, looking very pretty in pale blue silk and a frilly flowered hat, arrived punctually at the registry office for the civil ceremony. Marcos was fifteen minutes late; he looked as though he hadn't slept all night. He listened impassively to the formalities and gave his replies in a dry, flat voice. His only sign of emotion came when asked if he took Gladys Emilia Gaspari, widow of Teófilo Gómez, to be his wife. There was a long silence. The judge performing the ceremony stared over the rim of his glasses. Perhaps Señor Luciani had not heard him. He cleared his throat and spoke again.

'Do you take . . .'

'Yes,' interrupted Marcos hoarsely. 'I do.'

He repeated the same words at the religious ceremony an hour later. *Till death do us part* hammered the final nail home. Last night he had been briefly tempted to back out, even if it meant risking La Catalina. It was too late now.

'You may kiss the bride,' beamed the priest.

Marcos kept up appearances. He kissed the bride. The Lucianis kept up appearances. They gathered in the living-room at Barranco Rosales and made polite conversation. The children invited their new stepsister into the garden. Only Juan Gaspari appeared to be enjoying himself.

'Jimmy, it's ghastly!' whispered Angela. 'Why did Carlos and Teresa bother to come if they disapprove so much of Gladys?'

'They can't afford a clean break,' he whispered back. 'Marcos owns a huge packet of shares in Los Toros through Magdalena's

152

dowry. They've got other joint interests as well. I was talking to Carlos coming back from the church. He's livid, but not so livid or blind he can't see the advantages of political protection these days. Learning to be pragmatic in his old age, Carlos is. If his brother-in-law's fool enough to stick his neck out – why not?'

'But that's so heartless! People using each other for protection and money and politics! Poor, stupid, starry-eyed Gladys – she's nothing but a pawn.'

He chuckled. 'I imagine poor, stupid, starry-eyed Gladys can take pretty good care of herself, angel.'

The parents of the bride came in their Sunday best – Celestina in rigorous black bombasine, with a seed-pearl brooch which had belonged to her mother pinned defiantly on her generous bosom. Not for the world did they unbend to anyone. Angela felt sorry for them and tried to make polite conversation, but her overtures met with stiff resistance. Rich was rich and foreigners were foreigners. Celestina Gaspari kept her hands firmly clasped on her lap and stared at blue velvet curtains framing a sweeping vista of terraced lawn and trees.

She had never been so unhappy in all her life.

VIII

The election results in November 1951 confirmed Perón as president of Argentina for yet another term. Evita, whose vice-presidential ambitions were stubbornly blocked by the armed forces, made an impassioned public renunciation and openly wept in her husband's arms on the balcony of the Casa Rosada. She looked worn and frail, but Juan Gaspari stoutly denied rumours that she was seriously ill.

Despite the efforts of his friends, Artemio Mendes was not elected governor of the province.

PART II

1952–1955

'Set me as a seal upon your heart,
As a seal upon your arm . . .

(Song of Solomon 8:6)

CHAPTER FOURTEEN

I

Perón had created a myth.

To sustain it he muzzled the press, manipulated public finances and built up a powerful propaganda machine, but by 1952 time was running out. Argentina's vast reserves were nearly gone, the government's industrialization programme floundered, the country's agricultural wealth was hamstrung by depressed prices and the exodus of rural workers to the cities.

The opposition watched the country's disintegration in alarm, but Perón was too firmly entrenched and they themselves too divided yet to force a showdown.

At grassroots level Argentina still believed in the myth with passionate devotion. Evita promised Paradise and people's hopes soared into the luminous Argentine sky. *Perón Cumple, Evita Dignifica* was the magical password. The ever-hopefuls clung to it tenaciously, blinded by credulous dreams.

II

Gladys hated La Catalina.

They had barely unpacked from their honeymoon when Marcos drove off to the ranch, leaving her to follow three weeks later with Mercedes and the children. Barranco Rosales was bad enough, but at least there were shops and cinemas in the city to amuse her. La Catalina, sprawling in the middle of the endless pampa, was nothing short of exile in the remotest corner of Hell.

There was nothing for her to do.

The first morning Mercedes began to arrange flowers after breakfast. The sunlight streaming through the open windows, the lazy cooing of the doves, the distant hum of a tractor – all were part and parcel of a domestic ritual as beloved as the bowls and vases spread along an oilcloth on the floor. Gladys, of course, had no way of knowing that the ritual involved only one priestess. She followed Mercedes into the living-room and hovered uncertainly as a gardener brought in armfuls of freshly cut flowers and branches. Mercedes tied a faded blue apron around her waist, knelt down on the oilcloth and began to tackle a large bowl made from hammered silver. Her fingers clipped and trimmed deftly; after a few minutes silvery-green eucalyptus leaves sprouted from a fluffy cloud of mimosa.

'That's pretty,' Gladys indicated a brass-topped table by the bookcase. 'It'll look nice over there. I'll do the blue vase if your like.'

Mercedes set the bowl firmly on the mantelpiece. 'Marcos likes it here. I can fix the flowers myself, thank you.'

The dismissal was too obvious to be ignored and Gladys flushed.

'I only want to help.'

'I have always arranged the flowers at La Catalina,' said Mercedes, snipping a few sprigs of oleander. 'Even when Magdalena was alive.'

Daunted by this tight-lipped invocation of a household custom she did not feel equipped to challenge, Gladys wandered off to the kitchen.

There she met with an equally disconcerting reception. Rosario's grudging *'Buenos días, senōra'* was faintly tinged with contempt; she knew a señora from a good family when she saw one and Don Marcos's new wife came nowhere near the mark. All smiles perhaps, but the common touch stood out like a sore thumb. Shrewd, no doubt about that. Caught Don Marcos off his guard and tricked him into marriage – which proved that even the best of men were fools in the hands of scheming women. Rosario sniffed disapprovingly and announced she had already decided on the day's menu.

'Soup, chicken mayonnaise, fruit salad. Something simple, seeing how Don Marcos and Don Losa ain't here for lunch.'

'I didn't know that,' said Gladys lamely.

'Today's auction day. Don Marcos always eats at the Estrella in Laguna Grande on auction day.' Rosario picked up her rolling pin and gave it an expert twirl. 'You want anything else, senōra? I'm busy this morning.'

158

Gladys beat a flustered retreat and went for a walk in the park.

The morning was very warm; she trudged along, over-powered by the smell of eucalyptus and pine and dank, mossy earth. Beyond the trees a lavender-blue field of lucerne rippled gently under a cloudless cobalt sky. The sight – one of the loveliest in springtime – depressed her almost to tears. No sign of a living soul; no sound other than the sleepy drone of the cicadas and the mocking screech of the parrots as they streaked vivid blue-green flashes through the tangled gloom overhead.

How anyone could like such a place was a mystery.

The honeymoon in Brazil had been so wonderful, reflected Gladys wistfully. They stayed at the most expensive hotel on Río's Copacabana beach, shopped in all the exclusive boutiques, dined and danced at a different place every evening. Marcos turned out to be a man of unexpected moods – joking and teasing her one minute, sardonic the next, swinging from laughter to frowns without warning. He was generous with his money, but his lovemaking . . . Gladys snapped at a pine twig.

Everyone knew that sexual contact outside of marriage was immoral; within marriage it was strictly a marital duty. Teófilo Gómez had performed his marital duties decorously: lights out, a bit of chaste foreplay, an awkward poke under the covers. There was nothing intimate or satisfying about the experience . . . certainly there was no pleasure in it. Only loose women found pleasure in doing *that*, Gladys had reminded her rebellious female instincts. She was, as her mother never tired of pointing out, a 'decent' woman.

Marcos was not Teófilo Gómez.

He did not have a flabby paunch, false teeth or bunions. His darkly tanned skin was firm, the hair on his chest curled slightly, his long legs were strong and muscular. Gladys stared up at the tangled canopy of branches overhead. She had been so nervous on their wedding night. She remembered getting ready for bed in the bathroom and hearing Marcos move around the room beyond the closed door. Her heart had begun to beat very fast as she slipped into her new pink satin nightgown. It was very feminine and decorous: a pleated skirt, ruffled straps and little roses on the bodice. She had fiddled with the straps and combed her hair and tugged at the straps again because she was so nervous. She didn't know what to expect; she didn't know what to do.

159

After dinner they had drunk champagne and danced on the hotel's roof-garden under a starry tropical sky. The night was very warm and fragrant, the music slow and sensual. Gladys had enjoyed the dancing, but the pressure of Marcos's body embarrassed her. He did not talk much; he just pressed her against him and danced. At half-past-one he had drained the last of the champagne and said they might as well call it a night.

The pine twig broke between Gladys's fingers and she snapped off another one.

Teófilo Gómez had religiously turned off the light before climbing into bed. Marcos left it on. He didn't get into bed – he didn't even bother to wear pyjamas. When Gladys finally emerged from the bathroom in her new pink satin nightgown, she saw him standing stark naked in the middle of the room. The sight shocked her. She blushed furiously and Marcos frowned.

'What's the matter?' he demanded.

Gladys swallowed. 'I'm sorry. I thought you were ready for bed.'

'I am ready.' His dark eyes raked her up and down; his voice was expressionless. 'Come here, Gladys.'

She obeyed nervously. He slid down the nightgown's ruffled straps. 'You won't need this.' Pleated pink satin crumpled to the floor. His hands fondled her breasts briefly, then worked down to grasp her small, rounded buttocks. His kiss was perfunctory. Gladys returned it timidly; after a moment she worked up enough courage to stroke his head. Marcos jerked away. He walked over to the radio, found a music station and came back.

'Let's dance,' he said, pulling her against him.

'But – aren't we going to bed?'

'Later. I want to dance now.'

There was no protective clothing to disguise the hollows and bulges of their bodies. Gladys squirmed uncomfortably. She had to dance on tiptoe, her arms clinging around Marcos's neck and her breasts squashed against his chest. He swayed back and forth in the same place, hands on her buttocks and eyes closed, forcing himself to concentrate on the physical sensations of a woman's body rubbing against his own. He didn't want to remember who this particular woman was. The music helped. He danced her over to the bed.

160

'Aren't you going to turn out the light?' asked Gladys.

'No.'

To hell with modesty. She was a stupid woman with a high, stupid voice. He had condemned himself to living with her and hearing that voice for the rest of their lives; he wanted to see every punishing detail of his act of damnation.

Gladys shuddered as he climbed on top of her. If only she couldn't see what went on, but this was indecent. They weren't even under the sheets. Marcos sawed impatiently between her thighs. His dark, staring eyes were glazed, his hands braced against the mattress.

His neck muscles stood out like cords, the veins above his temples were knotted. He grunted. Several drops of sweat splashed on Gladys's face. Disgusting. She clenched her teeth against the monotonous heaving of her husband's body.

Duty might be duty – but the next time she would insist Marcos must turn off the light.

III

Times were growing increasingly difficult in Argentina.

Marcos, along with every other rancher in the country, had his hands full. Thanks to the government's price policies the world market for Argentine beef and grain was shrinking rapidly; as a result local producers sowed less crops and thinned out their herds. The drop in productivity dealt a severe blow to Perón's ambitions, but massive industrialization programmes were certainly no cure-all for the country's problems. By 1952 the government was not only forced to introduce 'meatless days' (previously unheard of in a country whose staple diet begins and ends with beef), it also raised agricultural prices and offered subsidies to encourage production. Tadeo Ortíz grimly predicted that the measures had come too late.

'Perón put this country's natural wealth in hock to promote his damned mania for factories,' he added. 'We'll never redeem it now. Ten, fifteen more years at this rate and Argentina will be as good as bankrupt.'

Juan Gaspari paid a flying visit to La Catalina to assure Marcos that rumours of the country's economic ills were groundless.

'Propaganda by anti-national elements who wish to sell us out to the foreign imperialist powers,' he parroted with an energetic flap of his white hands. 'Argentina is better off now than she ever was.'

'Bullshit,' snapped Marcos.

Gaspari looked pained. 'The general is a very astute man,' he said. 'We may be going through a few difficulties – I tell you this in confidence, of course – but Perón knows what he's doing. I can assure you there's nothing to worry about.'

'Like you assured me Artemio Mendes would be elected governor?'

'Ah, well – Mendes!' Gaspari leaned back in his chair and studied the map of La Catalina on the wall. 'A very stupid man who overshot his mark. Men like Mendes are dangerous elements in any party. They must be kept in check. Besides, the general found no reason to complain about the present governor. He a good Party man.'

'I seem to recall you saying that he had fallen out of favour with Evita,' remarked Marcos acidly.

There was a curious little silence and then Gaspari laughed. 'You know how women are, *amigo*. The general likes the governor.'

He began to talk about the import duties on a piece of equipment Marcos wanted to bring in from Holland. Isidoro Sánchez in the ministry would be very happy to arrange things, but there were certain expenses . . . Gaspari's voice ran smoothly on, detailing the ins and outs of a procedure they both knew by heart. Marcos studied him thoughtfully. *You know how women are* was a glib, almost indifferent observation. He doubted Juan Gaspari would have dismissed Evita so casually two months ago.

IV

Another family gathering, this time for New Year's Eve. If Gladys was nervous she managed to hide it well. Wearing the right clothes went a long way to boost her confidence and before supper she regaled the women with a description of the dresses and jewels Marcos had bought for her in Río.

'Marcos and Magdalena spent three months touring Europe on their honeymoon,' remarked Teresa to Angela in clear, ringing Spanish. 'They would have stayed longer if it hadn't been for the threat of war. I suppose he thought Río would be good enough for Gladys. The place is such a carnival.'

Angela smiled thinly. She enjoyed speaking Spanish; on the other hand Teresa's remarks would certainly have been more tactful in English. She supposed that in a way they were a compliment to her own fluency. She was an accepted part of the local scene now – a friend with whom one could dissect one's unacceptable sister-in-law in comfort.

Any other time the inner complexities of family warfare might have amused Angela, but not tonight. Tonight she felt bloated and ugly and thoroughly out of sorts with everything and everyone. To sit and listen to Gladys's endless recital of married bliss was torture; not to have come to La Catalina would have been even worse.

It was so difficult to be composed and mature when you wanted another woman's husband.

It was so bloody difficult when you were pregnant with your own husband's child and looked like hell.

Maybe I should have married Anthony after all. Grown sedately mouldy in a rose-covered cottage on the Cam.

If John and Cora Morgan had not invited themselves to Los Alamos for Christmas things wouldn't be so bad. They came, as Cora energetically put it, with the intention of being helpful, but by Boxing Day Tiburcia had threatened to leave and Jimmy could hardly bring himself to speak to his parents. Angela tried to hold everything together until the end of the month, when presumably her in-laws would be going on to their summer home in the hillside resort of La Cumbre, but her efforts were doomed to failure.

'I think it would be so nice for all of us to celebrate your first New Year with Angela, James,' Cora announced brightly on the day of their departure. 'Your father and I have decided to postpone La Cumbre until the second of January.'

'We're going to La Catalina on New Year's Eve,' said Jimmy bluntly. 'We're staying overnight.'

163

John Morgan looked hurt. 'I say, old chap – you can put off the invitation this year, can't you?'

'No, we can't.'

'I'll ring Mercedes,' said Angela quickly. 'I'm sure they won't mind if your parents come with us, Jimmy.'

She had forgotten all about Gladys. Her embarrassment when she remembered only increased her irritation, but Mercedes had laughed it off and extended an invitation to John and Cora Morgan as though Gladys did not exist.

Petty cruelties . . . Angela excused herself in the middle of a rambling account about Gladys's stomach on the cable-car ride up Río's Sugarloaf Mountain and went outside. It was slightly cooler on the veranda; a soft breeze touched her cheek and passed on, leaving the air faintly scented with oleanders. Hemmed in by the park's ungainly outline, night lost its remoteness and descended to earth, jewelling the treetops with stars.

'It's almost next year, Angela!'

The girls raced around the corner of the house, waving lighted squibs. Claudia trotted awkwardly behind. That child looks so unhappy and out of place here, thought Angela. It must be difficult for her to adjust. I suppose Gladys doesn't care how miserable her daughter is. Gladys doesn't seem to care for anything but clothes and jewels.

'May I join you, *gringuita*?'

Marcos came out on to the veranda, balancing a plate, glasses and a bottle of wine. 'Your mother-in-law and my wife are exchanging anecdotes about family illnesses. Did you know Jimmy bit the surgeon who was taking his tonsils out?' The plate was thrust gently but firmly into her hand. 'Cold turkey and salad. I thought you might want something to eat.'

Any host would have performed a similar courtesy, Angela told herself. There was no need for her heart to race so foolishly. Marcos was married to Gladys now. She took the glass of wine he handed her. Another social gesture. The place where their fingers had touched tingled. Angela barely managed a sip of wine without spilling any.

'The children are growing so fast,' she said in a chatty, social voice. 'Miguel's almost as tall as you are. He's going to be a very handsome young man.'

'Right now he's a very tired young man,' chuckled Marcos. 'Carlos put him to work on Los Toros when he was down

164

there, and I've put him to work on La Catalina. He's not very happy about it, but he has to learn.' He settled himself comfortably against the railing. 'What's the matter?'

'Nothing's the matter.'

He let that pass. A woman's voice drifted through the open windows – Teresa's this time, detailing the latest society scandal.

'Hugo's living with an absolute tart! A bleached blonde – years younger than he is and with two children of her own. Imagine! Now that Perón apparently plans to legalize divorce . . .'

'Disgraceful!' chimed in Mercedes. 'The Church has a moral obligation to stop him!'

'The Church,' rumbled Pedro's priestly bass, 'is trying its best to block the law.'

Teresa carried on. 'My brother saw Hugo at the Jockey Club the other day and Hugo told him he was going to ask Silvia for a divorce as soon as the law is passed.'

They continued to dissect divorce.

'Silvia won't give in,' remarked Marcos.

'If divorce becomes legalized in Argentina, why not?' asked Angela.

'The Church will never allow divorce even if it is law, and Silvia is a very devout Catholic. Besides, think of the scandal.' He cocked a quizzical eyebrow at her over the rim of his glass. 'A divorced woman is an embarrassment to most people.'

'Suppose she fell in love with a man who wanted to marry her?'

'Why are you so interested?'

'I just don't see the point of staying together if a couple no longer has anything in common,' said Angela shortly. 'Why shouldn't they be free to live their own lives the way they want to?'

Marcos laughed. 'People manage to "live their own lives" very well in spite of marriage.'

'That's not right either!'

'I've shocked your English conscience again, eh?'

Angela picked at the food on her plate. The night was too warm to argue – especially in Spanish and even more

165

especially on the subtle shadings of infidelity. She changed the subject.

'Did you enjoy Río?'

'No.'

The turkey stuck in her throat. 'I thought you would have loved it. It's supposed to be a beautiful city. Ideal for a honeymoon.'

'You know why I didn't enjoy it!' he said savagely. 'Stop baiting me.'

Angela couldn't stop. She was hot and miserable and the baby wouldn't keep still. Her insides hurt, and her heart was killing her. She wanted Marcos to hold her and love away the pain, but all she could do was bait him.

'Gladys seemed to enjoy it. She looks well.'

'She should,' he said. 'It's costing me a fortune to make her presentable.'

For some reason the dryness in his voice annoyed her. 'How can you say that!'

'I'm a realist. Gladys married me for social position and money, and I make sure she has everything she wants. It's my responsibility as her husband.'

'Especially since you married her for your own protection!'

'For the protection of my land, my family and my heritage.' Marcos's voice softened and he reached for Angela's hand. 'Those are three very strong reasons, *gringuita* – even in your England. They have nothing to do with love.'

'Marcos?' Gladys appeared in the doorway and peered inquisitively at the darkened veranda. 'What are you doing out there?'

He pressed Angela's hand before releasing it; his eyes did not leave her face. 'I brought Angela something to eat. She wasn't feeling well.'

Gladys's heels clicked importantly along the tiled floor. She saw no reason why Marcos should pay so much attention to the *gringa*; if the woman didn't feel well, why had she bothered to come? She patted her curls and sketched a polite, unenthusiastic smile.

'Do you want some aspirin?'

'No, thank you,' returned Angela with equal lack of enthusiasm and returned to the living-room, carrying eight and a half months' pregnancy with as much dignity as she could muster.

166

V

Nineteen hundred and fifty-two exploded high above the trees in shimmering starbursts of gold and blue and green and red against a dark velvet sky. Dogs barked hysterically, the dinner bell clanged, the children shouted 'Happy New Year!' until they were hoarse. The two boys Gastón and Miguel chased the girls across the lawn with lighted squibs. Isabel hugged Marcos; her eyes sparkled.

'Happy New Year, Papa!' She made a grab for his glass. 'Let me have some champagne! Cristina's tipsy.'

Cristina and Yvonne had collapsed in a giggling heap under a eucalyptus tree. Claudia hovered uncertainly nearby and chewed on her nails. No one had offered her any champagne.

The ranch-hands and their families trooped up from the Bajo to receive the traditional end-of-year bonus sealed in bright blue envelopes. Rosario, dressed in her Sunday best, appeared with a towering sweet bread bursting with raisins, nuts and glacéd fruit.

'Happy New Year!' she cried and everyone cheered as though her appearance with the *pan dulce* were the most important event of the evening.

Old Venancio Paredes, the eldest of the ranch-hands, began to recite a rambling toast in verse to La Catalina and the *patrón*. Lucas, who was at the ranch this New Year's Eve because he couldn't afford to go anywhere else, wandered along the veranda to where Miguel was lounging against the railing.

'How's the crown prince tonight?' he murmured.

Miguel hiccoughed. He had drunk more than his share of champagne. 'Wh-what do you mean?'

Lucas waved his glass at Marcos. 'There's the king,' he sneered. 'You're his son. Crown prince. Heir to the cattleman's kingdom.'

'I'm OK,' said Miguel uneasily. He wasn't too sure about Uncle Lucas. Great fun – but not the sort of fun that kept you out of trouble.

'Sweating like a pig with the *peones*, eh?' Lucas pulled out a gold cigarette case and flicked it open. 'Your old man's really got it in for you, hasn't he? Have a fag,' as Miguel eyed the cigarettes wistfully.

'I'd better not, thanks.'

Lucas lit one and blew the smoke lazily through his nostrils. 'How old are you now, Mickey?'

'Fourteen.'

'You look older. Been around?'

Miguel flushed. 'Sure.'

'I mean really been around,' chuckled Lucas. He studied his nephew thoughtfully. 'How about us going out for a few laughs one night when you get back to town?'

'I-I don't know . . .'

'Scared of your old man?'

'No!' said Miguel sharply and walked off.

Ten to one if he went out for a few laughs with Uncle Lucas he'd get caught. Papa was keeping a close eye on him these days. He wasn't sure he wanted to go out for a few laughs anyway. He knew what that meant. Women. He'd been around – a bit. A few experimental clutchings with Rosita the maid in the cellar at Barranco Rosales. A few kisses at parties. Not the big stuff . . . Miguel hiccoughed again. He'd like to try the big stuff, but he wasn't sure. He wondered if Gastón had. His glance wandered over to where his lanky dark-haired cousin sat listening to the grown-ups talking. Gastón was proud of being a cattleman's son. He should have been Papa's crown prince. Miguel sighed and joined his cousin. It was boring – but safer than talking to Uncle Lucas.

'I wonder what sort of rot ol' Lucas was whispering to Miguel,' Jimmy remarked to Angela. 'Mind you, Marcos won't stand for any nonsense. He reins that boy in tight – too tight, if you ask me. Have to give young colts room to kick up their heels every now and then.' He filled his glass to the brim with champagne and took an appreciative sip. 'You might not think it, but Marcos was quite a heel-kicker in his time. Him and me – we used to cut all hell loose in the good old days. Ah, bless m'whiskers – we're the soul of respectability now.'

Angela laughed because Jimmy was laughing, but her heart wasn't in it. He bent his head to kiss her.

'Mmm, that's nice, angel. Know what I want to do?' He whispered in her ear, then protested thickly as she shrugged him off. 'Oi – what's the matter? Come on, angel.'

168

'No.'

'Just a little cuddle. I'm going to have one hell of a dry spell in a couple of weeks, won't I? Come on, let's go have our own New Year's party.' He began to stroke her swollen belly. 'I'm feeling amorous, gorgeous. Don't say no.'

Out of the corner of her eye Angela saw Marcos watching them. 'Please, Jimmy,' she whispered, 'I'm not feeling well and you've had enough to drink.'

His face changed so suddenly she was startled. 'What the hell's the matter with you? So I've had a bit to drink — so what? It's New Year's Eve. Let's celebrate!' His voice rose, slurring the words. 'I want to make love to my wife. Why the hell shouldn't I? Won't hurt the baby — scout's honour, angel. Won't hurt the baby.'

'Jimmy, stop it!'

'What the hell you 'spect me to do? Go find a widow? There's plenty o' widows around. Maybe I'll find me one . . . Look, angel!' He gripped her arm, his eyes bloodshot and pleading. 'Don't say no! Please don't say no!'

She gave in. It was easier than avoiding Marcos's eyes.

VI

New Year's Day was overcast and humid. The trees in the Bajo drooped listlessly in the heat, no breeze cleared the smoke from the *asado* fires. A cloud of bluebottles droned dismally over the tables. Thunder rumbled in the east and Pablo Losa cast an appraising glance at the sky.

'Too bad it's moving north. We could use some rain.'

Julia Ortíz brought over a plate of sizzling sweetbreads and sat down beside Angela. 'What do you think of the newlyweds?'

Angela shrugged. 'I suppose they're happy.'

'Happy?' Julia snorted. 'She is, at any rate. Preening as though she's won the Christmas draw ten times over. Stupid woman.' She bit into a sweetbread. 'What's the matter?'

'I'm tired.'

'Why doesn't Jimmy drive you home? It's too hot to be out today, especially in your condition.'

And suddenly home was the one thing Angela wanted most in the world.

Their departure caused a minor upheaval because Cora insisted on coming as well. She briskly overrode Jimmy's objections and installed herself in the back of the car, from where she proceeded to organize their lives with devastating precision. Angela must return to Buenos Aires at once and see a reputable gynaecologist. They would book a room for her at the British Hospital; after the baby was born she would stay with the Morgans for as long as necessary.

'You must buy a house in BA, James! You simply cannot bring up a child properly out here – it's quite ridiculous to even think of it!'

'There's nothing wrong with Los Alamos,' growled Jimmy through clenched teeth.

'I daresay you may not think so, but Angela agrees with me – don't you, dear?'

'Please,' said Angela wearily, 'Let's not argue about it any more.'

Cora Morgan rattled on. 'I know you've done your best, but quite frankly the house isn't suitable. What you need is a nice little place in the suburbs where you'll feel at home . . .'

She was still rattling on when the car turned into Los Alamos.

VII

Angela left Jimmy to deal with his mother and went out to the orchard at the back of the house. She wanted to be alone; she didn't even want to think about Marcos. The new fruit trees needed to be sprayed. She would do that after she had inspected the large new well being opened behind the shed. She stepped on a plank running along one side of the well and peered down the shaft. Nearly ten feet had been dug through sandy soil – the diggers predicted at least thirty more feet before they found water . . . Angela started as thunder rumbled beyond the horizon. A new storm was building up. Maybe they would have rain tonight after all.

Jimmy strode into the orchard, drink in hand and murder in his eyes.

'Goddamn mother's hide!' he muttered as soon as he came within earshot. 'For tuppence I'd send the old bag packing this minute if it weren't for my old man.'

'Your mother means well,' said Angela.

'Means well, shit! She means to drive me into the ground the way she drove him. Nag, nag, nag – old bitch!'

He drained half the drink in a single gulp. Angela watched uneasily. He had been drinking since before lunch. It seemed a very long time ago. Thunder growled again; the sky darkened. Jimmy stepped on to the plank.

'She's got a bee in her bonnet about that bloody house in BA,' he said. 'Why the hell didn't you tell her you don't want to live in the suburbs? You have to spell it out to my mother – otherwise she doesn't understand. She thinks you don't like it out here.'

'I do like it out here!'

'Then tell her so, for God's sake!' He thrust his face at Angela; his breath smelled of gin. 'Do you know what she's been nagging me about in there? Says you're not happy because we live out here instead of in a nice little house with a nice little garden. Fake England!' He drained his glass. 'It's my fault you're not happy, she says.'

'That's not true . . .'

'Then go and tell her it's not true!' rasped Jimmy, grabbing Angela's arm and shaking her. 'Stand up for me, for Christ's sake! I'm your husband!' He gave her another, harder shake. 'Why don't you go and say something?'

'I'll speak to Cora later . . .'

'I want you to speak to her now!'

'Jimmy, calm down! You've been drinking too much.'

'Shut up!' he shouted. 'Goddamn it – just *shut up*!'

He didn't mean to shove Angela so hard. He wouldn't have shoved her at all if she hadn't said that about his drinking. Her words sparked a surge of blind, unreasoning fury and he shoved. Angela screamed. She lost her balance, beat frantically at the air, and plunged into the well.

'Oh, Jesus!' whispered Jimmy. The glass slipped from his hand and broke. 'Angela? *Angela*!'

There was no reply. He found a ladder and lowered it into the open shaft, then climbed down. Angela lay on the sandy bottom, her right arm bent beneath her. The swollen shape of her belly traced a grotesque hump in the growing darkness. Jimmy scurried up the ladder and raced towards the house.

'Saúl!' he yelled. 'Give me a hand! The señora's fallen into the well! Hurry!'

Cora Morgan bustled out. 'What is going on, James?'

'Angela!' he panted. 'She's fallen into the well. Ring Feldman. Tell him to hurry!'

'Ring who?'

'Feldman! Feldman!' yelled Jimmy and rushed out again.

Cora Morgan rang La Catalina and told her husband that Angela had had a slight accident. She suggested he ask someone there for the name of the local doctor.

VIII

Saúl and three of the ranch hands placed Angela on a makeshift litter and began to haul her out of the well, but it was slow work. Jimmy paced up and down, shouting instructions; his mother contradicted him with sensible advice. Marcos and John Morgan arrived. Jimmy tried to explain what had happened. Marcos pushed him aside and began to haul on a rope; Jimmy's father gave a hand. By the time Jacobo Feldman arrived a good hour later they had managed to get Angela out and carry her to bed. The doctor made a quick examination and shook his head.

'I can't risk moving her,' he said. 'Labour's started and I don't like the way it's going. She has a broken arm and bad concussion as well. How did it happen?'

Jimmy licked his lips. 'She s-slipped.' His hands caught at the air awkwardly. 'Tried to-to catch her. T-too late.'

'She's lucky not to have broken her back,' remarked Feldman shortly and turned to Marcos. 'I want you to drive into Laguna and fetch Sister Ana from the convent. My nurse is on holiday again. Pick up the midwife on your way back. Sister Ana knows where she lives. I'll ring the convent to let them know you're coming. Hurry!'

Marcos had never driven so fast in his life. The storm broke halfway into Laguna; he barely noticed it. Every nerve strained towards Angela. Ten feet was a bad fall at any time, but in her condition . . . What the hell had she been doing on that plank anyway? Jimmy should have known better than to let her go near the well. She was his wife. He should take care of her. Marcos's hands tightened around the steering wheel. If anything happened to Angela . . . He began to pray, repeating the same desperate words over and over. 'God don't let her die, oh God, don't let her die!' The same desperate words he had prayed when he learned of Magdalena's accident. Magdalena was dead. What if Angela died?

'God, don't let her die!'

He didn't know he was sobbing the words at the top of his voice above the crashing of the storm.

IX

The baby lay positioned across the womb. There was not enough dilation. Angela regained consciousness, but she was too shocked and frightened to be of much help. She struggled against the contractions and groaned. Her groans echoed through the living-room with a helpless, inhuman sound. Jimmy buried his head in his hands.

'If we were at the British Hospital, this wouldn't be happening,' pronounced Cora Morgan. 'Angela would have expert care.'

'Jacobo Feldman's one of the best doctors I know of,' said Marcos from his place by the window. 'I'd trust him with my children's lives any day.'

'I'm sure he is a competent doctor,' she retorted. 'But the conditions out here — really, James!' turning to Jimmy. 'I hope you will now realize your father and I are right about your moving.'

'Mother,' sobbed Jimmy, 'shut up!'

For the first and only time in his life John Morgan stood up for his son.

'Leave the boy alone, Cora. He's upset.'

The clock ticked minutes off hours. Tadeo and Julia Ortíz stopped by to ask after Angela; Mercedes came with them. The living-room seemed suddenly overcrowded. Jimmy walked up and down. He drank. He cracked his knuckles. He drank some more. No one could think of much to say. At eight o'clock Jacobo Feldman came out of the bedroom. His sleeves were rolled up and he was spattered with blood.

'We can't turn the child around,' he said. 'It's wrapped in the cord and probably badly damaged by the fall. Your wife's too exhausted to push any more.'

Jimmy made a sick noise. 'Is — is she . . .'

'She's exhausted,' repeated Feldman irritably. 'I want the kitchen table scrubbed with disinfectant and brought into the bedroom. I'll need boiling water, sheets, towels — something to cover the floor as well.' He pushed his glasses up on his head with a weary, discouraged gesture. 'I'm going to do a caesarian, Morgan, but I doubt we can save the child.'

X

Angela and Jimmy's child was born on 1 January 1952. Its brain had been badly damaged; it only survived a few hours. Angela never saw her son. She started haemorrhaging after the operation and was rushed to hospital in Buenos Aires. Complications developed. There was a danger of septicaemia. An antiseptic surgeon performed an emergency hysterectomy. There was nothing else that could be done.

XI

Isabel was puzzled. She hunted out her father and found him down in the Bajo about to mount the tall, ugly bay he always rode.

'Where are you going?'

'Out to Chañarcito, ñatita. Want to come?'

They started off at a brisk canter towards Chañarcito, a tangled expanse of carob and chañar trees straggling along the river that cut through La Catalina's western fields. It was one of those extraordinary days that often occur on the pampa, when the clear summer light shimmers a pale, diaphanous blue and the horizon seems so near that you have only to stretch forth your hand to touch it. *Carancho* hawks swooped overhead, a long-legged hare sprinted through yellow grass. Isabel sighed.

'Papa, why doesn't God want Angela to have any more babies?'

'God doesn't have anything to do with it, *ñatita*,' replied Marcos carefully. 'Angela was badly hurt when she fell and – and she just can't have any more.'

'Oh.' Isabel wrinkled her nose at the sun. 'I wish she hadn't fallen. Then she could have had lots of babies and I could help her take care of them.' She darted a quick glance at her father. 'You won't be angry if I say something, will you?'

He grinned. 'What are you going to ask me for?'

'I wish you could have married Angela.'

There was a long silence.

'Angela's married to Jimmy and they're very happy together,' said Marcos finally. 'Marriage is a very special thing, *ñatita*. It means sharing your life with the person you love. Raising a family. Going through the good times and the not-so-good times together. Remember that. Once you make the commitment, you can't change your mind.'

Isabel sighed again. 'It must be awful to marry someone you don't love, mustn't it, Papa? I'm going to marry and be happy for ever and ever. Like Jimmy and Angela – or you and Mama.'

He noticed with somewhat grim amusement that neither of them had mentioned Gladys. Perhaps it was just as well. He could not bring himself to pretend that he loved her – not even for the sake of maintaining his image before Isabel.

CHAPTER FIFTEEN

I

Summer dragged on – hot, thundery and humming with rumour.

Evita was said to be seriously ill – some predicted death in a matter of weeks. A specialist had flown in from Europe. Perón was preparing for a political shake-up once she died. The rumour mills creaked and clattered, despite official disclaimers.

Gladys did not know what to believe.

Argentina without Evita seemed impossible, yet Marcos discussed it as a distinct possibility. On the other hand Juan assured her that Evita was merely overworked and had been ordered to rest by her doctor. Gladys would have liked to talk over the matter with Norma Mendes, but the one time they had met on the street in Laguna Grande Norma had cut her dead. Hurt and bewildered, she wrote to Juanita in Quilmes inquiring about Evita's illness; after several weeks Juanita replied with a stirring account of the most recent strike at a nearby textile mill.

Summer dragged on.

Gladys missed her period and Jacobo Feldman confirmed she was pregnant. Marcos received the news with ill-disguised indifference; his heart had not gone into the making of this child and he felt little except irritation at the additional burden.

In his overstuffed sitting-room behind the Party headquarters, Artemio Mendes savoured the bitter dregs of humiliation and defeat. It was all a conspiracy, he muttered savagely. The governor was in the landowners' pockets. They had banded together to buy the votes that kept him in power, they were corrupting the Party. The veins in Mendes's neck bulged. Juan Gaspari was a blatant example of that corruption.

'Brother-in-law to the worst bloodsucker of them all!' exploded Mendes.

Norma poured a stream of boiling water into the *maté* gourd, gave a few experimental sucks at the metal straw, and handed the gourd to her husband.

'I always said that Gladys Gómez was a sly one,' she remarked sourly. 'Giving me all that talk about how devoted she is to Evita and the Party – ha!' Her full bosom heaved with indignation. 'She even had the crust to stop me in the street the other day. Me! As if I'd betray my principles by talking to her!'

The gourd passed back and forth in disgruntled silence.

'Gaspari!' growled Mendes, reaching for the kettle. 'I tell you, *compañera* – I don't know what this country's coming to!'

II

Jimmy and Angela did not come to La Catalina for Easter.

'My parents invited us to La Cumbre,' he explained to Marcos. 'There's a golf tournament on. The old man wants me to play in it with him.'

Marcos tried not to look disappointed. 'I thought you didn't like going up there.'

'I don't, but he practically begged me to come. Mother and I had one hell of a row after the baby died and she's been nagging him stupid ever since.' Jimmy chewed glumly on his cigarette. 'Angela's not too keen on going, but it'll do her good to get away. She's been a bit down since the op. Feldman says there's nothing physically wrong – just nerves. That kind of op makes women weepy and all that. He thinks a change of air will do her good.'

'Feldman's probably right,' said Marcos flatly and changed the subject.

The only remarkable incident in an otherwise dispirited Easter was Lucas's astonishing announcement that he had decided to go into business.

'Iván Torres wants me to manage a new art gallery he's just bought. A very exclusive little place downtown. The opening night is a Fabio Grandi one-man show.'

The family, dutifully eating its way through the inevitable Good Friday cod, did not appear to be impressed.

'We're promoting progressive art by contemporary Argentine artists,' continued Lucas loudly. 'Grandi says there's a big future in it.'

Teresa arched a sarcastic eyebrow. 'Judging by his own work?'

'Never seen such rubbish in my life,' remarked Carlos. 'That man ought to be jailed for trying to pass off pornography as art. They're not even good paintings.'

He spoke with a clipped, pedantic manner that made Lucas bristle. 'That's just your opinion! Fabio Grandi's the best painter in the country. All the experts say he's bold, inventive, original . . .' He stabbed his fork into a piece of fish. 'Grandi's damned keen on the gallery!'

'If you expect me to put up money for this gallery of yours,' said Marcos irritably, 'the answer is no.'

'Why not?'

'You know nothing about art and even less about business. Iván Torres is a crook. If I were you I wouldn't have anything to do with him, but I suppose that's asking too much.'

Lucas flushed angrily. 'You don't give me much credit, do you?'

'None at all. Pass the bread please, *ñatita*.'

Lucas's involvement with Iván Torres had been a spur-of-the-moment decision prompted by boredom and too much whisky. Fabio Grandi suggested it to him. Torres, he said, was looking for a partner in a small, very exclusive art gallery. Nothing but the best. The Luciani name was well known in cultural circles; if Lucas chipped in with a small share he would reap a windfall in no time at all.

'Your stiff-necked brother can stuff the pittance he doles out to you,' added Fabio inelegantly. 'Just think, old boy. All you have to do is smile at the rich bitches who come to ogle the paintings and persuade them to buy one.' He winked a languid, malicious eye. 'Maybe even get yourself invited to tea, who knows?'

The urge to make a fortune began to obsess Lucas. He dreamt continuously of the magnificent mansions he would buy, the women he would have, the men he would crush under his heel. One of those men was his brother. In his favourite fantasy Lucas kept Marcos begging in rags at the back door of a palatial villa while he himself lay among satin pillows and caressed beautiful, naked Magdalena to his heart's content.

On his return to Buenos Aires he went to a certain address in the moneylenders' district and pledged his mother's diamond cross as surety for the loan which would open the door to fame and fortune.

178

III

In June, Gladys gathered up enough courage to visit her parents.

She had written several times since her marriage, without receiving any reply; when she asked Juan how they were he dismissed the question with a vague 'just the same' that did little to appease her pangs of conscience. Eight months had passed since she left behind Verdulería Nápoli's potato sacks and mouldy cabbages, but in the fragrant luxury of Barranco Rosales eight months seemed more like eight hundred years. Even her political activities belonged to another life. The Gladys Gómez who cheered and sang Party songs on the back of a truck crammed with loyal Peronists bore little resemblance to the perfumed, jewelled Señora Luciani who struggled to master the mysteries of a very different social game.

Juanita was the only friend she kept in touch with and even that friendship had its limits. She invited her to tea only to discover with some dismay that Juanita, crooking her little finger and sipping tea through pursed lips, was a shrill, exotic creature with whom she now had little in common. Better to meet at an impersonal tea room downtown. The shrill voice and mincing manners did not matter so much then; they could laugh at Party gossip and eat their fill of cream puffs as though the fairytale which lay between them had never happened.

Her parents were quite another matter.

They received her stiffly and asked about Claudia, complaining because she had not come along.

'Claudia had a piano lesson this afternoon,' hedged Gladys, to whom her daughter's pining for Quilmes was a constant source of irritation. 'She has homework to do as well.'

Celestina indicated a plate of thick round biscuits sandwiched with layers of *dulce de leche*. 'I baked them especially for her. *Alfajores*. They're her favourites.'

Gladys sat down, taking care not to crush her fur coat, and placed a package wrapped in brightly coloured tissue paper on the kitchen table.

'I've brought you a present. It's a clock for the kitchen.'

179

Her father sucked dismally on his *maté*. 'Why waste good money? We've already got a clock.'

Inside the wrapping was a blue leather box containing a miniature pink porcelain temple covered with roses. A round gilt-edged clock with a luminous dial glowed faintly between the temple columns. The Gasparis stared at it blankly.

'That's expensive,' said Celestina after a moment. 'It'll get broken in no time.'

'Shouldn't have bothered,' added Gaspari senior. 'We've got a good one.' He pointed to a large blue clock ticking away sturdily on the dresser. 'Hasn't lost a minute in twelve years.'

Gladys's lower lip trembled. 'I want you to have a nice clock! I want you to have something expensive!'

Her mother placed the porcelain temple carefully back in its box and went over to the sink. There was a wheezing gurgle and a rattle of pipes; after several seconds a stream of rusty water gushed from the taps. A bell tinkled faintly inside the shop and Gaspari senior shuffled off to his customers. Gladys wrinkled her nose against the familiar smell of soup stock and vegetables.

'Papa's rheumatism is worse, isn't it?'

'Just the same as always.' The pipes rattled again. 'How's your husband?'

'Busy. Shall I get out the cups?'

'Stay where you are. You'll mess those fancy clothes of yours.' Celestina bustled around with the crockery, sliced a loaf of bread, plunked down jam and butter. Her sharp eyes took in Gladys's carefully waved hair, the gold and amethyst earrings, the diamonds on her manicured fingers. 'What do you do with yourself all day?'

'Oh, take care of the house and things like that.' Gladys watched her mother splash water from the kettle into the teapot. 'You know. Take care of the house.'

'Doesn't Luciani have servants?'

'Of course he does!'

'Then why're you taking care of the house? I thought you'd be living like a rich lady. Doesn't seem right for you to be doing the same work you did here – not if Luciani has servants.'

Gladys kept her temper, but only barely. 'It's not the same thing, mother! You have to tell the servants what to do and you plan the meals and see that the maids keep the place clean.'

'You do all that?'

Not if Mercedes could help it, but Gladys was not about to confide in her mother. She mumbled something inconsequential and bit hungrily into an *alfajor*. Rich was rich and poor was poor. The more distance she put between herself and Verdulería Nápoli the better.

IV

Mercedes had delayed public recognition of her sister-in-law for as long as possible, but in the end her sense of social duty got the better of her. At the end of July she gave a tea party for Gladys.

In Magdalena's time, teas at Barranco Rosales had been celebrated highlights of the winter social season. This time the same fragrant, elegant crowd of women filled the drawing-room with well-bred voices and cultured chatter, but most came more out of curiosity to see Marcos Luciani's new wife than any real fear of missing out on the latest gossip.

Mercedes was grimly determined to do her duty; her guests took their cue and performed their part in the social ritual with flawless skill. A brief touch of cheek against cheek, a featherlight laugh, a hastily murmured greeting brimming with insincere charm. Gladys ran the gauntlet with a stiffly formal smile, both offended by and envious of their performance.

The last couple of weeks had been difficult. Evita's illness was no longer rumour, but shocking fact. She was in hospital. Gladys could not bring herself to believe it, but even Juan looked worried these days.

'Juanita and six *compañeras* from the Quilmes branch are going to visit the hospital,' he told her. 'They want you as well, seeing how Evita gave you a personal commendation. There'll be a reporter from the local press, pictures, a short speech – you know the sort of thing.'

Gladys looked uncomfortable. 'That's the day Marcos arrives from La Catalina and Claudia has an appointment with the dentist.'

New loyalties were vying with old. Gaspari settled himself into his armchair and thoughtfully sipped his whisky and soda. Maybe it was just as well. It was not too healthy to be known as one of Evita's 'men' these days; he didn't relish the thought of being connected with Gladys's devotion to a sinking ship.

'Your family comes first,' he said through sips. 'When's the baby due?'

'September.'

'I'll tell Juanita you can't go in your condition. She'll understand.'

But neither Juanita nor the Quilmes branch understood why *Compañera* Gómez (they refused to call her by any other name) would not drop everything and fly at once to Evita's sickbed. Minutes after Gaspari finished his elaborate explanations Juanita called Gladys and demanded to know how she could be so callous.

'Think of all Evita's done for you!' Her voice crackled angrily over the telephone. 'She needs our support, our strength – our courage, *compañera*!'

It was an emotional appeal that stirred twinges of guilt, but little else. Gladys still did not believe Evita was as ill as everyone claimed and Quilmes seemed very far away. More important, she doubted Marcos would approve of the hospital visit, and his approval came before everything else. He was a difficult husband who took careful handling; all her energies must be channelled into that one effort until she had mastered the art.

There were fleeting moments of weakness when Gladys Luciani was tempted to wonder whether the art was worth the effort. Marcos was not an affectionate man; on the other hand he wouldn't have married her if he hadn't felt an attraction. She was sure of that. Even her brother had said so. 'The man can hardly wait,' were Juan's exact words. Marcos's roughness was part of his nature; she would just have to be patient. After all, money and social position were far more practical than affection, and marriage was a practical matter. That was why she had married Marcos Luciani in the first place; there was no room in her warm, luxurious world for fleeting moments of weakness . . .

Light flooded the drawing-room at Barranco Rosales. The deep blue velvet curtains formed a sumptuous barrier against the gloomy winter evening outside, enclosing Angela in a fragrant, elegant universe of furs, silks and sparkling jewels. The main doors of the formal drawing-room were open, beyond them she could see the dining-room with its massive crystal chandelier and the great rosewood table draped with a lace tablecloth which had belonged to Magdalena's great-great-grandmother. The cups and saucers were so delicate they seemed translucent — pale primrose yellow with a delicate gold border and tiny golden roses hand-painted on the centre of each one. Angela recalled Mercedes telling her that Bruno Luciani had ordered them especially for his daughter-in-law as an anniversary present.

'Magdalena always said this was her favourite set,' she sighed, stroking a cup reverently. 'They will be for Miguel's wife when he marries.'

Gladys sat behind an imposing silver tea service and warily picked her way through the intricacies of an unfamiliar ritual. There were so many details to remember. The butler handed her a cup and murmured '*a la inglesa, señora,*' which meant a drop of milk must be poured into the cup before the tea. A paper-thin slice of lemon with the next one, a single lump of sugar in the one after that, '*a la inglesa*' again . . . She knitted her brows in an effort to juggle hot water, tea pot, milk pitcher and sugar tongs under the butler's basilisk eye.

'It makes me sick to see that woman!' Aurora Grandi sat down beside Angela and glared into the dining-room. 'The way she tricked Marcos into marrying her — it's degrading!'

'What is?'

'Everyone knows she was after him. Teasing and teasing, then holding back and saying the only way he could have her was with a wedding ring. My brother Fabio saw them one night. The things he told me about it!' Aurora's voice shook. 'Marcos and I were engaged, you know.'

'No,' replied Angela tartly, 'I didn't.'

Something in her voice led Aurora to add hastily, 'Not officially, of course.' The fantasy of her engagement to Marcos began as a bitter little piece of make-believe on the night of Teresa's dinner party last October; by now it had reached the stage where fact and fiction were so hopelessly entwined that any attempt to unravel them was more damaging than the deception itself. No one believed her and she knew it, but in the eyes of Aurora's own particular world it was far more respectable to be jilted within a hair's-breadth of the altar than never to have been in the running at all.

'Teresa tells me you and Julia Ortíz have started some sort of child-care centre in Laguna Grande,' she said to change the subject. 'A place for stray children, is that it?'

Angela smiled politely, wishing she could like this tall, intense woman whose frustrated passions were so cruelly etched on her face. 'Something like that,' she admitted vaguely.

Aurora gave one of her high, witty laughs. 'Trust Julia! She's always been one for that sort of thing.'

'Do you know her well?'

'We went to school together. I saw quite a bit of her afterwards until she married Tadeo Ortíz and buried herself in the *campo*. Whatever Julia sees in that man is beyond me. He's so unbearably provincial.'

'I like Tadeo,' countered Angela shortly. 'He's a gentleman.' Then, regretting her abruptness, she asked, 'How is your brother – the one who plays the piano?'

'Lorenzo? He gave a recital last Monday at an appalling little theatre in the suburbs. Only a handful of people came. He can't get better bookings because he's unknown – or so they keep telling him. What rubbish!' Aurora puffed indignantly on her cigarette. 'Lorenzo went to Paris on a scholarship and played for Rubenstein.'

She rambled on, passionately defending her brother's career while Angela listened politely. Far better to keep one's mind on the musical misfortunes of young Lorenzo than think about Marcos or talk about Laguna Grande's stray children.

The children were Julia's idea.

A week-old baby, abandoned on the outskirts of Laguna Grande, had died of starvation. Its death might have gone unnoticed if a pack of dogs fighting over the remains had not disturbed people living nearby. Someone complained to Norma Mendes, who promptly announced that the Party, with Evita's blessing, would open its doors to strays, unwed mothers, fallen women and other social outcasts.

'All that woman cares about is being hailed as another Evita!' protested Julia. 'One Eva Perón is one too many and I'm not going to let her get away with it!'

'How can you stop her?' Angela had asked curiously.

'We'll set up a shelter for children at the convent. I've already discussed it with the nuns. They'll let us use one of the rooms and give us whatever we need. The girls are eager to help as well . . .' The dark eyes held Angela's without wavering. 'Someone has to show them what to do and Sister Ana doesn't have that much time. Will you give me a hand?'

She said 'yes' quickly before the memory of her dead child could say 'no'. It was no good brooding over what might have been. One got on with life and left death behind.

Jimmy apparently found it very easy to do so. He had been upset over the child's death, but there were other matters to claim his attention. He did not spend his days staring at an empty cradle; he did not wander aimlessly about the room opening and shutting drawers. He had not carried life inside him for nearly nine months, had not felt it stir and grow as part of himself, had not nourished it with his own body. Her body would never carry another child. He could not understand her feeling of non-fulfilment or her tears.

'Buck up, old girl. I know it's been tough – but it's not the end of the world. Come on,' with a pat on the back. 'Cheer up. We've still got each other.'

Bracing, practical advice delivered with ill-disguised impatience. Angela sighed. Impatience, irritability, arguments – they were more the rule than the exception in their relationship these days. The proverbial teething pains of marriage, compounded by her own frustration.

Perhaps.

V

Gladys circulated among the guests, still smiling her stiff, formal smile. Her back hurt. She wished she could take her shoes off. She wished everyone would go home. By now a number of husbands had arrived and tea gave way to cocktails. She wished Marcos would come. Conversation was difficult because she didn't know what to say once ritual amenities were over – yet everyone else seemed to have so much to say to each other. A tall, auburn-haired woman whose name escaped her sneered as she went by. The gesture was half hidden by a cocktail glass, but Gladys noticed it just the same. A half curling turn of the upper lip, a drawing down of the corners of the mouth, a hardening of the eyes. Contempt, hatred – quite possibly envy. Gladys turned away quickly and saw Marcos walk into the drawing-room.

She rushed over to him, relieved and eager to show off her possession. Barranco Rosales suddenly swung into perspective

185

with Marcos's appearance; he was the centre of its brilliant, fragrant world and she was his wife. Nothing else mattered — not even a woman's contempt.

'*Querido*!' Darling.

He flinched as she clutched his arm and returned her greeting stiffly. Mercedes hurried over, her thin face flushed with pleasure.

'We thought you were never coming . . .' she began, then broke off at the sight of his expression. 'Marcos, what's wrong?'

Impossible not to hear the high, spinsterish voice or ignore its note of alarm. *What's wrong?* sparked a sudden, electrically charged silence; someone laughed in the library and then voices faded there as well. Marcos looked around at the questioning faces. His eyes found Angela, held her glance for a second, then moved back reluctantly to the two women hovering at his side.

'I've just been with your brother,' he told Gladys. 'Evita's dead.'

A voice exclaimed, 'Thank God!' fiercely and fervently. Gladys shook her head.

'You can't mean it!' she stammered. 'There must be a mistake. Evita . . . No, no! There must be a mistake!'

'There's no mistake,' replied Marcos impatiently. 'She died earlier today. There's to be a public announcement in an hour.'

Gladys's mouth trembled. 'It's not true! *Dios mio*, it can't be true!' She began to cry, twisting her fingers in the voluminous folds of her dress. 'Evita . . . it can't be true . . .'

No one spoke. Marcos took Gladys by the arm, and propelled her roughly towards the door. 'For God's sake control yourself!' he hissed. 'You're my wife. I won't have you making scenes in public!'

Tears were forbidden in the gold-and-white drawing-room at Barranco Rosales. Tears belonged to Quilmes, to Gladys Gómez who sang and waved banners for Evita the fairy princess. There must be no mourning for what had been; there must be no scenes in the gold-and-white drawing-room where men thanked God fiercely and fervently for the end of other men's dreams. Gladys swallowed and met her husband's outrage with a shaky smile.

'I'm sorry. It's just that . . . Let me go, please.'

He moved aside, still glowering. Gladys climbed the stairs with slow, dragging steps; in the drawing-room someone laughed and she heard Marcos's voice in reply.

Evita is dead.
She tried to weep, but the few tears that came were sour and tasted of self-pity.

VI

María Eva Duarte de Perón died of leukemia on 26 July 1952.

While moderate Peronists wondered uneasily whether Perón could keep the country together after her death, Evita's faithful followers indulged in a hysterical flood of grief.

The queues to view her body as it lay in state stretched for miles through Buenos Aires's bleak and windy streets. Gladys, returning from downtown with the girls one evening, found the way blocked by a large group of grim-faced mourners. They flocked round the car and shook their fists, hissing threats and jeering at the 'oligarchs' inside. Claudia began to cry, but Isabel and Cristina sat stiffly upright on the edge of the seat and stared ahead with proud, determined little faces as the car inched through the chanting crowd. It occurred to Gladys with somewhat of a shock that but for Marcos's chance visit to Verdulería Nápoli she would have been one of them.

The wreaths for Evita's funeral lined the city pavements and stood in great floral banks from floor to ceiling all around the bier. Perón, his features suitably composed for the occasion, made periodic appearances to stand beside his wife's coffin. The stench of flowers and death was overpowering, the footsteps of the mourners trooping past echoed with a slow, monotonous shuffle. Many had waited days for a glimpse of their beloved Evita. An old, gaunt-cheeked woman dressed in black, her teenage granddaughter, a lathe operator whose rough face was stained with tears ... For these people grief was real; for others, like Juan Gaspari, grief was a question of skilful balance. Neither too much nor too little, with a weather-eye firmly fixed on the shifting political winds.

By government decree all clocks in public places were stopped at 8.25 p.m. and for weeks a lugubrious radio announcer reminded Argentina that this was the hour in which 'Eva Perón passed into immortality'.

The *descamisados*, the 'shirtless ones' who formed the backbone of Perón's political power, demanded even greater recognition for the 'Madonna of the Americas'. Appeals for her canonization were urgently sent to the Pope in Rome. Throughout Argentina streets, cities — even provinces — were renamed Eva Perón. Altars dedicated to her memory sprang up in railway stations and parks, in schools and public buildings. In Laguna Grande the Hotel Estrella was changed to 'Hotel Evita' and Artemio Mendes instructed Father Antonio to hold a solemn memorial mass for the 'Madonna'. The priest replied tartly that he would pray for Eva Perón's soul as he prayed for all souls, but refused to go any further.

The government capitalized on popular grief and decreed that Evita's autobiography was to be compulsory reading in all schools. When the rumour mills whispered that the United States government had prohibited translation of the book, an enraged mob set fire to the Lincoln Library in downtown Buenos Aires. It was one of many burnings that were to haunt Argentina in the years to come.

CHAPTER SIXTEEN

I

A chilly April wind gusted through Buenos Aires's deserted streets, swirling papers and rattling metal shutters on the shop fronts. The wind whined around corners and caught in the banners stretched across the Plaza de Mayo, tossing them above the heads of a chanting, restless crowd. The man in shirtsleeves who stood on the balcony on the Casa Rosada at the east end of the Plaza raised his fists to the wind and unleashed his powerful, rasping voice to whip the crowd to fury.

'*Compañeros*, the enemies of our people will not succeed!'

Only minutes before a bomb had exploded near the plaza, interrupting his speech for the second time. A first bomb had gone off as he stepped on to the balcony to address his loyal *descamisados*; several Party officials dived for cover, but the man shrugged off bombs with a characteristic sneer. He was Juan Domingo Perón and he held Argentina firmly secure in his spell.

'The traitors must pay!'

One hundred thousand voices bayed in reply.

'We'll hang them from the trees!'

Half an hour later the crowd surged through the city streets, screaming vengeance and primed for blood.

II

Carlos would have enjoyed his dinner at the Jockey Club had he not been saddled with the rear admiral's monologue. The rear admiral had been thrust upon him by a grinning Freddy Rodríguez Nelson, who promptly disappeared into the bar. Carlos did not want to hear about the rear admiral's exploits in the Brazilian brothels; he wanted to eat his steak in peace. He had come up from Los Toros on business that morning;

189

business had gone wrong, and he was debating whether to approach Marcos about contacting Gaspari for help when the rear admiral appeared.

Only God knew why Freddy had invited him, Carlos mused sourly as his unwelcome dinner companion paused to sample the wine. Certainly only God knew why he had allowed Freddy to install the man at his table. There were plenty of vacant places in the dining-room. The club was not full tonight — surely the rear admiral could have sat somewhere else. Carlos frowned, mentally weighing principles against expediency, his grey eyes fixed with polite boredom on a point behind the rear admiral's grizzled head. There was no doubt in his mind that Gaspari was the only answer to his problem — the question was, what would it cost him? On the other hand he needed the bank loan. The harvest had been a poor one and Perón's economic policies were crippling . . . He started as his companion's voice suddenly sharpened.

'It's a question of how much longer. How much longer can the man hold everything together now that she's gone?'

Presumably not a brothel. Carlos focused on the rear admiral's face and ventured a non-committal answer.

'You tell me.'

A strong, weatherbeaten hand flicked the air. 'Perón's made a number of stupid mistakes. Evita's brother's "suicide" is one, removing the key men she appointed another. Legalizing divorce and prostitution — only a complete idiot would mess with the Church!'

'Or a man who's very sure of himself,' remarked Carlos dryly.

The rear admiral took another long, appreciative sip of wine and leaned forward again. He had very pale green eyes set deeply in a face the colour and texture of well-seasoned leather. The eyes probed shrewdly.

'I don't need to tell you this country's being ruined,' he said. 'You know it better than I do. There's only one way to save Argentina from total disaster and that's to wipe out Perón and Peronism. Crush them until there's nothing left!'

Carlos agreed, but thought it more prudent to show an interest in the Jockey Club's excellent beef. His companion grinned.

'Oh, the man still has the magic touch,' he added in the same guarded tones. 'No doubt about that — Perón can move the masses. The question is, can he count on the armed forces as well — and for how long?'

The problem of an urgent bank loan for Los Toros was far more pressing than rhetorical speculation on Perón's future — and far healthier in the long run. Carlos glanced at his watch; if he put a call through to La Catalina he might catch Marcos awake. He pushed back his chair.

'Excuse me for a moment, I must make a phone call.'

He was halfway across the dining-room when the mob attacked.

It roared up Florida Street like a juggernaut, thundering a single, chilling refrain.

'Pe-rón! Pe-rón! Burn the Jockey! Pe-rón!'

An ashen-faced porter hurriedly closing the front doors was knocked to the ground. The mob raced up the marble staircase, burst into the main hall, ripped paintings and hangings from the walls. A wild hand flung a torch into one of the reading rooms; as the flames ate greedily into the carpet an elderly waiter appeared with a fire extinguisher. The mob howled in protest and beat him back. Flames leapt from floor to ceiling, licking the woodwork and spreading rapidly through the leather-bound volumes on the shelves. Several dozen men made for the stairway to the second floor; others went to work in the dining-room, jostling diners and over-turning tables, smashing windows and dishes to the cries of 'Perros oligarcas! Viva Perón!'

Men and women fought frantically to flee the burning building; the mob paid little attention to them, other than to harass and jeer. Through dense clouds of smoke Carlos saw a thick-set man in overalls slashing at a portrait with a broken bottle. The man looked around as he yelled and drew back thick lips in an ugly, taunting sneer.

'Son of a bitch!'

Carlos struck hard. His first blow knocked the bottle from the man's hand, the second sent him flying against the wall. The man screamed and several of his compañeros raced to the rescue. They pinned Carlos's arms behind him and began to whip his face with their fists, jeering as he fought to break free. Someone shouted that the fire was spreading. The mob turned tail and ran, screaming, 'Viva Perón! at the top of its lungs. Carlos groped through the smoke; his left eye was half closed, the right one blinded by blood. Someone grasped his arm.

191

'This way, quickly!'

Freddy. He dragged Carlos across the threshold and down the steps as the flames roared skywards through the darkness.

III

During that grim April night of 1953 political paranoia went on the rampage. No one could say for sure who had planted the bombs in the Plaza de Mayo, but identities were unimportant. The Peronists struck back with savage, unreasoning fury. Landowners, businessmen, Radicals, Socialists – they were all the same to the mob. Enemies of the fatherland, traitors to Perón. Throughout the city loyal followers burned opposition headquarters while the police and the army turned a blind eye.

The fire brigade eventually showed up at the Jockey Club after dawn; by then the building was a smouldering ruin; its priceless collection of books and paintings reduced to ashes.

The following day a pro-government newspaper praised the mobs and spoke of 'purifying flames'. Artemio Mendes read out the editorial at a Party rally in Laguna Grande and promised his cheering listeners that the flames of Buenos Aires would soon clean out the rot festering in certain ranches around the area.

Father Antonio, deafened by the strident strains of the 'Peronist March' thundering across the square, found himself praying fervently for a well-aimed thunderbolt from above.

IV

The telephone rang at La Catalina just as Marcos was finishing breakfast. Over a distance of three hundred miles he heard the crackle of Teresa's voice, shrill and brittle with fear.

'Something terrible has happened! The police arrested Carlos. Gastón rang from Buenos Aires . . .' Her voice broke. '*Dios mío* – I don't know what to do. I don't even know where Carlos is!'

192

Marcos shouted above the static. 'Are the children all right?'

'Yes . . . I think so . . . very frightened. Gastón's been trying to reach me since three o'clock this morning . . . Dear God, what do I do?'

'Tell me what happened. Slowly.'

There was a loud crackle and then suddenly the line was clear. 'I came down to Los Toros three days ago to see about new furnishings for the house. We planned to stay until the end of the week and return to Buenos Aires together, but Carlos had to go back unexpectedly yesterday. He told me he would be dining at the Jockey Club last night . . . They burnt it. Do you know that? The Peronists burnt the Jockey Club, Marcos!'

'I've heard about it,' he said tersely. 'Go on.'

'Carlos got into a fight with some men in the mob. They beat him up – Gastón says quite badly. Freddy brought him back to the flat. Gastón wanted to ring the doctor, but Carlos wouldn't let him – you know how he is!' Teresa caught her breath. 'The police came to arrest him a couple of hours later. They wouldn't give any reasons, they wouldn't even let him ring his lawyer. They took him away . . . the ch-children saw it . . .' Fear and outrage exploded in a harsh sob. '*Por Dios*, Marcos – it's inhuman!'

He told Teresa to return immediately to Buenos Aires and go straight to Barranco Rosales; Mercedes would fetch the children. When he finished making all the necessary arrangements he rang up Los Alamos. Angela answered the telephone and he spoke to her rapidly in English, just in case anyone might be eavesdropping on the line.

'Tell Jimmy I cannot meet him this afternoon. I must leave in a few minutes for Buenos Aires. You have heard about the trouble last night?'

'Jimmy's father rang early this morning to tell us.'

'There's been a problem with Carlos.'

She caught this meaning at once and was shocked, but her voice remained calm. 'Is there anything we can do to help?'

'Say nothing about this to anyone – do you understand?'

'Of course.' For a moment calm faltered. 'Please . . . be careful.'

'Do not worry, *gringuita*,' said Marcos and rang off.

193

V

He made the ten-hour drive from La Catalina to Buenos Aires in just under eight and drew up in front of Verdulería Nápoli at four in the afternoon. Juan Gaspari sat sipping *maté* in the kitchen; he looked around uneasily as Marcos strode through the entrance, followed by Celestina.

'He wants to talk to you,' she said in a disapproving voice. 'I told him you're sick, but he says it doesn't matter.'

Gaspari sneezed and pulled a lavishly patterned silk dressing gown around his plump shoulders. 'I've got the flu.' He pushed aside a stack of comic books and magazines. 'Bring Marcos some coffee, mother.'

Celestina plunked down a steaming cup and bustled back into the shop, muttering under her breath. Gaspari refilled the *maté* gourd from a kettle at his elbow; he looked ill-at-ease. Not flu, Marcos told himself grimly. The clown knows.

'My brother-in-law was arrested at three o'clock this morning,' he said roughly. 'What do you know about it?'

The plump hands flapped listlessly. 'I've been ill.'

'I want Carlos released!'

Juan Gaspari swallowed. 'I can't meddle with the police.'

'I don't give a damn if you're afraid of the police, I want Carlos released! I don't care how you do it – just do it!'

'Perhaps his lawyer . . .'

'The goddamned law's hamstrung in this country!' shouted Marcos, crashing his fist on to the table. 'That's why crap like you grow fat on the rest of us – because there is no law except Perón's law!'

'Sshh!' Gaspari darted an uneasy glance in the direction of the shop. 'Someone might hear you.'

'Go to hell! I pay you good money to make yourself useful, but I can just as easily find someone else! Scum like you litter the streets these days!'

Gaspari's face glistened. Over the years he had built up an exclusive and highly profitable network of wealthy, pragmatic men like Marcos Luciani, who relied on his services and were willing to pay good money for them. If just one of those men spread the word that his services were no longer reliable, the good money would find its way into someone else's eager pocket. He mopped his brow with a bright red bandana.

It was a bitch of a problem because the police were a law unto themselves.

'It won't be easy and it will be expensive,' he hedged.

'Well worth your while!'

Gaspari licked his lips. 'I cannot promise success, *amigo*. There have been other important men arrested, you know . . .'

'Just get Carlos released!' growled Marcos. 'If you fail, I'll find someone else to do the job.'

VI

At Barranco Rosales the hours inched by with excruciating slowness.

Every time the telephone rang, Teresa's heart stopped. She put on a brave front for the children's sake, but there was no hiding the tell-tale shadows under her eyes or her abrupt, restless silences. She could not sit still, she could not stroll with Mercedes in the garden, she could not bear Gladys's nervous attempts to make conversation.

'Everything will turn out all right. There must have been a mistake. My brother's doing everything he can to help you, you know.'

Teresa stared through Gladys without bothering to reply. Frustration and uncertainty were bad enough; the knowledge that her husband's fate depended on a man she despised made them a doubly bitter burden.

Carlos's lawyer, stymied by official stonewalling, reluctantly admitted that Gaspari was their only hope. The arrests following the disturbances all involved prominent men; the charges came under the blanket heading of 'antigovernment activities', but just what those activities might be was anyone's guess. The only thing certain was that the men were being held at the government's pleasure – indefinitely, and without trial.

'If your man can get Carlos released it'll be a miracle,' he told Marcos on the morning of the second day after the arrest. 'Perón's turning the screws as tightly as he can to prove he's in control. If you ask me Evita's death was the beginning of the end – but God only knows when the end will come.'

The miracle occurred at three o'clock that afternoon.

Gaspari had spent most of the previous night and all of the morning asking questions which appeared to have no answer. No one knew anything. Maybe the man he wanted had been arrested, maybe not. It was a government matter. One must be very careful about these things. He should try Devoto jail, where political prisoners were held.

At Devoto he learned that a number of the men arrested after the disturbances were being held *incommunicado* in different places throughout the city; when he asked for details his informant grinned.

'Can't tell you that, *compañero*. Nobody knows.'

Gaspari decided to take a break for lunch. He went to a steakhouse near the dockyards, ordered the thickest sirloin on the menu, and settled down to plan his next move. There were several secluded booths nearby; Gaspari sipped his wine and stared at a couple in one of them. A tall, heavy-set man in his mid-forties had his hands cupped around the face of a young blonde; as Gaspari watched he kissed her and murmured something.

A moment later Juan Gaspari hovered anxiously at the man's elbow.

'It wouldn't be Captain Sammartino – but of course it is! Remember me? Juan Gaspari – we met in Mar del Plata last February. How are your father-in-law and your wife, captain?'

The man flushed darkly. 'Gaspari? I . . . er . . . yes.' His eyes flickered nervously across to the blonde. 'This young lady is my . . . er . . . niece.'

'*Encantado, señorita.*' Gaspari leered politely. 'As a matter of fact I'm glad to run into you, captain. There's a little matter I'd like to consult you about.' He glanced at his watch. 'Perhaps we could step outside for a quiet chat, eh? Just a few minutes, señorita,' as the blonde pouted. 'I won't keep your . . . uncle . . . more than a few minutes.'

As a miracle Captain Sammartino had two distinct advantages. He was married to the only daughter of a high-ranking police officer and he was a member of the internal security forces. He also had a third advantage and this one Gaspari exploited ruthlessly for all it was worth.

The captain had an inordinate passion for women. Unfortunately his career depended on his father-in-law's good graces and Gaspari knew through the grapevine that the father-in-law took a very dim view of the captain's roving eye. The next affair – or so the grapevine rumoured – would be the end of his career. The officer could always find his daughter a new husband, but Captain Alfonso Sammartino would spend the rest of his life policing sheep in the wilds of Patgonia.

The 'quiet little chat' lasted a quarter of an hour; when it was over Gaspari drove to the Central Police Department and presented Captain Sammartino's card to an officer who studied it with pale impassive eyes.

'What's your interest in this man?' he asked after a moment.

'We're brothers-in-law by marriage,' replied Gaspari glibly. 'His late sister was my sister's husband's first wife. I'm sure there's been a mistake. My sister was very close to Evita, you know.' He lowered his voice confidentially and leaned across the desk. 'Her husband is a very wealthy man – and Arcos Arizu is as well.'

The pale eyes did not blink.

'Very wealthy,' repeated Gaspari, rolling the words off his tongue. 'The general himself was telling me the other night how much the Party owes to men like that. There must be some mistake about Arcos Arizu's arrest.'

'None that I know of.'

Juan Gaspari leaned back in his chair and lit a cigarette. The matter would require some very tough bargaining.

VII

When Gaspari's call came that evening Marcos and Freddy Rodríguez Nelson had been closeted for several hours discussing options for exile. Gaspari's voice sounded thin and guarded.

'Come to the four hundred block of Alsina Street at ten tonight. Alone.' He named a sum. 'Bring it in banknotes.'

Marcos was relaying the conversation when Teresa walked into the study.

'I'm going with you to get Carlos,' she announced.

'No,' he said. 'For God's sake – try and understand, Teresa!' as she began to argue angrily. 'We don't have much time.'

What little colour she had left drained away, leaving her face pinched and ugly; after a moment she demanded shrilly, 'What do you mean?'

'He has to leave the country . . .'

'No!'

'Under the circumstances he has no choice – and if you don't believe me ask your lawyer.' Marcos rubbed his eyes wearily. 'I'm sorry, Teresa, but that's the way it is. Freddy will take Carlos out on his boat tonight; with any luck they'll reach Uruguay by dawn.'

'It's an easy crossing from my island in the Delta,' added Freddy. 'The *Misty* can do it blindfolded. Don't worry,' he flashed a bold, reassuring smile. 'The boys in the coast-guard know me, I often take friends to the island at night.' The smile twisted slightly. 'As a matter of fact I've invited one along tonight, but don't tell Marta. She disapproves of blondes.'

Teresa continued to argue; in the end they compromised and Freddy drove her out to the marina where the *Misty* was moored. A sculptural Swedish blonde in the back seat kept up a cheerful, lilting patter in broken English as the car sped through the late evening traffic.

'Don't worry about Ulla,' grinned Freddy. 'She's as dumb as she is beautiful. It's all an adventure to her. Top secret. She's thrilled.'

Teresa darted him a disapproving glance. 'You ought to be ashamed of yourself. Think of your family.'

'I do think of them. My wife's an iceberg, my son's a prig, my mother-in-law treats me as though I had the rabies.'

'You have a lovely daughter.'

'They won't let me near her. Bad influence and all that. Maybe I am, but I enjoy life. There's only one, might as well live it up.'

'I cook you eggs with schnapps for breakfast, yes?' cooed Ulla.

Teresa stared out of the window.

VIII

Buenos Aires throbs from dawn to dawn in a continual wave of nervous, intoxicating energy. At ten p.m. its nightlife is just getting underway, with crowded cinemas and restaurants, congested streets, bustling throngs of people. Even during the height of its troubles, the city stubbornly continued to work and play at a frenzied pace, determined to make the most of borrowed time.

In 1953 Marcos Luciani could not know what the future held in store for himself or the country. He did know that the present was dangerous, even for men like Juan Gaspari. A word spoken at the wrong moment, a miscalculated pause, an inflection that could be wilfully misconstrued – any one of these could bring on disaster. If something should go wrong now . . . Marcos fought down apprehension and concentrated on the blank, shuttered buildings on either side of the street. After the brightly lit downtown area Alsina was nearly deserted. A couple embraced in a darkened doorway, a stray cat scavenged in the gutter, the melancholy strains of a tango drifted from a dimly lit bar. A foreshortened shadow stepped up to the kerb and made motions for the car to approach.

'Do you have the money?' hissed Gaspari, poking his head through the window.

'Do you have Carlos?'

'Of course! What do you take me for? Give me the money quickly.'

'I'll hand it over myself.'

Gaspari was too tired and hungry to argue. The bargaining session had been longer and much more difficult than he imagined; he still was not convinced of success. Money spoke for itself – did it matter who made the payment? If they wasted more time the officer inside might change his mind. He sneezed violently.

'This way.'

They hurried along a dark hallway, up a flight of stairs and into a small room lit by a single low-watt bulb. A man in plainclothes sat at a desk; on the wall behind him hung a large coloured photograph of Perón in dress uniform. The man nodded at Marcos and ignored Gaspari.

'A regrettable error, señor.' His voice was dry and flat. 'You have brought the documents requested?'

Marcos help up a manila envelope. Fifteen thousand pesos in banknotes – they were lucky to get off so lightly, although the sum probably represented more than a year's salary to the man behind the desk.

'I'll hand them over when my brother-in-law is released and not before,' he said curtly.

Gaspari gurgled something inaudible in his throat and smiled apologetically at the man behind the desk; the man pressed a buzzer, unimpressed by the apology. The minutes ticked by. Outside in the street a car braked sharply; somewhere in the building a radio blared a popular tune and a woman laughed. The man started to whistle the tune under his breath, drumming out the beat with maddening, inconsistent rhythm.

The door opened and a policeman walked in; behind him, looking dazed and dishevelled, stumbled Carlos.

His face was covered with bruises and ugly patches of raw skin. He looked around dully, as though unable to grasp the situation; his left eye was half closed and inflamed a dark, angry red.

'We had nothing to do with that!' said the man behind the desk, hearing Marcos's angry exclamation.

'They didn't touch me,' agreed Carlos thickly. The words made a weary, sibilant sound.

Marcos handed over the envelope; the man counted the contents with quick, agile fingers and nodded.

'Thank you, señor. It was a regrettable error, you understand.'

The etiquette of bribery called for a handshake and a cup of strong black coffee laced with *caña*. Marcos made himself drink the coffee slowly; if anything it would do Carlos good. There must be no sign of hurry, no indication anything out of the ordinary was about to happen. They made desultory conversation about the weather and football; when these topics talked themselves out they drove off towards Barranco Rosales at normal speed, their hearts in their mouths.

No one followed.

200

IX

Carlos broke the silence in the car with a single word. 'Why?'

'Why?' Gaspari shrugged. 'Who knows? Someone with a grudge against you who overheard something you should not have said. A maid, perhaps? She places an anonymous call to the police, tells lies out of spite – it happens often. They are very stupid, these girls . . .' He pointed to a house on the corner. 'Leave me off here, Marcos. A friend of mine lives in one of those flats. It's too late to go back to Quilmes tonight.'

There was a light in the ground floor flat; as the car rolled to a stop a woman's figure appeared silhouetted against the window. Gaspari grinned sheepishly.

'Women! Always worrying about nothing.' He cleared his throat and touched Carlos's shoulder with a surprisingly diffident gesture. '*Que le vaya bien*, Don Carlos. Good luck. If you ever need any more help just let me know.'

No reply. Gaspari got out of the car and hurried towards the darkened entrance of the building. They saw his short figure pressed against the glass doors; a moment later the doors opened as though expecting him and he disappeared into the hallway.

The car headed north through sleepy, tree-lined suburbs bathed in clear moonlight. Carlos leaned back wearily against the seat. He must not think about the past forty-eight hours nor about what lay ahead. They were too many matters to discuss, business arrangements to be made, instructions for the ranch manager at Los Toros. He spoke slowly, articulating with care because of the pain. There was no time for fear or loneliness or despair.

Only once did he falter and that was when they passed the cathedral in the old colonial suburb of San Isidro. He had married Teresa there in 1936 – a love match which began five years earlier when Roque Hernández brought his seventeen-year-old sister to Los Toros for a summer weekend. She was thin and dark and painfully shy, but Carlos fell in love with her on the spot. Twenty-two years later their love still held firmly and without regrets . . . He swallowed a sudden lump in his throat.

'You'll take care of Teresa and the children for me?'

'Don't worry,' replied Marcos quietly. 'They'll live at Barranco Rosales until your return.'

On the threshold of exile, *return* seemed a bitter, futile word. Carlos sighed and began to explain about the problem which had brought him to Buenos Aires three days ago.

At San Fernando they veered right down a steep, winding slope and took a dirt road leading to the river. The road ran for some way over marshland before ending at a wooden barrier. Low buildings loomed through a cluster of willow trees straight ahead; beyond them naked masts traced perpendicular lines against the darkness. As the car braked a sleepy face peered suspiciously from the window of a guard hut.

'We're Señor Rodríguez Nelson's guests,' said Marcos. 'He's expecting us.'

The guard cranked up the barrier and waved them on with a dismal grunt of envy. Day or night, two or three times a week . . . He knew all about Señor Rodríguez Nelson's guests.

The *Misty* rocked gently at her moorings near the outlet to the river; as they came alongside Teresa ran out from the shadows. Her eyes widened with horror when she saw her husband's face.

'*Dios mío*! What have they done to you?'

'Hush, Teresa . . .'

'I'm coming as well. I won't leave you!'

'No,' said Carlos unsteadily. 'The children need you here.'

'Hurry!' hissed Freddy from the deck of the *Misty*.

'But this is impossible!' cried Teresa. 'Dear Holy Virgin – it can't happen! Not to us! Not to you! Carlos . . .'

He pressed her to him to stifle the cry; then, no longer trusting his own nerves, thrust her gently aside and climbed into the waiting boat. The engine coughed softly and turned over; Freddy waved at the shore.

'Let's go!'

There was a splash as the ropes slipped into the water. Teresa sobbed harshly and ran to the edge of the jetty.

'*Carlos!*'

'Be brave for me,' he whispered. 'Please be brave for us both.'

The *Misty* slid swiftly through the channel into the river; when Carlos could bring himself to look back the moon was gone and night had enveloped the coastline in darkness.

CHAPTER SEVENTEEN

I

Gladys accepted Teresa's presence at Barranco Rosales with a colourless smile that barely disguised her rage and frustration. Sharing a house with Mercedes was bad enough; to have this additional burden thrust upon her was next to intolerable. She protested, but Marcos refused to listen.

'I'm responsible for Teresa and the children now,' he said curtly. 'They'll remain under my roof until Carlos returns.'

Since arguing made matters worse Gladys embarked on subtler tactics. She went out of her way to be courteous and understanding; of doing everything in her power to please. Teresa cooperated by being as rude as possible and flying off the handle at the slightest imagined provocation. Gladys restrained an urge to claw out her sister-in-law's eyes and smiled patiently. When Rosita, now her personal maid, commented on Señora Teresa's rudeness, the hazel eyes filled with tears.

'One must make allowances, my dear,' Gladys murmured. 'Poor Señora Teresa – she's crazy, you know.'

Rosita repeated this remark in the servants' dining-room, adding that in her opinion Don Marcos's wife was a saint.

Fortunately there was little Lalo to cuddle and spoil.

It was a pity Marcos did not pay more attention to his youngest son, Gladys reflected as she bounced the baby on her lap. Such a bright, endearing child – so different from Claudia. There had never been any money to buy Claudia proper baby clothes or a lovely cradle; never time to fuss over her or cuddle her or sing nursery songs. Lalo smelled fresh and sweet, his room was crowded with toys, his sheets were hand embroidered with clowns and dancing elephants. The medal around his neck was eighteen-carat gold and not a cheap imitation. It read 'Eduardo Salvador Luciani' on the back and the date of his baptism. 'Salvador' was her father's name and the only acknowledgement she gave to her parents. They had sent a small silver crucifix as a gift, but Gladys hid it at the back of her stocking drawer.

'Mama's love, my little Lalo,' she cooed softly. 'You'll be much better looking than Miguel. Smarter, too – and much, much nicer.'

At fifteen Miguel was a hot-tempered handful whose increasing resentment of anything resembling authority had led to several rows with his father during the summer; recently there had been a more serious one over his budding friendship with Lucas. One of Marcos's friends had reported seeing them coming out of a downtown striptease theatre at an hour when Miguel was supposed to be at rugby practice.

'I do not want you to get mixed up with Lucas!' Marcos told his son sternly. 'He's rotten all the way through. The only reason he lives in this house is because he's my brother – otherwise I'd throw him out. Where else has he taken you?'

Miguel swallowed. With the constant threat of being permanently exiled to La Catalina hanging over his head he thought it better not to tell Papa about Lucas's blonde friend Erika. Marcos saw the guilty expression on his son's face and guessed the reason for it.

'Look, Miguel,' he said in a friendlier tone, 'I was your age too, you know. I know all about starting with women. It's like opening a new box of chocolates – you want to bite into all of them at once. Fair enough, if you pick the right box. The time will come when you find the woman you want to marry and settle down with. Just stay away from Lucas and his friends – they're rubbish.'

It was on the tip of Miguel's tongue to ask what box Papa had picked Gladys out of, but on second thoughts he decided against it. He didn't know what to make of his father's marriage. An ordinary man might marry a woman like Gladys, but Papa was not an ordinary man. He was an inaccessible god. A god picked the best chocolate from the most expensive box; he didn't settle for cheap imitations. It was difficult to reconcile the god with the man in Papa. Perhaps there was some weakness in him after all.

II

Miguel had a habit of showing up late for meals when his father wasn't around. Mercedes scolded him. He replied with a kiss on her cheek and a winning 'Sorry, Aunt. It won't happen again.' It did happen again. This time Gladys objected. Miguel glared at her.

'What the hell are you carping about?' he said rudely. 'This is my house.'

'This is my house too,' she replied. 'It is not a hotel. We expect you to come to meals on time.'

Mercedes did not welcome her sister-in-law's support and told Gladys not to interfere. Gladys appealed tearfully to Marcos when he arrived from La Catalina later that day.

'I don't see why I shouldn't have something to say in the matter,' she sniffed. 'Especially after Miguel was so rude to me. After all, I am your wife.'

The veiled approach irritated Marcos because it made him feel guilty about innumerable sins of omission in their relationship, but he was forced to agree that Gladys had a point. He told Mercedes not to undermine her authority in front of the children – and promptly found himself trapped in a barrage of feminine crossfire. Mercedes indignantly announced she would leave Barranco Rosales and live in a flat on her own. Gladys would have liked nothing better, but by now she was equal to the challenge and protested in great agitation that she would not dream of Mercedes abandoning 'our home'.

'Oh, that "our home" was very clever,' Mercedes complained to Angela when they met during the winter holidays. 'Slipping it in with a little smile while she fluttered her eyes at Marcos. My brother's a blind fool!' she added in exasperation. 'That woman has him believing she's delighted to have Teresa and the children in the house when I know she loathes the sight of them!'

'How is Teresa?' asked Angela, anxious to get away from the subject of Gladys and Marcos.

'Bearing up as best she can, but Carlos's exile has been a terrible blow to her. They are so devoted to each other. Such fine, decent people . . .' Mercedes crossed herself and dabbed her eyes. '*Que desgracia, querida*! What misfortunes we must bear!'

Strange to think of Carlos and Teresa feeling anything more for each other than a courteous formality, reflected Angela. They seem so correct, so detached from passion – yet I suppose I can't imagine them not being together.

She felt a stab of envy for their oneness, still intact after so many years.

In all honesty she could not say the same for her own marriage. She and Jimmy were each moving at a different speed and in a different direction. It was no longer a question of teething pains – if it had been teething pains in the first place. For the last six months or so she had been making a conscious attempt to keep the marriage on an even keel, determined to make it work in spite of her own misgivings. Lately, however, she found herself wondering uneasily whether it was worth the effort.

One quarrel in particular distressed her.

Jimmy was not happy about Angela's work at the convent, but she could never pinpoint the exact reason for his disapproval. When challenged he would merely pull a face and mutter that she shouldn't be wasting time with that sort of thing when she had other matters to tend to.

'Like what?' demanded Angela.

'Looking after the house, for one – and looking after me.'

'The house looks after itself, and you're not here most of the day. Besides, I don't spend all of my time at the convent.'

'You spend enough of it,' grumbled Jimmy and buried himself in his newspaper again.

Angela sighed. There was no accounting for men. In the beginning Jimmy had encouraged her to become involved; now he was offended because she spent several days a week in Laguna Grande instead of docilely twiddling her thumbs by the hearth, waiting for his lordship to return from the fields. She reached over and tweaked his lordship's ear, still determined to keep the ship on an even keel.

'Don't be such an old grouch. You should see the state some of those poor children are in! This morning the butcher brought us a little boy he found crawling in the gutter behind his shop. Someone said the child belongs to a woman called the Widow. No known father, of course. It's disgusting how these men get a woman pregnant and then wash their hands . . . What's the matter?'

The expression on Jimmy's face was a very curious one. If the idea weren't so ridiculous she would have sworn his lordship had just seen a ghost.

'What the hell are you talking about?' he demanded harshly.

'A child belonging to some woman called the Widow. What on earth is wrong?'

'Nothing's wrong! Why should anything be wrong? Stop looking at me like that!'

'Jimmy!'

'I don't want you to have anything to do with the Wi-widow's child! You keep away! I won't have you mixed up with her!'

'I'm not mixed up with her!' snapped Angela. 'I've never even seen the wretched woman! All I'm telling you is that she obviously has no money and even less sense when it comes to caring for her child. It's not the first time someone has found it crawling in the gutter. How in hell do you expect me to sit back and not do anything?'

'I don't want you to go near her! I don't want you to go near that blasted convent! I'm fed up to the teeth with all this Lady Bountiful crap, with your messing around with whores' brats! You're my wife! I want you here! With me!'

Angela turned white. 'If we had a child . . .'

'Goddamn it, stop nagging!'

'I'm not nagging! You stop acting so idiotic about this! If we had a child of our own I would spend less time with other people's children. Since we don't and we won't ever have one, I do and I will!'

'It's my fault the child died!' shouted Jimmy. 'Go on, say it! That's what your thinking! It's my fault the child died and it's my fault you're stuck here on Los Alamos. You should have married that bloody pipe-smoking whey-face in England, you shouldn't have married me — that's what you're thinking, isn't it?'

She stared hard at him without replying, then turned and walked out of the room; after a moment he heard the bedroom door slam and the sound of the key in the lock.

III

For the first time since his marriage Jimmy got deliberately drunk.

He drove to a rundown *almacén* on the outskirts of Laguna Grande and bought himself a bottle of imported whisky left over from pre-war stocks. The *almacén*, which sold everything from horseshoes to gingham, obliged its customers with a few unsteady tables at the back. Jimmy sat down near a pile of foul-smelling sheepskins and filled his glass to the brim.

Women were hell.

He envied Marcos, who seemed to do whatever he pleased without anyone nagging him to death. If Marcos chose to litter the streets of Laguna Grande with his bastards he would; if his wife happened to mention that one of them had turned up at the convent he would probably laugh it off as a joke.

'Doesn't go in f'r that sortathing,' muttered Jimmy thickly. 'No whoresons for old Marcos – no, sir. Smart bastard. I should've taken pr-precaushuns.' He hiccoughed and wiped the back of his hand across his mouth. 'Bloody bitch – I gave her mo-money . . . Tha's my m-money,' he said at the top of his voice. 'Better get it ba-back.'

He lurched to his feet and stumbled out to the car, the whisky bottle tucked under his arm. The ignition key kept climbing up on to the dashboard, but he finally captured it with both hands and, after another tussle, he started the engine. Whisky tasted stale. He tossed the bottle out of the window and backed on to the road, narrowly missing a car headed in the same direction. Jimmy roared with laughter and waved a confused pattern of obscene gestures at the cursing driver.

It was good to be drunk again. Good to be free.

The Widow's shack stood on the far side of a stream running through Laguna Grande's narrow back streets. The place was in darkness when Jimmy drove up, but as he switched off the engine a dim light went on behind the curtained windows. Except for a dog barking in the distance and the wary rustling of the acacia tree the night was still. Jimmy climbed out of the car and picked his way unsteadily across a small yard littered with rubbish and

208

broken bottles. There was no moon, but he knew his way blindfolded. He shivered slightly and tapped on the door.

After a while it opened a crack and a pair of long, black eyes looked him over. He pushed impatiently to enter, but the door did not yield. The low, curiously honeyed voice that went with the eyes asked, 'What do you want?'

'T-talk to you. Lemme in.'

The door opened and he stepped into a circle of dull yellow light streaming from a paraffin lamp on a table near the window. The table was covered with a bright red oilcloth; on it lay several mounds of dried herbs, a broken saint and a pack of grease-stained playing cards. Nothing had changed. There was a low bed covered with a dirty blanket, a lopsided paraffin stove in the corner and two rickety wooden chairs painted blue at the table. There was no sign of a crib or the child.

'Do you want to drink *caña?*'

He accepted, hoping to ease the sudden throbbing in his head. The Widow stood on the edge of the yellow circle. She wore a tight-fitting dress; the cheap, shiny stuff clung to her large breasts and the plump V between her legs. Jimmy looked away. The Widow's bare feet traced circles on the dirt floor. He remembered how he used to fondle them and the things he had whispered under the dirty blanket.

'The m-money I gave you for the ch-child,' he stammered thickly. 'Wh-what have you done with it?'

She shrugged. 'I buy things. Why have you come?'

He frowned at the cut-glass beads around her neck and the coloured bangles on her fleshy wrists. Her long earrings clicked with a tantalizing little sound. 'That m-money's for the ch-child. Not for you. Where is h-he?'

The Widow's dark eyes flickered briefly across his face and slid away. She had put the child on the floor to play while she entertained a travelling salesmen early in the morning; the child managed to crawl through the door and had disappeared. A neighbour later came to tell her that the butcher had taken it to the convent. The neighbour had said a number of other things as well – had even threatened to report her to the authorities. The Widow found the threat amusing. The authority in Laguna Grande was Captain Cordero and he was her friend. *El loco* Morgan had also been her friend – once. More than a friend because of the child. She glanced up at him from under her thick lashes and ran the tip of her tongue over full, pouting lips.

'I took the child to the nuns,' she lied. 'The people here are cruel. They laugh because it has no father. Why have you come to see me, *loco*?'

He gripped her arm, bruising the swarthy skin with his fingers. 'I came about the child. That m-money's for him!'

The Widow laughed.

'Damn you, you stupid bitch!' rasped Jimmy. 'That boy's my son! You're his mother – you'll take care of him! I don't want the nuns to have anything to do with it! He's my child and you're his mother! Do you understand?'

She chuckled. 'You don't like your *gringa* wife anymore? You still want me?' Her breasts gleamed like dark gourds in the lamplight. 'You want to touch them, *loco*? You want to kiss?'

Heavy drops of sweat rolled down his face. 'No! I don't want to touch you.'

'*Si, si loco*. You want to kiss your *negra puta*.' Her plump V rubbed across his thighs. 'We kiss, eh?' Her fingers moved before he could stop them, her lips and tongue caressed greedily. Jimmy's heart drummed inside his head; he began to whisper words he had tried to forget. The Widow raised wet, glistening lips and leered.

'You like me to kiss, *loco*? You want more?'

He crawled under the dirty blanket with the mother of his son. She was a liar, a whore and a cheat, but he couldn't stay away from her. He wanted more.

CHAPTER EIGHTEEN

I

Angela often wondered what would have happened had she not met Julia's great-aunt Lucía in June of 1953. Certainly she would have had no excuse for visiting Buenos Aires later that year.

Lucía Evarista Olmedo de Claire was a small, ugly woman with bird-like features and a pair of disconcertingly bright black eyes. At eighteen she had been married off to a wealthy banker more than twice her age. The marriage lasted for twenty years, during which time Lucía humoured her dour husband and did exactly as she pleased; when Alberto Claire died at sixty-five he left his thirty-eight-year-old widow an immense fortune and no heirs. Lucía promptly caused a family scandal by refusing to turn the administration of her estate over to her brothers; instead she announced she would look after matters herself, adding that she would be damned if her father's sons were going to fill their pockets at her expense.

She continued to do as she pleased with life and Julia could remember when the tales of the scandalous Lucía were strictly forbidden at home. More recently there had been the gloriously outrageous occasion when Julia's father heard himself called a pompous, stiff-necked idiot by great-aunt Lucía, scarlet with indignation at her nephew's refusal to let his daughter marry Tadeo Ortíz.

That memorable moment had endeared Julia to Lucía Claire forever.

Angela, invited to meet the notorious family celebrity, found a remarkably energetic and charming woman in her seventies who immediately proceeded to extract information about her life with a surgeon's dispassionate skill. Lucía loved to talk. She possessed a witty, malicious tongue, a keen eye for detail, and a seemingly inexhaustible store of society gossip which she distributed among her listeners as though handing out sweetmeats at a banquet.

211

Angela returned home feeling she had been immersed head first in a vat of champagne and held there for several hours – a sensation that went a long way towards raising her low spirits.

'That young woman is unhappy,' remarked Lucía to Julia afterwards. 'I have invited her to stay with me in Buenos Aires whenever she feels like getting away. A change of diet will do her good.'

II

There had been a reconciliation with Jimmy, but it solved nothing.

Angela made it very clear she would continue to work with the children at the convent; he gave in grudgingly, but the subject remained a sore point between them. On the day following the quarrel the Widow turned up to claim her child.

'She's a brazen bitch,' reported Julia, who had been there at the time. 'Snatched the boy away from Sister Ana and strutted out, looking as pleased as a cat stealing cream.'

The Widow had plenty to be pleased about. *El loco* Morgan promised more money for the child if she looked after it; more money meant more trinkets for herself. Perhaps a new dress as well. *El loco* promised to visit often. He did not like his *gringa* wife any more because she was cold and did not like to do the things which gave him pleasure. He wanted his bitch, his *puta*, his whore . . . The Widow lay back on the dirty blanket and smiled up at the cracks in the thatching overhead.

As long as she fed the child, wiped its nose and made sure it didn't escape, *el loco* Morgan wouldn't complain.

When challenged by his conscience Jimmy argued that he wanted to make sure his son was being cared for. His conscience knew better. The Widow's coarseness had fascinated him from the very beginning. She coupled like an animal, she did things with her body that drove him out of his mind, she filled him with disgust the minute it was all over . . . but he could not stay away. He had tried. He had fallen in love with Angela, settled down to family life, deluded himself into thinking that a decent woman and a happy home would be enough satisfaction. He would have succeeded if things had not become just another

212

nagging domestic routine; if Angela had continued to be his angel instead of turning into his wife.

Perhaps he should never have married her in the first place.

III

At the end of August Julia and Angela spent several days visiting Tadeo's brother, who owned a large vineyard in a neighbouring province. On their return Tadeo met them at the station and offered to drive Angela out to Los Alamos.

'Thanks, but Jimmy promised to pick me up,' she replied. 'He'll be along any minute now.'

She waited for over an hour; in the end it was Pablo Losa, on his way back to La Catalina from town, who took her home.

Several unfamiliar cars were parked in front of the house. Angela frowned at them and ran up the steps. A tub of geraniums had been overturned; she righted it, opened the door, and stopped dead on the threshold.

Eight men she had never seen before slept sprawled in every available chair; a ninth snored on the sofa, his mud-caked boots propped up on the armrest. The room was littered with empty bottles, the air reeked of tobacco smoke and stale sweat. Someone had overturned a drink on the table by the window; the liquid had seeped into the wood and formed a dark, sticky puddle on the floor.

A tenth man stumbled through the door at the far end of the room and blinked at the newcomers in astonishment; after a moment he came warily forward, staring at Angela through bleary, red-rimmed eyes.

'Hullo, angel. Wha' you doin' home?' He tripped over a bottle and kicked it noisily into the corner. 'You're comin' tomorrow. That's wha' you s-said. T'morrow.' A grimy hand flapped vaguely at the room. 'Pals o' mine from the g-good ol' days. *Compadres.* We been playin' a bit o' po-poker ... Oi, angel! Come 'n meet the boys!' as Angela pushed past him. 'Be nice to 'em ... they wan' meet you.'

She stared at him for a long, icy moment, her face very pale, then ran into the bedroom and slammed the door. Jimmy grimaced at Pablo Losa.

'*Carajo, che*! She said tomorrow!'

'It is tomorrow, Don Jimmy,' replied Losa dryly and went to fetch Angela's case from the car.

The aftermath of the poker game was yet another reconciliation of sorts. Jimmy wept and pleaded and swore he could not live without his angel, but although she eventually gave in to his frantic appeals their lovemaking no longer held any meaning for her.

Two weeks later Angela went to visit Lucía Claire.

IV

In her own inimitable way Julia's great-aunt was a practical woman.

The first day of Angela's visit she let her sleep until half past ten, then sent in the maid with a breakfast tray and a crystal jar of bath salts. Angela soaked for three-quarters of an hour in a steaming, fragrant heaven; when she finally emerged the maid reappeared with a chilled glass of champagne on a silver tray and a note in Lucía's spidery handwriting.

'I hope you have slept well,' it read. 'We will lunch at Sauvage. One o'clock. It is the most fashionable restaurant in town.'

Great-aunt Lucía, it seemed, was an accomplished sybarite.

'Sauvage is quite simply the only place worth my while,' she purred as they followed an impeccably disdainful *maître d*' across the restaurant's blue and gold dining-room. 'One eats like the gods and amuses oneself observing one's neighbours. The smoked salmon is excellent and the rum soufflé an open invitation to sin.' Lucía laughed gaily as they settled themselves at the table. 'I can pay for my sins, so why should I not enjoy them?'

After lunch they went shopping — not in the elegant shops along Florida Street or Avenida Santa Fé, but in private boutiques where admission was by invitation only. They were, Angela discovered, very exclusive and outrageously expensive.

'Why spend my money on clothes other women can afford?' remarked Lucía, eyeing a black silk dinner dress. 'This should suit you admirably. Try it on, please.'

'But I couldn't! I mean . . .' Angela flushed with embarrassment.

Two very bright black eyes peered quizzically at her over a tiny pair of gold-rimmed spectacles.

'You English have such an unimaginative sense of what is right and proper,' observed Lucía Claire with a dry chuckle and then patted Angela's hand. 'You must learn to enjoy life, my dear.'

The week sped by in a whirlwind of late mornings in bed, lunches at Sauvage and tea with Lucía's friends. Dinners, concerts, art exhibits. Auctions in a turn-of-the-century townhouse whose architectural extravaganzas rivalled the priceless antiques on display. Shopping expeditions, an evening at the opera. Theatre parties. Champagne . . . fragrant baths . . . late mornings . . . There was method to Lucía's madness. She had obviously decided that self-indulgence and a fever of social activities was the perfect cure for unhappiness.

A year ago Angela would have resented Lucía Claire's interference – but a year ago Angela had convinced herself she knew all the answers. Her marriage was merely going through normal teething pains; she could handle them with common sense and detachment. She had come to terms with her hysterectomy and was sensibly devoting herself to caring for needy children. Even falling in love with Marcos was nothing more than infatuation; given time it would pass and be forgotten.

Reasonable, level-headed answers given by a woman of thirty-four with her feet planted firmly on the ground.

Stale, last-year answers that did not fit this year's doubts at all.

Perhaps she should have stuck it out in England and married scholarly Anthony Hobson.

Angela quirked a guilty little smile at the traffic flowing along the tree-lined avenue seven floors below. Aunt Win had been right. She had not played fair with Anthony. She wasn't playing fair with Jimmy, either. Things were so unsettled between them – was patching them up worth the effort? She didn't know. What about Marcos? She was still in love with him, no matter how hard she tried not to be. How was she supposed to handle that? Oh, God! thought Angela miserably. I wish I'd never met him . . . Damn, that's a lie! I know what I want, but that's not right either. Does Jimmy really love me? I wish I knew. It would make everything so much easier if I knew ... If I had never met Marcos.

Around and around and around. She couldn't even write to Aunt Win because Aunt Win was dead.

It was useless to panic in Lucía Claire's drawing-room, of course. The magnificent Aubusson tapestries on the wall made a mockery of panic, the stylized elegance of a Louis XV sofa did not take kindly to quaking knees. Sèvres and Meissen and rose damask curtains frowned on fear. They demanded gay, rippling laughter and worldly wit, a sophisticated temper that did not crumble to pieces ... Angela turned her head at the mention of a familiar name in one of Lucía's intricate society anecdotes.

'Luciani? Do you know Marcos Luciani?'

'I know everyone worth knowing in Buenos Aires. His father was one of the handsomest men I have ever met.' Lucía held a fluted champagne goblet up to the light. 'What a shame Bruno Luciani married such a splendid wife. A very astute wife as well.' Even after nearly forty years her laughter held more than a hint of envy. 'Isabel knew how to handle her husband – much to my regret.'

'I don't think I know how to handle mine,' said Angela abruptly.

'And that bothers you?'

'Of course it does!'

The black eyes twinkled. 'I was married to a very dull, overbearing man and yet I enjoyed myself immensely. One learns the art – if you don't take yourself too seriously, my dear. It is a great mistake to take oneself seriously. This husband of yours – has he made you unhappy?'

'It's not just a question of making each other unhappy,' said Angela reluctantly. 'Something's gone very wrong with our marriage, but I'm not sure what it is. Maybe it's me. Maybe I ...' She tugged at a silk tassel, her blue eyes filling with sudden tears. 'I don't even know if I really love Jimmy.'

'Does that matter?'

'Yes, it matters.'

Lucía's small shoulders moved with a graceful shrug. 'People pay too much attention to love. It is not essential in a

216

marriage. I was a very successful wife, but I did not love my husband.' She cocked her head to one side and studied Angela through bright, inquisitive eyes. 'Are you in love with another man?'

An eighteenth-century shepherdess simpered at Bacchus in Arcadia on the opposite wall. Angela stared at the painting for a moment, then turned back to the window.

'No, of course I'm not in love with another man,' she said woodenly.

As if on cue Jimmy rang.

He sounded harassed. Tiburcia had scalded her hand, a burst pipe in the bath had flooded both bedrooms, the new paraffin refrigerator Angela had made him buy was leaking and he didn't have time to fuss with it.

'I never had any trouble with my old icebox. When are you coming home?'

'I'm taking the Friday night train.'

'Hell, Angela – today's only Tuesday! Can't you make it sooner? Why do you have to stay so long with Julia's aunt anyway? You hardly know the old woman.'

'Lucía's been very kind and I'm having a lovely time, Jimmy. Quite different.' She forced a light, careless laugh. 'Wait until you see what I bought at an auction yesterday. A Pancho López wood-carving of gauchos around the fire . . .'

'A *Pancho López?* My God – how much did that cost you? We can't afford to throw money away at auctions! I wish to hell you had consulted me first.'

The wood-carving was a delightful one, full of character and that rugged gaucho charm she found so appealing. It was just right for Los Alamos. On the mantelpiece perhaps – or on the window ledge with the handcarved *maté* gourds she had bought in Laguna Grande. Angela stared at the small porcelain clock on Lucía's desk.

'I thought you would enjoy a Pancho López,' she said after a moment. 'His work's very special.'

Jimmy heard the hurt in her voice and spluttered an exasperated apology. There was a short silence.

'Can't you come back before Friday?' he insisted impatiently. 'I'm up to my neck with spring planting and calving and there's trouble over the canal with Remigio Juárez. You've got to come home and look after the house. Ring up Marcos. He's been in town a few days, but he's returning tomorrow. Ask him to drive you back. He won't mind.'

'No,' said Angela.

'Why not?'

She twisted the telephone cord around her finger. 'I've already bought my train ticket for Friday. You know how difficult it is to get a refund.'

'Marcos can fix that. Damn it, Angela – I need you here!'

'Jimmy, I don't . . .'

'For Christ's sake, stop saying no! *I'll* ring up if it's too much bother for you!' he exploded and slammed down the receiver.

Marcos himself rang back fifteen minutes later. He sounded amused and asked Angela how she was enjoying her stay with Julia's scandalous great-aunt.

'Lucía is a delightful old lady and I'm having a wonderful time,' Angela repeated wearily.

Marcos laughed. 'I'm sure you are. Jimmy seems to think you'll make him go bankrupt if you stay any longer. He asked me to bring you back tomorrow.'

'No, thank you. Lucía's giving a dinner party for me on Thursday night, and I am not going to ask her to cancel it just because Jimmy can't handle a household crisis.'

'Knowing Lucía she would think you a fool if you did,' he drawled. 'I won't be returning to La Catalina before the weekend anyway.' There was a pause. 'I'm driving down early tomorrow morning to a place I've just bought near Parrales. Would you like to come?'

'You've bought another ranch? I thought times were bad.'

'Good land is always a worthwhile investment,' observed Marcos dryly. 'Besides, you've forgotten that I have good political connections these days. I paid a high price for them and I make sure the returns are worth it.' He let a moment go by before repeating the invitation. 'Will you come to Parrales with me tomorrow?'

Angela started to say 'no' and heard herself saying, 'Why not? It's a chance to see more of the country', in a voice that was too bright and brittle around the edges.

Perhaps the champagne was going flat or perhaps, as Lucía Claire had already observed, there was no longer any point in taking herself seriously.

V

Four-fifteen a.m.

Marcos's car sped along deserted city streets, past shuttered houses where people slept and dreamed and took themselves seriously. In one house a light went on behind a high, narrow window; in another a caretaker sloshed water down a flight of stairs and began to scrub the top step with listless, disgruntled strokes. The car circled a roundabout and headed south down a wide avenue flanked by shadowy plane trees. Angela turned up her collar against the cold air coming through the half-open window. Her heart thudded uncomfortably fast with a mixture of excitement and apprehension.

I must be mad! she thought. Totally mad to do something like this!

'I'm glad you decided to come,' remarked Marcos, breaking the silence. 'For a moment I thought your very proper English conscience might disapprove of my invitation.'

Angela smiled faintly. 'It does disapprove.'

'But you came anyway.'

'Against my better judgement. I should be lunching with Jimmy's parents today. Cora was very upset when I told her I couldn't make it.'

They slowed down as a horse-drawn milk cart rattled across an intersection.

'What reason did your English conscience give?'

'Lucía had planned a surprise outing to the gaucho museum at Luján and the arrangements were already made.'

Marcos laughed. 'What did Lucía say to that?'

'It was her idea. She told me to enjoy myself and not to take life so seriously.' The blue eyes met his glance without wavering. 'She said she envied me.'

'Lucía Claire is a very discreet woman.'

'There won't be any need for that kind of discretion,' said Angela firmly.

He touched her cheek with a tender, teasing gesture and did not reply.

Angela's heart gave another apprehensive lurch. There was certainly going to be need for discretion. This kind of madness could only have one outcome: moralists called it adultery. One of the ten commandments. Nice people didn't break it. What kind of a mess was she getting herself into? She should never have come . . . No, that was a lie. She might feel guilty, she might see herself poised on the brink of disaster – but underneath guilt and apprehension seethed an exhilarating current of elation.

The suburbs dwindled to villages, the villages gave way to isolated hamlets strung along the back of an endless, rolling plain. Dawn inched over the horizon, streaking night with pearl and rose and pale, luminous green. Trees and cattle floated like ghostly islands in a sea of mist, the land huddled in pockets of grey and brown and dun. In the distance the paling sky frosted the shadows with silver.

'How beautiful everything is,' said Angela softly. 'Like a fairy world – one of those enchanted lands at the bottom of a hidden lake.'

Marcos handed her a cigarette. 'This is very different country to La Catalina. Low land, fertile soil and good rainfall. Los Toros is not too far away. I was down there last week; if I had known you were in town I would have asked you to come with me.'

'Is there any news of Carlos?'

'A letter smuggled through by a pilot friend of Freddy's. Would you have driven down to Los Toros with me?'

'No.'

'Why not?'

'Are you always so curious at this time of the morning?'

Marcos grinned. 'I'm many things at this time of the morning. Your English conscience would probably disapprove of them all.'

'Very likely,' agreed Angela, but the laughter in her voice robbed disapproval of its sting.

They stopped for breakfast at a sleepy roadside café and talked about Marcos's new ranch.

'It belonged to a car dealer from Buenos Aires,' he explained. 'One of our "new rich" who play at being landowners. This fellow never came down more than three or four times a year and then only to hunt partridges. His manager cheated him blind and ran off with his wife. Not very pleasant for the car dealer, but lucky

for me. I bought El Remanso for far less than its real value.'
Marcos stirred his coffee thoughtfully. 'When Miguel finishes
school I may bring him down here to work. He has to learn how
to be a *peón* before he can sit in the *patrón*'s saddle.'

'Did you?'

'Oh, yes. My father sent me to live at different *puestos* on
La Catalina every holiday from the time I was ten. No favours,
no privileges, no taking into account who I was. I lived with the
puesteros' families and learned about the *campo* from them. It
was a good experience.'

Angela bit hungrily into a croissant. 'I wouldn't have thought
a wealthy man like your father found such a practical upbringing
necessary.'

'My father went out of his way to be practical where I
was concerned,' replied Marcos dryly. 'When I turned fifteen he
allowed me to eat and sleep at the big house with the family, but
I still had to be up before dawn and to go out to work with the
men.' He frowned at the cigarette between his fingers. 'My father
kept me on a tight rein and wasted little time on affection.'

Cups clattered behind the counter as the café's stout owner
set down a tray. Two men wrapped in ponchos sat by a window
hunched over coffee and the inevitable *caña*; a truck driver
dunked huge chunks of bread into his cup; the café owner's wife
scolded shrilly in the kitchen. Her voice rose and fell against the
background of guitars strumming the opening bars of a lively
chacarera dance on the radio.

'What if Miguel doesn't want to be a rancher?' asked Angela.
'He may choose to study something else.'

Marcos shook his head. 'He must carry on with the
family business. It's his responsibility as my eldest son.'
He hesitated. 'I'm worried about Miguel, you know. We've
had several serious talks this past year about La Catalina.
I've tried to make him understand how important the ranch
is for our family – but he still doesn't seem to realize
it.'

'Maybe you're trying too hard. After all, the boy's only
fifteen.'

Marcos fiddled restlessly with a sugar wrapper. He had not
spoken to anyone of his fears about Miguel – not even to Pedro,
who was the boy's godfather. To acknowledge a flaw in his son
would be to acknowledge a certain degree of failure in himself.

221

It was a difficult admission for a proud man like Marcos Luciani to make. All his life he had kept his weaknesses closely locked in his heart; he found himself strangely anxious now to confide them to Angela.

'Miguel's old enough to know what I mean,' he said. 'It's not that.' He studied the traffic outside the window for a moment and then added slowly, 'Sometimes I'm afraid he will turn out like Lucas.'

Angela smiled. 'I doubt it very much. You're much too good a father for that to happen.'

'Is that the answer? I don't know, *gringuita*. My father was a good father. He did what he thought was best for his sons. I don't think I really loved him, but I'm grateful for everything he taught me.'

'You once said he had spoiled Lucas . . .'

'And the logical conclusion must be that Lucas is a mess because of it? Maybe. I tell myself that's the reason because I don't know the real answer. I certainly don't spoil Miguel – but I'm still afraid.' He made a sudden grimace of distaste. 'God only knows what Eduardo will turn out like. Gladys spoils him rotten.'

'At least she has Eduardo!' burst out Angela with a bitterness that startled him. She saw his surprise and bit her lip. 'I'm sorry, that was rude of me. It's just that sometimes . . . thinking about children . . .' Her voice quavered. 'You must think I'm very silly.'

'No,' replied Marcos quietly. 'I think you are a very special woman.'

I'm going to cry, thought Angela. Oh, God – I'm going to be stupid and break down in the middle of the café. She groped blindly for her handkerchief. Lucía Claire's extravagant cure had not worked. She was still unhappy and desperately weary of keeping that unhappiness bottled up because she could entrust it to no one. It spilled over now in a torrent of frustration and grievances.

'You don't know what it's like, lying in a hospital bed and thinking "I'll never be able to have children again." All my dreams – if the baby had been a girl I was going to call her Caroline. That was my mother's name.' Angela tried to smile. 'If it was boy I wanted to call him Bruce. Bruce Morgan . . . I've always wanted to call my son Bruce.'

'Don't, *gringuita*, said Marcos. 'Don't hurt yourself like that. Please.'

'It doesn't hurt any more,' she answered unsteadily. 'Not really. It's just that – I won't ever have any children, you see. Never. I'll never have children of my own to l-love and care for and worry about. No one to plan f-for . . .' Her voice broke. 'Oh, God! How silly . . . I'm sorry, Marcos . . .'

He took hold of her hands without saying a word; after a moment Angela drew away and dabbed at her eyes with her handkerchief.

'It's the small things that get me,' she said. 'Did you know Jimmy's brother Nigel already has his second child? They've only been married three years. Cora keeps writing about how pleased everyone is.'

'Cora Morgan is an ass.'

'It's not just Cora. Even Tiburcia says things. Not to me, but I heard her telling Dominga that I can't have children because the old Russian cursed Los Alamos . . .'

'Tiburcia's an ignorant old fool,' interrupted Marcos harshly. 'You know better than to listen to her.'

'Do I? Maybe it's true. Things like curses work that way.'

He grasped her hands again and held them tightly. '*No digas pavadas*! Stop talking nonsense.'

'If you must know the truth,' Angela rushed on in a thin, brittle voice, 'things haven't been too good between Jimmy and me lately. If only I could have children . . . I know he wanted a son . . .' She broke off at the sight of Marcos's expression. 'What is it? Why are you looking like that?'

'Has Jimmy ever blamed you for not having children?'

The question was curiously flat. Angela stared; after a moment she gave a little shrug. 'Why should he? It was an accident. I – slipped.' Their quarrel was the only secret she and Jimmy shared. She would never betray it – especially not to Marcos.

He pressed her hands, smoothing his thumbs over the soft skin with a gentle, caressing motion. 'Why did you come with me today, Angela?'

'Because Lucía asked me a question and I lied.'

'May I know the question?' When she did not answer he raised her hands and kissed them before letting go. 'After lunch I'll ring Lucía and tell her we're returning tomorrow.'

'Marcos . . .'

'If you were my wife, having children would not matter,' he said and went to pay the bill.

VI

They turned off the main road and headed southwest along a narrow secondary road congested with local traffic. A straggling line of eucalyptus trees bordered the right-hand side; beyond them the ground rolled in gentle grassy swells towards the horizon. Cattle and grass, grass and sky, sky and cattle. The poetry of the landscape never varied, but its rhythm was no longer foreign to Angela's heart.

At seven o'clock Marcos turned on the radio. 'There's pen and paper in the glove compartment,' he said. 'Write down the stockyard prices for me please, *gringuita*.'

They might have been following the same familiar routine together for the past twenty years.

If a few hours ago Angela had thought *I must be mad*, that madness now seemed as natural and necessary as Marcos's presence beside her. She could not tell exactly when the complete transformation had taken place, but pinpointing time no longer mattered. Like guilt it belonged to another world – a remote existence inhabited by shadowy people whose lives and fates were totally alien to the sun-dappled quiet of El Remanso, where time and the universe stood still.

A white gate marked the entrance off the road; a wide dirt track snaked between grey-green tamarisk bushes for a quarter of a mile or so, then passed through another gate and came to an end before a square pink stucco house set among *paraíso* trees and tall, feathery pines. A miniature grass jungle tangled cheerfully with nettles and thistles, the iron bars protecting the windows were white with pigeon droppings, a few plump chickens pecked industriously on a bare patch of ground near the drive. The heavy green door creaked as Marcos pushed it open; inside the house smelled of wood smoke and musty leather.

It was not a large house – a main room with a good-sized fireplace, a bedroom facing east, a bathroom dwarfed by a battered tin tub, and a kitchen which for some unknown reason had been painted a depressing shade of pale blue.

Shabby furniture, doubtful plumbing, lizards scurrying through cracks in the floorboards – nothing could have been more unlike the efficient comfort of La Catalina, yet shabbiness and neglect were very much a part of El Remanso's charm. When Angela threw back the bedroom shutters a flood of September sunshine streamed through the open window, bringing a fragrant hint of resin and the sleepy murmur of invisible doves. She drew a deep breath and lifted her face to the sun.

'What does El Remanso mean?'

'I love you very much,' said Marcos. 'Do you know that, *gringuita*?' He braced his arm across the window and smiled down at her. 'When we finish work today I am going to show you just how much I love you.'

Angela laughed. 'That's not what El Remanso means.'

'No?'

He bent his head; her lips opened eagerly, full and yielding to his hunger. His hands slid under her jacket and caressed the firm, full outline of her breasts. His fingers found the buttons of her blouse, undid them, eased into her bra. Their tongues danced back and forth in the moist cavern of their mouths.

'To hell with work,' murmured Marcos and closed the shutters. 'I want to show you now.'

They undressed and stood gazing at each other for a long moment, enraptured by the sight of their naked bodies. Marcos reached out and caressed Angela's breasts very gently; his fingers traced a network of veins faintly visible under the pale skin, then slid down to stroke the soft, feminine contours of her belly.

'I never imagined you were so beautiful,' he said in a low, wondering voice and held out his arms.

She moved towards him as though gliding through a dream. The arms that held her were strong and secure; the body she clasped in her own arms was warm and alive with love. They kissed again, pressing their nakedness against each other with tense, breathless excitement. Their hands explored eagerly, charting out the physical landmarks of love on which to feed memory; their voices sighed together in an urgent conspiracy of desire.

'I have so much love for you,' whispered Marcos. 'So much to give you . . . Angela . . .'

Her breathing came faster now. She fondled his penis with uninhibited eagerness, guiding it towards the warm flesh between her legs. 'Love me like this . . . quickly . . . hurry . . .'

'*Gringa bruja*,' he murmured and carried her over to the bed.

They lay in the hollow of the mattress and devoured each other greedily with their mouths; they engulfed each other with their arms and legs. His fingers stroked her cleft, his tongue darted over its golden nest. Exquisite softness. *Let me kiss it, eat it, your sweet fruit, let me love you.* She straddled his rigid flesh; her thumbs and forefingers formed a ring around the thick stem rising from a dark, curling mat of hair. He lay on his back, his eyes half closed, and smiled at her game.

'You're sealed inside me forever,' she smiled in return.

'I'm sealed inside you forever. Oh, God – I love you so much!'

Their bodies danced in frenzy. They were gods enclosed in magical madness, they were heat and sound and rhythm of love. They heaved, thrust, rode each other, pounded like waves higher and higher, soaring to burst, to shatter, to die with me, die in me, pour streams of love, flood me with sweetness. They cried out together, *love me, love me, oh my God love me* – then sank, depleted, into silence.

'I hate to withdraw from you,' whispered Marcos after a moment. He raised himself slightly and pushed back a damp strand from Angela's brow. 'I want to stay like this always. I want to be part of you forever.'

She reached up to caress his cheek; her eyes brimmed with tenderness. 'I love you,' she said softly in English. 'My dearest heart. My one, my only love.'

He kissed her very gently, then lay down again with his head cradled against her shoulder. They were immensely happy. They closed their eyes and slept.

VII

Angela woke briefly to the sound of water drumming against the old tin tub in the bathroom; when she next opened her eyes it was to see Marcos, a towel around his waist, holding out a cup of coffee. He grinned at her.

'It's after ten, señora. I should have been out in the fields a couple of hours ago.' He sat down beside her and tousled her hair. 'You're a witch, you know. A few more sessions like that one and there won't be anything left of me.'

She smiled sleepily. 'Mmmm.'

'I must get going. Do you want to stay here?'

'Of course not!' She took the coffee and drank it slowly, savouring the languid, dreamlike aftermath of love. It had never been like this with Harry Redfield. It was certainly not like this with Jimmy. So deeply intimate and complete. She had given herself with such passion and abandon; she had never known there could be such fulfilment of body, mind and heart in the physical expression of love. She watched Marcos dress; even the simple act of strapping on his watch belonged to their intimacy now. He leaned over and kissed her.

'There's enough hot water for a shower,' he said. 'Don't bang your head on the pipe. I'll meet you out by the car in ten minutes.'

Love and the morning were bound up forever in the sunlit madness.

VIII

The second part of the morning was spent inspecting the herds and checking repairs on the cattle pens with El Remanso's new foreman. The man – extravagantly named Washington Chávez – was anxious to show the *patrón* some damaged fences. Angela trudged behind the two men and watched a pair of *teros* circling overhead. A tractor moved in precise rows across a distant field; she shaded her eyes against the sun and watched the tractor swing slowly around to start its return journey. The chugging of its engine reached her as a steady, companionable echo to the poetry of grass and sky.

How unbelievably happy I am, thought Angela, and was astonished to think that only yesterday she had been so distressed about things which had no place in her new world.

Washington Chávez turned out to be a friendly, talkative little man. His father Elpidio had been one of the district's most famous horsetamers, and on the way back to the house in the car he kept up a running patter on that remarkable gaucho's exploits.

'There weren't a *domador* in the province to match him, Don Marcos,' he boasted. 'Don Alfredo Castro's father bet fifty pesos Elpidio couldn't break in a brute called Comanchero. Said he'd come unstuck after two seconds. Ha! My old man rode that horse until it dropped. Sixty-two he was then, and Comanchero couldn't throw him!'

'What about yourself? Did you learn anything from Elpidio or did the old man keep it all to himself?'

Washington Chávez guffawed, displaying two rows of crooked, blackened teeth. 'Seventy he was and on to his fourth wife when I came along, *patrón*. Tied me to the saddle when I was a year old and made me ride all the way from Parrales to Horneros. That's seven leagues, that is.'

'Twenty-one miles?' exclaimed Angela. 'And you were only a year old?'

'Ain't done me no harm, senõra. Reared us rough, my father did, but he never lost a son and there ain't one of us who's ever shamed him. What I don't know about horses you can write on a pinhead.'

Marcos grinned. 'No wonder Alfredo Castro didn't want you to come to El Remanso. The windmill you see beyond those trees is Castro's ranch La María Fernanda,' he remarked to Angela in English. 'Alfredo is a very dull man with an ugly wife and a son named Elías. The son is as dull as the father, which is a pity. La María Fernanda is a valuable piece of land. Chávez was a *puestero* there until I offered him work on El Remanso.'

'And Castro didn't like that?'

'He's too tight-fisted to make a counter-offer. We have little to do with each other fortunately.' Marcos darted a cautious glance at Chávez through the rear-view mirror and took hold of Angela's hand. 'Are you happy?'

'Very happy.'

'Then nothing else matters,' he said and began to whistle the *charcarera* tune they had heard that morning.

IX

During the night they woke to the sound of rain pattering through the trees outside the window.

'Nice,' murmured Angela drowsily. 'I don't want this to end.'

Marcos's voice echoed through the shadows. 'It won't end. I love you, *gringuita* – or have you forgotten already?'

'No.' She closed her eyes for a moment, listening to the rain and the beating of his heart. 'I don't want to go back. I want to stay like this forever. Just the two of us.' Her voice rasped suddenly. 'Oh, God! Why couldn't we have met before?'

He rolled over and reached for a cigarette, lighting it slowly and deliberately to make room for his thoughts. The rain drummed heavily now, driven by angry gusts of wind. Marcos watched the tip of his cigarette glowing in the darkness; when it was nearly finished he asked, 'Are you thinking about Jimmy?'

'Did you expect me not to?'

'Of course you think about him. So do I. Jimmy is my friend and I am in love with his wife. I've been thinking about it for the past two years.'

There was a long silence.

Marcos slid back under the covers and took Angela in his arms. 'Listen to me,' he said anxiously. 'You are married to Jimmy, I have a wife and family. These are facts of life. I told you once before they have nothing to do with love.' He held her against him; his lips brushed her forehead. 'You are the woman I love. I want you with me always, Angela . . . my heart . . . my life . . . I need you . . .'

'My love,' she whispered. 'I'm here,' and drew his face down towards her.

He entered her very tenderly, as though their love were a new and wonderful discovery. As though every kiss, every caress, every promise they murmured formed a miracle of love that must be prolonged beyond tonight into endless time.

CHAPTER NINETEEN

I

At the end of 1954 Gaspari senior died suddenly in his sleep.

His death barely dented Gladys's life, totally absorbed now by Eduardo and the domestic battles with her sister-in-law. Events at Verdulería Nápoli were inconveniences to be tolerated for duty's sake, but little else. She put in an appearance at the funeral with Claudia, informed Juan there was no question of their mother coming to live with her, and fled thankfully back to the fragrant sanctuary of Barranco Rosales. Celestina shuffled over to the stove and turned on the gas under the kettle.

'Your sister could have left Claudia with me,' she commented. 'The girl wanted to stay. Cried her heart out for her grandfather, she did. Gladys has no right taking Claudia away when she wanted to stay and keep me company.'

Gaspari flicked a speck of dust from his sleeve. 'They're off to La Catalina tomorrow for the holidays. Are you selling this place?'

'Selling?' Cups and saucers clattered noisily on the table. 'Why should I sell? This is my home and I'm not about to leave it.'

'You can't handle the work alone.'

'Seems to me a decent son would give his widowed mother a hand,' countered Celestina tartly. 'Seems to me that's what a son and a daughter should do. Help their parents and know their place in the world, not gallivant after crooked politicians or a rich man's money.'

Gaspari flushed. 'I'm busy these days!'

'Seems only yesterday I was holding Claudia in my arms,' continued his mother, ignoring the interruption. 'How old is she now? Thirteen? The girl looks liverish. They don't feed her properly.' She set the coffee pot down on the table with a thud, her eyes brimming with tears. 'It wouldn't have harmed to let her stay with me a few days!'

Claudia knew there was no point in saying she wanted to stay with her grandmother. Family routine had already been disrupted by the funeral, and Gladys had no intention of providing extra ammunition for anyone's guns. She bundled her daughter unceremoniously on to the train, double-checked their luggage to make sure nothing had been forgotten, and sent Rosita off to find a bottle of mineral water.

'The waiter should have put one in our compartment,' she complained, fanning herself energetically. 'The railway knew we were travelling today. It's all Mercedes's fault, of course.'

'But they left three days ago,' pointed out Claudia, uncertain of her parent's logic.

Gladys glared. 'Don't contradict me! Stop biting your nails and sit up straight. Don't sulk. You're always sulking – why can't you look nice, like Isabel or Cristina?'

'Because I'm me.'

'Don't be so stupid!' snapped Gladys and began to fuss over Eduardo.

II

No one paid much attention to Claudia at La Catalina. She was afraid of hunting, she didn't like to ride, she was slow to understand jokes. The adults forgot about her, the children pretended she wasn't there. Claudia shrugged it all off with a wistful smile and wandered around in her own little world; after a while she no longer noticed she was alone.

Down by the lake she had discovered a tangled *chañar* thicket; no one could see her once she was safely curled up between the twisted roots and she could daydream or read to her heart's content. On this particular afternoon in late February she brought with her a well-thumbed copy of *Corazón Feliz*, a popular confession magazine cadged from Rosita in exchange for not telling she had seen the maid trying on her mother's new mink coat. Favour for favour, because both Gladys and Mercedes had strictly forbidden the girls to read *Corazón Feliz* – the first time they ever saw eye to eye on anything in the Luciani household.

As old Pampa ambled down the slope leading to the shore Claudia suddenly hauled on the reins. Two horses stood tethered under a carob tree. She recognized her stepfather's tall, ugly bay and a grey mare her mother sometimes rode. Her lower lip trembled anxiously.

'They'll spoil everything!'

She looked around, but there was no one in sight. Perhaps they had gone for a walk; if she hid in the thicket they wouldn't find her. Old Pampa was no more than half a dozen yards from the *chañar* when Claudia heard her step-father's voice.

'Why do I love you so much?'

She turned brick-red and froze. The voice echoed from inside the thicket. A woman laughed softly and murmured something, but it did not sound like her mother. There was a brief silence before Marcos spoke again.

'You're a witch, *gringuita*. You make me feel like a twenty-year-old.' Another, somewhat breathless silence. 'I'm crazy about you, Angela. Do you know that?'

She laughed. 'I should. You've been saying it for over a year. Seventeen months and twenty-three days, to be exact.'

'I wish I could say it more often. I'll be free Wednesday afternoon. Can you meet me?'

'I should go to the convent.'

'To hell with the convent. I want to see you.'

There was a sound of scuffling in the thicket and then Angela protested, still laughing, 'Marcos, behave yourself!'

'You have beautiful breasts, *gringa bruja*. I want to kiss them . . .'

More laughter. The underbush crackled and someone sighed. Claudia swallowed. She wanted to run away, but her legs refused to budge. Her heart began to thud. An invisible army of ants seemed to have taken possession of her body, raising prickly little ripples under the skin. She held her breath and strained to listen. The noise in the underbrush was louder now. Sighs and rustlings and the voice that was Angela whispering, 'Marcos, Marcos,' over and over until suddenly the whispers ended in a long shuddering gasp. Claudia clenched her fists; her hands were clammy. Another, deeper gasp this time – and then silence. After what felt like forever she heard her stepfather say in a voice that did not sound at all like his own, 'Even after I finish, I want to go on making love to you. I've never felt that with any other woman . . . Angela . . .'

'We better return to the house and pretend to be respectable,' she replied unsteadily. 'It won't do to have Gladys start wondering about this afternoon ride you so gallantly offered to escort me on.'

'Damn your English conscience!'

'Damn you, my love, for making me forget it!'

Claudia turned and fled.

The incident puzzled her for the rest of the day because it formed part of something vague and disturbing which she did not understand. Angela had come over for lunch and Jimmy would arrive in the evening. They were staying for supper. There was nothing strange about that, it happened often. On the other hand Marcos Luciani was a very busy man. Why would he take Angela riding in the middle of the afternoon when he always had so much to do? He never went riding with Mama. What had they been doing in the thicket – and what was an English conscience?

'I don't know what it is,' retorted Isabel when asked. 'Where'd you hear about that?'

Claudia looked uncomfortable. 'Oh, I just did. Forget it.'

Isabel was curious. An 'English conscience' sounded very intriguing and far too important for Claudia to have invented. She waited until supper and then dropped the question during a lull in the conversation. Her father choked on his wine. Angela dropped her napkin. Everyone else looked blank. Mercedes leaned forward with a puzzled smile.

'What did you say, dear?'

'An English conscience,' repeated Isabel, enunciating clearly. 'Claudia wants to know.'

'Sounds like something my wife would have,' joked Jimmy loudly. 'Prim and starched and locked in mothballs – eh, angel?'

She gave him a cool smile. 'Quite.'

'Porky's crazy,' volunteered Miguel, helping himself to salad. 'There's no such thing.'

Claudia's cheeks flamed. 'There is too! I heard it. I was down by the lake and I heard hi . . . someone say an English conscience!' She darted a frightened, half-reproachful glance at her stepfather. 'I did!'

'You're imagining things,' he said dryly.

Miguel whirled his forefinger around his right temple and Yvonne giggled. Gladys glared impatiently at her daughter.

'Why did you go down to the lake?' she demanded. 'What were you doing down there? Reading? What were you reading?'

'*Corazón Feliz*,' suggested Isabel maliciously. 'She reads them by the dozen.'

'I don't!' cried Claudia, her eyes filling with tears.

'Yes, you do,' said Cristina. 'You hide them under your bed. I'll bet "English conscience" is the name of a story. She acts them out,' grinning at Gladys. 'We've heard her. She makes believe at night, just like in the movies.'

'*Amor mío*, why do I love you so much?' emoted Isabel and Yvonne in raucous unison.

'That's enough!' rasped Marcos as Miguel and Jimmy burst out laughing. He did not dare look at Angela. 'Ring for the maid, Mercedes.'

'Elías Castro's cousin is a naval pilot,' said Gastón quickly as Claudia began to snivel. 'He thinks there'll be a revolution this year.'

'*Quiera Dios*!' breathed Teresa fiercely. 'God rid us of the Peronist filth!'

She glared at Gladys, who returned the glare with a patient little smile while Marcos began to discuss the prospects of a military uprising as though the fate of mankind depended on the outcome.

Angela made a good pretence of appearing unconcerned, but inside she felt sick with apprehension. 'Out of the mouth of babes' – wasn't that how the saying went? Love in the *chañar* thicket had been a delightful interlude of erotic mischief – until innocent, bumbling Claudia came along. How much did that silly child overhear? she wondered uneasily. I can't look at her. It was such a wonderful afternoon. Why did she have to spoil it? I wish Jimmy would stop grinning at me. I can't face making love with him tonight . . . Angela gave an involuntary shudder. That was the difficult part of a love affair: faking enthusiasm with one's husband. Keeping identities straight was another pitfall. Once she had almost called Jimmy 'Marcos' by mistake. She still turned cold every time she thought about it, but when she had told Marcos he laughed.

'It's not funny!' Angela protested.

'It would be even less funny if you called me Jimmy,' he had replied, kissing her. 'Then you really would be in trouble, *gringuita*.'

The secret of a successful love affair was to relax and enjoy it, Angela reminded herself. With every passing day she and Marcos were becoming more attached to one another. They suited each other perfectly as lovers, they understood and respected each other as friends. Their relationship was a complete unity of body, heart and mind. There was no need to panic.

III

By 1955 opposition to Perón had hardened and the military were uneasily considering how to go about saving their own skins. Not surprisingly, the Church was also running out of patience. Divorce and prostitution were bad enough; Perón's proposals to end religious influence in public education, his threat to separate Church and state, his call for taxation of Church property were the three straws that broke the camel's back.

In Buenos Aires outrage over Perón's proposed reforms exploded in a mass meeting that would have been unthinkable a few years earlier. One hundred thousand Catholics gathered in front of the Casa Rosada and marched through the city to the national congress building, where a number of zealous young men had dared raise the Vatican flag.

Revolt was not far off.

On 16 June 1955, naval planes flew over Buenos Aires and bombed a number of buildings – including Perón's secret love-nest in the wealthy Barrio Norte. Perón's immediate reaction was to summon his *descamisados* for a mass rally in the Plaza de Mayo. They streamed into the city from the suburbs on lorries, buses, vans, private cars – anything they could lay their hands on. The roar of 'Pe-rón! Pe-rón!' thundered through the streets. To the women and children praying in the drawing-room at Barranco Rosales the echoes of the mob sounded as terrifying as the baying of the hounds of Hell.

Jesus, our refuge . . .

A truck full of shouting men rumbled past the gates. Gladys swallowed and clutched Eduardo to her breast. She didn't care what happened as long as they were left alone. Juan had laughed off talk of a revolution when she asked him, but this time Juan was wrong. Her voice shook as she echoed the endless litany.

Jesus, spare us . . .

Teresa clenched her hands until the knuckles whitened. If the revolution succeeded Carlos would be able to return. He was very optimistic; his latest letter had been full of encouragement and projects for the future. Tomorrow or the next day or the day after . . . She closed her eyes and sobbed her own, desperate prayer.

'Someone's coming,' whispered Yvonne suddenly. 'I hear voices.'

Everyone turned towards the door of the drawing-room, their faces white with anxiety.

'Children, stay here!' ordered Mercedes. 'Isabel!'

'It's Papa!' She leapt to her feet and raced for the stairs, scattering rosaries and cushions. They heard her shouting excitedly, 'Is it over? Have we won? Is Perón dead?'

'No such luck, *ñatita*,' Marcos came into the drawing-room, followed by the priestly Pedro looking strangely out of place in civilian clothes. 'The army and the air force had second thoughts at the last minute and left the navy in the lurch. The pilots fled to Uruguay. It's all over and Perón's howling for blood.'

'Lord, have mercy on us!' gasped Mercedes, crossing herself.

Teresa stared at the two men, her eyes large and black in a face the colour of clay. 'Do you mean there's no hope?'

'There's always hope,' murmured Pedro.

'Don't lie to me!' she screamed. 'Everything will go on like this for years! I want my husband back! Don't you understand that? I want Carlos back and I can't have him because of that filthy swine! You're glad, aren't you?' whirling on Gladys. 'You've been praying for that son of a bitch . . .'

'That's enough,' Marcos rapped out sharply as Gladys burst into indignant protests.

Teresa rounded on him, eyes blazing. 'It's all your fault! You married her because you don't care for anything but your damned ranch! Our feelings, our family, our position – they don't count, do they? You married that stupid Peronist tramp because it was the cheapest way to get protection!'

Gladys turned white.

'If it hadn't been for that protection,' roared Marcos, 'Carlos would still be rotting in jail!'

'And I'm supposed to be grateful!'

'God damn it, you stupid woman – yes!'

'Marcos, calm down!' cried Pedro.

'Oh, God!' shrieked Teresa. 'I want my husband!'

'Children,' said Mercedes firmly, 'go and wash your hands for tea.'

'Isn't Papa ever coming back?' quavered Yvonne, staring at her mother with wide, frightened eyes.

'Of course he's coming back.' Mercedes hustled them towards the stairs. 'Claudia, bring your brother – no Isabel, you cannot stay with your father . . .' The voices faded down the stairwell and then there was silence.

Teresa collapsed on to the nearest chair and buried her face in her hands.

Pedro cleared his throat. 'The country's in for some very rough times and we must all keep calm.' He patted his grey suit and managed a wry smile for the women. 'Even priests must take precautions these days.'

Gladys turned her back on Teresa and walked over to the gilt-edged mirror hanging above a rosewood table near the door. No one spoke.

'I was on my way to a meeting downtown this morning when the trouble started,' continued Pedro, determined to fill the silence. 'The planes started strafing and bombing, no one knew what was happening, people ran for cover . . . I think I recited every prayer I know and then some. Worst of all was the sound of the *descamisados* chanting as they drove down the streets.' He smiled faintly. 'I reached San Gregorio school just as Marcos drove up to fetch the boys. I don't think I've ever been so happy to see anyone on my life!'

Teresa raised a drawn, tear-streaked face. 'I can't go on like this. Waiting and waiting . . .' She pushed herself wearily to her feet. 'Where's Gastón?'

'I took the boys to your flat,' replied Marcos shortly. 'It's better to have someone from the family there tonight instead of just the servants. Don't worry,' as she started to speak, 'they'll be all right. I told them to stay in the flat and not to open to anyone until I return in the morning.'

'You think of everything, don't you?' she said bitterly and left the room.

Gladys gave a small, deprecating laugh and studied her image in the mirror. 'Poor Teresa's in a terrible state, isn't she?'

'We must be patient and try to understand,' replied Pedro mildly. 'Things are not easy for her.'

'Oh, but I do understand. She's like that all the time.' A bright red fingertip traced the arch of a carefully plucked eyebrow. 'The things she says are quite ridiculous – aren't they, Marcos?'

'Yes.'

Gladys studied his reflection for a long, searching minute and then smiled a possessive little smile. She took hold of his arm, her crown of ash-blonde curls barely reaching his shoulder. Husband and wife. A handsome, wealthy couple. The smile deepened.

'Poor Teresa,' she said lightly. 'Let's go and have tea with the children, *querido*.'

IV

Carlos and Teresa owned a large flat in the fashionable Recoleta district. From the study window Miguel could see across the rooftops towards the centre of town. He had been standing there for some time, listening to the crowds prowling the streets ten floors below. They didn't seem to be doing much more than prowl and chant unintelligible slogans. Miguel jingled a handful of coins in his trouser pocket. He was bored.

He cast a disgruntled glance at his cousin. Gastón was a pain in the ass. Always taking his responsibilities so damned seriously. Always playing safe. No taste for adventure. He's only eighteen, reflected Miguel morosely. Only one year older than me. You'd think he was my great-grandfather.

The coins in his pocket made an impatient, jangling sound.

Take tonight, for instance. They could be down in the streets where all the action was instead of twiddling their thumbs in the flat. It wasn't the political goings-on that mattered – it was the excitement of being where there was movement and activity and turmoil. He wanted to feel the thrill of danger, perhaps even experience fear. Anything was better than stagnating between panelled walls and velvet curtains. Miguel wrinkled his nose.

The study smelled of tobacco and brandy and polished leather: expensive, luxurious smells. Rich man's mould, he thought sarcastically and was startled by the harshness of his comparison.

He turned away from the window. 'Nothing's happening outside. There won't be any trouble.'

'You heard the bastard on the radio,' growled Gastón from the depths of an armchair. 'He ranted on long enough about stringing us up with baling wire.'

'Five of us for each one of them – I heard him, all right. Think they'll go after us like he said?'

'I hope not.'

'Why not? We'd give the sons of bitches a good fight. At least there'd be some excitement.'

Gastón buried himself in his magazine. He wasn't interested in that kind of excitement.

Miguel sauntered across to a graceful mahogany bar and inspected his uncle's selection of drinks. 'Black market whisky, eh? My old man keeps ours locked up.' He chose the most expensive brand, poured himself a generous measure, dropped in a few ice cubes and took a long, appreciative sip. 'That's the stuff!'

Gastón turned a page. Down in the street a police siren whined past and faded into the distance. Miguel rattled the ice cubes in his glass and stared glumly at the Impressionist landscape above the bar.

Life was boring.

'Let's go down for a look around,' he said.

'We're not supposed to leave the flat.'

'Just a few minutes.' When there was no reply, 'You're scared!'

Gastón's lean face darkened with an exasperated scowl. At the moment he was more interested in an article on cattle breeding than in what went on outside in the streets. Damn Miguel anyway. He never sat still, never took time to read or learn. The family ranches were their concern, their heritage – but he just didn't seem to care.

'Uncle Marcos told us to stay here,' said Gastón. 'We're responsible for this place tonight.'

'My old man's soft in the head. He thinks I still wear nappies.' Miguel drained his drink and strolled back to the window. 'Hey! Something's going on!'

The downtown skyline glowed a deep, angry red; as the two boys watched in astonishment a column of dark, billowing clouds rose above the distant rooftops. Gastón opened the window and sniffed the air.

'Smoke,' he announced uneasily. 'There must be a big fire somewhere.'

'Come on, let's go see!'

Gastón hesitated, then shook his head. 'No. We're supposed to stay here. The crowd are starting up again – listen!'

'Don't be such a goddamned *maricón*!' cried Miguel and raced for the front door.

V

Tension crackled in the streets.

There were few people about, but as Miguel headed down Callao towards Avenida Santa Fé he saw several groups of men hanging around on the corners; further on men and women chanted ominously about baling wire and lamp-posts. Near the police station a large crowd had spilled into the street and was dancing around a bonfire. Miguel paused under a tree to watch. Most of the dancers were men; some of them dressed in cassocks. A fat, bald-headed man brandished a missal and pretended to chant in Latin. The crowd jeered; a woman snatched the missal away and hurled it into the fire. The man laughed and began to dance with her, shouting obscenities at the top of his voice.

'Holy Jesus, have mercy on us!'

Miguel turned sharply. A girl stood in the shadow of the doorway, staring at the crowd around the fire. Her face was wet with tears. She glanced at him and clutched a small golden crucifix around her neck.

'They don't know what they're doing!' she whispered. 'They can't know what they're doing!'

'They're burning cassocks,' he said, glancing back at the crowd.

'For the love of God, *why*?'

Miguel shrugged. 'They're Peronists.'

'When they were children they must have been taught to love God!' cried the girl as a roar of laughter went up from the crowd prancing around the fire. 'To honour the Church! They must fear Hell!' Tears rolled unchecked down her cheeks. 'Are you Catholic?'

'Of course I am!'

'Did you know they're looting churches all through the city? My sister's a nun. They attacked her when she was coming home a few hours ago. The police thought it a big joke.' She drew a low, gasping sob. 'It must be like this in Hell! Did you know they've set fire to the cathedral? They're burning the Vatican flag and the crucifixes and the saints . . . *Why?*'

He left her then, still transfixed by the crowd. The burning cathedral must have been the smoke they saw from the window. Miguel gave the fire dancers a wide berth and continued along the wide, tree-lined avenue with its elegant blocks of flats and shops. He had never given the *why* of anything much thought – except for why did he have to be a rancher when he wanted to do something else? Just what else didn't matter – as long as it wasn't what his father wanted him to do.

Further along he came to a small church tucked between two old buildings. There were more people here. Men and women were crammed into the small forecourt of the church, waving torches and chanting the same senseless slogans he had been hearing for the past half hour. Miguel eyed them uneasily. Perhaps it was time to return to the flat. He started to move away when two men ran out of the church carrying a large stucco statue of the Virgin Mary. An elderly priest, his cassock kilted around his waist, chased after them.

'Stop, thieves! Come back here!'

The crowd howled with laughter. The two men raised the statue triumphantly aloft, yelled 'Viva Perón!' and hurled it to the ground. Someone tripped the priest. He pitched headlong down the steps and landed face down among the broken fragments of the Virgin's robes. The crowd roared in approval and began to advance, waving torches.

'Leave him alone!' yelled Miguel. 'Can't you see he's an old man?'

He pushed into the yard and tried to drag the priest away. A hand grabbed his jacket. He fought back, kicking and struggling as the crowd jeered. Someone struck him across the mouth; he cursed with rage, slipped on a piece of stucco and went down.

241

The crowd picked Miguel up and tossed him impatiently over its shoulder without a backward glance.

VI

Lucas Luciani was on his way to a poker game.

He had just turned down Callao looking for a taxi when there was a commotion in the middle of the block and a young man landed in the gutter. Lucas was totally impervious to the political situation. He sidestepped the gutter, walked on half a dozen steps, wheeled and stared down at his dishevelled nephew in astonishment.

'What the hell are you doing here?'

Miguel spat out a mouthful of blood and groaned. 'They were beating up an old priest,' he mumbled, staggering to his feet. 'I tried to help.'

'Long way from home tonight, aren't you?' Lucas said, helping Miguel to stand and brushing off his clothes.

Miguel explained slowly and painfully about the flat.

Lucas grinned. 'Guarding the fort with glum Gastón, eh? You're better off with me. A couple of drinks is what you need, kid.'

'Where are you going?'

'Fabio Grandi's giving a little party – ever met him? No? Fantastic guy – best painter around these days.' Lucas eyed his nephew speculatively. 'Got any money on you?'

'Not much. Why?'

'Give me some. There'll be a couple of poker tables and probably baccarat. You may like to try your hand.' He clapped Miguel on the shoulder. 'This is what I call a kiss of the gods, old boy. A chance to show my favourite nephew off to my friends.'

Fabio Grandi lived on the top two floors of an old house in the southern part of the city. A narrow staircase climbed past the respectable lodgings of a retired schoolteacher, a flat shared by three strip-teasers, a love-nest owned by a prominent banker, and stopped on the third floor in front of a scarlet door decorated with buxom, one-eyed mermaids. The mermaid motif was repeated all over the walls of the living-room, which had been painted a virulent shade of turquoise.

'Erotic,' explained Grandi, waving his cigarette holder at the mermaids. 'Stimulates the libido, don't you think?'

Miguel thought they looked ridiculous. 'I like that one,' he said doubtfully, pointing to a blonde lorelei swimming through a maze of three-dimensional ice cubes.

Fabio Grandi burst out laughing. 'Priceless! Lucas, your nephew's a gem! Have a drink, Mickey. Don't mind if I call you Mickey, do you?' He thrust a glass of nauseous green liquid into Miguel's hand. 'That sea-queen you fancy is your lovely Mama, painted from memory – eh, Lucas? The ice cubes are quite symbolic, don't you think?'

Miguel flushed dark crimson and took a hasty gulp of his drink. It tasted even worse than it looked. Mint, Cointreau, brandy – he thought he detected rum as well. A very heavy hand with the gin bottle, an even heavier one with whisky. He swallowed, trying not to make a face, and glanced at his watch. A quarter to ten. Gastón was probably sitting down to a solitary dinner at the flat: roast beef and horseradish sauce, roast potatoes, a bottle of vintage wine.

Miguel's stomach rumbled, but all he could find to eat were green olives.

There were two parties going on at the same time. In the mermaid room Fabio Grandi had collected an arty assortment of guests, most of whom looked either very intense or very bored. One stocky, bearded man with a broad provincial accent earnestly recited poetry; a faded blonde in velvet pyjamas proclaimed to the world at large that suicide was the highest form of creativity.

'The supreme expression of the painter's will!' she cried ecstatically, flapping long, paint-streaked fingers at her host. 'I've already begun to paint my death, Fabio darling.'

He kissed his fingertips at her. 'Fabulous, sweet Ofelia! A masterpiece!' Then muttered to Miguel, 'Stupid cunt hasn't got a brain in her head, but her husband's worth a fortune.'

The second party took place in a smaller room. No mermaids or ranting Ofelias here, Miguel noticed with relief. The walls were painted a dark, sober green and hung with an impressive collection of eighteenth-century erotica. There were two poker tables and one of baccarat. A large, swarthy man at the baccarat table glanced up and studied Miguel through heavy-lidded, amber eyes. Lucas quickly came over.

'My nephew.' He thrust Miguel forward and winked at the man. 'This is Iván Torres. We're just about to start. Want to join us?'

Miguel shook his head. 'Not now, thanks.'

'Smart kid,' hissed Grandi in his ear. 'Torres would rob his blind grandmother if it suited him. Have another drink and let's go watch old Lucas lose his shirt.'

By the time Aurora Grandi arrived both parties were warming up. In the front room blonde Ofelia tangoed bare-foot on the table, oblivious to the ear-splitting thumpings of a mambo. The gamblers studied their cards through a fog of cigarette smoke and grunted their bids in colourless monotones. Aurora frowned. Fabio kept insisting these people were important to his career, but she wished he would be more selective. Her eyes lit on a young man lolling uncomfortably on a sofa in the corner; as Fabio drifted by she asked sharply, 'Isn't that Marcos Luciani's boy?'

'In the flesh. Handsome devil, isn't he?' Grandi leered at his sister. 'Chip off the old block. Maybe you'll be more successful this time.'

'Don't be so stupid!' she snapped. 'What's he doing here? He looks sick.'

'Probably is. Lucas brought him. Harmless entertainment – a few drinks, a game of cards. The boy did pretty well at poker, but I don't think my concoctions agree with him.'

Fabio's concoctions were churning up a storm in Miguel's stomach. He lurched to his feet and stumbled across the room, knocking against the baccarat table and spilling a mound of chips. Iván Torres laughed. Miguel groaned and groped for the door. The floor began to rock as his stomach fought for relief. A woman grabbed his arm and guided him into a bathroom decorated with obese golden cupids. His stomach lurched violently and everything went black.

VII

Miguel stirred uneasily and opened his eyes. Somehow he had gone from Fabio Grandi's bathroom to the front seat of a minute Fiat. A woman was driving. He ought to know her

244

from somewhere, but the aftermath of Grandi's drinks made recollection very difficult.

'Fabio should be shot for serving his concoctions,' laughed the woman, catching Miguel's eye. 'My name's Aurora Grandi, but you probably don't remember me. I'm a friend of your Aunt Teresa.'

'Oh, God!' he groaned.

Aurora patted his hand. 'The next time stick to whisky at Fabio's parties. It's safer.'

He leaned back and closed his eyes; after a moment his head slumped against Aurora's shoulder. They drove back to the flat in silence. When the car came to a halt Miguel opened his eyes and stared blankly through the window.

'Christ!' he exclaimed in sudden dismay. 'That's my old man's car!'

Aurora frowned at the dark grey Mercedes parked ominously in front of the building. Her hand gripped Miguel's to reassure him; the sensation of his warm skin against her palm was a strangely exciting one. She caught her breath and said unevenly, 'Let me do the talking.'

He climbed reluctantly out of the car and went to press the bell. There was a pause before a voice crackled sharply over the intercom. Miguel rolled his eyes at Aurora.

'It's me,' he said thickly. 'Open the door.'

They rode ten flights up in uneasy silence – a forced intimacy surrounded by four walls rising through space. Aurora smiled at Miguel. 'Don't worry.' She saw the frightened movement of his Adam's apple as he swallowed. So young, so young, so ridiculously young . . . The lift came to a stop. Marcos stood in the open doorway of the flat, his face livid; Gastón, looking frightened, hovered behind him. Miguel swallowed again and tried nonchalance.

'Hello.'

'Where the devil have you been?' thundered his father. 'It's almost two a.m.!'

'Don't be angry with the boy, Marcos,' said Aurora. 'He was at my place.'

She explained quickly, making a joke of it. Miguel had run into a spot of trouble, luckily she was able to help him. They had gone back to her flat to wait until the situation in the streets grew calmer. They had tried to ring Gastón, but couldn't get through. Aurora laughed and gesticulated with her large hands.

'We started talking and the time just flew,' she said. 'Your son's a very entertaining young man.'

Marcos glared at the entertaining young man. He had rung Gastón at ten-thirty to inquire if everything was all right; after much hedging Gastón admitted it wasn't. Marcos spent nearly three hours combing the police stations and hospitals. He had been on the point of contacting Gaspari when the doorbell rang. Three endless hours of anguish – and all the time the boy had been entertaining Aurora Grandi.

'You stupid brat!' he raged. 'I told you to stay here! When I give an order I expect you to obey it!'

Miguel stared glumly at the ground. There was no point in arguing; the old man would rant for hours if you wound him up. Besides, Aurora Grandi had done a good job pulling some nasty chestnuts out of the fire for him. The woman had guts, no doubt about that . . . He shuddered and swallowed a mouthful of bile. Life was hell.

VIII

After she left the flat Aurora sat in her car for some time without starting the engine. Her thoughts travelled back over the drive from Fabio's flat. The weight of Miguel's head against her shoulder, the line of his jaw, the impact of his physical presence. So young . . . Her hand caressed the place where he had sat. She rested her cheek against the back of the seat, kissed it, laughed softly. The dreams a handsome young devil could inspire were quite extraordinary.

CHAPTER TWENTY

I

The political storm raged on. Plots and counterplots, clashes between Peronists and opposition groups, violence, reprisals . . . Gastón arrived home one day bleeding from a savage blow delivered by a policeman's truncheon. A skirmish with factory workers near school, he explained proudly. Teresa had hysterics when she saw him. Gladys was caught in a tear-gas attack on Florida Street and later chased by a screaming mob.

'Now you know how we feel!' snapped Teresa as her sister-in-law sobbed on the drawing-room sofa. 'Why didn't you say you were one of them?'

'I'm not!' cried Gladys, goaded at last to exasperated fury. 'I don't care about politics! I just want to live in peace!'

In Laguna Grande Artemio Mendes took his cue from the diehards and announced to a chanting crowd that the time had come to string up the oligarchs. The crowd burst into shouts of '*Viva Perón!*' and bellowed the 'Peronist March'; the rest of the townspeople scurried home and barred their doors. Captain Cordero pushed his cap over one eye and lit a cigar.

'One of these days Artemio'll bite off more than he can chew,' he muttered to his assistant. 'Put the water on for some *maté*, lad. We'll wait and see what happens.'

The crowd, which included El Rubio, piled into two trucks and headed west out of town, singing and waving Argentine flags. First stop – La Catalina.

'When Luciani falls the others'll drop like rotten apples!' roared Mendes. 'The land belongs to the people!'

Viva Perón!

Along the way they collected a few disgruntled gauchos from one of the smaller ranches and a pack of mangy dogs. The sky was overcast, the July wind biting cold. Artemio Mendes rode in the first truck, head thrown back and legs

247

braced against the uneven jolting, his foghorn voice bellowing above the wind.

'*La vida por Perón*! Our lives for Perón!'

The gauchos whirled their *rebenques* against the sky and spurred their startled horses, the men in the trucks shook their fists and cheered.

'Hang the oligarchs from the lamp-posts!'

La vida por Perón! exploded with a defiant roar, tangled in the wind, and faded across the winter fields into silence.

II

Tadeo Ortíz happened to be in town that morning and rang La Catalina shortly after ten. Losa took the call; he stared at the receiver for several startled seconds before jumping to his feet.

'Where did Don Marcos say he was going?'

The accountant peered over his glasses. 'Number forty-five by the main road. They're having problems with the new well. Why?'

'Trouble!' barked Losa and raced for the gunroom.

In number forty-five Isabel leaned on her horse's neck and squinted against the grey morning light. A couple of trucks were rattling down the road at great speed; they seemed to be filled with flapping flags and upraised fists. The wind brought the echo of voices, but the echo made no sense at all. She shivered and turned up the collar of her windbreaker. Winter holidays were tense and uncertain this year. Or perhaps it was because at fourteen she herself was tense and uncertain about so many things. Her own body, for instance. Or her moods, which seesawed from laughter to uncontrollable tears and back to laughter without warning. Even the way she felt about La Catalina was changing. She still loved the ranch, but other things were beginning to intrude on her dreams of living there forever. The purely feminine delight of wearing a pretty dress, for instance. Parties. Gossip and laughter with her friends. Dancing with boys ... The horse whinnied nervously and Isabel stood up in her stirrups to see better.

'Papa,' she called after a minute, 'who are those men?'

Marcos took one look at the trucks and ran for his horse, shouting to the two men who had been working on the well to follow him. He waved his arm frantically at Isabel.

'Get back to the house!'

'Why?' she demanded. 'What's happening?'

He vaulted into the saddle and galloped towards the gate, the startled ranch hands hard on his heels. Dust swirled along the road; behind the dust stormed the crowd, braying fury.

'Pe-rón! Pe-rón!'

'Isabel!' yelled Marcos. 'Go home!'

Too late.

The trucks rattled to an uncertain stop some twenty yards before the gate. Invading a man's land unopposed was one thing; it was quite another when he barred the way. Even worse when that man was Luciani. The gauchos reined in their horses and waited uneasily to see what would happen. One didn't mess around with *patrones* like Don Marcos.

Maybe *la vida por Perón* wasn't such a good idea after all.

The shouting and cheering died away.

Artemio Mendes understood the sudden silence and gripped the side of the truck, his swarthy face congested with rage.

'*Viva Perón!*' he roared. 'The land belongs to the people!'

Marcos did not move. There were close to forty men in the trucks, plus the handful of riders; he had only himself and the two ranch-hands. And Isabel. His heart sank as he suddenly recalled the shooting of Roberto Gabán.

'The land belongs to whoever owns it!' snapped Marcos, ignoring Mendes and addressing the men in the trucks. 'I own La Catalina. This is my land. If Mendes told you it's yours he's lying.' He stared at the gauchos in disgust and they looked away. 'Only mongrels follow liars.'

'What're we waiting for?' hissed the man beside Mendes. 'There's only three of 'em and the girl, *compañero*. Run 'em down and get on with it!'

The trucks rolled forward. La Catalina's two ranch-hands glanced uneasily at the *patrón*. He sat stone-faced on his horse, showing no sign of giving way or even trying to argue. The men rubbed moist palms against their thighs and took a firmer grip on the reins. A roll of tumbleweed blew across the road; the wind teased the horses' manes and sighed through the dry winter grass. The trucks swung around to face the entrance and stopped. Mendes hitched up his trousers. The occasion was a momentous one. He made the best of it, pounding the air with clenched fists and bellowing at the top of his lungs.

'Bloodsucking oligarch!'

'Go to hell!' shouted Marcos.

It occurred to El Rubio that Artemio Mendes was going about things the wrong way. Fist-pounding and name-calling wouldn't impress the *patrón*; you had to catch him where it hurt. As the trucks' engines raced noisily El Rubio jumped out, slipped under the fence and vaulted on to Isabel's horse with a whoop of triumph.

'Got her! Let's go, Don Artemio!'

Isabel screamed and El Rubio grunted. The girl fought like a wildcat. He liked that. The *patrón* was sheet-white and yelling fury, but he couldn't move because of the trucks. So much the better. El Rubio grinned. Maybe he wouldn't wait for Artemio Mendes to take over the *patrón*'s land. A wildcat girl fighting and clawing was more exciting than *la vida por Perón*. He groped with heavy, sweating hands as the horse shied and Isabel screamed again.

After that, chaos.

Down the road from the ranch house streaked Pablo Losa with a truckful of men, from La Juana more men, from Laguna Grande Tadeo Ortíz. The driver of Mendes's truck shouted a frightened oath and slammed down on the accelerator. The front wheels hit a deep rut and sank into several inches of loose, sandy soil. The second truck manoeuvred frantically to steer clear, skidded and slewed around, blocking the entrance. Mendes shook his fists and roared.

'Move away from there, you fools!'

Losa ran up to Marcos, gun in hand. 'You'll need this!'

El Rubio laughed. The wildcat was still fighting. He wheeled the horse and clutched her like a shield; he was still laughing when the *patrón*'s bullet struck him.

Artemio Mendes continued to shout encouragement from the safety of his truck. A bullet whizzed past his ear, another one smashed the windscreen. The driver flung himself out in terror and fled down the road; others followed. Mendes climbed down and lumbered towards the entrance, determined to breach resistance barehanded. He knocked one man to the ground and grappled with a second. His feet went out from under him. He fell heavily and rolled away from a descending boot.

The barrel of a .38 gleamed six inches away from his head.

'I've already shot one bastard,' rasped Marcos. 'You'll be the next.'

Artemio Mendes swallowed. *La vida por Perón* did not include having his brains blown out. He rose slowly and backed off, neck muscles swollen like thick cords, his black eyes blazing with frustration. The second truck coughed fitfully and reversed, narrowly missing Tadeo's car. Mendes clambered aboard and squawked a final insult that was lost in the rattle of the engine. A few seconds later the truck clattered away in a cloud of dust.

Marcos did not notice. A moment's hesitation, a fraction of an inch either way and the bullet meant for El Rubio would have hit Isabel. He tore off her blood-splattered windbreaker and put his own jacket around her shoulders. His mouth was dry, his hands would not stop trembling.

'Is he d-dead?' asked Isabel, her eyes glued to the motionless figure being lifted into the pickup. 'Did you kill him?'

'No.' He coaxed her over to Tadeo's car. 'Don't think about it, *ñatita*. Everything will be all right.'

'I want to go home.'

'In a few minutes,' said Marcos and left her.

She perched stiffly on the front seat and stared at the grim men grouped around the pickup. Nothing was all right. In a single morning La Catalina's enchanted world had been shattered; it would never be the same again. Her childhood had been invaded by violent men, its innocence destroyed by El Rubio's rancid breath and groping hands. By her father's savage cries of rage. She felt unclean as though the violence, in touching her, had made her a part of its horror. The blood-forces aroused by men's passions troubled her dreams for weeks afterwards. Although in time their memory faded from conscious thought, their shadow prowled below the surface like the ghost of a half-forgotten nightmare.

III

In August 1955 Juan Domingo Perón took a sniff at the political winds and offered to resign. His letter of resignation was immediately rejected, and the powerful trade union movement called for a general strike in support of their beleaguered leader. The strike was followed by a mass rally in the Plaza de Mayo, which thundered with impassioned harangues about holocausts, supreme sacrifices and a bloody struggle to the death.

Encouraged, Perón toyed with the idea of arming the trade unions; this, however, proved too much for the military to stomach. On 16 September the key garrisons revolted; when the navy and air force joined in, his fate was sealed. Gun battles raged in and around Argentina's major cities; on 19 September Perón hastily resigned and fled to a Paraguayan gunboat anchored in the middle of the Río de la Plata. Clambering hurriedly on board he slipped and fell into the river's muddy waters, from where he was fished out by an overzealous sailor.

Dictators in disgrace make unwelcome guests. Juan Domingo Perón, who for twelve years had held Argentina firmly under his heel, bounced like a hot potato from country to country and finally found asylum in Franco's Spain.

IV

Celestina Gaspari stared at her son. Rain dripped off his hat and made muddy splashes on her clean kitchen floor. There were dark circles under his eyes and lines around his mouth; his moustache drooped, his round cheeks sagged with weariness. He looks frightened, she thought with a mixture of pity and satisfaction. Caught once too often with his hand in the biscuit tin.

'Well?' she demanded.

Gaspari shrugged. 'Well, what? You need someone to look after the shop, don't you?'

'I thought you were too busy.'

252

'It just happens I have time on my hands these days.'

'What about your sister?'

'She's got nothing to worry about. None of them do – for the time being, anyway.' He dropped his hat on the table and went over to warm his hands by the stove. 'Don Carlos flew back yesterday from Uruguay. They're throwing a big do for him at Barranco Rosales next Tuesday.' Bitterness crept into his voice. 'I'm not invited.'

Celestina's mouth tightened. 'You'll catch cold in those wet clothes. Go upstairs and change. I'll make you some nice hot soup.'

V

On 23 September General Eduardo Lonardi became provisional president of Argentina. He stood on the balcony of the Casa Rosada flanked by a glittering military panoply and solemnly swore to restore law and order, as well as the nation's self-respect and honour. The warm spring sunshine streamed down on a Plaza de Mayo packed from end to end with cheering, flag-waving Argentines. The mood was one of relief, excitement, exhilaration – political champagne at its frothiest and most potent. Perón was finished, the nightmare had ended, the future glowed blue and white and golden.

'Half the people cheering for the revolution were probably yelling for our heads last month,' remarked Marcos dryly. 'Let's hope the army boys are smart enough to hand the government over to capable men. We've had enough speeches to last us a lifetime.'

The new government's first step was to erase the past.

All reminders of Perón and Evita were destroyed. The Party was disbanded. Peronism as a political movement was forbidden. The presidential mansion was opened to the public and the Peróns' fabulous wardrobes exhibited as further proof of how they had swindled Argentina's good faith. The people trooped silently past rooms of jewelled evening gowns, furs, hundreds of pairs of shoes, jewellery, silk shirts embroidered with Perón's head. They stared and murmured, but perhaps were not too impressed. These were the trappings

253

of a fairytale and for many the fairytale still lived on in their dreams.

The one thing they could not and would not forgive was that Perón had been unfaithful to Evita's memory and had taken a fourteen-year-old girl as his mistress.

VI

Lucía Claire invited Angela to spend a week in Buenos Aires and enjoy the celebrations. Lucía was as bright-eyed and amusing as ever, filled with inexhaustible energy and an enviable zest for life. Over lunch at Sauvage she told Angela how, when the revolution was over, she had rushed into the street to celebrate and had danced with enthusiastic crowds of young men all up and down Avenida Santa Fé.

'They even carried me on their shoulders,' she recalled with a delighted laugh. 'I was quite thrilled, my dear! Such handsome boys! If only I were fifty years younger.'

Carlos and Teresa gave a large luncheon to celebrate their wedding anniversary. Two years in exile had aged Carlos considerably, but he greeted Angela as courteously as ever and inquired after Jimmy. Teresa clung to his arm, radiant with happiness.

'It still seems like a dream,' she said. 'Carlos and I are driving down to Los Toros tomorrow afternoon. We're staying there for two months – just the two of us.' The dark eyes sparkled with an unexpected hint of mischief. 'I must finish measuring my curtains.'

'You deserve time together.'

Teresa laughed. 'We'll make the best of it! You and Jimmy must come down this summer to Los Toros. Perhaps before Christmas.'

'Perhaps before Christmas,' agreed Angela and to change the subject asked Carlos about his appointment as minister of agriculture for the province.

Lies ... There was no use pretending to herself that she enjoyed them. If only she hated Jimmy things might not be so bad. Hatred carried its own moral justification. Perhaps then she would not feel so guilty about loving another man.

Angela found herself envying Teresa's happiness with a bitterness born of knowledge.

If Marcos noticed her mood, he made no immediate comment. They dined together that evening at one of the small, exclusive restaurants tucked away near the river; over the main course he told her about plans to open an office in Buenos Aires.

'Carlos and I want to merge all three ranches into a single business, but it means far more paperwork than either one of us can handle on our own.' He refilled their wine glasses. 'What's the matter, señora? You're not paying attention.'

Angela's glance met his, very blue and direct. 'I was thinking about Carlos and Teresa – how very happy they are. I wish . . .' She crumbled a piece of bread between her fingers. 'I wish we could be together like that. Openly, without any need for hiding what we feel for each other.'

The candle on their table flickered as a sudden breeze blew through the window.

'Marcos . . .'

'I'm very happy tonight,' he interrupted, reaching for her hand and kissing it. 'It doesn't matter to me how we are together as long as we are together whenever possible.' His dark eyes glowed tenderly in the candlelight. 'I love you so much, *gringuita*.'

He was so damned sure of her love. If he hadn't looked at her like that, she might have dared shake his happiness a bit. Another woman would have kept him on tenterhooks – maybe even told him 'whenever possible' was not good enough. That it must be all or nothing. Angela sighed. She was not that type of woman; she couldn't hold love over Marcos's head like a weapon. 'Whenever possible' was the only solution – but that didn't make things easier. Oh, God! she thought. I wish I didn't love him as much as I do. I wish I had the courage to love him less. Maybe I wouldn't care then that we can't be together all the time.

'What is it?' asked Marcos. 'Why did you sigh?'

'I've got a bit of a headache.' She pressed his hand against her cheek. 'I meant to tell you that Lucía's taken a box at the Colón for tomorrow night's gala performance. She made sure it was next to yours.'

VII

The Colón is a glorious relic of grand opera-house tradition with sweeping marble staircases, red velvet seats, painted ceilings, ornately scrolled balconies and a mirrored foyer reminiscent of some minor sun king's palace. From the huge revolving stage all the way up to the gallery seats perched six floors about the stalls it is a formidable theatre – an arena of giants where only the most talented can avoid being engulfed by the grandeur of its dimensions.

Lorenzo Grandi, who dreamed of taking the Colón by storm, firmly believed in his own considerable talent.

At twenty-five he was still struggling to make others believe in it as well, but so far all he had achieved were a few concerts in the provinces, recitals in unimportant theatres, and an endless round of dreary music lessons. Lorenzo heaved a disgruntled sigh and stared up at the boxes ringing the stalls; after a moment he nudged his sister.

'Who's the blonde dripping diamonds?' he asked, nodding at a box on their left.

Aurora adjusted her opera glasses. 'Marcos Luciani's wife. She's vulgar.'

Lorenzo glanced past the diamonds and spotted a young girl hanging over the box's velvet edge. His eyes narrowed. Twelve or thirteen, perhaps. Long, honey-golden hair glowing in the mellow light. He watched her laughing and making excited signs to several other girls behind her. A little Juliet, he thought and smiled to himself.

'Is that kid her daughter?'

'Heavens, no! That's Marcos's youngest girl, Cristina.' The opera glasses focused on Miguel, standing awkwardly in the shadows. 'She plays the piano quite nicely.'

Lorenzo grunted. 'I don't suppose it would be any use offering to teach her,' he remarked after a moment.

Aurora followed Miguel as he leaned over to greet Angela and Lucía Claire, who had just entered the adjoining box. He should always wear a dinner jacket, she thought. Handsome devil. Lucas must bring him to Fabio's again. I'll be there and we can talk; smile at each other. We share a secret. Smile. Touch. I'm not too old . . .

'I've already suggested you several times,' she told Lorenzo, 'but Marcos isn't too keen on Cristina taking up music seriously.'

There seemed no point in pursuing the matter further.

The programme was standard repertoire: an overture by a local composer and the suites from Falla's 'Three-Cornered Hat', followed after a lengthy interval by Tchaikovsky's first piano concerto. During the interval Lorenzo acidly informed his sister that tonight's soloist had no more idea of phrasing music than a monkey.

'The notes stick together like treacle,' he complained as they strolled through the foyer. 'If I had a chance to play that concerto in this theatre — Christ, I'd turn the audience on its head!'

Halfway along the foyer they met Mercedes and the girls; Gladys trailed behind, smiling self-consciously and nodding at people she thought she recognized. Aurora performed somewhat stilted introductions, but Lorenzo was all charm. He bowed to Mercedes, kissed Gladys's hand and praised Cristina's playing. Aurora, he earnestly assured everyone, had just finished telling him what an accomplished little pianist Señor Luciani's youngest daughter was.

'Believe me, my sister is no mean critic,' he added, winking at open-mouthed Cristina. 'I long to hear this prodigy myself.'

'Oh,' said Gladys, somewhat taken aback by the hand-kissing. 'I don't know. She does play a bit, I suppose.'

Lorenzo had a good memory. He recalled a certain recital four years before at Teresa's flat and a blonde woman hanging on to his every note. He smiled.

'You're too modest, señora. I know you recognize talent when you hear it.'

Gladys blinked. The name Lorenzo Grandi suddenly rang a bell. He was Aurora Grandi's famous brother and Aurora — or so Teresa had repeatedly taken pains to remind her — would have married Marcos had Gladys not come along. She put an arm around her stepdaughter and returned the smile.

'Perhaps you might like to come to tea next week and hear our little Cristina, Señor Grandi. Shall we say Wednesday?'

Mercedes drew in her breath. Gladys was definitely getting out of hand. She wished Marcos were here to intervene, but he had taken Miguel to visit Lucía Claire as soon as the lights came on.

257

'I'm afraid tea isn't really a suitable occasion,' she observed sharply. 'We haven't seen you in a long time, Aurora. Why don't you and Lorenzo come to dinner next Friday? Marcos will still be in town.' She smoothed Cristina's golden head, her lips drawn in a steely smile. 'My niece will have time to prepare a few little pieces by then.'

'Splendid!' agreed Lorenzo, still smiling at Gladys. 'This is one recital I'm looking forward to with pleasure.'

'What was all that about?' demanded Aurora as they continued their stroll. 'Making fool's eyes at that woman! She wouldn't know good music if she heard it! I will not go to Barranco Rosales for dinner!'

Lorenzo lit a cigarette and flicked the match over his shoulder. 'Gladys Luciani is rich and stupid. Those, my lovely cow, are qualities I plan to milk for all their worth. Besides,' he blew a thoughtful smoke-ring at a simpering Venus, 'you never know. Little Juliet may be able to tickle the ivories decently after all.'

VIII

As the houselights dimmed Marcos returned briefly to Lucía's box and beckoned to Angela. They kissed in the musty, crimson darkness of the tiny entrance, shielded from the world by faded velvet curtains. It was one of the most intimate and exciting moments they had ever experienced together. Cut off from everything but pure physical contact, their awareness of each other sharpened by secrecy, they concentrated all their desire in that one hasty embrace.

'Come with me tomorrow to El Remanso,' whispered Marcos. 'I have to go down for the day.'

Her lips roamed hungrily across his mouth. 'Yes.' Last night's dissatisfaction belonged to the past. Tonight the frustration of 'whenever possible' didn't matter as long as she could be in Marcos's arms. As long as she could love him like this. Feel the wild pounding of his heart racing against her own. 'Yes,' she breathed again and pressed against him, moist and throbbing with excitement.

Tchaikovsky's first chords crashed heroically above the expectant silence.

Marcos kissed her again. 'I love you madly,' he murmured and left the box. Angela returned to her seat. She felt flushed and breathless with exhilaration; even Gladys's diamonds sparkling next door were unimportant. On stage the music surged in an impassioned crescendo and flowed on. Her emotions surged with it on a rising wave of anticipation and thoughts of tomorrow.

Towards the end of the first movement Marcos came into the box again and touched her bare shoulder – but this time his fingers were icy cold.

'Please come with me a moment,' he said in a low voice.

Two men stood in the softly lit corridor outside the boxes. Angela glanced at them and turned to Marcos in alarm. His face was ashen.

'What is it?' she demanded sharply. 'What's happened?'

'These men are from the police,' he said. 'There's been an – an accident. Near Los Toros.'

Angela grabbed his arm. 'Oh, God! Marcos . . .'

His voice shook. 'Please – I need your help. Warn Mercedes. Tell her to take the children home at once. I'll return as soon as possible.'

'Where are you going?'

He hesitated and then said bleakly, 'To identify the bodies.'

IX

The accident occurred five miles from Los Toros's main gate.

A narrow road, poor visibility, a lorry overtaking a car on a sharp curve – there was no time to avoid a head-on collision. Carlos and Teresa were killed outright, the lorry driver had to be cut from the wreckage and died on the way to the hospital.

Next day's newspapers carried indignant editorial comments on the scandalous state of the national roads. The obituaries ran to two columns in one newspaper, another printed a lengthy account of Carlos's exile. Juan Gaspari sent an elaborate wreath and came to the funeral wearing a black band sewn ostentatiously on to his sleeve. In the lugubrious grandeur of Recoleta cemetery Angela thought he made a strangely forlorn little figure.

Perhaps we all do, she mused wryly as the funeral procession moved slowly along a cypress-lined avenue towards the family vault. We cluster in the shadow of the marble angels and listen to endless speeches. We murmur words that do little justice to grief, glance surreptitiously at our watches. *Rest in peace.* The rain drips off a crucifix, gurgles down a gutter, glistens like sweat on a stony Pietà . . . A woman began to sob as the crowd made way for the two coffins to be lowered into the vault.

Bell, book and candle.

Perhaps the ceremonial amulets men hang on death would wring a smile of pity from indifferent gods.

PART III

1958–1964

'From a spark of fire come many
burning coals . . .

(Sirach 11.32)

261

CHAPTER TWENTY-ONE

I

A fiery February sun beat down on La Catalina.

In the Bajo the temperature registered ninety-two; at the big house it was scarcely one degree lower. The hot, heavy air smelled of dust and eucalyptus and remnants of smoke from the *asado* fires. Not a breath of wind stirred in the park, not even a hint of breeze to ruffle the oleanders outside the study window. The dogs sprawled under the pepper trees and lolled their dripping tongues.

Sunday afternoon hummed with cicadas.

Claudia sat on the edge of the swimming pool and scowled at her reflection in the water. The pool was a recent addition to La Catalina which she hated. She also loathed the new tennis court behind the chapel, and dancing on the terrace after supper – but the pool was her own special torture. All very well if one could swim properly or enjoyed horseplay in the water. She could barely manage an awkward breast-stroke, and as for horseplay . . . Miguel especially took cruel delight in swimming up from behind and hauling her backwards by the heels despite her screams of terror.

Everyone thought it a huge joke.

If she were as attractive as Isabel no one would care whether she could swim or not. If she were slender, with large, dark eyes and hair that gleamed like ebony in the sunlight, she wouldn't sit out at dances or wait wistfully for phone calls that never came. Isabel had a virtual monopoly on boys and the telephone; shyness, a dumpy figure and blotchy skin were no match for such stiff competition.

Claudia thrust out a mutinous lower lip.

Being ugly duckling among the Lucianis was bad enough; when summer holidays included their friends things like the pool turned life into hell. This summer there were five friends; since the Lucianis also included Gastón and Yvonne everyone paired off perfectly and left her odd one out.

She tugged at the elastic of last year's bathing suit and glared at the group sunning itself at the far end of the pool.

There was Cristina, slim and golden all over, wearing a new green bathing suit that fitted like a glove. It didn't matter to her if Isabel attracted all the attention, she had a crush on her piano teacher. Claudia swatted impatiently at a fly. The piano teacher's name was Lorenzo Grandi and he was very handsome. She would have liked to take piano lessons with him, but when she said so her mother had replied, 'Don't be silly! Señor Grandi only teaches talented pupils.' Lorenzo Grandi called Cristina 'little Juliet'.

Next to Cristina sat Ana Inés and Elisita. Claudia knew them from school – they were very high society, very much Isabel's crowd. Both were slender and pretty, with an instinctive knack for knowing what to say to boys. Claudia's lower lip quivered. She didn't know how to get along with them. Gastón and Miguel's friends were just as difficult – nice enough if you knew how to laugh and flirt and chatter about nothing, but not very responsive if you could think of nothing to say. She could never think of anything to say to someone like Manolo San Martín or Alfredito Rodríguez Nelson, whose sole interest seemed to be politics. Elías Castro was Gastón's friend, but there was no point in talking to him because he only had eyes for Isabel.

Claudia turned her scowl on the deck chairs under the trees.

The others were just as bad. Her mother only cared about Lalo, Mercedes never showed more than a vague interest in her brother's stepdaughter. Neither of them understood her unhappiness. Don Tadeo and Señora Julia were pleasant enough, but she never knew what to say to them. Don Jimmy (she could not bring herself to forget 'don' or 'señora' no matter how hard she tried) made her feel uncomfortable because he laughed too loudly and drank too much. As for Señora Angela . . . The round hazel eyes darted an uneasy glance across the pool. Rosita the maid had told her something this morning about Señora Angela. She didn't want to believe it, but Rosita swore by the Virgin Mary it was true.

'I saw her walking in the park with Don Marcos, *niña*. Thursday after lunch, when she came to fetch those papers for Don Jimmy.'

'Why shouldn't they walk in the park?'

264

Rosita simpered. 'Arm-in-arm? He kissed her. Just like in the movies. I saw them.'

Claudia flushed with sudden embarrassment. Ever since the incident by the lake nearly four years ago her stepfather and Angela had treated her with chilly wariness. At the time their attitude hurt because she did not understand it; she understood now and looked quickly away in case anyone noticed.

Angela noticed, but the afternoon was too warm and pleasant to be spent wondering about Claudia's scowls. There were few opportunities to relax and enjoy life these days.

Even with Marcos.

Their first passionate years of madness had imperceptibly slowed down to a steady, predictable rhythm. The secret meetings, the flush of excitement from a kiss stolen when no one was looking, the lover's language of glances and smiles were all very much still a part of their relationship, but the edge to madness was blunted.

Perhaps because they were growing older and each age has its own rhythm, even for love. Perhaps because life itself intruded on their secret world with irritating persistence and not even love could keep it out. Small things. Family problems. Work. Even with an office in Buenos Aires and a very capable office manager, Marcos had his hands full running the three ranches. It was to be expected. These were facts of life and, as he had once pointed out, had nothing to do with love. Angela disagreed. They had everything to do with love because they sapped at its foundations. The frustrations of 'whenever and wherever possible' continued to nag with a dull aching pain that threatened to poison her happiness. The worst part was that she could not bring herself to force an all or nothing showdown.

The whole situation was so damnably stupid. She felt more married to Marcos than she did to Jimmy – the proverbial wife in all but name. If only she could marry Marcos, the facts of life wouldn't matter.

Angela argued endlessly with herself on the subject and got nowhere. Marcos was a Catholic, he could not divorce his wife. She had known that from the beginning. He could *leave* his wife if he wanted to, but the only time she had brought up the subject he cut her short.

'I won't have you involved in that kind of scandal, *gringuita*.'

Infidelity, when discreet, was permissible. Adultery in the open obviously was not.

What made it even more difficult was that Marcos made the whole thing sound so bloody reasonable. More difficult still, she couldn't imagine life without him.

Then there was Jimmy.

He didn't suspect about Marcos – Angela was sure of that. In the beginning she could not help feeling guilty; afterwards she put both lives into separate compartments and tricked herself into believing they could be kept apart.

Their marriage had drifted uneasily along, each one trying so hard not to rock the boat. Steering away from dangerous waters by clinging obstinately to domestic routine. She thought they were doing quite well until Julia asked if there was anything wrong.

'Jimmy and I are going through a bit of a rough patch these days,' admitted Angela after a moment's hesitation.

Julia looked sympathetic. 'You two need a holiday. Six weeks away from everything – make it a second honeymoon. It would be a chance to sort out the problems. Be alone together.'

Togetherness won't solve anything, Angela told herself glumly. Besides we can't afford holidays right now.

'I'm spending three days in Buenos Aires next week,' murmured Marcos. 'Can you come?'

He lay no more than a foot away on the edge of the pool, dark head cradled on his folded arms, his body relaxed. A strong, muscular body without an extra ounce of fat. A forty-five-year-old man in full prime. No beer belly, no slackness. Angela glanced in the direction of Jimmy's deck chair. Comparisons again. She frowned slightly.

'I don't know if I should.'

'Why not?'

She watched an adventurous ant exploring the face of his watch. 'Problems – money, mostly. Jimmy's worrying himself sick about it. The crops haven't done well and we didn't get what he expected for the herd that was sold in Cardales. Saúl was in charge of it, but things just didn't turn out.'

'Saúl's no good. Jimmy should have seen to that sale himself.'

Jimmy had gone to Laguna Grande the evening before; when he returned shortly before dawn he was in no condition to do anything except sleep.

'Did Jimmy tell you what happened when his parents came last week?' asked Angela.

'No.'

'He asked his father for a loan. I heard them arguing about it after breakfast.

'And John Morgan refused?'

Her cheeks burned. 'Refused isn't the word. He got on his high horse and lectured for a good quarter of an hour before Cora joined in. She spent another quarter of an hour telling Jimmy what an ungrateful son he was. When Jimmy finally got a word in he told them both to clear out. After they left he got drunk and then . . .' a disgusting quarter of an hour in the bedroom. 'Oh, well,' she finished shakily, 'the rest doesn't matter.'

'You didn't tell me this on Thursday.'

'I couldn't. I don't know why I'm telling you now. There's nothing you can do. Let's forget it. I'll come to Buenos Aires next week and to hell with everything. We need new towels. There's a sale at Harrods.'

There was a long silence. The ant edged off the watch and began to inch its way along Marcos's forearm. He jumped up suddenly and dived into the pool, cutting the water with quick, powerful strokes; when he swam back he was laughing, but his eyes were angry.

'Come into the water and cool off, *gringuita*.' He gripped Angela by the wrists. 'You've been sitting too long in the sun.'

A friendly, spontaneous gesture. Angela thought nothing of it until she happened to glance up and saw Claudia watching them.

II

Tea time under the trees.

Sandwiches, scones, and Rosario's walnut cake spread with layers of *dulce de leche*. Raspbery jam and politics – a generous helping of each. Elections after three years of military rule had brought the Radicals to power. A shrewd lawyer from the left-wing faction owed his seat in the Casa Rosada to a large majority which, according to Tadeo Ortíz, included every Peronist in the country.

'I've been told that Perón himself gave the order to vote for Frondizi,' he grumbled. 'God only knows what promises he got in return. Probably that the ban on the Peronists would be lifted and the old man himself allowed to come back. They should have let Perón drown in the damned river when he fell off the gunboat.'

Alfredito Rodríguez Nelson's face quivered with excitement; at twenty he was as passionately devoted to politics as his father was to women. He now took the opportunity to announce proudly that he had just joined the Glorious Homeland movement.

'You mean those idiots who parade around in red cloaks?' drawled Miguel scornfully. 'The ones carrying banners with all that stuff written on them in gold letters? "God, Homeland and Heritage" – or some crap like that . . .'

'It is not crap!' retorted Alfredito. 'We happen to be a very serious organization, dedicated to ridding Argentina of all Peronists, Communists and Jews!' He bit energetically into a ham sandwich. 'This new government's Marxist, you know. We'll all be calling each other "comrade" soon . . .'

Miguel stared at him. 'Do you really believe that?'

'Of course I believe it! Don't you?'

Miguel's interest in politics was no more than vaguely conventional. He had been born into the land-owning class, he was meant to keep faith with its tenets. They existed as part of the rigid heritage governing his own life; he had never bothered to question them. Movements like the Glorious Homeland went to ridiculous extremes – but he found himself suddenly envying Alfredito's commitment and passion. At least he has something to get steamed up about, Miguel reflected. The thought unsettled him, unsettlement sparked irritation. He didn't want to be unsettled on a sweltering summer afternoon, he wanted to laze about under the trees and stare at Isabel's friends. They were certainly worth staring at, especially Ana Inés . . . Miguel tossed a twig at her and grinned when she blushed.

'It's too hot for politics,' he said. 'Who the hell cares anyway?'

'It's irresponsible attitudes like yours that let the Reds in!' spluttered Alfredito, shaking his index finger and spilling half his tea in the process. 'We have a responsibility to our homeland, to our . . .' The rest of the tea splashed on to Yvonne, who let fly a short, pungent oath.

'Yvonne!' Mercedes's eyebrows flew up in scandalized amazement. 'What did you say?'

'You wouldn't understand if she told you,' drawled Lucas from the depths of his deck chair. He winked at Yvonne, who looked embarrassed but defiant. 'You're way behind the times, Mercedes old girl!'

'There's no excuse for vulgarity!'

Encouraged by Lucas's grin, Yvonne giggled. 'You're so old-fashioned, Aunt. Everyone talks like that these days.'

'And I suppose if everyone jumped off a cliff you'd follow,' observed Marcos in a tone of voice that brought an angry flush to his niece's cheeks. 'What's that fool child crying about now, Gladys?'

They all turned to look at little Lalo, who had apparently come out the worst in a tussle with one of the dogs. The disapproval in his father's voice was more frightening than old Parche's growl; he peered at Marcos from behind Gladys's chair, his brown eyes wide and still brimming with tears. A caress or a smile from the tall, forbidding man called Papa would have restored Lalo's courage in a second. He longed for some sign of recognition or friendship; with a child's unerring intuition he knew that Papa did not love him and no sign of affection would be forthcoming.

'That dog's dangerous,' complained Gladys, hugging Lalo to her. 'One of these days he'll bite someone. I wish you would have him shot.'

'There's nothing wrong with Parche,' retorted Marcos in disgust and, turning to the boys, began to discuss teams for a game of polo after tea.

Elías Castro edged over to Isabel. He was a slight, brown-haired young man, not particularly good-looking but with a nice smile and impeccable manners. Elisita and Ana Inés thought him dull and old-fashioned; Isabel hadn't quite made up her mind. Physically Elías might not be as attractive as Manolo San Martín or Miguel, but she wouldn't want to be married to either one of them. Manolo's green eyes strayed after anything that wore a skirt and as for Miguel – you couldn't depend on him at all. Lately Isabel was finding it very difficult to like her brother. They had got on well enough as children, but now that they were almost adults she was becoming increasingly critical of him. He showed such little interest in the family business; all he seemed to care about was having a good time. Elías wasn't like that at all. He helped his father run the Castro ranch and he always seemed to enjoy her stories about La Catalina. He was really quite *simpático*.

Isabel grinned as he came over. 'Make yourself useful and bring me some more tea,' she said, holding out her teacup. 'A drop of milk and two lumps of sugar.'

Elías took the cup and continued to stand, staring down at her through anxious light-brown eyes. 'Are you going to watch the polo?'

He was a good player; he wanted to show off for her. She decided to tease him a bit. 'Why should I?'

'It's young against old. We'll win – your father and the others don't stand a chance. Should be a good game.'

He looked so earnest Isabel had to laugh. 'All right, I'll go and watch. Just make sure you win.' She reached out a slender, bare foot and pushed his leg. 'Where's my tea?'

The afternoon sunlight brought out faintly reddish highlights in her dark hair and warmed her skin to a deep, golden bronze. She wore an open shirt over her bathing suit; Elías stared at the hollow in her throat, not daring to let his eyes stray any further.

'We're having a big do down at La María Fernanda next month,' he stammered. 'It's my m-mother's fiftieth birthday. Would you like to come?'

Isabel shrugged her shoulders.

'I'd like you to,' insisted Elías. 'We could drive down together.'

She began to inspect her fingernails. 'I don't know. Maybe. Go on, bring me my tea.'

'Poor old Elías,' murmured Ana Inés as he trotted obediently off. 'You're a bitch, Bela. Go to his mama's birthday party and make him happy.'

'He's an only child and Papa Castro's loaded,' chuckled Elisita from the other side. 'The silly fool's eating his heart out for you – what more do you want?'

'She wants to marry a man like Papa with a ranch like La Catalina and live happily ever after,' said Cristina, who had just returned from a dip in the pool. 'Bela couldn't live on love in a garret.'

'Neither could you,' observed her sister.

When one is sixteen and passionately in love with one's piano teacher, romantic love in a garret sounds as wonderful as love in a crystal palace. Cristina coloured under her golden tan.

'I could too,' she retorted. 'If Lo-if a man loved me I could live anywhere with him.'

Isabel gave her sister a worldly look. 'You better not let Papa find out you like Lorenzo,' she cautioned, lowering her voice. 'He's not too keen on your wanting to be a concert pianist, and I don't think he approves of Lorenzo very much.'

Cristina stubbed at the ground with her toe. 'Papa's so old-fashioned! Why shouldn't I be a pianist if I want to? What's wrong with it? Look at people like Rubenstein and Horowitz — and Cósima Cantini. She's marvellous! Even Papa thinks she is. It's so stupid of him to say I can't be a concert pianist just because I'm his daughter!'

'Why does he let you take lessons if he doesn't want you to play?' asked Ana Inés curiously.

'He's proud of her playing,' replied Isabel as Cristina continued to look stubborn. 'It's just that he doesn't want her to make a career of it. He wants Cristina and me to get married.'

Ana Inés stole a quick glance at Miguel standing by the tea table. Her brown eyes softened. 'There's nothing wrong with getting married.'

'Well, I'm going to be a pianist!' said Cristina defiantly. 'And if I marry it'll be who I want, not someone Papa's picked for me!'

She jammed a straw sunhat on her golden head and stalked off. Elisita laughed. 'What's her piano teacher like?'

Isabel shrugged. 'Gladys thinks he's divine. She badgered Papa into letting him teach Cristina.'

Elías came back with her tea-cup and a slice of cake. 'I thought you might be hungry.'

Isabel eyed the cake as Ana Inés and Elisita giggled. 'No, thanks. I'll put on weight.'

Elías Castro's light-brown eyes dared slide further than the V of her blouse. He swallowed. 'You're perfect.'

It was the breathless way he said 'perfect'. Almost as though he were afraid to pronounce the word. Isabel studied Elías through her eyelashes. He had a nice smile. He wasn't that bad-looking, either. A dependable type. His heart was written all over his face. She smiled back at him.

'I'd like to go with you to your mother's birthday party,' she said and took the slice of cake.

III

Polo à La Catalina was played without helmets and at suicidal speed.

A field had been laid out about a quarter of a mile from the Bajo; the rough ground was hard and tufted with stiff grass, the boundaries were marked by a rope slung between stakes leaning at drunken angles. As far as Angela had ever been able to make out there were only two objects to the game. The first, to whack the ball like hell; the second, to charge one's opponent broadside at full gallop and damn the consequences.

This particular match is rougher than usual, she reflected uneasily. The boys are baiting the men, who have their own conflicts to sort out. Even Tadeo looks grim.

She held her breath as Gastón and Jimmy raced neck and neck down the field. Jimmy swung first, Gastón's stick came into the arc of his swing and engaged the mallet; Miguel, thundering up to scoop out the ball, caught the full brunt of his father's reckless charge. The horses reared, someone shouted, Gladys squealed and covered her eyes. The players disentangled and galloped off again. Angela discovered that her knees were shaking.

'Don't look so worried,' murmured Julia beside her. 'They always play like that.'

Angela laughed uncertainly. 'I'll never get used to it.'

On the field Jimmy whooped with elation as he slammed the ball through the posts at the far end. Julia bent over as though to inspect her shoe; after a moment she asked, still bending over, 'You're in love with Marcos, aren't you?'

A statement of fact, neither censoring nor approving. Angela let another minute go by.

'Is it so obvious?'

'It's obvious you don't hate each other.'

The players were cantering down the field. Tadeo said something to Marcos, who laughed and turned to look at the women watching from behind the ropes. His eyes found Angela and smiled at her — an intimate, possessive smile that shook her to the core. She looked quickly away, afraid that her answering look might betray their secret.

It was moments like this that made the frustrations of 'whenever possible' so difficult to bear.

'Perhaps you'll tell me it's none of my business, but I still think you and Jimmy should take a trip somewhere,' said Julia softly. 'Try and make a new start before it's too late. This way – who knows? I'm very fond of you, Angela. I don't want you to be hurt.'

'Don't worry, I can take care of myself.'

Julia shook her head. 'In these cases,' she said gravely, 'the woman always gets hurt.'

IV

During drinks on the terrace before supper Jimmy drew Marcos aside. 'Can we talk a minute?'

They left Alfredito trying to convince everyone that Argentina's salvation lay in the extreme Right and went into the study. The light on the desk made pools of shadows in the corners, deepening the lines around Jimmy's mouth. He sank down in a chair and stared blankly at the opposite wall. Marcos waited uneasily.

'What's the matter?' he asked when several minutes had ticked by in empty silence.

There was another pause before Jimmy stirred. He rattled the ice in his glass, took a long sip and hunted for cigarettes in his shirt pocket. His fingers trembled as he struck a match.

'I'm up shit's creek,' he muttered and fell silent again.

'Trouble with the Widow?'

'What? Hell, no.' A faint, bitter smile flickered briefly across his face. 'Much worse than that. There was a poker game a month ago down at Cardales. Angela was in BA and I . . . hell, you know how it is! All the old crowd was there, plus a couple of chaps from Córdoba. Iván Torres as well.'

Marcos frowned. 'Playing far from home, isn't he?'

'He owns the bloody hotel in Cardales.' Jimmy stared at the glass in his hand. 'I had a bad night. We ended up playing Mad Dog or something like that. Can't remember.' He shuddered and emptied his drink in a single gulp.

'It was Torres and myself at the end. He picked me clean.'

The sound of laughter drifted through the open window. Marcos watched Jimmy, his face expressionless. A month ago Angela had been with him at El Remanso while her husband lost his shirt to Iván Torres. He felt a sudden surge of unreasoning anger against Jimmy, compounded by an equally sudden sensation of guilt. The guilt startled him. Jimmy and Angela were two separate worlds; so far he had been able to keep them apart. He fiddled with a paperweight and concentrated on anger.

'I asked my old man for help,' continued Jimmy bitterly. 'Told him I needed the money for an investment. He lectured and mother bitched and in the end . . .' His hands sketched a nervous gesture. 'The usual crap.'

'What about the bank?'

'Can't afford their interest rates.' Jimmy cracked his knuckles and looked miserable. 'I need help, old boy. Torres wants his money by the end of the month – that's only ten days away.'

Marcos lit a cigarette very slowly and deliberately; when he spoke his voice was colourless. 'How much help?'

Five figures. Marcos shook his head.

'Six months, old boy! I'll repay you in six months!'

'Where will you get the money from? Gambling?'

Jimmy flushed angrily. 'God damn it, don't use that tone with me! You're no stranger to a poker table!'

'I never lost more than I could afford and I was never fool enough to sit down with Iván Torres,' snapped Marcos. 'I know all about gamblers, Morgan! My brother's one. The only difference between you and Lucas is that he doesn't have the brains for anything else.'

Jimmy jumped up and began pacing the room. 'What the hell do you want me to do? Angela and I . . . well, it's not the same anymore. She's more interested in Laguna's brats than she is in me – or she's off to BA to gallivant around with Julia's old aunt. Or poking her nose into the way I run the ranch. Questions about this and questions about that – hell, it's a man's job!' He flung up his hands in disgust. 'She doesn't even like me to make love to her anymore. Cold as a fish – that's the treatment I get! Ever tried screwing an iceberg? I don' t recommend it!'

'Look, I'm not interested . . .'

'So what if I have a couple of drinks and a game of poker now and then? What the hell's wrong with that?'

No answer.

274

Jimmy struck his fist against the wall and stared out of the window. 'So I see the Widow — why not? She's my brat's mother, isn't she? I've got a right to her, damn it! I've got a right to that kid too, even if he is a whore's son. I won't get any out of my own wife, will I?' He hunched his shoulders and whistled silently at the darkness. 'That kid's a good-looking little bastard,' he added after a moment. 'Calls me *loco*. "Hey, *loco*," he says. "Show me how to make a slingshot."' There was another brief pause. 'I'd like to adopt him, but there's Angela. She wouldn't understand.'

'No,' said Marcos dryly. 'I don't think she would.' He stood up with a brusque movement, eager to end the interview. 'I'll lend you half the amount. I can't afford any more right now. Pay me back in six months.'

He heard his own voice telling Angela *it's very difficult because I am Jimmy's friend*. There were times when he hated that friendship with all his heart, but the nagging shadow of guilt refused to go away.

CHAPTER TWENTY-TWO

I

At twenty Marcos Luciani had known for a long time exactly what he wanted.

La Catalina was his sole interest; he had rooted his dreams in the land and set about proving to his father that he could fulfill them. He had sowed his wild oats as enthusiastically as the rest of his friends, but had never allowed the sowing to interfere with what was important. At forty-five he could look back on those days with a certain amount of wry pride. His discipline had served him well; he saw no reason why other men should not do the same.

Other men included his son.

At twenty Miguel still had no idea what he wanted out of life. His future had been mapped out for him since the day he was born; from womb to cattleman's saddle to tomb. Perish the thought. It was a dismal prospect.

He wouldn't have minded so much if he were living in pioneering days, when life was full of adventure and danger. Clearing land and building stockades and fighting Indians would have been exciting. He could identify with the struggle for survival, Miguel told himself. What he couldn't identify with was routine. The deadly rhythm that marked today and tomorrow and the day after with the sameness of yesterday. Life on La Catalina would be like that. Up at the crack of dawn, overseeing the endless business of cattle and crops and machinery, into bed by eleven at the latest and up at the crack of dawn again. The same monotonous pattern year after year until he died.

'I'll end up like Papa, married and with three kids by the time I'm thirty,' he reflected glumly. 'By the time I'm forty I'll be an old man. Finished.'

He envied Gastón, who at twenty-two knew what he wanted and was actively involved in running the family ranches.

Gastón shared Marcos's consuming passion for the land. Miguel tried his best to work up similar enthusiasm because it was expected of him, but the spark refused to kindle fire.

Apart from a strong physical resemblance, Miguel had very little in common with his father. Their relationship was an uncertain one. Adolescent rebelliousness had given way to a wary truce, but there was no closeness between them. Miguel instinctively sensed Marcos's disappointment and resented it; on the other hand he felt guilty for not measuring up to his father's expectations. He often reflected with grim humour that he and Isabel should have changed places.

'She's the one my old man really wants as his right hand. It's always been like that, ever since we were kids.'

Perhaps that was part of his resentment as well.

Had Miguel known exactly what he wanted he might have found the courage to fight for it, but vagueness and generalities were no basis for a confrontation. He would only make a fool of himself. It was important for his own pride that he preserve a certain image before the world and especially before his father. It was vitally important that no one should ever know the secret, unhappy restlessness in his heart.

Miguel cultivated that image carefully, sowing his wild oats with apparently cynical disregard for the consequences. There are, however, different kinds of wild oats and he took great care to keep the wilder ones concealed from his father. That first night at Fabio Grandi's flat three years ago had opened an adventurous world of sorts to him and he quickly became one of its most promising products. Lucas was flattered by his nephew's growing reputation as a card-player and womanizer; at the same time he thought it prudent to warn Miguel against biting off more than he could chew — especially where a tough like Iván Torres was concerned.

'There's a rumour you've been making a play for Torres's new girl,' he remarked. 'Sonia — the one who works at the art gallery downtown. Better watch it, kid. I'm a partner in that place.'

'So?'

'Iván Torres is very touchy where his tarts are concerned. I wouldn't like you to get into trouble.'

Miguel grinned. 'I can take care of myself.'

'I won't pick up the pieces if you can't,' laughed Lucas, but he sounded uneasy just the same.

II

Aurora Grandi knew all about Miguel's wild oats. At forty-three her infatuation for him still persisted; he excited her as though she were a fifteen-year-old, with far less attractive results. Whenever he went to Fabio's flat she was there; if he wanted a drink she brought it to him, if he needed money she gave him her purse. She laughed shrilly at his jokes and flirted with anxious hunger. Miguel was flattered at first and then bored; after a while he began to egg her on because she irritated him, but Aurora was too besotted to take the hint.

'I thought we might have dinner together one night,' she suggested. 'My place on Friday, perhaps?'

Miguel winked at Lucas. 'You're a goddess, Aurora.' He kissed the inside of her wrist, letting his lips linger on her skin with cruel humour. 'I can hardly wait.'

Nothing but the best for what promised to be a very special occasion. Brussels lace on the table, candles, the Limoges service that had been part of her mother's dowry. A small fortune of food, flowers and champagne. In a burst of extravagance Aurora bought herself a black lace négligé and a bottle of imported scent. She made up the bed with new sheets, plumped the pillows and dimmed the lights. A warm, intimate aroma of fresias and *coq au vin* filled the flat. Aurora put on her favourite Sinatra record and lit a cigarette. Autumn rain drilled against the living-room window. She swayed happily to the music and listened for the lift. It was eight o'clock.

The minutes ticked by and became hours.

At eleven o'clock Aurora gathered up courage and dialled Barranco Rosales. Perhaps Miguel was ill or had met with an accident . . . She pressed a crumpled handkerchief to her lips and listened to the telephone ringing halfway across Buenos Aires. Mercedes answered. Aurora swallowed and clamped the handkerchief over the mouthpiece with trembling fingers.

'M-may I speak to Miguel, please?'

'I'm sorry, he went to Mar del Plata for the weekend. Who's calling?'

Aurora rang off without replying. She sat down very slowly on the sofa and studied the rings on her hands. A bus braked in the street below, a man shouted some unintelligible obscenity.

'Perhaps he forgot,' she said out loud.

The clock chimed the half-hour; after a moment she turned up Sinatra full blast because she could no longer bear the sound of time.

III

The weekend dragged by. Monday came, no word from Miguel. Aurora forced herself to go about life as usual, but she felt grey and old. Lorenzo was giving a recital that evening. She went, not because of the music but because he had been Cristina Luciani's music teacher for the past two years. Even such a remote connection with Miguel might ease the empty ache in her heart.

The recital was in a private home owned by Alberto Navone who made his money importing and exporting whatever came his way. His wife Toti was a close friend of Gladys. Not top-drawer society but more than wealthy enough, decided Aurora as she glanced around the packed drawing-room. The new wealth. New business, new industry, new names with a scattering of the old established ones grafted on by marriage. Not one of these people would have known the Lucianis in the old days, she reflected wryly. Magdalena would have seen to that. Lorenzo didn't mind who he played for as long as it meant money and a chance for fame. She watched him bending over Gladys Luciani's hand and gave a sudden, involuntary shudder of distaste.

'Our little brother's missed his calling,' murmured Fabio in her ear. 'He should have been a gigolo.'

Aurora drew away slightly. 'Don't be stupid. Lorenzo's doing very well for himself.'

'Oh, yes — no doubt about that. But then most young men do when they find an old hen to dote on them.' Fabio waved his cigarette holder, ignoring her furious blush. 'Furs and all, la Gladys is still delightfully kitsch, don't you think? Old Marcos has surprisingly bizarre taste for a philistine. I'm dying to paint her.'

279

'I doubt you'll ever get the chance,' retorted Aurora through clenched teeth and went home to another lonely night.

Tuesday was cold and damp. Mist seeped in from the river and clung to the buildings; the wind was raw and stank of mud. By four p.m. the city was shrouded in a grey, melancholy half-light; Aurora turned up her coat collar and walked aimlessly down Paraguay Street, staring at shop windows. The art gallery was not far off. She decided to go in and browse.

Anything to keep her mind off a telephone that did not ring.

The gallery appeared to be deserted. She wandered through two rooms, paused to inspect a landscape by a new artist and passed Fabio's latest cubic nude without a second glance. A room at the back contained several cast-iron sculptures. Aurora stopped before a convoluted diagram of motherhood; two seconds later she heard Miguel laugh.

The laughter came from what seemed to be a small office behind a half-open door. She tiptoed towards it, her footsteps muffled by thick black carpeting.

'You're a jealous little bitch, you know,' said Miguel's voice.

A woman answered, half annoyed, half teasing. 'What do you expect? Everyone knows that old cow's hot for you. The way she carries on.'

'Forget her.' There was a long silence and then he added in reply to a murmured question, 'No, I didn't go on Friday. I have better things to do than spend the night with an old bag like her.'

From where she stood Aurora could see their reflections in a mirror. Miguel and Iván Torres's girl. Sonia – the redheaded secretary who sometimes modelled for Fabio. Aurora had once seen her posing naked – smooth hips, high rounded breasts, rounded belly, the reddish glow between her legs coyly shielded by a milk-white hand. *Venus on rollerskates*. The milk-white hand tickled Miguel's ear. He laughed and leaned forward; their lips met, opened, eagerly explored each other's mouth. Aurora swallowed. There were two milk-white hands now. They moved inside Miguel's jacket, touched, did things she herself dreamt so often of doing. His voice rasped.

'God, you're an incredible bitch!'

He pulled up Sonia's sweater. The high, rounded breasts challenged Aurora through the mirror. She watched Miguel fondle them, kiss them, dart his tongue over the stiff pink nipples. Her own breasts ached for his touch.

280

'God, you're a sexy bitch!' repeated Miguel. 'Let's go somewhere now. There's a place around the corner . . .'

'I can't. I work here until seven.'

'Afterwards then.'

'I don't know . . .'

'Sonia, for Christ's sake!'

She chuckled deep in her throat. 'Greedy bastard.' They kissed again. 'Iván's off to an all-night poker game. Come by my place after eleven tonight if you still want to.'

'Why don't you leave that pig?'

'Because he pays my bills. What's that noise?'

By the time they looked around the office door Aurora Grandi was gone.

Somehow she made it home. The world was clammy and dark and very cold; she thought she would never find warmth in it again. Her mind refused to remember the things it had heard, but memory laughed and goaded cowardice to hot, savage fury. She thumbed through the telephone book, found Iván Torres's office number, dialled. A crisp, impersonal secretary put her through.

'They called you a pig,' Aurora whispered as soon as his voice came on the line. 'If you want to know what goes on behind your back, go to Sonia's tonight. Eleven o'clock, pig.'

She hung up on his startled silence and stared at herself in the mirror. A stranger stared back — a pale, middle-aged stranger with bags under her eyes and a sagging chin. Aurora watched as tears streamed down the stranger's cheeks. She made no move to wipe them away.

IV

At Barranco Rosales a telephone began to ring.

The sound reached Marcos through a fragmented world of uneasy dreams. He surfaced slowly, groping towards the shrill, insistent ringing until his hand found the receiver and a man's incisive voice replaced the bell.

'Marcos Luciani?'

He grunted acknowledgement and fumbled for the light. Two a.m. on the alarm clock. The man spoke rapidly, cutting through the remnants of sleep. Marcos listened, asked a question; when he replaced the receiver Gladys stirred beside him and mumbled 'What's wrong?' A thin film of wrinkle cream glistened on her face, the pink netting around her curls resembled an incongruous cocoon.

'Miguel's in trouble,' said Marcos, pulling on his trousers.

'Police?'

'No. I didn't catch the man's name. Go back to sleep.'

'Be careful,' yawned Gladys and turned her back.

A well-intentioned warning. Together with the face cream and the pink hairnet it formed a cosy domestic hell that did little to improve his temper.

V

The man had directed Marcos to a street in the dock area. He drove along it slowly, looking for number 157. Most of the houses were old one-storey buildings separated from the cobblestone street by a narrow strip of uneven pavement; number 157 stood in the middle of the block between an abandoned warehouse and a bakery. It was taller than the rest – four storeys of dirty yellow stucco and a dark green door. The windows on the ground floor were tightly shuttered; as Marcos studied them uneasily a man stepped out of the doorway and came towards him.

'Señor Luciani? My name's Stefan Stervic. I rang about your son.'

'Where is he?'

The man motioned with his head. 'Upstairs.'

They groped their way down a dark corridor, turned right and climbed four flights of stairs dimly lit by a paraffin lamp on each landing.

'Power cut,' explained Stervic. He thrust a key into the lock of a door on the top floor and paused. 'I cleaned him up as best I could. His nose is broken, probably a couple of ribs as well. They did a rough job on him.'

'*Who did?*'

Stefan Stervic shrugged. 'Whoever threw him out of the car that nearly ran me down,' he replied dryly and opened the door.

They entered a small, sparsely furnished room. A table littered with papers under the window, a makeshift bookshelf stacked with books and rolls of blueprints, a narrow bed covered by a roughly woven black-and-red rug. Miguel lay on the bed. His nostrils were sunken in a swollen mass of discoloured flesh, his lips raw and shapeless, his eyes narrowed to half-slits under monstrous eyelids. When he heard footsteps he opened the left slit a fraction of an inch. It took a long minute for consciousness to register; when it did he groaned and tried to look away.

'I'll make some coffee,' said Stervic quietly and left the room.

Miguel's blood-stained jacket and tie lay on a chair. Marcos stared at them; after a moment he sat down gingerly on the bed.

'What the devil have you been up to?'

The terrible lips made a hissing noise and were silent. In the minute space that served as a kitchen water gurgled, cups clattered. The lips moved again.

'Papa . . .'

Marcos leaned over the bed. 'Tell me who did this to you,' he urged, making his voice gentle. 'I want to know.'

There was a brief, agonized pause and then, 'T-torres.' Tears trickled between the swollen slits. 'H-he came to Sonia's. Someone t-told him . . .'

'Go on.'

Miguel had reached Sonia's place at eleven. They had a couple of drinks, put on records, danced. He was about to suggest moving into the bedroom when Iván Torres burst in, followed by four of his thugs. They collared Miguel and began to whip him with their fists. A brutal kick caught him in the groin, another one brought him to his knees. Sonia screamed. Two of the thugs hauled Miguel up and opened the front door. He felt himself plunging down an endless staircase; then, mercifully, everything went black.

Marcos took hold of his hand. 'How did you get mixed up with a bastard like Torres?'

Another pause before the words came again. Miguel clung to his father's relentless grasp and talked, finding a strange, bitter relief in confession. The only part he kept back was Aurora Grandi – out of shame perhaps, or a twisted sense of pity. After he finished speaking there was a very long silence.

'I found some *caña*,' said Stervic, bringing in a tray with three mugs of coffee and a glass. 'Rot-gut stuff, but it's strong enough

283

to get him home.' He handed the glass to Miguel, who forced down the contents with a shudder.

'The car almost hit me when I was crossing at the corner. Fifty yards further on the rear door opened and someone threw him out. I thought I was seeing things.'

Marcos looked up curiously. Stervic was much younger than he sounded – early twenties, perhaps. Slightly above average height, strong build and features, light-brown hair and very pale, hard eyes. The eyes returned his glance without blinking. Stefan Stervic would not get himself into trouble over Torres's bitch, Marcos decided ruefully. He glanced around the room. A threadbare rug on the floor, a silver crucifix hanging from a nail in one corner, a calendar and a large framed photograph above the bookshelf. The photograph showed a mountain landscape and a large man in his fifties with his arm around a handsome fair-haired woman.

'My parents,' said Stervic. 'My father was an architect. The Communists shot him in fifty-two. Yugoslavia.' The slightly foreign inflection in his voice was suddenly more noticeable. 'We escaped and came to Argentina.'

'Do you have family here?'

'My sister and brother-in-law. They came over in forty-nine and opened a hotel in the lake district. My mother lives with them now.' The right side of his mouth twitched. 'She's not very strong. The climate's better for her down there.'

Marcos indicated the rolls of blueprints. 'You're an architect too?'

'Three more years to get my degree – if I'm lucky. I work in a civil engineering office, don't always have time to study.' He put down his coffee as Miguel groaned. 'You'd better take him home.'

Marcos reached for his wallet. 'Let me give you something for your help.'

'No thanks.'

He studied the young man for a minute and then held out a business card. 'All right. If you ever need a recommendation, let me know.'

Stervic thrust the card into his trouser pocket. 'I'll help you down to the car.'

When he returned upstairs Stefan Stervic took out the card and studied it for some time. He had been very close to his own father. They had been good friends. His father had been shot in the doorway of their house; he would have rather died himself. He would have rather died than have caused his father the same bitter disappointment he had seen on Marcos Luciani's face as he bent over his son. Failure, sadness – Stefan Stervic was not meant to have seen them, but he did. They cut him to the heart.

He placed the card carefully inside his wallet and stretched out on the bed. He missed his father. There were so many things he wanted to talk about, so many plans for the future he wanted to discuss. Stervic was an ambitious young man. He knew what he wanted from life, but there were times when he felt an aching need for his father's encouragement. A man like Marcos Luciani, he thought wistfully, would have understood that need.

His pale, hard eyes strayed to the photograph of his parents above the bookshelf; after a moment he went over and took it down. The photograph remained under his pillow for the rest of the night.

VI

Lucas spent the evening persuading an elderly American couple to buy three of Fabio Grandi's paintings; later that night he amused himself taking photos through a peep-hole in the wall of a room the painter rented by the hour. Afterwards he made the rounds of his favourite bars and finally stumbled back to Barranco Rosales at six a.m. He dropped his clothes on the floor and crawled into bed. Two minutes later the door of his bedroom flew open.

'Get out of here!' yelled Marcos. 'Now!'

Lucas blinked. '*What?*'

'*Out!*' A hard, leathery hand cracked across his face. 'Take your things and get out of this house!'

He let out a cry of rage and scrambled from the bed as the hand swung again. 'You're crazy! Why the hell should I? God damn it!' ducking another blow, 'What have I done?'

Marcos told him in no uncertain terms, beginning from the day he was born and ending with Miguel; when he heard about the beating, Lucas shrugged.

'Serves him right. I warned the stupid ass not to fool around with Torres's whores.'

'That stupid ass,' roared Marcos, 'is my son! All these years I've put up with your crap, but I won't put up with you mixing Miguel in it!' He blocked Lucas's sudden lunge for the door and forced him against the wall. 'Get out of this house! I don't care where the hell you go, I don't care what happens to you! Tell Torres to feed you – you're not getting another god-damned peso out of me!'

'What if I don't leave?'

'I'll kick you out.'

'You wouldn't dare.'

Marcos bared his teeth. 'Try me! You have one hour. I'll send the butler to help you pack. If you give me any trouble I'll beat you up like Torres beat Miguel – only a hundred times worse. If it kills you, so much the better.'

'You're crazy!'

'*One hour!* I've given orders you're not to be allowed back in this house for any reason whatsoever. Any letters for you will be sent on to the office.'

Lucas attempted a sickly sneer. 'Anything else?'

They stared at each other for a long, bitter moment before Marcos walked over to the door. His face was grey.

'Yes,' he said heavily. 'As far as I'm concerned, you're dead. I never want to see you again.'

The quarrel woke Miguel from a nightmare of misery and physical pain. He lay listening in bed and wondered if Lucas would come to see him before leaving. Nothing happened. The door to his room remained closed; some time later he heard the sound of suitcases being taken downstairs. The front door slammed, tyres crunched on the driveway, the church bells down the street began to peal softly.

The least Lucas could have done was say good-bye. Not leave him in the lurch like this. It was all Lucas's fault anyway. If it hadn't been for Lucas he would never have met Iván Torres or Sonia . . . Miguel uttered a painful groan. He didn't want to remember Sonia or the things his father had said coming home in the car. Stern, impressive things about being a man and not disgracing the family name. Marcos Luciani had not been angry, just solemn. Solemnity intensified guilt and rubbed bitter salt into Miguel's wounded pride; Lucas's desertion completed his misery.

There was nothing left now but the bleak prospect of life on La Catalina. Last night his father had made that abundantly clear.

'I thought I could trust you on your own,' he said in those same solemn tones. 'I was wrong. From now on you'll live on La Catalina where I can keep an eye on you. I'm sorry, but that's the way it's going to be. You'll have to prove you're man enough to behave responsibly before I can trust you again.'

Miguel had tried to push words through his swollen lips. 'P-Papa, I . . . don't . . .'

'You don't what?'

He didn't want to be the cattleman's son. He wanted to live his own life . . . It was no use. He couldn't bring himself to make any more confessions. Miguel shook his head and stared dismally out of the window. The moment of truth between father and son had come and gone. It would never return.

VII

Pedro came to see Miguel later that day and found his godson in a truculent, self-pitying mood. The priest tried to talk him out of it.

'Put yourself in your father's place,' he said. 'Marcos got the fright of his life when he saw the state you were in. Those thugs might have killed you – or maimed you for life.'

Miguel muttered something under his breath.

'Your father's only doing what he thinks is best,' Pedro continued after a moment.

'I know that.'

'You're his son. He wants you to take pride in the family business, in your future . . .'

'I know that!' shouted Miguel. 'I know I'm his son! I know it, I know it! Stop telling me!' He buried his swollen face in the pillow. 'Leave me alone!'

Pedro was a tactful man. He repeated a watered-down version of their conversation to Marcos, adding that it might be a good idea to let Miguel decide for himself what he really wanted to do.

'He may be cut out for something else besides ranching – or he may not. It's only fair to give him a chance to find out.'

'You seem to know more about my son than I do,' observed Marcos dryly. 'He's never mentioned any of this to me.'

Pedro smiled. 'I'm a priest. I've developed a sixth sense for reading between the lines.' He leaned forward, his good-natured face unusually serious. 'Marcos, don't stifle that boy. Let him breathe.'

'La Catalina's as much a part of Miguel's responsibility as it is mine. It's high time he settled down and started taking his responsibility seriously.'

There was a short silence.

'You're a fortunate man,' Pedro said finally. 'You've always known what you wanted. Others aren't that lucky. Just because Miguel may be unsure or have doubts doesn't mean he's any less your son or any less a man.' He studied Marcos with strangely compassionate eyes. 'You may find it very difficult to be measured by your own standards on Judgement Day, you know. It's a point worth thinking about.'

Marcos thought about it — briefly. A week later he took Miguel back to La Catalina and put him to work. He blamed himself for what he saw as his son's failure to measure up to standard; as a result, he drove Miguel harder than he would have under ordinary circumstances. Miguel seemed apparently resigned to his fate — but frustration and resentment continued to fester below the surface like an unhealed sore.

CHAPTER TWENTY-THREE

I

Claudia, still awkward and unhappy at seventeen, had taken to paying her grandmother surreptitious visits on Saturdays. Celestina Gaspari seemed pleased to see her. They made a feast of each occasion, reliving past memories over cups of tea and stacks of *alfajores*. The visits became the focal point of Claudia's existence. Each day brought her nearer to the next one, each hour spent in Quilmes made the misery of Barranco Rosales easier to bear. No one there seemed too interested in her whereabouts and she was free to enjoy the past unchallenged.

Then, one mild Saturday afternoon in mid August, Claudia walked into her grandmother's kitchen and found Celestina slumped in a chair.

The old woman's face was blotched, a thin line of spittle dribbled from the corner of her open mouth. Claudia stared at her in terror.

'*Grandmother?*'

There was no reply. Claudia fled into the street. A man was coming along the opposite pavement; she ran over and grabbed hold of his arm. Her voice made shrill, babbling noises.

'Help! My grandmother's dying! Please help me!'

He uttered a startled exclamation and followed her back into the shop. Celestina sat bolt upright in her chair, her thick hands gripping the table. She grunted indignantly at the sight of a stranger in her kitchen.

'What do you want?'

The man threw Claudia a puzzled glance. 'Your grand-daughter said you weren't well, señora.'

'I'm all right. Just a touch of indigestion.'

She might just as well have said 'mind your own business'. The man shrugged and walked out of the kitchen. Old women were old women. This one looked like a tartar. All the same the

289

girl had been frightened. A well-dressed girl. Too well-dressed for this kind of neighbourhood. He stood on the pavement outside the shop and wondered.

In the kitchen Claudia continued to fuss anxiously over her grandmother.

'Let me call the doctor. You should be in bed . . .'

'I'm all right!' Celestina tugged her thick black cardigan into place. 'I don't need a doctor.'

'What's going on?' inquired a man's voice and Juan Gaspari strolled through the kitchen entrance.

Claudia's round cheeks flushed. 'Grandmother's not well.'

'What's wrong with her?'

'She's not well! She works too hard and you're never around and the girl in the shop's no good! Why don't you help? Can't you see she's old and needs to be taken care of?'

'I'm all right,' muttered Celestina.

'No, you're not. Maybe Uncle Juan doesn't care about you, but I do!'

'Just a moment!' protested Gaspari. 'What do you mean I don't care about her? Didn't I find somebody to help in the shop when I'm not around? Can I help it if I'm a busy man these days?'

'It's a touch of indigestion,' said Celestina loudly. 'I'll lie down for a while and feel better afterwards. Leave me alone, child!' as Claudia rushed to help her. 'I don't need any fussing. Come and visit next Saturday if you like. I'll make special *alfajores*.'

They heard her footsteps dragging heavily up the stairs; the floorboards creaked overhead, a door shut. Juan Gaspari stared uncomfortably at his niece.

'She gets like that now,' he said. 'Cranky and always imagining things. Take Rita, the girl who helps in the shop – she's a nice kid, but mother doesn't like her.' He cleared his throat. 'I'm a busy man these days. She doesn't understand that either.'

Claudia's eyes brimmed with tears. 'I do,' she replied bitterly and walked out.

A strong gust of wind whipped around the corner. The afternoon had turned colder; clouds covered the sun, threatening rain. Claudia trudged glumly along, kicking the leaves underfoot. Her Saturday afternoon dream was spoiled; she had a sinking feeling it would never return. She was no longer Claudia who played in Grandmother's kitchen or helped Grandfather behind the counter. Grandfather had been dead for a long time. There was a Rita to help now and even if Grandmother didn't like her, she would not exchange Rita for Claudia. Claudia was a visitor for whom one baked special *alfajores*. She must not be allowed to help because she belonged to her mother's world.

'I don't,' she muttered under her breath. 'I don't belong anywhere.'

'Your grandmother'll be all right,' said a man's voice at her elbow. 'I shouldn't worry too much about it.'

Claudia jumped. The stranger she had asked to help was smiling at her. She mumbled something and started off again; after a moment he followed. Out of the corner of her eye she noticed he was not very tall, young, with a narrow, earnest face. He wore stained grey flannel trousers and a shabby tweed jacket over a faded blue woollen jersey. His clothes hung loosely on a thin body, the sleeves of his jacket exposed two inches of bony wrist. He caught her eye and smiled again.

'My name's Luis Cabales. Do you live around here?'

Claudia shook her head. He waited for a moment and then tried again. 'May I ring you to find out how your grandmother is? Just to make sure everything's all right.'

'Ring me?' Her voice squeaked in astonishment. 'You want to ring me?'

'If you don't mind.'

'Oh. All right.'

There was a pause.

'I don't know your number,' he said.

Claudia gave it to him and signalled a passing bus; halfway across town she remembered she had not given him her name.

II

Luis Cabales shared a house with two aunts.

The house was very old and half hidden from the street by a garden consisting almost entirely of palm trees, ferns and weeds. The two aunts occupied the front rooms, which were cluttered with shabby old-fashioned furniture and an ever-changing collection of stray cats. Luis lived in two rooms at the back, reached by an outdoor passage and a small open patio. He was twenty-five and for the past four years had been ekeing out an existence as a journalist. His aunts thought him a genius; his father, who owned a small business in the eastern city of Paraná, thought him a damned fool.

'A journalist!' snorted Cabales senior in disgust when he learned of his son's intentions. 'Good-for-nothing oafs, that's what journalists are! You go to the capital to be a journalist and you're no son of mine! You're your mother's son – God rest the fool woman's soul. She came from a family with all sorts of pretensions.'

The aunts, who are the fool woman's sisters, welcomed their nephew with open arms.

Most of his articles, signed 'Dámocles', appeared in left-wing publications. He had recently started a small periodical with another colleague; he was, in fact, on his way to the man's house when Claudia stopped him.

The incident intrigued Luis Cabales. There were incongruous elements in it which appealed to his sense of social satire. An expensively dressed girl calling a working-class woman 'Grand-mother', an oily uncle, a dilapidated green-grocer's shop: the situation begged investigating. Luis mulled it over for a couple of days and finally dialled the number the girl had given him.

A man's voice answered. Luis cocked an eyebrow at the receiver and asked for the señorita. The voice demanded to know which one. He gave a brief description, the voice lost interest.

'Momento.'

A long silence followed and then the girl's voice came on the line, out of breath as though she had been running or was badly flustered.

'Luis Cabales here. I'm afraid I don't know your name.'

'Claudia.'

'How's your grandmother?'

'All right, thank you.'

Another silence. Cabales could hear the girl's uneasy breathing at the other end. He frowned slightly and asked, 'Would you like to meet me for a cup of coffee tomorrow?'

Her conversation seemed to be made up entirely of silences. 'All right' came after the longest one; when she said it he didn't know whether to be annoyed or amused.

Luis Cabales prided himself on being cool, even indifferent where women were concerned. Emotional involvement was a bourgeois affectation that clogged one's reasoning processes and wasted energy which could be put to far better use. Certainly there was no danger of becoming involved with a seventeen-year-old schoolgirl who had so little to say for herself and kept watching the clock in the café like a frightened rabbit. After their first meeting he made up his mind not to ring Claudia again.

A week later he found himself asking her out on Saturday afternoon.

III

Claudia took great pains to keep her friendship with Luis Cabales a secret. He was her own private world, untouched by disappointments or disapproval. She intended to keep matters that way. It was not too difficult. Gladys had firmly established herself in the world of new wealth and found little time for her daughter; when she did pause for breath it was to focus full attention on her son. The rest of the family revolved in its own universe and seemed relieved that Claudia no longer hung about on the fringes.

She did not quite know what to make of Luis, mainly because he treated her like a person. Her opinions interested him, he asked questions and waited for the answers. Claudia had few opinions and often found his questions confusing. He would laugh and explain what he meant very patiently; after a time she realised that he relished an audience and went out of her way to provide one.

On their fifth outing Luis took her to meet the aunts.

Lidia, short and plump with faded yellow ringlets, was passionately devoted to astrology and fortune-telling. She fussed over Claudia like a mother hen and offered to cast her horoscope. Alba was two years older, tall and gaunt, with henna-red hair hanging in a thin braid below her waist. She wrote obscure poetry and insisted Claudia had it in her to do the same. Both women were in their fifties – disorganized, eccentric and immensely kind. After fifteen minutes in their company Claudia felt she had known them all her life.

'I like your aunts,' she told Luis shyly. 'They're different.'

He laughed. 'They're both mad, but I like them too. It's a crazy house. You never know what to expect with Lidia and Alba.'

'It's a happy house,' said Claudia. 'It must be nice to live in such a happy house.'

The wistfulness in her voice disarmed Luis. Claudia certainly was no beauty and not particularly bright; he told himself he could live with that. She listened avidly to everything he had to say, laughed at all his jokes, was impressed by his political arguments. He found her very refreshing to be with – which was more than he could say for other women he had known.

Refreshment sharpened his pen.

'Dámocles' became even more inspired than usual – blistering, caustic and gloriously controversial. An editorial in one of the leading conservative newspapers ridiculed his wit and underlined the infiltration of Marxist elements in the national press. The president himself was rumoured to chuckle at Dámocles's sense of humour. Claudia, who did not understand much of what Luis wrote, told him her stepfather pronounced it rubbish.

'He would,' retorted Luis in disgust. 'He's the perfect example of the whole rotten system. A landed capitalist. Look at the thousands of acres he squats on!' He jabbed his pencil into the desk top. 'The only solution for this country lies in equal distribution of land and wealth, in the abolition of private industry. Men like your stepfather are an anachronism.'

Early October sunshine streamed across the patio and through the windows of Luis's room. Claudia stretched and yawned. Her cheeks were flushed, her brown hair curled in damp tendrils along the nape of her plump neck.

'It's so nice here,' she murmured, 'I'd like to live in your house.'

A stinging denunciation of the landowning class suddenly became irrelevant. Luis found himself studying Claudia's mouth, watching the small beads of moisture on her full upper lip. The aunts were out for the afternoon, they had the house to themselves. The lip quivered. His palms grew moist, his heart began to hammer very hard. Claudia's round, brown eyes widened in surprise.

'What's the matter?'

He leaned forward and traced the outline of her lips with an unsteady forefinger. They were soft and moist; he kissed them, pushing his tongue gently through the softness. Claudia caught her breath and sat very still, not knowing what to do. His hand touched her leg, hesitated, and began to move along her thighs.

'Don't be afraid,' whispered Luis. 'I won't hurt you.'

She blushed and returned his caresses awkwardly, stirred to passive excitement by the unfamiliar sensation of naked flesh against her own. The house was very quiet. Claudia closed her eyes and wished it could be like this forever.

IV

Gladys enjoyed a series of satisfying social successes that year.

A new charity invited her to sit on its main committee, a new concertgoers' society approached her for the same purpose. She sat on the organizing committee of another charity's annual bridge tea. Not one of these organizations belonged to Buenos Aires's long-established cultural and social institutions, but only a purist would quibble over that detail.

Gladys's crowning triumph came when Alfredo Castro's wife Fortunata invited her to join the Ladies of the Rosary.

Fortunata Castro was not only an extremely ugly woman, she was also sanctimonious and strait-laced. The Ladies of the Rosary was her brainchild – an exclusive body of society matrons pledged to defend the traditional teachings of the Catholic Church and combat moral corruption. She preached respectability in a shrill, incisive voice and constantly drew attention to her own marriage as a shining example of the virtuous household. Marcos burst out laughing when Gladys repeated Fortunata's assertion and remarked that Alfredo Castro lacked the imagination to be anything more than his wife's doormat.

'I recall Magdalena saying that Fortunata Castro would curdle the patience of a saint,' added Mercedes. 'Magdalena was a very devout woman, but she had no use for the Ladies of the Rosary.'

Gladys ignored Mercedes. 'I've invited the Castros to spend the first weekend in December with us here at La Catalina.'

'Christ!' muttered Marcos, 'I suppose Elías will show up as well. Every time I turn around these days he seems to be underfoot.'

Elías Castro was an important part of Gladys's plans. She looked over at her daughter and said with a pointed little laugh, 'He's a very nice young man. Sit up straight, Claudia. Can't you look pleasant for a change? What's the matter with you?'

Claudia began to tear at her nails. Ever since they arrived at La Catalina a week ago she had felt queasy. Maybe it was the heat – or her liver. She wished everyone would stop staring at her. She wished she could be with Luis.

The Castros arrived in due course for a weekend that tried the family's patience to its limits. Fortunata Castro insisted on drinking barley water instead of wine and immediately made everyone else feel like disreputable drunkards. At lunch on Sunday she lectured on public morals at the top of her voice until even Gladys began to squirm. The dining-room windows were open, but no breeze stirred the heavy summer air. Claudia began to sweat. Her stomach lurched into her throat, her knees wobbled. Fortunata Castro's voice droned on.

'The increase in pre-marital relations is scandalous! Father Ignatius was telling me only the other day that four out of five brides have already had an Experience before marriage. Disgusting!'

Claudia took one look at the dish of marinated partridges Yvonne had handed her, and proceeded to be violently sick.

No one could ever accuse Gladys of not being equal to the occasion. She uttered a shrill cry of motherly dismay and flew to her daughter's side while Fortunata clucked sympathetically in the background.

'It's my liver,' moaned Claudia. 'I'm all right. Just the heat and my liver and . . . and everything.' She pushed her mother away and began to sob. 'Leave me alone!'

'It could be food poisoning,' suggested Fortunata. 'My sister's niece-by-marriage died of food poisoning. Very suddenly – remember, Alfredo? She ate tinned peppers that were bad and took ill. Died within hours.'

Gladys eyed the partridges suspiciously. 'Maybe we should send for the doctor.'

'I should do so at once,' agreed the indomitable Señora Castro. 'My sister's niece-by-marriage had exactly the same symptoms.'

Feldman, summoned by an hysterical Gladys, reached La Catalina to find Claudia sobbing on her bed, surrounded by a handful of twittering women. He ordered everyone out of the room and began to examine her. Nearly an hour later he went in search of Marcos and found him taking a solitary walk in the park. Feldman studied the long, sweeping line of fields visible through the trees.

'Nice view,' he commented. 'How are things on the ranch?'

'Fine, as long as the weather holds. What's wrong with Claudia?'

The doctor took out a short, stubby pipe and began to pack in tobacco with an agile finger. His eyes studied Marcos over the rim of the bowl.

'Rich man, poor man – we all start the same way,' he remarked cryptically. 'Funny thing, Nature. Take you and me for instance. You own all this land and God only knows how much else besides. I'm next to nothing in your world, yet we both started life as a damned zygote. Even Hilter did – depressing thought, eh? We both have something in common with Hitler.'

'There's more to life than zygotes,' said Marcos dryly.

'So we keep telling ourselves.' Jacobo Feldman puffed for a moment in silence, his gaze lost in the trees. 'I'll carry out a test, of course, but I can tell you right now your stepdaughter's pregnant.'

V

The Castros had already left by the time Feldman dropped his bombshell on the rest of the family. Gladys insisted he was mistaken until she saw the result of the test; then she had hysterics. To think that her own daughter had done something like this – a child she had raised to be decent and respectable! A child she had so many dreams and hopes for. A child to whom she devoted so much care . . . Gladys grew incoherent with rage.

'Deceiving me behind my back! Carrying on like a street-walker! My own daughter, acting like a common tramp!'

'I'm not a tramp!' retorted Claudia angrily. 'I'm sorry if I deceived you, but you wouldn't have let me go out with Luis, and I wanted to and I'm going to live in his house and I'm not a tramp!'

'Who is this Luis?' shrieked Gladys. 'Nobody's ever heard of him!'

'He's a journalist.'

'A journalist!' Gladys sank down on the edge of the bed and clutched her head. 'Blessed Mary and all the saints — a *journalist*! No money, of course.' She began to moan. 'I had such high hopes for you, such dreams! I wanted you to get on well with Elías — such a nice young man. Serious, rich, good family . . .'

'Elías likes Isabel,' interrupted Claudia. 'Besides, I don't think money's everything.'

Her mother's head shot up. 'What do you mean, money isn't everything? *It is everything*! Where would we be now if I hadn't been smart enough to marry money, my girl? You answer me that!'

'What about happiness? Are you happy?'

'Of course I'm happy! I have everything I want.'

'Do you, Mama?'

They stared at each other for a long, empty moment before Gladys turned away. Claudia watched her walk over to the door and grasp the handle; it was a blind gesture.

'You are a very stupid girl,' snapped Gladys and walked out, slamming the door with all her might.

VI

Dámocles's pen wilted.

It was the summer heat, Luis told himself. Muggy, sticky days when the city streets melted underfoot; humid, sticky nights when he thrashed around in bed and thought about Claudia. He lost weight and grew irritable. His aunts fretted and his colleagues teased; his social conscience rebelled against the treachery of bourgeois affectations. He tried to settle down to work; four hours later he still sat staring at the same blank page in his typewriter.

There seemed to be only one, undeniably bourgeois solution to his misery. He was debating what to do about it when Claudia and her stepfather walked into the aunts' living-room.

Luis listened to what Marcos Luciani had to say, took one look at Claudia's apprehensive face and made up his mind.

'There's nothing to be afraid of,' he said, putting his arm around her. 'It's all right, Claudia.'

Her voice quavered. 'You're not angry?'

'Because of the child?' He patted her cheek. 'Don't cry, everything will be all right. Run along to the kitchen and help Lidia. I want to talk to your stepfather.'

She went off obediently. The two men heard a door open and Lidia's high, silvery voice laughing with pleasure. Luis cleared his throat nervously and indicated a chair.

'Sit down, señor.'

'No, thanks. I prefer to remain standing.'

Luis's face tightened. If that was how the man wanted to play it . . . He lit a cigarette with slow, calculated movements, waiting for the silence to thicken.

'Look here, Cabales,' began Marcos, 'about Claudia . . .'

'I don't deny the child's mine. I'll marry her – that's what you want, isn't it?'

A shadow of distaste crossed Marcos's face; he did not bother to reply.

'Mind you, I don't believe in marriage as an institution,' continued Luis loudly. 'It's the by-product of a hypocritical, anachronistic society. A bunch of bureaucratic mumbo-jumbo with a mess of religious superstition thrown in for good measure. If Claudia weren't a minor we'd live together without all that rigmarole. I suppose you wouldn't allow her to live with me without the blessing of Church and state?'

'Certainly not!'

'Well, there you are then,' sneered Luis and lapsed into uncertain silence.

A magazine lay open on the table, with a recent Dámocles article heavily circled in red pencil. Marcos frowned at it. 'You're a journalist?'

'What of it?'

'Just this, Cabales. If it weren't for the fact that you got Claudia pregnant I wouldn't allow this marriage. Her mother's very upset – I'm sure even you can understand that. The girl has no money of her own. I'll settle a reasonable dowry on her, but she's not my daughter and she won't inherit from my estate. I want to make that perfectly clear.'

'Do you think I'm marrying Claudia for her money?' exploded Luis, turning white. 'Yes, you would! Money . . .'

'Pays for housing, education, food and clothing. You'll be thinking about that with a family to raise, boy.'

Dámocles rose to the challenge with a vengeance. 'In the society of the future money will no longer be necessary!'

'Quite possibly,' agreed Marcos dryly. 'I hope I don't live to see it.'

VII

Claudia and Luis were married by Church and state on 20 December 1958, in the most threadbare of ceremonies. Gladys and Marcos put in a dutiful appearance, but the rest of the family showed a singular lack of interest. The witnesses were friends of the groom. Juan Gaspari turned up at the last minute with Celestina, who muttered ominously all through the ceremony. The aunts invited everyone back to their house for a wedding breakfast that was enlivened by the cats eating most of the sandwiches. Gladys held her tongue until the bitter end, then collapsed in raging floods of tears and sobbed all the way home on her husband's shoulder.

Her tears awakened in Marcos an uncomfortable sensation of guilt. Gladys might be a tiresome woman, but she was his wife and Claudia's mother. He told himself that she had every reason to be bitterly disappointed in her daughter; for once he was also honest enough to admit that his own attitude towards their relationship did not help matters much.

The family was already at La Catalina preparing for Christmas; they had Barranco Rosales all to themselves. Marcos made an effort to be agreeable. He sat with Gladys in the family living-room before dinner instead of going to his study. He coaxed her to have a cool drink, brought aspirins, fetched pillows for her back. He opened all the windows, turned on the electric fan, made an ice-pack with his handkerchief for her headache. Gladys continued to complain. She picked at her dinner and went upstairs without drinking her coffee; when Marcos entered the bedroom an hour later he found her by the open window, staring out at the darkness. She made a lonely figure, rendered even more vulnerable by the frothings of lace on her nightdress and the luxury of her surroundings. Guilt pricked his conscience again.

'There's a storm building up over the river,' he remarked as thunder rumbled in the distance. No reply. He crossed over to the window and touched her shoulder. 'Are you all right, Gladys?'

She said forlornly, 'I wanted Claudia to make a good marriage. I wanted her to have everything. It's so important to have everything. So important for happiness . . .'

Her voice trailed off. Without thinking he began to caress her bare shoulder. 'Are you happy?'

'Yes, of course. I'm very happy.'

What damned good liars we both are! reflected Marcos uneasily and felt a small stab of shame. The dark garden beyond the window was fragrant with the voluptuous perfume of roses and flowering jasmin. He tilted Gladys's face back and said pleasantly, 'It's late. Why don't you come to bed?'

He should have left it at that, but shame prompted a goodnight kiss as a sop to his guilty conscience. Gladys put her own interpretation on the caress. Perhaps out of loneliness and frustration – or perhaps the night's fragrant heat had loosened her many inhibitions. Her arms circled his neck, her parted lips demanded love with awkward, almost embarrassing passion. Marcos cursed mentally. He did not want to make love to Gladys. The idea of thrashing about in the heat and working up a lather for no pleasure at all was definitely an unwelcome prospect. On the other hand, to reject her outright would be adding cruel insult to injury. He tried to unclench her arms and hedged tactfully.

'We have to leave early tomorrow.'

It was a totally useless excuse. Gladys in bed proved to be even more demanding than Gladys by the window. He ended up thrashing about and working up a lather until he was sufficiently aroused to produce a passable performance. As far as his wife was concerned, he might have been Eros in the flesh. Gladys sighed and heaved and moaned; she rolled her eyes and uttered ennervating little cries. Marcos continued to thrash until he finally found release; then he crawled over to his edge of the bed, which was the only cool spot left, and fell into an exhausted sleep.

VIII

On 1 January 1959, a bearded rebel named Fidel Castro rode triumphantly into the Cuban city of La Habana and permanently altered the continental axis. Dámocles heralded the Cuban Revolution with an article calling for similar action in Argentina – a challenge which led Marcos to remark that men like Dámocles were far more dangerous than Artemio Mendes because they were intelligent.

CHAPTER TWENTY-FOUR

I

Towards the end of January Marcos drove down to El Remanso. Angela, who was spending a week with Lucía Claire, went with him.

They spent three days basking in Eden, oblivious to the world; on their return Marcos left Angela at Lucía's and drove to Barranco Rosales. He spent the rest of the afternoon reading reports from Jorge Robles, his office manager. Shortly after five he rang Angela to arrange for dinner.

'I'll come by for you at half-past eight. Do you think Lucía would like to join us?'

'She'd be thrilled.'

'I love you very . . .' began Marcos and stopped in mid-sentence.

Gladys stood on the threshold.

There was some distance from the door to his desk and he had been speaking in a low voice; it was impossible to say how much of the conversation she might have overheard. Angela broke in anxiously on the other end of the line.

'What's wrong?'

'I'll bring those papers over right away, Robles,' said Marcos, his eyes still on the motionless figure in the doorway. 'Meet me downstairs in twenty minutes.'

He replaced the receiver as though it scalded and Gladys laughed. 'Have I interrupted anything?' She came around the desk to kiss him – deliberately, Marcos thought.

'What are you doing in town?' he demanded.

She leaned against the desk, staring down at him with eyes he could not fathom. 'I was bored. I wanted to be with my husband.'

'I'm returning to La Catalina tomorrow.'

'Well,' laughed Gladys archly, 'that gives us tonight, doesn't it?' She took a cigarette from the box on his desk and held it out for him to light; smoking was a new habit she handled awkwardly. 'How was your trip?'

'What trip?'

'Didn't you go away? The butler says you haven't been here for three days.'

'I was down at El Remanso,' replied Marcos curtly.

Gladys smiled, her small bow-shaped mouth pursed in a knowing little grimace that infuriated him. She held her cigarette between thumb and forefinger and puffed without inhaling; the smoke spurted forth like the nervous breath of a miniature bellows.

'You've never taken me to El Remanso,' she complained.

'You'd be bored.' Marcos gathered up the papers in front of him, annoyed to discover that his hands were unsteady. 'I have to leave now. Robles is expecting me.'

He started for the door and found Gladys standing in the way. 'Let's dine out tonight,' she murmured. 'Just the two of us.'

'Not tonight, I'm tired.'

Her eyes widened and she ran the tip of her tongue over her lips. 'Don't be silly, we have a little something to celebrate. Guess what?'

'I can't imagine what we have to celebrate.'

She laughed in a coy, infuriating way and patted his cheek. 'Can't you? We're going to have another child, *querido*. Aren't you pleased?'

II

Angela was waiting downstairs when Marcos arrived. He motioned her impatiently into the car and sped off without replying to her anxious questions. They took the wrong direction on a one-way street, swerved blindly into a deserted cul-de-sac and careered to a halt within inches of a bright red sports car parked on the pavement. Marcos switched off the engine and sat staring blankly through the windscreen. There was a very long silence.

'It's Gladys, isn't it?' asked Angela when the silence became unbearable.

'I didn't hear her come into the study. She may have overheard our conversation – I don't know.' He ran a distracted hand through his hair. 'Christ almighty! Of all times, now! *Why?*'

Angela watched a fat woman on very high heels mince past trailing a white poodle on a leash; the poodle wore a rhinestone collar and a pink bow on its head.

'It was bound to happen sooner or later,' she laughed in an attempt to sound lighthearted. 'We've been damned lucky these past five years.' Her laughter quavered slightly. 'The Devil's own luck, they say.'

Marcos leaned his elbows on the steering wheel and covered his face with his hands; after a moment he dragged them away as though wiping off something unpleasant and reached for his cigarettes.

'It's not only that.' His voice rasped harshly and he continued to stare through the windscreen. 'She told me she's pregnant.'

The woman and the poodle disappeared into a courtyard. Traffic hummed in the distance, but the cul-de-sac was very still. Angela watched a sparrow pecking crumbs on the pavement. Yesterday we were at El Remanso, she reminded herself. Last night we ate supper under the trees and watched the stars coming out in a sky so clear it might have been a painted canvas. He called them the eyes of Heaven. We confided so many things to each other . . . She clenched her hands in her lap until the knuckles showed white.

Marcos's hand groped for hers. 'Angela.'

'It's all right,' she said dully. 'I understand. Love had nothing to do with it.'

She could go on saying *it's all right* until Doomsday – the words were a meaningless convention. Like marriage, when it was dead. Or love. Alive, love and marriage were as beautiful as the eyes of Heaven. Dead, they hung like millstones on the heart. Five years of love, reflected Angela bitterly. Five years of days and hours stolen at random – for what? A child is a child is their child. Oh, God! Why does it hurt so much? Because Gladys shares something with Marcos that I will never have? I have an empty marriage. Why the hell do I cling to it? Because there's nothing else I can do . . . Apart from the fact that she stood to lose everything if she deserted her husband, there was the question of a reason for leaving him. If she told Jimmy the truth, he would probably kill Marcos. Even if she told a lie he would never agree to a divorce. As far as Jimmy Morgan was concerned, their marriage was A OK. And what about Marcos? What if she found the courage to leave him? 'I love you, but I don't want to go on loving you like this. Whenever possible.' He wouldn't understand . . . Why the hell couldn't love be simple? I love you, you love me. We're as happy as can be. Very simple. The woman always gets hurt.

Angela drew a long, painful breath and repeated, 'It's all right. I do understand,' because love whenever possible was better than no love at all.

III

Old Rosario swore by all the saints on the calendar that troubles came in bunches like the Devil's claws. One of those claws was a letter from Italy.

It was addressed to Lorenzo Grandi and offered him a contract for a concert tour during the coming winter season. Nothing very grand, but Lorenzo was sick of Argentina. Despite Gladys's enthusiastic patronage he had not made much headway in his career. He was fed up with playing at private soirées and had few illusions about the future. He told himself that if he didn't get out now he would be doomed to spend the rest of his life in a pretentious backwater.

'Or wind up like Fabio,' he added with a heartfelt shudder.

Somewhat to his surprise Lorenzo discovered that Cristina Luciani was the only person he really minded leaving. He had put in over two years' hard work trying to develop her talent; he thought she was progressing well. He would have liked to make a success out of her – both for professional and personal reasons. Cristina was a charming and very attractive young lady. Lorenzo found himself unable to get her out of his mind.

'I've been offered a contract in Italy,' he remarked one afternoon during a pause between Czerny and Chopin. 'They want me to travel to Milan next month and discuss the details.'

Chopin slid to the floor. 'Oh,' said Cristina. Her cheeks were pale. 'Doesn't that mean you won't be teaching me any more?'

'I'm afraid it does.'

She played a few desultory notes. 'Do you want to go?'

'It's a big chance for me.' He waited a moment. 'You're good enough for the conservatory now. I can get you a recommendation.'

She continued to worry the piano keys, her head bowed. Lorenzo heard a faint sniff. He frowned and touched Cristina's shoulder.

'What's the matter?'

There was no reply. He took hold of her chin and forced it back gently; a pair of amber eyes stared woefully at him through a film of tears. Cristina blinked and the tears rolled down her cheeks. Lorenzo swallowed.

'Don't cry, little Juliet,' he whispered, and kissed her.

He intended the kiss as a gesture of comfort; he found himself embracing Cristina as though he could not bear to let her go. Perhaps it had been there all the time and he had not wanted to see it because the idea was so preposterous. Certainly the way she responded told half the story. Lorenzo tore himself away with a smothered phrase of caution.

'Someone might see us!'

Cristina laughed. Juliet sparkled and glowed and touched him with youthful, happy hands. 'You do like me, don't you?'

Her eyelashes were spangled with tears. He resisted an impulse to kiss them and smiled back, badly shaken by his discovery. 'I . . . how old are you?'

'Seventeen last week. Don't you remember?'

'I'm twenty-nine,' said Lorenzo uncertainly. 'That's almost twice your age.'

Cristina laughed and kissed him again – experimentally at first, then with disarming certainty. Lorenzo took a deep breath and gently pushed her away. Matters were getting out of hand. He smoothed down his hair and straightened his tie. Chopin leered at him from under the piano stool and he slammed the music on to the rack.

'Let's hear this nocturne. Have you practised it?'

'Do you love me?'

He made a feeble attempt to be stern. 'Be serious, please!'

'I am serious. I love you. I think about you all the time and now you're going away . . .' She twisted her hands in her lap and stared at him, her eyes wide and pleading. 'Do you love me just a bit?'

More than just a bit. Lorenzo placed her hands firmly on the keyboard. 'We must get on with this damned lesson,' he said. 'Do you think your aunt would let you come to a recital with me tomorrow evening?'

'We'll have to take her along.'

He brushed Cristina's lips very gently. 'That's better than nothing, isn't it? Much better, little Juliet.'

IV

At the beginning of July Lorenzo Grandi travelled to Milan and his sister went with him. Ever since the Torres incident Aurora had cloistered herself in a bitter world of self-pity, but even that world was no longer bearable. She desperately needed to start a new life unencumbered by the past; half an hour after take-off from Buenos Aires she discovered that the past, as far as her brother was concerned, belonged to the present and the future.

Lorenzo talked non-stop about Cristina Luciani. He managed to fill the days with a torrent of praise and plans. For the first time in his life he was really in love, Lorenzo assured his sister. Cristina was the perfect companion. Lively, intelligent, beautiful . . . He rambled on while the sunshine beat down on the Duomo in the hazy heat of a Milanese summer.

'The girl's barely seventeen!' protested Aurora when she could fit a word in edgewise.

'I want to marry her.'

'*Marry* her? Do you think Marcos Luciani will allow his daughter to marry a pianist? You're out of your mind!'

'What's he so particular about?' jibed Lorenzo, squirting soda into his vermouth. 'Look what he married.'

Aurora's expression soured. 'We all know how *that* happened. Anyway, she isn't Cristina's mother. Lorenzo,' as he set his jaw and glared at the pigeons pecking on the pavement, 'you have your career to think about. This is a wonderful opportunity . . .'

'You don't understand, do you?' he interrupted savagely. 'I'm in love with that girl, Aurora. I'm going to marry her.'

The Milan trip not only produced a contract for the coming season, but future engagements as well. At last Lorenzo's career seemed to be headed in the right direction. He returned to Buenos Aires in mid-August, brimming with optimism and more determined than ever to marry Cristina.

His arrival coincided with a number of occurrences, most of them unconnected with his own immediate concern but particularly important to the persons involved.

The president, ostensibly elected on a left-of-centre political platform, made an abrupt about-face in favour of private investment and economic austerity. His change in direction may well have been intended as a temporary concession to reality, but it spawned a new wave of violent political squalls.

Juan Gaspari had found his political footing again in the underground workings of the Peronist Party. The Party was split between those who championed Perón's return to power and those who favoured a form of 'Peronism without Perón'. Gaspari preferred the latter, but was politically shrewd enough to keep his preferences to himself. In the meantime he made a tidy profit on the black market.

'Don't blame me, *amigo*,' he grinned when Marcos complained about the price of imported cigarettes and whisky. 'Blame the minister of economy – better still, blame the president for appointing him. Whoever heard of a man from the Left making his major political opponent from the Right responsible for the nation's pocket? It's crazy!'

Marcos had a number of other things to complain about that year. Miguel was not settling down. He made no effort to do more than the work assigned to him and headed for Laguna Grande whenever he had the chance. Pablo Losa reported that he had been seen with a gambling crowd from Cardales.

'Don Jimmy's been known to sit down at cards with them,' added Losa with a disapproving shake of his head. 'A bad lot. They won't do Miguel any good.'

Jimmy, when questioned, admitted that Miguel had played in a few poker games and told Marcos to stop acting like a mother hen.

'For Christ's sake – the kid's of age! Let him live his own life.'

'Not gambling.'

Jimmy grinned, but it was a distorted grimace. 'You know what your trouble is? You're getting old.'

More aggravation, this time from an unexpected quarter.

In August Gladys gave birth to a daughter. Marcos regarded the child as an irritating accident; to his astonishment Angela disagreed.

'It's your child. Surely you knew what you were doing?'

He scowled, embarrassed and exasperated by her logic. 'That has nothing to do with it.'

'Why not? You have no right to father a child and then turn your back.'

'It was an accident!'

Angela raised a scornful eyebrow. 'I should have thought that you of all people would know how to prevent accidents.'

They were in a furnished studio flat Marcos had rented in downtown Buenos Aires. One of those rabbit-warren buildings where no one notices faces or asks questions. It was an expensive, impersonal place, functional and safe. He never knew how much Angela hated it until their quarrel.

The biting sarcasm of her retort stung Marcos on the raw. 'Of course I know how to prevent accidents!' he flared. 'I've been preventing them ever since Eduardo was born! You don't think I enjoy making love to my wife, do you?'

'I wouldn't know!'

'You know damned well I don't! I didn't want to make love to her this time, but she cornered me. *It was an accident!*'

'Stop saying that! Why don't you face up to the fact that for once in your life things haven't gone your way?' Angela cried furiously. 'You're always harping on about responsibility, always deciding what others should do or not do! You're so bloody good at preaching, but you're no damned good at practising what you preach!'

Marcos stared, his face pale. 'What the hell do you mean by that?'

'You think you can run everything, don't you? My life, Gladys's life! We're supposed to jump whichever way you pull the strings! You don't care if she's hurt or I'm hurt as long as you're happy. You don't even want to care about your own child!'

'You're talking nonsense!'

'Am I?' raged Angela. 'What about me? You've got everything you want. Land, wealth, a family, even a mistress you're so

310

goddamned sure of! What do I have? Love on the sly whenever possible. Half an hour on the sofa in your study or a couple of hours in your bed if we're lucky. A quick kiss when Jimmy isn't looking. A few days at El Remanso or at this flat . . . Have you ever asked me what I thought of this place? I hate it! It makes me feel sleazy and cheap, like some backstreet whore you picked up for a few thrills . . .'

'That's not true!' he interrupted in angry astonishment. 'If you didn't like this flat, you should have told me. I'll find some place else . . .'

'I don't want some place else! Can't you understand? I'm fed up with loving like this! I . . . oh, God, I wish I'd never met you!' she sobbed and stormed out, slamming the door with all her might.

Marcos remained rooted to the floor for a full thirty seconds before it dawned on him that Angela was gone.

Only a madman could have raced down five flights of stairs at such speed; only a madman could have charged down the street yelling her name at the top of his lungs. For the first time in his life Marcos Luciani acted like a madman. He caught up with Angela halfway to the corner and spun her round. She pulled away roughly; her sobs caught in her throat.

'Leave me alone!'

'Angela, for God's sake come back!' he pleaded. 'Don't leave me. I'm sorry if I hurt you . . . Please, *gringuita*. Please come back.' A bus roared past and he heard himself shouting, 'I love you!' to the amusement of the newspaper vendor on the corner. 'Angela, please . . .'

Only a madman would pull her into his arms and kiss her so desperately in full view of the world. He coaxed Angela back to the flat, still kissing, still pleading. His words tumbled frantically over each other.

'I'm sorry . . . I lost my temper . . . Angela . . . please!'

His kisses and caresses continued upstairs in a desperate attempt to erase the memory of their quarrel. He wanted to silence Angela's bitterness and anger, and reassure her of his love. His lips touched her eyes and found them still wet with tears.

'Don't cry anymore, *gringuita*. Please don't cry.'

She stood very still, offering no acknowledgement of his despair. Her impassivity frightened Marcos. He said brokenly, 'I love you so much,' and fell silent. After a moment Angela stirred and raised her head.

'You really do love me, don't you?'

'Do you doubt it?'

She sighed. 'I don't know. No, I don't think I do. It's just that . . .' Her voice shook. 'It's so difficult to continue like this, Marcos.'

'Don't you think I'm unhappy about the situation?' he asked gravely. 'I'd give anything to be able to change it, Angela. It's just not that simple and I will not place you in a position that would hurt you more than the one we're in.' His dark eyes searched her face. 'Do you really think things are any easier for me?'

She let a few seconds go by before smiling wearily. 'I don't suppose they are.'

'They're not,' he said and took her into his arms.

Late afternoon sunshine filtered through the blinds and spread pale yellow bands across the flat's functional, impersonal couch. They made love on the yellow bands, their bodies zebra-striped with light and shadows. This time love was too urgent for nakedness. They coupled in guilt-ridden haste, fumbling for the openings in their clothing with frantic fingers. Random details whetted physical excitement: the small hard knobs of Angela's nipples outlined against her blouse; the texture of bare skin between hips and knees; the rasping, laboured sound of their breathing. They rubbed each other to a frenzy while a typewriter clattered in the flat upstairs and late afternoon traffic blared in the street five floors below. *Te voy a coger hasta reventar . . .* Marcos's voice broke through their breathing with muffled, gasping phrases. I'm going to fuck you like crazy until we split atoms together, don't leave me Angela, for God's sake don't ever leave me!

They split atoms in a violent, shuddering climax that drained them of everything, even tenderness.

We've finally reduced love to a four-letter word, reflected Angela wryly when she went to wash. It's not surprising. We both know the years are slipping away. We try to deceive ourselves by fucking like crazy – for what? Time passes, our situation remains the same. Oh, God! Why must we love each other so much? Why must we need this love?

The image staring back at her in the bathroom mirror was silent. Some things would appear to defy even God's logic.

V

Lorenzo Grandi had all the symptoms of stage fright.

Dry mouth, weak knees, an empty pit that weighed like lead in the pit of his stomach . . . He wiped his hands nervously on his handkerchief and stared at the glass doors of the café. An elderly couple walked in, arguing querulously; behind them, two businessmen. No Cristina. A waiter strolled over and stared pointedly at Lorenzo, who ordered a coffee. His hands shook as he dropped in the sugar lumps. Suppose she didn't come? What if she had met someone else? She sounded pleased to hear him over the phone, but it was difficult to tell. Seventeen was a volatile age and Cristina Luciani was a lovely girl. A rich man's daughter. There would be plenty of rich men's sons in the running. At seventeen six weeks is a very long time and there had never really been any firm commitment. Just a few breathless, hasty kisses, a few respectable outings chaperoned by Mercedes and a tearful farewell. What, he wondered bleakly, did it all amount to?

'Not much,' grunted Lorenzo and was about to leave when Cristina rushed into the café.

She collapsed on to the chair beside him and dropped her schoolbooks with an exasperated crash. 'Sister Encarnación kept us overtime, the old cow! I've been running like mad.' Her hands caught hold of his and shook them urgently. 'Did you get my letters? I've been counting the days. What was Milan like? Are you glad to see me?'

'Yes.' Lorenzo touched her cheek lightly. 'Yes, I got your letters and yes, I'm glad to see you.' His eyes searched her face. 'I have so much to tell you, little Juliet.'

'Can I eat something? I'm starved. Gladys had a little girl the day before yesterday. Clara. Isabel and Yvonne and I think it's revolting. She must be nearly forty! Yvonne wants to go to art school. She had a hell of a row with Gastón about it and Papa backed him up and there was blood all over the place. Gastón's a troglodyte — even worse than my old man, I swear he is! I'll have three toasted ham sandwiches and a Coke, please. What's so funny?'

'You are,' laughed Lorenzo. 'I missed you very much.'

He told her about the concert tour and his plans for the future. Aurora had remained in Milan to hunt for a flat; he would live with her until he found something of his own.

'I'm going to make Milan my base. It's a glorious city. Elegant, dynamic – it would suit you well, little Juliet. Do you think you'd like it?'

'I don't know. I've never been there.'

Lorenzo cleared his throat. 'Cristina . . .' His voice trailed off because the flowery phrases he had practised all the way across the Atlantic suddenly failed him. They looked at each other. 'I want to marry you,' he said unsteadily. 'I want to take you back to Europe with me.'

In a Hollywood production there would be saccharine strings swelling the background and a close-up of misty-eyed lovers gazing passionately at each other. Real life produced the clinking of coffee cups and a heated discussion about cars at the next table.

'You'll have to ask my father, I guess,' said Cristina with somewhat dampening realism.

'Yes, I suppose so.'

She sighed dismally. 'Papa came down yesterday because of the baby. He's in a foul mood.'

Lorenzo reached for her right hand and kissed it. 'Trust me, little Juliet. I love you.'

On the strength of trust and love he made an appointment to see Marcos Luciani the following afternoon. He took great pains to dress for the occasion – dark grey suit, pale grey shirt, sober tie. Cristina would not arrive back from school until five o'clock; that gave him nearly three quarters of an hour to put their case to her father. As Lorenzo followed the butler into the library he reflected uneasily that three quarters of an hour seemed a hell of a long time.

Marcos greeted him with the detached politeness busy people reserve for unimportant interviews. They discussed the weather, politics, the situation in Europe. The minutes ticked by. Lorenzo told a joke; Marcos smiled politely and glanced at his watch.

'What did you want to see me about, Grandi?'

Lorenzo took a deep breath. 'I want to talk about Cristina, señor. You see, I – I'm very fond of her.' He stared at da Fiesole's *Madonna* for inspiration, his face suddenly pale. 'No, not just fond. I want to marry her.'

A clock chimed softly in the silence.

'We're in love with each other.'

'I'm not surprised Cristina's "in love" with you,' said Marcos. 'At seventeen girls fall for anyone who gives them half a glance.' He leaned back in his chair and studied Lorenzo over the tips of his fingers. 'How long has this been going on?'

'Before I went to Europe we . . . we realized it.'

'While you were playing duets, no doubt.'

Lorenzo began to lose his temper. 'Look, I know it's a shock but one doesn't plan for these things to happen. They just do. I've fallen in love with your daughter – what's wrong with that?' There was no reply and he rushed on, his words tumbling angrily over each other. 'I have a good career ahead of me! Cristina won't lack anything. We'll be living in Milan – my sister's there, if that makes you feel better. It's not as if . . . For Christ's sake, can't you understand that I love her?'

Marcos shook his head. 'I'm sorry. The answer is no.'

'Why not?'

'In the first place Cristina's still at school; she's far too young to marry. Secondly – you may be a talented musician, but you're not the kind of husband I want for my daughter.'

Frustration clouded Lorenzo's face. 'Because I don't have a fortune or a double-barrelled name? Is that all you care about?'

'I want my children to make good marriages,' said Marcos curtly and stood up. 'I don't know what you've told Cristina – presumably you led her to believe I would agree. Since I don't and she'll be upset, do me the favour of leaving now before she returns from school.'

'At least let me explain . . .'

'Stay away from my daughter, Grandi! If you know what's good for you, you'll take the first flight back to Europe and forget about her.'

'Go to hell!' shouted Lorenzo and slammed out of the house.

On the face of it he could do nothing about the situation. Cristina was chained to her father's authority until she became of age – and that date was a long five years away. Lorenzo hailed a taxi and slumped on to the back seat, glowering out of the window at the passing traffic.

He was not going to give up without a fight.

CHAPTER TWENTY-FIVE

I

Cristina's interview with her father proved disastrous. Marcos insisted he knew what was best for her; she drowned his explanations in a flood of tears. He grew exasperated and told her she was too young to know her own mind. Cristina exploded in shrill recriminations that had little to do with the original argument. It all ended with roars of impossible threats and Cristina fleeing upstairs to lock herself in her room.

Isabel told her sister not to be so stupid. Papa was on edge these days; yelling at him would make matters worse.

'Besides, how can you be sure you're in love with Lorenzo? You hardly know him.'

'Shut up!' sobbed Cristina. 'You don't know the first thing about love!'

She was wrong. Isabel knew all about love because Elías Castro was in love with her.

He had declared his love last weekend after a polo match. They were having drinks on the club terrace against a background of green lawn, flower beds and stately trees. The evening was warm for early spring, the sky shimmered with pale amber light. Elías's team had won; he looked happy and triumphant. When Isabel congratulated him, he took hold of her hand and pressed it.

'I played for you,' he said.

Isabel's heart missed a beat. All of a sudden the boyish Elías Castro she had flirted with over the past two years had turned into a serious, masterful man. The change was disconcerting. She could think of nothing to say, except, 'Did you?' and immediately wished she hadn't because it sounded so inane.

Elías cleared his throat. 'I always do. Everything I do is for you.' He continued to grip her hand while a round golden sun sank behind the trees. 'I care for you very much, Isabel. I've cared for a very long time.'

Her heart missed a few more beats. Everything was so romantic, so perfect – the way a declaration from the heart should be. Elías holding her hand and gazing into her eyes . . . Isabel smiled at him, her own heart fluttering in her throat. This was and could only be love.

That evening they danced on the club terrace under the stars. Isabel's eyes sparkled; she glowed with happiness. Elías was so considerate, so gallant. He only had eyes for her. If he made a scene because a waiter accidentally spilled soup on his tweed jacket – well, it was just that he expected decent service. There was nothing wrong with that – or with the way he fussed about food. He liked things done properly.

On the way home from the club Elías kissed Isabel. His lips were dry, his kiss was disappointingly respectful. She had expected a bit more passion; after all, they were in love with each other. One of Miguel's friends had kissed her once behind the potted palms at Barranco Rosales. She certainly hadn't been in love with him, but his kiss had stirred far more emotion than this chaste caress. Isabel wanted Elías to be exciting and intimate, but she didn't know how to take the initiative. She was afraid of seeming immoral.

Elías, she discovered, had very decided views on sex. He believed in female chastity before marriage. A woman who gave her virginity to any man other than her husband was no better than a whore. As for adultery . . . Elías waxed eloquent.

'Adultery is a sin against man and God. A defilement of one of His most holy sacraments. Marriage is a sacred bond between husband and wife. A true Catholic marriage is the supreme example of unity and order. A true Catholic marriage is the foundation of all harmony and peace.'

Isabel laughed. 'Elías, you sound so pompous!' she teased. 'Where did you get all that from?'

'It was in my mother's lecture last Wednesday,' he replied stiffly. 'You know – the talks she gives to the Ladies of the Rosary. Why are you laughing? Don't you agree?'

Mama Castro's word was sacrosanct. Isabel bent a hasty retreat from ridicule and kissed Elías's ear.

'Of course I agree,' she said meekly. 'It's just that you sounded a bit – daunting.'

Elías grinned, mollified by her submissiveness. 'My mother tends to be long-winded,' he admitted, 'but you can't deny

317

she's right. Marriage and family are tremendously important –
especially these days.'

Isabel nodded. Stability and order, family and heritage. They
formed the pillars of her father's life and the bedrock of her
childhood. They were what she wanted for the future. They were
what Elías Castro offered because he was in love.

II

Gladys took Lorenzo Grandi's marriage intentions as a personal
insult. She had discovered him and had offered her generous
patronage. Thanks to her he had been received in the best social
circles. He owed his career to her influence – but how did he
repay her? By carrying on with Cristina, who was immature and
rude and ungrateful. Mercedes was to blame, of course. She had
made a point of encouraging Marcos's children to be rude and
ungrateful. The Grandi affair was just one more of her tricks.

'Mercedes deliberately waited until I was in hospital having the
baby!' shrilled Gladys. 'I wouldn't be surprised if Aurora Grandi
had something to do with it as well. She's always hated me.'

Marcos glared at her over the edge of his newspaper. 'Don't
be so damned stupid.'

'It's all very well for you – you have no idea what
goes on in this house. Your sister may be very clever at
deceiving people, but I can see through her! As for Grandi
. . .' The shrill voice cracked sharply. 'A gigolo, that's what
he is! No wonder Mercedes was so keen to have him around
all the time.'

'I seem to recall that Lorenzo Grandi was your idea,'
said Marcos in a dangerously even voice. 'You claimed
he would be the perfect teacher for my daughter. Ideal –
wasn't that it?'

Gladys turned bright scarlet and flounced out of the room.

Mercedes did not take kindly to her sister-in-law's accusations,
and the domestic war between them raged for weeks. Isabel lost
count of the battles rocking Barranco Rosales. Marcos returned
to La Catalina, Cristina sulked. There were no more piano
lessons. Gladys bought a garish seascape and hung it in
place of the Japanese print in the family dining-room. This

time the battle lasted a fortnight until Marcos intervened and the seascape was banished to one of the upstairs storage rooms.

Isabel threw herself into a frenzy of social activity – partly to escape the atmosphere at home, partly because it never occured to her to do anything else. A girl in her position had only one aim after leaving school: to make a good marriage. No one expected her to follow a career; certainly no one expected her to work. The most she might do was dabble in cultural niceties or learn the intricate refinements of interior decoration. Isabel enrolled in a fashionable course on Japanese floral arrangements which were all the rage.

Life was such a breathless, hectic whirl; cocktail parties, dinners, weekend *asados*, polo matches. Life was so perfectly romantic: dancing under the stars. Elisita became engaged to Manolo San Martin. Elías invited Isabel to Sunday lunch at his parents' townhouse. Mercedes informed Marcos over the telephone that Elías Castro was a very correct young man and seemed to be serious about Isabel.

Marcos sounded sceptical. 'Is she serious about him?'

'Oh, yes!' said Mercedes. 'They make a lovely couple. Prepare yourself, my dear. One of these days I am sure Elías will ask you for Isabel's hand.'

At the beginning of October Isabel and Elías planned to join Elisita, Manolo and four other friends for a short holiday in the lake district. At the last minute Alfredo Castro decided to send his son up north on a business trip.

'You go down to the lakes and enjoy yourself,' Elías told Isabel. 'Just don't forget to come back in time for the dance at the Yacht Club.'

Isabel laughed. 'Do you trust me on my own in the wilderness?' she teased. 'Just think, I may be swept off my feet by a sexy forest ranger. What if I don't come back?'

Elías's cue called for an impassioned embrace and hoarse threats of bloody vendetta if she dared so much as glance at another man. Instead he looked faintly surprised and replied solemnly, 'Of course I trust you. Why shouldn't I? Besides, you must come back because my mother has already organized our table for the dance.'

It occurred to Isabel that her beloved lacked a sense of humour.

III

Sprawled along the southwestern Andes lies some of Argentina's most spectacular scenery.

Lakes glitter like jewels in a giant's coffer; turquoise, emerald, opal, sapphire so blue it seems almost black. Jagged ice-peaks crown sparkling snow fields; dark crags rear their forbidding heads above a vast, untamed forest where the only sound is the sound of silence. A majestic kingdom of light and shadow, pungent with the peculiar mustiness produced by centuries of leaf-mould and bark and fungus embedded in roots and earth.

The vegetation is mostly native to the region. Tall, stately *coihue* trees; the graceful *arrayán*, with its mottled reddish-beige bark and tiny white flowers; slender grey and green *lenga*, found near the timberline. There are conifers and bamboo and wild fuchsia; bright golden *amancay* and the disconcerting brilliance of a leafy parasite showering matchsticks of flame against darkness. It is Nature's dower — as yet unspoiled by the clumsy greed of men.

Isabel felt as though by some strange, inexplicable magic she had been transported to another planet. Their hotel was well off the beaten track — a comfortable, eight-bedroom chalet on the shore of a small lake tucked into the mountains. A large, bustling resort town lay fifteen miles away, but in this quiet enclave the days slid peacefully by and she let them carry her in their stream. The world dissolved into sunlight on blue-green water and the immovable tranquillity of ancient hills.

She was perfectly happy to sit on a log by the lakeside and enjoy the scenery. The sharp air smelled of burning wood, October's sunshine felt warm and pleasant against her face. A condor cruised lazily above a distant peak, the morning was so quiet she could hear voices from the fishing boats halfway across the lake. Barranco Rosales no longer existed and even La Catalina seemed remote, like the ghost of a half-forgotten dream. Isabel tossed a pebble into the water and gazed at a large clearing in the forest on the opposite shore.

'I'd like to build a house over there,' she mused aloud. 'A place just for me.'

'It's already been taken,' said a voice behind her.

A young man stood several yards away. He smiled faintly at her astonishment and motioned with his head at the clearing across the water. His eyes were very pale and hard.

'I picked that spot for myself. Years ago.' The pale eyes studied Isabel curiously. 'Why do you want to build a house on the other side? It's miles from nowhere.'

'Perhaps that's why,' she retorted.

'I would have thought you prefer to be where all the noise is.' He tugged a cigarette pack from the pocket of a worn sheepskin jacket, inspected it, and offered her the least crumpled of two cigarettes. 'What kind of a house would you build?'

Isabel puckered her brows. 'Not a very large one, but plenty of space and light. Windows everywhere, so I could see the lake and the mountains. A house with room to move around in and breathe and feel free . . .' She gave a small, self-conscious laugh. 'I hate being penned up.'

'At least you have the right idea.' He sat down on the log and stretched out his legs. 'Something clean and uncluttered, with long lines sweeping upwards.' His right hand sketched a series of movements against the distant shoreline. 'Perfectly balanced between perpendiculars and arches.'

'You're an architect?'

'Two more years to make it official.'

They laughed. A dog barked in the woods behind them and a woman's voice called 'María!' The lake shimmered softly in the sunlight, a hazy reflection of snow-capped mountains suspended within its blue-green bowl.

'So much for me. What do you do?' asked the young man.

Isabel shrugged. 'Oh – things.'

'Like what?'

The faintly mocking inflection irritated her. She tossed another pebble into the water and replied indifferently. 'I keep busy.' Then to forestall further irritation, 'Are you on holiday?'

'My mother lives here. I always visit her around this time of year. My sister and brother-in-law own the place.' He stood up as the boats on the lake made for the landing-stage. 'May as well give your friends a hand. We can't have them falling overboard in this weather. By the way, my name's Stefan Stervic. What's yours?'

'Isabel.'

'Just Isabel?'

'No,' said Isabel shortly. 'Isabel Luciani.'

He gave a short grunt of astonishment and strolled away without comment.

IV

During the next few days Isabel saw little of Stefan Stervic. Occasionally she heard his voice in the kitchen and once she caught a brief glimpse of him walking by the lake with a thin, grey-haired woman. He had his arm around her shoulder and seemed to be explaining something at great length. They looked happy together.

Isabel had planned to fly back early to Buenos Aires because of the dance at the Yacht Club. Her flight was scheduled for Monday; on Saturday the national airline went on a forty-eight-hour strike. She checked at the hotel's registration desk. The only other airline operating in the lake district was booked solid, and the train, forever uncertain, would never make the two-day journey in time. Isabel threw up her hands in exasperation.

'This is ridiculous! I must get home! Elías is expecting me!'

'Ring him and explain why you can't make it,' said Elisita. 'It's not your fault there's a strike.'

'I know, but he'll be terribly upset because he's expecting me on Monday. You know how he gets. Then there's this do at the Yacht Club. His mother's organized a huge table and we're sitting at it. I can't let them down!' Isabel ran her fingers through sleek waves of dark hair. 'What am I going to do?'

'Do you drive?' queried Stefan Stervic from behind the registration desk.

'Of course I drive!'

'Good. I'm returning to Buenos Aires tomorrow. You can come with me.'

No gallantry – just a blunt statement that took its own logic for granted. Isabel later told herself that she had accepted through lack of choice, but even then that excuse sounded feeble.

V

They set out at eight a.m. and by noon were well into the desolate foothills bordering the Patagonian desert. Stefan drove fast and spoke little; Isabel found his silences strangely reassuring. The rough dirt road snaked through large ochre buttocks of land dotted by clumps of stunted trees. An occasional farm squatted on the floor of a hollow; elsewhere sheep grazed on slopes faintly shadowed with pale green down.

'Just think what good irrigation and roads could do for all of this,' remarked Stefan as the car inched up a track scratched along the face of a high cliff. He pulled over to the edge for a moment and indicated the stark contours of contrast unfolding under a leaden sky. Grey and brown and purple indentations pressed into the earth by a giant's capricious thumb. '*At dusk, when the land is bruised with shadow* . . . It may not be dusk yet but the image still holds, don't you think? Or do you think about such things at all?'

'Why shouldn't I?' demanded Isabel.

He shrugged and changed gears to tackle a steep rise. 'When we reach the top you take over for a few hours. I'm not going to do all the work.'

'You would if I weren't here.'

'But you are here,' grinned Stefan and began to whistle under his breath.

They left the foothills behind and entered Patagonia's flat, gusty barrens. Sky and scrubland and wind; mile after mile after endless mile, broken infrequently by a clutch of hovels huddled around a petrol pump. Sky and earth: dun, ochre, dun. Uniform and unchanging. There was an unexpected stretch of green as they drove through orchards in the Río Negro valley and then the road sliced into desert again – arrow-straight this time for a hundred miles. No hamlets, no petrol pumps. Nothing but sky and scrub and the relentless, gritty wind.

Their journey was made up of long silences and intermittent bursts of conversation; they both skirted intimacy as skaters skirt danger. Stefan did not know what to make of Isabel. She was beautiful, rich and probably spoilt rotten. He had no patience

323

with girls of her kind. There was no point in wasting so much time wondering about her; they would probably never run into each other again. He continued to wonder what Isabel Luciani was really like.

It was Isabel's turn to drive. She tried to think about Elías, but his face had receded into a shadowy no-man's land and even the memory of his voice sounded hazy. She was uncomfortably aware of Stefan Stervic's presence: the space between them burned. He lounged against the front seat, arm resting carelessly along the open window, his pale eyes fixed on the road ahead. She found him disturbingly attractive in a rough, unromantic way; even his blunt comments and half-mocking smile had a certain charm. Certainly Elías would never treat her with such directness. Elías was . . . The words 'prim and proper' leapt to mind, but she immediately rejected them as being disloyal. 'Gallant' was the correct word. Stefan Stervic was anything but gallant.

'You drive damned well — for a woman,' he remarked suddenly.

'I learned to drive when I was twelve,' said Isabel. 'My father taught me.'

He gave her a smile she did not know how to interpret. 'What's your father like?'

She began to tell him about Marcos Luciani and La Catalina, unaware just how much of herself she revealed in the telling. Stefan listened and thought about a certain night over a year ago, when he had rescued Marcos Luciani's son out of the gutter. Strange to think that blood-soaked mess was this girl's brother. He wondered how the incident had ended.

'Sounds like you've had an idyllic childhood,' he commented. 'Lucky girl. What do you want out of life?'

Isabel laughed awkwardly. 'To be happy.'

'A very original ambition. And just how do you plan to go about being happy?'

She threw Stefan a suspicious look. He was grinning at her and after a moment Isabel grinned back. She was beginning to enjoy this conversation. Gallant Elías had never asked her what she wanted out of life.

'I want to get married and raise a family,' she said. 'My parents were very happy together — I want my marriage to be like theirs.' There was a short silence and then she added with a little laugh, as though making fun of her own dreams, 'I used to wish I had been born a boy. Then I could have helped Papa run La Catalina.'

'What's to prevent you from helping him now?' asked Stefan.

'I'm a girl!'

'So? There are girls who study agriculture, you know. It seems to me that if you loved your ranch so much and wanted to help your father, that would be the solution. Much better than tying yourself down to marriage.'

'But I want to get married!' protested Isabel sharply. 'Anyway, I've got an older brother. He's supposed to take over from Papa one day.'

Stefan did not miss the underlying doubt in that last sentence. Running a ranch must be very hard work — not at all the sort of life for the likes of Miguel Luciani. He lit a cigarette and handed it to Isabel. That one brief instance of physical contact jolted them both more than they dared admit.

'I still don't see why you don't study for an agricultural engineering degree,' he argued. 'You've got the brains for it. If I were your father I'd be damned proud of my daughter's wanting to go into the family business.'

'You don't understand,' said Isabel with what was perhaps her first flash of critical insight into her own situation. 'Girls like me aren't meant to go into the family business — or any other business, for that matter. It's just not done.'

The conversation threatened to become too personal. Isabel pretended to concentrate on her driving, Stefan stared at the bleak Patagonian landscape. Neither of them spoke for the next fifteen miles and then it was to comment on the weather. They did not touch on personal subjects again.

VI

They drove straight through the night, taking turns cat-napping in the back of the car; by mid-morning they were out of the desert and on to the fringes of the pampa.

'Any preference about which way we go from here?' inquired Stefan.

Isabel yawned and pulled a pocket mirror out of her handbag. 'The quickest one. *Por Dios* – what a face! I look like hell.'

'You look all right,' he grunted, but it did not sound like a compliment.

Lack of sleep and the sexual tension between them had contributed considerably to straining the atmosphere. Stefan grew morose, Isabel began to fidget. They bickered over trifles. The car became a cage. Stefan sensed Isabel's urgency to return to the safety of her own world and resented it. A perverse desire to thwart her prompted him to take the coastal road, adding unnecessary time and milage to an already endless journey. Isabel protested indignantly. The car stopped with a jolt.

'What the hell's the matter now?' he demanded.

'It'll take forever this way!'

'If you don't like it, I'll leave you off at the next town. You can find your own way back.'

No one had ever treated Isabel like that. Her cheeks flamed scarlet. 'You wouldn't dare!'

'Wait until we get to the next town,' he snapped and started off again.

Clearly Stefan Stervic was not the sort of man to be bullied. Isabel let several minutes go before trying another tactic.

'I'd like to get home as soon as possible. It's very important to me.' She placed her hand over his on the steering wheel. 'Please, Stefan.'

His look made her withdraw her hand at once. 'You always get your own way, don't you?'

Isabel thought about Elías and panicked. '*I have to get home*!'

'You'll get home,' drawled Stefan acidly, still looking at her. 'Just because you're an attractive bitch doesn't mean you'll get your way with me. You're not my type.'

'You're not mine either!' retorted Isabel with icy dignity and turned to stare out of the window.

High clouds scudded across a rain-washed sky; white-caps pricked a restless pattern on the Atlantic's heaving surface, flecking grey and blue with tiny plumes of foam. A lonely seagull planed above the troughs, its harsh cry mourning with the wind.

'When I was a little boy I used to dream about the sea,' remarked Stefan after several miles of stony silence. 'I wanted to be another Sindbad.' He glanced at Isabel out of the corner of his eye. 'Still sulking, *linda*?'

'I'm not sulking!'

326

He laughed. 'You make it look convincing enough. Let's call a truce, shall we? I want to hear more about this dream house of yours.'

Her dream house was a secret and very personal thing. To her amazement and dismay, Isabel heard herself telling him about it in great detail.

Shortly after one o'clock they stopped for lunch at a roadhouse some distance inland from the coast. Stefan led the way to an empty table at the back; as they reached it Isabel suddenly exclaimed 'Angela!' and stopped near a side door. He turned and saw a fair-haired woman sitting by herself. She stared at Isabel in astonishment and, Stefan thought curiously, alarm. It was impossible to tell whether her high colour was due to the sun or to embarrassment.

'What are you doing here?' laughed Isabel. 'Are you and Jimmy on holiday? This is Stefan Stervic. He's driving me back from the south — because of the air strike.'

Angela smiled vaguely at Stefan. She seemed to be making up her mind what to say.

'Don't tell me you've finally dragged Jimmy away from Los Alamos,' continued Isabel, making a dart for the bread. 'I wish someone could convince Papa to take a holiday. He's in one hell of a temper these days. May we join you?'

She chattered away volubly, relieved to be on her own ground again after so many hours of Stefan Stervic's disconcerting company. Angela nodded, made the right noises and tried not to look at the side door. It opened quite suddenly.

'We should do this more often, *gringuita*,' laughed Marcos as he came through.

He stopped dead in his tracks when he saw Isabel; the skin on his cheekbones bleached white. No one spoke for a moment and then Marcos cleared his throat with an effort.

'Well, this is a surprise.' He smiled faintly at Stefan, eager for an excuse to cover up his own embarrassment. 'Do you two know each other?'

Stefan explained. Isabel continued to stare at her father. There was another, more awkward pause.

'Do you mind if we have lunch with you — or are we interrupting something?' she asked in a shrill voice. 'Maybe you two want to be alone.'

327

'Sit down,' ordered Marcos sharply and signalled to the waiter. 'Quite a coincidence, Stervic – isn't it?'

They discussed coincidences, architecture and, inevitably, politics. The two men did most of the talking. Isabel interrupted frequently with short bouts of high, nervous laughter. She drank too much wine and avoided looking at Angela. The meal dragged on forever. Angela excused herself and went to the ladies' room. Isabel followed. She leaned against a basin, her chin thrust out defiantly, and glared. Angela began to wash her hands. The glaring and the silence grew unbearable.

'Look, Isabel,' she said finally, 'I know what it must seem like to you, but it's not really that at all. Your father and I . . . we . . . oh, God – it's so difficult to explain!'

Isabel gave the empty soap dispenser a vicious slap. 'What's so difficult about it?' she demanded. 'Papa's my father and you're Jimmy's wife.'

'It's not that simple, you know.'

'It's very simple,' retorted Isabel with a priggish little smile. 'It's adultery. It's immoral.'

'Isabel . . .'

'He's my father!'

Her dark eyes accused unhappily through the mirror and Angela gave up. It was so damned simple she didn't know whether to laugh or cry.

VII

Marcos's car followed Stefan back to Buenos Aires at a cautious distance. Isabel kept turning her head to watch; she did it so many times that Stefan finally had to laugh.

'Curious, aren't you?'

She gave him an angry glance. 'You don't understand.'

'Understand about what?'

Isabel stared at the traffic ahead. After a moment she said in a choked voice, 'Angela is Jimmy Morgan's wife. He's my father's friend. They've been friends a long time. Jimmy – well, maybe he drinks too much, but that's no reason . . . Angela's his wife . . . it's not right . . .' She turned her head to look again. 'I can't believe it!'

'It's not really any of your business is it?' he remarked, glancing through the rear-view mirror.

'It's wrong,' insisted Isabel. 'You don't understand.'

Stefan wouldn't understand that Papa had always stood for everything that was strong and good and true. That Papa had once told her marriage was a very special thing. He had even held up Angela and Jimmy as an example – yet here he was alone with Angela in a roadhouse miles from nowhere. His *we must do this more often, gringuita* clearly implied they had done it before. How many times before? How long had Papa been deceiving everyone, pretending to be the untouchable god who broke no rules? Why had he broken them to begin with?

Isabel stared out of the window. The answer to 'Why?' lay buried at the back of her mind, but she was afraid of unearthing it. Her own world must be kept intact. Her marriage was going to be a happy one. It would rest securely on the rules the god had broken . . . She shivered and heard Stefan say in a normal, everyday voice as though nothing had happened, 'With any luck you'll be home in time for supper.'

Stefan Stervic could not possibly understand about Papa because he was not part of her world – but Isabel found herself thanking God that she was with him right now instead of Elías.

VIII

Neither Marcos nor Angela spoke much during the drive back to Buenos Aires. Occasionally he asked, 'Are you all right?' and caressed her hand. She nodded and pretended to make light of the meeting with Isabel, but its ghost rode between them.

'If we had stayed at El Remanso this wouldn't have happened,' said Marcos impatiently. 'My fault, I suppose, for wanting a change of scenery.'

If was a hateful word. 'It doesn't matter,' replied Angela. 'We had a lovely weekend together.'

A small hotel tucked behind the dunes, walks along a wind-swept beach, salt spray and the high, pounding surf . . . Swift, bittersweet images that clicked through memory and were gone.

IX

A three-mile-long traffic jam blocked the entrance to Buenos Aires. Several irate drivers tried to by-pass it on the hard shoulder and created another tangle. Horns blared. A red-faced lorry driver leaned out of his window and cursed the world at the top of his lungs. A policeman flapped his arms in frantic traffic signals, but no one paid any attention. By the time Stefan and Isabel reached Barranco Rosales it was growing dark. Marcos's car was nowhere to be seen.

Stefan stared curiously at the house half hidden in the shadow of the trees. 'Some place you live in.'

Isabel shrugged. 'It's a mausoleum.'

'Not much fresh air, eh?'

She smiled faintly. 'Would you like to come in?'

'Your family's seen enough of me for one day.' He got back into the car and poked his head out of the window. 'I'll ring you some time.'

'If you want to.'

'Oh, I want to,' he chuckled and drove off, leaving a strangely empty world behind him.

Barranco Rosales smelled of ginger lilies and scandalwood and cedar. Isabel wrinkled her nose against the heavy, smothering fragrance and began to climb the stairs to the hall; as she reached the top Mercedes hurried out of the drawing-room. Pedro's tall, cassocked figure loomed behind her.

'Bela, thank God you're home!'

Isabel stared. 'What's the matter?'

Pedro and Mercedes began speaking at the same time, the priest's deep bass struggling to override Mercedes's frenzied, strident tones. Isabel caught Cristina's name and grabbed her uncle's arm.

'*What about Cristina?*'

'She's run away,' said Gladys from the doorway. 'Pretended she was spending the weekend at a friend's house and ran off instead with that – musician.' The high, tight voice grated harshly. 'We received a cable last night. They're married.'

'Dear Holy Virgin,' muttered Mercedes, crossing herself.

'I don't believe it!'

Gladys stepped into the hall. The light from the drawing-room slanted on her face, sharpening the features and adding unkind pockets of shadow underneath her eyes.

'The cable came last night,' she repeated, staring at Isabel. 'We've been trying to reach your father ever since, but no one seems to know where he is.'

X

Lorenzo's determination to put up a fight had led him to confide in his brother. Fabio raised his eyebrows and tried unsuccessfully to talk him out of Cristina Luciani, but Lorenzo was adamant. In the end the painter grudgingly agreed to see what could be done.

'Lorenzo's mad, of course,' he told Lucas. 'He actually wants to smuggle the girl out of the country and marry her!'

'Little Cristina, eh?' Lucas grinned. 'He's got good taste. She's every inch her mother.' The grin broadened. 'It's almost worth giving them a hand just to turn the knife in old Marcos's gut.'

Fabio eyed him uneasily. 'What do you mean?'

'I've got a couple of friends in Paraguay who can fix up a marriage licence. They owe me a favour or two.'

'You'd still have to get the girl out of the country.'

Lucas leered. 'Iván knows a man. Tell you what – we'll fix it all up and make the happy couple a wedding present of their marriage. Courtesy of the fairy godmother.'

'Count me out,' muttered Fabio and began splashing vermilion on a bright blue canvas.

Lucas contacted his friends in Paraguay; next he approached Iván Torres, who gave him a name and a personal card. The card gained him admission to a dingy office on the top floor of a building two blocks away from the police department. A pale, white-haired man with protuding teeth listened impassively to Lucas's request; after a moment he began to scribble on a sheet of paper.

'Name, date and place of birth, parents' names.' The words wheezed out in thin, colourless spurts. 'Six passport photographs. Two sets of officially stamped legal paper. Copy of birth certificate.' He handed the list to Lucas and stared blankly

331

at a calendar on the wall. 'Bring everything on Friday at three p.m. It'll take four weeks.'

During the month that followed Lorenzo met secretly with Cristina and made their plans. Lovers have their own gods; even Mercedes who kept a strict eye on her niece, never suspected what she was up to. As for Cristina – if she had any qualms, they were quickly set aside. She loved her family, but she was in love with Lorenzo. It was as simple as that.

At nine o'clock on the morning of the second Saturday in October Cristina left Barranco Rosales carrying an overnight bag. Four blocks from the house, after a quick glance over her shoulder, she entered a waiting car. It merged swiftly into the traffic and headed for the municipal airport where she boarded Iván Torres's private plane. No one questioned her new documents; by the stroke of a forger's pen she was no longer a minor and that was all that mattered.

A few hours later the plane landed in Asunción, Paraguay. Lorenzo and Lucas were there to meet her. At four o'clock that afternoon, when she was ostensibly playing tennis with her friends, Cristina Elena Luciani signed the marriage register.

By the time Marcos learned of his daughter's elopement the newlyweds were halfway across the Atlantic, headed for Milan with Lucas's blessing.

XI

Once, when Isabel was a little girl, she discovered a late-blooming rose in the garden. The rest of the flowers had already withered, but this one continued to hold up its magnificent head in defiance of approaching winter. Enchanted, she had grabbed the rose in her small hand and tugged. The petals broke loose and showered on to the ground; no matter how much Isabel had tried, she could not make them become a rose again.

It was the same now. Her world had fallen to pieces and the fragments refused to return to their original form.

There was no one she could talk things over with at home; she couldn't even talk to Elías about them. When he had heard about Cristina's elopement he murmured a few shocked sentences and had tactfully refrained from mentioning it again. Isabel felt grudgingly grateful for his discretion, but she still needed to talk things over with someone.

Stefan Stervic rang up a fortnight later. They met in a crowded downtown café; over a cup of bitter black coffee Isabel told him about Cristina. Putting it all into words gave things a different perspective. Even her father's desperate journey to Milan accompanied by Pedro and Miguel lost some of its impact when blurted out against a background of clattering cups and lively impersonal voices.

'Papa tried to have the marriage annulled, but he couldn't because Cristina and Lorenzo hadn't been married by a priest. Uncle Pedro finally persuaded Lorenzo to agree to a religious ceremony if Papa promised to forget about the annulment. Miguel said the church wedding took place in a small chapel somewhere on the outskirts of Milan. Creaking benches and mice and mouldy stones . . .' She broke off and stared glumly at her coffee cup. 'You must think all this very trite.'

Stefan grinned. 'My great-great aunt eloped with a Polish army officer, but they weren't as lucky. Her father brought them back and had them both horsewhipped in the public square; then he shut her up in a convent. She outlived them both and married my great-great uncle.'

Isabel laughed, but it was an unconvincing sound.

'Papa's livid,' she continued after a moment. 'I've never seen him so angry – not even when Claudia got into trouble. He was outraged then because it was so embarrassing and Gladys had tantrums all over the place, but I don't suppose it really affected him personally. I mean it's not as though Claudia was his daughter or anything. But this time . . .' Her voice caught in her throat and she couldn't go on.

'Steady,' teased Stefan patting her hand, 'Don't go to pieces now, you haven't told me the best bits yet.'

Isabel sighed. 'You see, it's not just that Cristina disobeyed Papa, it's the *family* thing. She's broken the circle and that's something he won't forgive. Miguel told me he only went to the wedding because Uncle Pedro begged him to. Afterwards Cristina tried to make up, but he refused to speak to her. Lorenzo shouted at him and Papa shouted back and Uncle Pedro tried to shut them both up . . . Miguel said it would have been funny if it was someone else's family.'

Stefan grinned. 'Neo-realism with a vengeance.'

'Pathetic, isn't it? Papa stormed off to the hotel after the wedding and everyone else went to celebrate the local *trattoria*. Even Uncle Pedro loosened up and enjoyed himself. According to Miguel he's sure Papa will relent – you know how priests are.'

'Maybe your uncle's right.'

'You don't know Papa. He won't even allow Cristina's name to be mentioned at home.'

On the other side of the café window the streetlamps made dull yellow reflections on the pavement. Isabel stared at them unhappily.

Cristina was only one of the fragments of her shattered world. Perhaps she was not even the most important one.

Memory of the incident with her father and Angela continued to plague Isabel. It was unbelievable that Papa should carry on as though nothing had happened. That he could face her without being ashamed. Without looking guilty – not even in front of Gladys. His own daughter had caught him with his neighbour's wife and he didn't even bat an eyelid.

It was quite simply unbelievable.

She had tackled her father about the incident the evening after he returned from Milan.

Dinner had been a nightmare with Gladys determined to make bright conversation and everyone else picking glumly at their food. No one dared ask about Cristina. Marcos had left the table before the meal was over; even Gladys seemed relieved to see him go. While coffee was being served Isabel had excused herself and gone upstairs to the study.

She had tapped uncertainly on the door; there was no reply and after a moment she had gathered up enough courage to go in. The heavy velvet curtains had not been drawn and moonlight streamed through the window, giving strange shapes to familiar shadows. The study smelled of old books and old leather, of years of cigarette smoke and, very faintly, of lavender. Isabel hesitated, then advanced slowly into the moonlit room; she was halfway across the rug when her father spoke.

'What is it, Isabel?'

He was sitting at his desk, his hands clasped over the picture of La Catalina. The moonlight glinted on his watch and traced the outline of his fingers. She remembered noticing how tightly the fingers gripped each other, how the skin pulled taut over the knuckles. He did not move; he did not turn on the light.

She said shrilly because the darkness unsettled her, 'It's about Angela. You and Angela. I want to talk about it. Why are you sitting in the dark?'

He switched on the desk lamp, but his face was still in shadow. 'There's nothing to talk about.'

'Angela's Jimmy's wife and Jimmy's your friend.'

'I don't need any lectures from you,' he said tartly.

'But, Papa, it's wrong!'

'You're too young to understand.'

'I'm nineteen! I'm not a child any more.' She leaned across the desk, her cheeks flushed with self-righteous indignation. 'I know what's right and what's wrong!'

She remembered that even in the yellow lamplight his face was very pale. A muscle twitched along his jaw, there were deep creases on either side of his mouth. His gaze had held hers for a moment before sliding uneasily away.

'You may be nineteen, but you don't know a damn thing about life,' he said. 'Whatever there may be between myself and Angela is no one else's business.'

'But you're my father!'

'You're too young to understand,' he repeated dully. 'There's nothing to explain . . .'

'Isn't there?' interrupted Isabel. 'Isn't there anything to explain to Gladys? She's your wife.' When he didn't reply she rushed on. 'You never did care for Gladys, did you? Why did you marry her if you don't love her?'

Still no reply.

'Didn't you once tell me that marriage was something sacred, Papa?' demanded Isabel. 'Didn't you say it was a commitment of love? *Didn't you say that?*'

'Yes,' he replied after a moment. 'I told you marriage was a commitment of love, Isabel. Now will you please leave me alone?'

She walked over to the door and paused, her hand on the handle. 'Are you in love with Angela, Papa?'

He switched off the light abruptly; in the sudden darkness his voice made an anguished, rasping sound.

'For God's sake, daughter – leave me alone!'

The despair in his voice had frightened Isabel. This was not what she imagined love to be: a bitter, guilty secret rooted in darkness. Love was something beautiful and happy; something to be enjoyed together in the open and approved by the world. Love was what she had with Elías Castro. She would have liked to tell Stefan about it, but somehow she didn't think he would understand.

XII

Life went on.

Isabel met Stefan Stervic a number of times for coffee. She found herself doing most of the talking, bringing in bits of family gossip because they were vital fragments of the new world she was trying so painfully to reconstruct. A row between Mercedes and Gladys over redecoration of the drawing-room; Claudia, showing up with her six-month-old son; Yvonne's latest shocker: bleached hair and green fingernails. Miguel was working at the Buenos Aires office and loathed every minute of it. Her friend Ana Inés was in love with him. Mercedes kept insisting Miguel should get married. Elías . . .

'Who's Elías?' interrupted Stefan.

'Elías Castro. He wants me to marry him.'

'Are you going to?'

She met his eyes and replied evenly, 'Yes. We're getting engaged next week.'

Stefan tossed a few coins on to the table and stood up. 'Come on,' he said brusquely. 'Let's go for a walk.'

They strolled through a maze of narrow, cobbled streets near the docks. The afternoon breeze smelled of tarmac and river; sunshine filtered between the branches of the plane trees and splashed pale golden pools on the uneven pavement. A solitary bus lumbered past, a ship boomed mournfully somewhere in the port. Isabel threw back her head and smiled at the sun.

'Where do you live?' she asked.

'Next block.'

Her eyes flew open. 'Near the docks?'

'Why not? It's cheap and it suits me. I'm not rich – yet.'

'Of course you're going to be very rich,' she jibed, laughing at him.

'I'm going to be two things – the best architect in the country and a very wealthy man.' His pale, hard eyes searched her face with an expression she found difficult to read. 'Do you want to see where I live?'

They entered a yellow house and climbed four flights to the top floor. Isabel looked around her curiously. Sunlight streamed through the window on to a table littered with papers; in the distance she saw a wide strip of river and the skeleton arms of a crane. Her eyes strayed to the photograph on the wall, took in the narrow bed and the threadbare brown rug. Stefan went out of a door at the far end; after a moment she followed and found him in a tiny space crammed between a sink, a cooker, a miniature refrigerator and, miraculously, a counter. The window between cooker and sink gave on to more river and cranes.

'Coffee?' he asked, reaching for a jar from an overhead shelf.

'How can you live in a place like this?'

He lit a gas-ring under the kettle. 'The same way you live in your mausoleum. Bathroom's to your right. Mind the seat, it's cracked.'

She wandered back into the main room, feeling ridiculously shy and vulnerable. Stefan brought in the coffee, used his elbow to clear a space on the table and set down the tray. A half-finished sketch fluttered to the floor. Isabel picked it up.

'This looks like a house.'

He snatched away the sketch and flung it on to a pile of papers. 'Your coffee'll get cold.'

They drank in silence. Isabel glanced at her watch. 'I'd better be going home.' Her voice shook slightly and she added with a touch of defiance, 'I'm dining out tonight.'

'With Elías Castro?'

'What of it?'

Stefan made no reply. Isabel put down her mug. He did not move. She picked up her jacket and handbag. He stared at them and then at her, letting his eyes prowl from head to toe and missing nothing on the way. She blushed angrily.

'Aren't you going to see me to the door?'

He moved then, grabbing her wrist and wrenching her around so that she was jammed between him and the table. His lips brushed her mouth and forced it open; his hands crushed her against him. She could feel every inch of his body. It was hard. The hardness touched parts of her no one had ever touched before. Isabel wriggled frantically. The hardness grew harder:

raw male excitement that had nothing to do with romance or gallantry. Her cheeks flamed.

It was one thing to read about sex in novels or see it beautifully photographed in films; it was quite another to have Stefan Stervic trying to force sex on her in his flat. They weren't even engaged. Isabel continued to wriggle. The whole thing was shocking. Not just feeling Stefan's hands touching everywhere and the embarrassing hardness between his thighs, but her own body's reaction which had nothing to do with what she had been taught was ladylike or decent. The intimate parts one didn't reveal before marriage felt very strange. They throbbed and grew moist; worse still, she liked what was happening.

'Let go of me, you brute!' cried Isabel, panicking because of sensations that were shocking and indecent and undeniably disloyal to Elías. '*Let me go!*'

'One of these days,' rasped Stefan thickly. 'I'll be wealthy enough to afford you and damn Elías Castro to hell!'

His mouth trapped hers again; his right hand closed around her right breast and massaged it roughly. Isabel broke away and ran for the door. He didn't follow. She fled down the stairs and out into the sunshine. A cruising taxi slowed down hopefully and she climbed in; the driver stared at her through the rear-view mirror.

'Are you all right, señorita?'

'Yes, I'm all right!' she cried angrily. 'Take me home!'

He grinned and lowered the flag. 'My pleasure, if you tell me where home is.'

Isabel nearly screamed the address. The taxi jolted across the cobblestones, turned into an avenue and picked up speed. She fished a handkerchief out of her handbag and began to scrub her lips. Her heart was still pounding, her breast tingled. Elías had never kissed her like that. She had never felt his body thrust against hers. His hands had never touched the way Stefan had touched . . .

'How dare he!' she exclaimed, her eyes filling with embarrassed tears. 'How dare he touch me like that!'

The taxi driver looked round. 'Beg your pardon, señorita?'

'Nothing!'

It was her own fault for having accepted Stefan's invitation to the flat, Isabel told herself indignantly. Her own stupid fault for believing they could be friends. He was no friend, he was a vulgar, ill-mannered lout who had tried to take advantage of her. She never wanted to see him again.

Isabel rubbed her handkerchief furiously back and forth across her lips, but it was no use. The intimate places touched by Stefan Stervic's hard, urgent body still throbbed with excitement and the memory of his hungry mouth would not go away.

CHAPTER TWENTY-SIX

I

On 14 February 1960 Isabel married Elías Castro.

It was a wedding to end all weddings – from the full-scale nuptial mass and papal blessing to the reception for over a thousand guests at Barranco Rosales. Pomp and circumstance with a vengeance to cancel out the bitter memory of that other wedding hastily conducted among scrabbling church mice and mouldy stones. It was the undisputed social event of the year with the bride of the decade. 'Splendid elegance in ivory satin and Brussels lace', gushed one society columnist, while another pronounced her 'a proud tribute to the women of our glorious homeland.' A third, not to be outdone, ended with a rapturous recapitulation of the bride's parents' wedding – 'another magnificent example of wealth and tradition bonded by true love.'

Stefan Stervic read all three accounts twice and threw them down the incinerator shaft with the contents of his dustbin. He was not surprised Isabel had married Elías Castro after all. Like draws like, money breeds money. They were two of a kind and they deserved each other. He sawed savagely at a loaf of bread.

'Damn Elías Castro to hell!'

He began to follow Isabel through the society columns; dinners, dances, a weekend at the Castros' ranch entertaining the Spanish ambassador, a skiing holiday, a charity ball. Her name danced through lists of other equally well-known names. The long-established élite, moving in an exclusive circle within the larger social circle which these days depended on new wealth for its numbers.

'The maze of the mini-gods,' chuckled tall, grizzled Nikos Kestri. 'Wheels within wheels within wheels. Who you know and who you don't. No hope in hell of your ever cracking that code, Stefi boy. Stick to your buildings and forget this black-eyed witch who haunts you.'

Stefan scowled. 'Too good for me, eh?'

'No, not too good for you. Just different.' Kestri reached for his tobacco pouch. 'I'll say my piece and you can damn me later for speaking from your father's shoes. Truth is, I feel like your father sometimes – we were good friends, Milos Stervic and I. I make it my business to be a good friend to his family.' He packed tobacco into his pipe with firm, decisive movements, but his gaze never left Stefan's face. 'These mini-gods have their own ways and their own rules. A defence mechanism, if you like. Mental and social in-breeding to protect the species. It's a dying one in this day and age, boy. Assailed on all sides by new thoughts, new values, new horizons. The species defends itself tooth and nail against them.'

'Not everyone's like that,' argued Stefan. 'I know a number of Argentines open to new thoughts, new values, new horizons. People with brains and the intelligence to use them.'

Kestri nodded. 'Oh, yes – there are many fine, enterprising people in this country. I'm the first to admit that. The mini-gods I mean belong to a small core isolated from the rest on their own particular Olympus. Not even their own countrymen are welcome if they can't produce the right credentials.' He puffed thoughtfully on his pipe for a moment and then changed the subject. 'I mentioned your name to an architect friend of mine the other day. He has an opening in his studio – very much an apprentice job, but it would give you a foothold.'

'Thanks, but I don't want it.'

'You already have something else lined up?'

Stefan hesitated. 'No. I'm going to work on my own.'

'Difficult without connections,' remarked Kestri mildly. 'You don't have any capital to speak of either.'

The pale, hard eyes did not waver. 'I'm going to be the best architect in the country,' said Stefan Stervic stubbornly. 'I'm going to make it on my own.'

II

One year followed another, summer came and went. Despite evidence of economic recovery the president gave in to impatient pressure groups, sacked his minister of economy and scrapped a successful austerity programme. The military, angered by the

341

presence of known Peronists in the government, grew increasingly restless. The political soup thickened. The harvest was the worst in ten years and prices skyrocketed. The rumour mills worked overtime. Argentina remembered 'the good old days' and grumbled sullenly in cafés and on street corners. Winter was raw and bitter with discontent.

One dreary, rain-soaked August morning Gladys found a letter.

She would have never discovered it if Marcos had not mislaid the draft of a talk he was scheduled to give at the national Cattlemen's Association. He turned the study inside out looking for it; Gladys suggested that the paper was probably in one of his pockets. He searched, found nothing and stormed out of the house. She decided to have a look for herself. The heavy woollen jacket he had worn down from the ranch hung in the dressing-room closet. She went through the pockets carefully; thrust down at the bottom of the inside one was an envelope. Gladys drew out a folded sheet of paper and stared at the half dozen hastily written lines. By no stretch of anyone's imagination could they be the draft of a business speech.

Marcos darling – love has everything to do with us. We can't go on like this. I must talk to you as soon as you return.

Gladys sat down very slowly on the nearest chair and re-read the letter. Again and again, carefully digesting the words. The dressing-room was warm, but her hands felt like lumps of ice.

Husbands were notoriously unfaithful to their wives – every decent woman knew that. Look at Toti Navone's Alberto, for instance. Constantly running after the strippers at the Maipo Theatre. Or poor Josefina García's husband, who had an obsession for blonde actresses. Trials like these were part of marriage. One put up with them and set an example in the home . . . Gladys read the first two lines again.

Instinct cautioned that this letter involved far more than a husband's passing fancy.

A love letter, written by a woman expecting Marcos to return – where? He had come down from La Catalina two days ago, he was going back at the end of the week. Gladys turned over the envelope and studied the postmark. Laguna Grande. Her eyes narrowed. There were only two women in the Laguna Grande area who might conceivably write such a letter to her husband.

Had Marcos been Teófilo Gómez she would have demanded an explanation. She would have ranted and screamed and scratched his eyes out instead of keeping her rage bottled up inside, poisoning herself with bitter jealousy. If this were Quilmes she would have thrown the house at his head — but direct confrontation would get her nowhere at Barranco Rosales. Scenes of jealousy would be just what everyone expected from her — a vulgar, ear-splitting scandal by a greengrocer's daughter.

'I won't give them that satisfaction!' muttered Gladys through clenched teeth. 'Even if it kills me — I won't give them that satisfaction!'

Her eyes strayed back to the letter. *We can't go on like this*. Only a desperate woman would write such words. A desperate, stupid woman. Gladys's lips curled with contempt.

She had a feeling the woman was an insipid *gringa*.

III

Angela would never have written to Marcos had it not been for the incident with the Widow's child. The incident itself would not have upset her so much had it not come on top of accumulated aggravations and frustration. It was the proverbial last straw that broke the camel's back. She had no way of knowing just how violent the breaking would be.

Over the years the children's centre had expanded from one room in the convent to a well-organized day nursery in a house on the outskirts of Laguna Grande. Angela spent a great deal of her time there these days. Life with Jimmy was rapidly sliding into a grim little hell; love with Marcos possessed its own particular torment. There were moments when she hated them both; days when she ached to be alone, living her own life safely removed from the demands of husband and lover.

Laguna Grande's children were her refuge and anchor to sanity.

The Widow's son had developed into a tough, wiry ten-year-old whose chief delight in life was throwing stones and

343

skinning cats. In theory he went to school; in practice the school authorities had long given up any hope of teaching him anything. He rarely did any work and mercilessly tormented his classmates; when punished for disrupting a geography lesson he retaliated by kindling a fire under his teacher's car. The school director complained angrily to the Widow, who shrugged off her son's misbehaviour with a loud, coarse laugh.

'He's his father's son,' she boasted cryptically. '*Loco*. That's my Romero. *Huachito loco*. A crazy little orphan.'

'Devil's brat, more likely!' snapped the director. 'The boy's a menace, woman. A reformatory's the only place for him.'

The Widow drew herself up indignantly. 'Ain't no devil in my son! He's been baptized. Romero, that's his name. Baptized by the Virgin and the saints. You ask the priest. He'll tell you. The boy's named Romero.' She tugged a garishly patterned yellow blouse over her full breasts and smirked proudly. 'Romero was my father's name.'

Angela came across Romero one cold, blustery August morning.

She was getting out of her car in front of the day nursery when a stone whizzed past, missing her head by inches. A child hooted with laughter. Shaken, she turned and saw a dirty, black-eyed boy leering at her across the dusty street.

Angela lost her temper. It had been a bad morning at Los Alamos. There had been a beehive in the chimney. A steer being led to the slaughtering shed had broken loose, found its way into the front yard and wrecked the flower beds. Jimmy was in a belligerent mood. Over breakfast he had complained about her lovemaking and they had quarrelled about that as well.

She did not need any more aggravations.

Romero made on obscene gesture and streaked off down a side lane. Angela gave chase. They ran through Laguna Grande's narrow backstreets, winding in and out of leafless plane trees and dry, untidy scrub. Romero jumped a gutter and slid down a bank. Angela followed. He fled through a rickety gate, scuttled across a yard strewn with rubbish and pounded his fists against the door of a ramshackle hut. It opened after a moment and the Widow looked out.

'What do you want?' she hissed. 'I've got a visitor.'

'The *gringa*'s after me,' wailed Romero, trying to peer around the door. 'Lemme in. She'll give me the evil eye.'

The Widow glared at Angela. 'What're you chasing my son for? He ain't done no harm. Leave the boy alone.'

'He threw a stone at me. I want to know why.'

'Ain't none of your business.'

Angela's English sense of social responsibility momentarily took over. Later she realized how very ridiculous she must have sounded, laying down the law with Victorian righteousness in the backstreets of Laguna Grande. At the time she was too angry to care.

'Your son might have hurt me seriously,' she said in a stern, dignified voice. 'Stone-throwing is wrong – surely you must have taught him not to do it! Surely you must instil some respect in him, some regard for other people! Besides, he should be in shool instead of roaming the streets.'

'She's got the evil eye, she's got the evil eye!' shrilled Romero, pushing at his mother. 'Lemme in, you bitch!' He began to curse as the Widow cuffed him and slammed the door. 'Lemme in! I know what you're doin'!' Feet and fists pummelled frantically against the wood. 'The *gringa*'ll eat me! She'll give me the evil eye!'

Angela walked off in disgust. Social responsibility be damned. The Widow and her hag-eyed son could enjoy each other's company for all she cared. It was none of her business.

By the time she arrived back at Los Alamos it had started to drizzle. Water dripped dismally off the eaves and echoed in the bathroom with a dreary, monotonous ping! magnified ten thousand times in the silence. The house seemed cold and cheerless in spite of a fire. She ate a solitary, dispirited tea and then took her mending basket over to a chair by the hearth. The old Russian's ghost stalked the shadows. Angela shivered. If Marcos were here ghosts wouldn't matter – but Marcos was forty minutes away, surrounded by La Catalina's orderly warmth and comfort. Even a phone call was out of the question because someone might overhear. A gust of wind blew down the chimney, sending a shower of sparks and smoke into the room. The dismal ping! from the bucket in the bathroom mingled with the uneasy whispering of ghosts.

It was then that Angela wrote the letter.

IV

For months now Jimmy Morgan had been haunted by a recurring nightmare. Minor details might vary, but the end result was always the same. He fled down a narrow corridor, chased by the Widow with Angela's face. The corridor grew progressively narrower and became a steep chute. He slid down the chute, screaming for help. His screams were useless because they made no sound. The chute grew steeper. Wind whistled. He was cold and everything was very dark. No one could hear him scream. The chute had no end.

Real life was as bad as Jimmy's nightmare. Angela had withdrawn into a remote, disapproving world; every attempt to reach her meant a dreary, exhausting struggle. Drinking no longer appealed to him, but he could not stop. He was heavily in debt because the cards were against him all the time. The bank had refused his latest request for credit and the disastrous harvest wiped out whatever hope he had of recouping his losses.

Even the Widow was giving him trouble.

She had a new friend now – a burly, moustached *almacén* owner from Santa Rosa who wanted to take her back with him. The Widow wanted to go. An *almacén* in Santa Rosa was better than a shack in Laguna Grande. Her burly, moustached friend was rich and promised her she wouldn't have to work.

'I'll have all the dresses I want, he says. Shoes, too. And stockings.' The Widow's honey-throated voice quavered wistfully. 'I'll be a real señora, he says.'

Santa Rosa was a long way off. If the Widow went, she would want to take the boy with her. Jimmy's heart sank. The boy was his son – his own flesh and blood. He had given life to Romero; the boy carried a vital part of himself within him. That was not all. They got along together. Lately he had been trying to teach Romero the difference between good, bad and criminal. It wasn't easy because the Widow let the boy run wild, but every now and then he showed signs of having understood. If she took him away all that would be lost. If she took him away Jimmy Morgan would no longer have a son. He would have nothing to live for.

He stared at the Widow uneasily. 'You don't want to go down to Santa Rosa, woman. This is your *pago*. Your place and people. The boy . . .'

'My friend likes the boy,' she interrupted. 'He says Romero can work in the *almacén*.'

'No!'

The Widow set her jaw. 'He wants me and the boy to go with him.'

'Romero's my son!' rasped Jimmy. 'I don't want him to leave Laguna. Listen to me, you stupid bitch!' as she continued to shake her head. 'You can go to Santa Rosa or to Hell, but the boy stays with me! I want to adopt him – I'm *going* to adopt him. He's my son!'

A mixture of cunning and fright passed over the Widow's face. She fidgeted with a tattered corner of the blanket, plucking at the frayed threads with short, grimy fingers. The hut reeked of paraffin and hair-grease. Jimmy drained his *caña* and stood up. The Widow did not move.

'I'll make all the arrangements,' he said. 'The boy won't lack anything.' When she did not reply he added awkwardly, 'My wife will be good to him, don't worry.'

She looked up then and stretched her lips in a bitter, mocking smile of contempt. Jimmy flushed. 'I'll fetch the boy on Friday,' he said and flung a few banknotes on to the table. 'Here's money to buy him clean clothes and a pair of shoes. See that he's washed.'

The Widow was still smiling when he left the hut.

That was on Wednesday night. All Thursday Jimmy agonized over his decision, debating whether he should tell Angela and, if so, just how much he should tell her. In the end he decided to say nothing. It would be better to appear on Friday with the boy in tow. He could say the mother had run off and the priest suggested taking him in at the ranch. Because of Angela's work with the children. That was it. The priest said Los Alamos was the best place for an abandoned child and Angela the only person capable of handling him. Appeal to her frustrated motherhood . . . Jimmy sighed. If he made a good enough story out of it she would understand and then perhaps things between them would be right again.

Romero became the symbol for a turning-point in *el loco* Morgan's life. He was startled to discover how desperately he longed for Friday to come.

Angela wanted Friday for a different reason. Her letter, written in a fever of loneliness and frustration, had been somewhat of an anticlimax. Marcos had received it the morning he left for Buenos Aires, but instead of returning at the weekend he came down with the flu. Seven more days went by before he rang and then their conversation consisted mainly of family snippets; he did not mention her letter.

Incredible as it seemed, Gladys and Mercedes had apparently buried the hatchet over Yvonne's latest boyfriend. A Brazilian, Marcos added in disgust. Some half-baked artist who made Fabio Grandi look as respectable as Rembrandt. Yvonne's romantic escapades were almost as bad as the discovery that Dámocles and Luis Cabales were the same person. Gladys had hysterics over that one; later Marcos found her fervently praying with Mercedes for the family's wayward sheep.

'I'd rather have them praying together than clawing each other's eyes out,' he remarked acidly. 'It makes a nice change.'

Isabel and Elías arrived from Maria Fernanda with nine-month-old Julián. They had just bought a flat in town; in the meantime they were staying at Barranco Rosales. Sturdy, dark-eyed Julián had already wreaked havoc in the nursery.

'He crawls at the speed of lightning,' chuckled his grandfather. 'Nearly pulled over the coffee table this morning trying to stand up. Little devil – we call him Tiger.'

We sounded so excluding. Angela grimaced at the receiver. 'When are you coming back?'

'Tuesday.' He paused before adding almost apologetically, 'Gladys has decided to come back with me for a couple of weeks. There'll be children all over the place. She's bringing Clara because she thinks the child needs fresh air, and Julián so that Isabel can sort out the new flat in peace. They found one near where Carlos and Teresa used to live. Mercedes is holding the fort at Barranco Rosales – between Eduardo, Yvonne and Miguel she'll have her hands full. Did I tell you Gastón is engaged to Freddy's daughter?'

'No,' said Angela, 'Is she *simpática?*'

'Very. Carlos and Teresa would be pleased.'

There was a silence. Angela heard voices in the background and a baby's gurgled laughter. Marcos said 'in a minute' to someone. More gurgling and then his voice came over the telephone again, guarded this time and speaking quickly.

'I'll have to leave you now, *gringuita*. Alfredo and Fortunata Castro have just arrived – my wife's idea of a pleasant evening. Are you all right?'

'Yes, I suppose so.'

'Good. We'll fix up to see each other when I get back to La Catalina,' he said and rang off.

V

Jimmy left for Laguna Grande at half-past ten on Friday morning. He was in a strange mood – exuberant, restless, even secretive. Angela caught him looking at her from time to time as though unable to decide whether she approved or not of his high spirits. Before going out of the door he took hold of her hand and held it tightly for a moment, then patted her on the shoulder.

'Everything'll be all right, angel,' he said awkwardly, 'I promise. After today everything's going to be all right.'

She wondered about that for a long time afterwards.

The day dragged on. Angela inspected repairs on the hen house, planned an addition to the vegetable garden, argued with Tiburcia about Dominga, the maid.

Halfway through the afternoon Marcos arrived, ostensibly to see Jimmy on business. Since his return to La Catalina Angela had not heard from him – too busy, she told herself bitterly. Ranch, children, grandchildren all conspired to claim his attention. They excluded outsiders like herself or at any rate set them aside for later. She returned his kiss impatiently, angered by the exclusion and with herself for resenting it.

Marcos frowned. 'What's wrong, *gringuita?*'

She could think of nothing to say except, 'Did you read my letter?'

'Of course I read your letter.'

So matter of fact, as if the contents dealt with heads of cattle or sacks of grain instead of the torments of her heart. Angela pulled away from him and stared at the fire crackling on the hearth.

'That's it,' she said in a muffled voice. 'I told you in my letter. We can't go on like this.'

'What do you mean?'

'Oh, for God's sake – don't pretend you don't know! We can't go on loving each other behind people's backs. Carrying on as though our love were some sordid affair instead of the most important thing in our lives.' Her eyes filled with tears. 'It is the most important thing, isn't it?'

'Of course it's important,' he replied after a moment. 'Unfortunately there are other things as well.'

Masculine realism. Cool head and the heart be damned.

'I don't want to hear about other things!' cried Angela. 'I don't want to hear about family and responsibility and all the rest of the important crap! Can't you understand how I feel, Marcos? Don't you realize what it's been like for me all these years? Having to tell lies, having to pretend, having to face Jimmy . . .'

'What about me?' asked Jimmy from the doorway.

He had driven into Laguna Grande at breakneck speed, his mind racing with plans for his son. The Widow's hut was empty. A neighbour told him the Widow had left the evening before with her moustached friend. They had taken the boy with them.

'And good riddance!' added the neighbour, crossing herself energetically. 'That woman was the Devil's own filth and her bastard was just as bad. Mean and twisted runt like I've never seen. God only knows what kind of man spawned him! What you be wanting them for, Don Morgan?'

Jimmy walked off without replying. He wandered in a daze for nearly an hour through the streets of Laguna Grande; when he could no longer stand the streets he went into the hotel and ordered a bottle of whisky. The barman later reported that Don Morgan looked murderous. He sat in a corner and drank nearly three-quarters of the bottle, staring straight ahead in hard-eyed silence. At half-past three he drove home.

Reaction took a long time to surface; even when the car bumped over the cattle-guard and through Los Alamos's main gate Jimmy was still stunned. He stared blankly at the estate wagon parked under the trees. His son was gone. The turning-point would never happen. He stumbled up the steps and heard Angela's voice.

Having to tell lies, having to pretend, having to face . . .

350

'Go on,' said Jimmy thickly. 'Tell me about the l-lies. Wh-what it's been like all these years. Go on! *I want to know!*'

Angela stared at him, the white-faced ghost of his nightmare. He focused with difficulty on the man standing beside her. Judas's ghost. Jimmy laughed at the ghosts because their faces told him what the lies were all about.

'Tha' funny,' he hiccoughed. 'All these years you've been way up there, angel. Sky-high. Iceberg in the clouds. Sq-squattin' on the bloody pedestal.' He lurched across the room, his face grey and glistening with sweat. 'Bloody b-bitch! You're not better'n the rest of 'em!'

Marcos's voice said, 'Keep away. You're drunk.'

'You filthy son of a bitch!' shouted Jimmy. 'How many years have you been screwing my wife?'

'You're out of your mind,' mocked the voice. 'There's nothing between us.'

He swung around on Angela. 'Go on, tell me! What's it feel like, playing iceberg for your husband and being this bastard's hot little whore?'

'Shut your goddamned mouth, Morgan!' roared Marcos and hit him.

Jimmy struck back blindly. He sobbed out incoherent words, his face distorted with fury and despair. His son was gone; he would never see him again. The Widow had stolen his son while his wife screwed with his friend. Bitch wife, bitch widow-mother of his son – they had lied to him. Romero was his. He wanted him back. His only son, flesh and blood. He was going to kill the filthy screwing bitch who had taken him. The ghost staring at him. White-faced bitch wife. He was going to kill them both. All of them. Judas – whore – wife . . .

'I'll kill you!' he screamed and ran out to the car. His gun lay under the front seat. He picked it up with shaking hands, slipped the safety catch, started back up the steps. Marcos blocked the way.

'No!' he yelled. 'Don't be a fool, Jimmy!'

A single shot cracked across the yard, the noise reverberated in the hollow echoes of a nightmare. In that nightmare Angela ran down steps spattered with blood. At the bottom of the steps the gound was dark and wet. Something horrible lay in the wetness. The yard was silent except for a man's weeping and a tiny gurgling sound.

VI

The nightmare continued in disjointed flashes of memory.

Dominga's ashen face peering through the window, Marcos's voice on the telephone. An overturned tub of geraniums. More faces. Later – so much later Angela thought eternity must have come and gone several times – Jacobo Feldman arrived. Someone took her into the bedroom and made her lie down. Later again she woke up to find Julia sitting beside the bed. Strange for Julia to be in the bedroom when Jimmy was hurt.

'I must go to him,' said Angela and struggled to sit up.

Julia pushed her back gently. 'Not now. You need rest.'

'You don't understand. Jimmy's hurt. I saw him. He needs me.'

'Oh, my dear,' whispered Julia and took hold of her hands. 'Jimmy isn't hurt any longer.'

It was another day before Angela fully realized what she meant.

VII

Angela came back reluctantly to life, mainly because there were details which could not be set aside. Her statement to the police, for instance.

Captain Cordero told her several witnesses claimed Don Morgan had been drinking heavily in the Hotel Estrella. Another witness reported he had been hanging around the Widow's hut in the morning. Don Marcos said he seemed exasperated about something. Exacerbated was the word. There had been a violent quarrel . . . The policeman looked uncomfortable. Certain things had been said about the señora which Don Marcos took exception to because they were offensive and untrue. When he reproached Morgan the man ran out to his car. Don Marcos was afraid of what might happen and followed, but before he could reach him Morgan shot himself. That was his statement. Did the señora agree with it?

'Yes,' said Angela dully. 'My husband was upset. I don't know why. He seemed all right that morning. The things he said weren't true. Mar – Señor Luciani told him they weren't true.' Her voice seemed to come from a very long distance. 'They weren't true.'

Captain Cordero had been in Laguna Grande for a long time. His report did not include the things which were untrue.

Suicide, which was in bad taste, became a regrettable accident. The Morgans quickly buried the son they had never understood in the British Cemetery near Buenos Aires and quoted Kipling on his tombstone. Angela thought how much he would have hated it.

'You'll sell the ranch, of course,' said Cora in her precise, clipped voice. 'I think a nice little house near us would be the best thing. After all, we are the only family you have now.'

'Quite,' mumbled her husband uncomfortably.

Angela took a deep breath. 'You're very kind, but I'm not going to sell. Los Alamos is my home.'

'But my dear girl, you can't possibly run that place on your own! A woman alone in the middle of the camp? It's unheard of!'

'I'm going to keep Los Alamos,' she repeated stubbornly. 'Jimmy would want me to do that. I'll carry on some-how.'

Lucía Claire sent an expensive wreath and invited her to stay at the flat, but Angela did not want to see Lucía Claire just now. Perhaps she would never see her again. That part of her life was over and buried. She wept for it, but she had no desire to resurrect stale ghosts.

Two days after Angela returned to the ranch Tiburcia announced that she and Saúl were leaving. Los Alamos was cursed. They wanted no part of it any longer.

'That old heathen Russian put the evil eye on this place, Señora Angela,' said Tiburcia, rolling her eyes. 'Tain't me alone who says that. Everyone around here says you're crazy to stay on. Best sell the land and return to your *pago*.'

Tadeo told Angela she was better off without Tiburcia and Saúl or anyone else who believed in curses. He advised her to keep Dominga until she trained a girl to take her place; in the meantime, he offered to look around for a competent foreman.

'I have a man in mind,' he said. 'Raúl Jones, my manager's nephew. He's intelligent, well educated and a hard worker. That should be quite a change from old Saúl. Married and with a small child. A boy, if I remember correctly. His wife's an excellent cook.'

Angela smiled faintly. 'Thank you, Tadeo. I appreciate your help.'

The gruff, weatherbeaten face softened. 'Jimmy was *loco* and we argued a lot, but I liked him. Whatever help you need is yours for the asking, Angela. Running Los Alamos on your own won't be easy.'

'I'll manage.'

He hesitated a moment before inquiring with a studied casualness that did not deceive her, 'Has Marcos been over lately?'

'No.'

Tadeo eyed her for a moment and then sighed. 'You have great courage, you know. Any other woman would have sold out and gone back to the city.'

It was guilt, not courage – but she couldn't expect Tadeo Ortíz to understand.

VIII

Marcos came to see her two weeks later.

They faced each other awkwardly in the centre of the room, neither daring to touch nor knowing what to say. The afternoon sunlight was harsh; it made him look older, sharpened the lines around his mouth and eyes. Angela noticed in surprise, as one notices irrelevant details, that his hair was streaked with grey. But then I don't look so young myself any more, she reflected wryly. Jimmy's taken our youth with him. Perhaps that's his revenge.

'I thought it prudent not to come before this,' said Marcos. 'Not that I haven't wanted to, but under the circumstances it was better to wait.'

'Of course.'

'Are you getting along all right? Do you have everything you need?'

'Yes, thank you.'

He smiled uneasily. 'I don't know what to say, *gringuita*. Driving over here I thought of so many things to tell you, but they all seem to have escaped me.'

Angela walked over to the window and stood staring out at the yard. The poplar trees stirred restlessly in the wind; beyond them lay a line of brown winter fields faintly shaded with the first greening of spring. Resurrection and renewal. Some things were impossible to resurrect. A dead marriage, for instance – or a dead love. Her love for Marcos lay buried beneath a mountain of disillusion and betrayal. All her hopes had been reduced to rubble by a single sentence. She had neither the energy nor the courage to attempt their resurrection. Ashes to ashes, dust to dust . . . Angela gave a small, involuntary shudder. Her voice was toneless.

'Everything has already been said.'

'What do you mean by that?' demanded Marcos.

She continued to stare at the distant fields. '*There's nothing between us*. That's what you told Jimmy, isn't it?'

'What did you expect me to do? Tell Jimmy the truth? Hurt him more than he was hurting himself?'

'I don't know,' she replied after a moment. 'It doesn't make any difference now.'

Marcos's voice shook. 'Jimmy was my friend. I tried to keep that friendship separate from my love for you. I tried up to the last minute, Angela. But I couldn't.' He faltered and then added bitterly, 'Jimmy blew his brains out in front of me. Do you think I will ever forget that?'

What a cruel light death sheds on truth, Angela reflected darkly. It shows up all the hidden dirt. A lover's cowardice, a husband's bastard . . . She dug her nails into her palms. The Widow's hag-eyed son was Jimmy's bastard. That truth was particularly cruel. She was barren because Jimmy had accidentally pushed her into a well, but a whore had given him a son. She would never forget that.

The wind blew a piece of paper across the yard; a dog chased after the paper, yapping madly. Angela watched for a moment, then glanced over her shoulder. 'Did you know about Jimmy's son, Marcos?'

There was a very long pause. 'Yes.'

Of course he had known. Probably everyone in Laguna Grande had known about Jimmy's son – except Jimmy's wife.

She turned back to the window. Marcos waited uneasily. The silence dragged on forever.

'It happened before Jimmy met you,' he said.

There was no reply. He walked over to the window and touched her shoulder.

'Please go away,' said Angela wearily. 'I want to be alone.'

'I don't want you to be alone.'

'What you want no longer matters. Please go.'

After another long minute she heard his footsteps retreating from the room. The door opened and closed. The footsteps went down to the yard, a car door slammed. The engine started. In her heart Angela followed the car along the drive, through the gate, turning right past the windmill on to the main road. Her heart wept, but her eyes were dry.

CHAPTER TWENTY-SEVEN

I

Little Julián Castro, aptly nicknamed Tiger, ruled La Catalina and his grandfather's heart.

Marcos took him everywhere. Cattle pens, hunting, auctions at the stockyards – the *patrón* and ruddy-cheeked Tiger were familiar figures in the saddle or on Laguna Grande's dusty streets. Jacobo Feldman grinned wryly as he watched Tiger toddling along with sturdy determination in the wake of his grandfather's long strides.

'If the rest of Laguna were that healthy I'd be out of business,' he remarked to Pablo Losa. 'That kid's the image of his mother. How are things out at La Catalina these days?'

Losa shook his head. 'Don Marcos works too hard. Everyone's after him to take a holiday, but he won't.'

'I should think it would do him good to get away.'

'That's what Señorita Mercedes and Señora Isabel were telling him yesterday. It's not as if we couldn't look after things while he's gone. Gastón knows the business backwards and even Miguel's settling down. And there's Jorge Robles in Buenos Aires.' Losa sighed. 'Don Marcos isn't to blame for what happened out at Los Alamos, but you can tell it's hanging around his neck. He's not the same man. Maybe that's why Señora Isabel leaves little Julián here so much. Keeps him going, if you know what I mean.'

Feldman fumbled for his pipe. 'I hear Morgan left the ranch in a mess. Debts all over the place. Hell of a thing for his widow.'

'Everyone's willing to give the woman a chance. With any luck we'll have a good harvest, which should help.' Losa tugged his ear and looked embarrassed. 'Doña Angela's a fine woman. She deserves better than what she got left with.'

The doctor puffed on his pipe in silence. At the far end of the square the old Peronist Party headquarters had been turned into a new café. Chrome fittings, formica-topped tables, coloured lights. There were mercury lamps on the road in front of the station and asphalt paving along the left side of the square, neon signs for the police station and La Federala. Rumours said that Eustaquio Flores's son-in-law was going to open a cinema. Other rumours claimed El Ombú would be sold to the Americans. A German businessman from Buenos Aires spent a week at Hotel Estrella; someone remarked that the man planned to build a supermarket on the outskirts of town.

'Life goes on,' observed Jacobo Feldman.

II

Angela Morgan began to pick up the broken pieces of her life and shape them into some form of coherent pattern again. She imposed a stringent provision on that pattern: no Marcos Luciani. It was the only way she would be able to survive. The wounds of anger and disillusion over his denial of their love might still be fresh in her mind, but Angela could not trust her heart. She must shut Marcos out of her life and keep him out.

Had it been possible for her to leave Los Alamos Angela would have done so, but she had already committed herself to carrying on with the ranch. To go back on that commitment now would be an act of cowardice, a further betrayal of Jimmy's dreams. She couldn't do it. No matter how badly things had gone between them, no matter how bitterly she resented his illegitimate child, he had been her husband. Los Alamos was his land; he had placed all his hopes in it. Whatever his faults, whatever the mistakes he had made, Angela felt dutybound not to let those hopes down. It was the only means she had of atoning for her own part in Jimmy's failure, the only peace-offering she could make to redress broken promises.

Reconstruction of her new life was a slow, painful process, yet Angela quickly discovered that she was not without friends. People's kindness amazed and touched her. Neighbours whom she had not known very well went out of their way to be of help; the inhabitants of Laguna Grande stopped her in the street to ask how she was getting along. The bank manager offered Los Alamos credit on reasonable terms; his wife showed up one morning with two enormous jars of pumpkin preserve and a small bay tree for the garden. The nuns from the convent school said a special mass for Jimmy, and the children at the day-care centre produced a ginger kitten.

'So you won't feel alone, Doña Angela,' they chorused. 'Don Morgan's happy in Heaven now. You mustn't be sad any more.'

For the first time since Jimmy's death Angela broke down and cried. The ginger kitten made loneliness easier to bear.

It was not easy to shut Marcos completely out of her new life. They lived within thirty miles of each other, they knew the same people, they had to do business together. There was also the rest of the Luciani clan. She didn't want to lose their friendship, but she couldn't risk the inevitable contact with Marcos on such an intimate level, with all the memories it held for them both. All she could do was use work as an excuse for not paying social visits and hope for the best. So far her strategy had worked, but then Gladys was very much in the family forefront these days. She had installed herself at La Catalina and stuck to Marcos like a limpet.

'That woman's either very stupid or very clever,' remarked Julia Ortíz when she went over to visit Angela one afternoon. 'It's so obvious Marcos can't stand having her around, but she just hangs on to him and smiles her priggish little smile. You never know what she's really thinking.'

Angela shrugged. She didn't want to talk about what Gladys might or might not be thinking. Marcos's wife, like everything else intimately connected with him, belonged to a past that was dead and buried. She poured Julia another cup of tea and began to discuss a new project for the day-centre. At least that was something alive and had a definite future.

III

Marcos viewed both the present and the future as a dreary, interminable hell.

Ever since he had walked out of Los Alamos he had been waiting for Angela to make some gesture of reconciliation. God knew he had tried to reach her often enough. He had poured out his heart in dozens of letters; they came back unopened. He had rung her up; she always found an excuse not to come to the phone. He had tried to entice her over to La Catalina on the pretext of urgent business; she had sent her manager instead. Raúl Jones was a capable man, but Marcos didn't want to see him. He wanted Angela.

His desperate efforts stopped short of returning to Los Alamos and forcing a showdown. He had never really cared for the place; he felt an almost superstitious aversion to it now. The image of Jimmy's mangled body sprawled at his feet was too terrible a memory. There was too much blood, too much bitterness — perhaps even too much belated guilt at the part his own betrayal of friendship had played in the tragedy.

There was something else as well.

Time and time again Marcos forced himself to review the death-scene in his mind; Jimmy slipping the safety catch on the gun, his own frantic attempt to grab it, their brief struggle. Jimmy had wrenched free, rammed the gun into his mouth and pulled the trigger. Marcos was certain Angela had not seen it happen; she had been standing by the fireplace when he rushed out after Jimmy. If she hadn't seen the actual suicide, she might think . . . He didn't know what she thought.

Angela wouldn't let him get near her, not even on neutral ground, like at the stockyards or in the impersonal surroundings of the Hotel Estrella. She attended the weekly cattle auctions and sometimes went back to the hotel for lunch. Marcos had tried to pin her down there several months after Jimmy's death. It had been a humiliating experience.

He had been having lunch at the Estrella with Pablo Losa and two other local ranchers when Angela walked into the dining-room. Perhaps she had intended walking out as soon as she saw Marcos, but one of the ranchers had already waved her over and signalled to the waiter to set another place at their table. There was nothing she could do but accept the invitation as graciously as possible.

During the meal Angela virtually ignored Marcos. Her blue eyes stared through him with chilling indifference; the few times she spoke to him directly she did so in a flat, colourless voice he hardly recognized. Her remarks did little to inspire his confidence. 'Pass the bread, please.' 'May I please have the salt?' Nothing more personal than that. Even Pablo Losa noticed the contrast and looked uncomfortable.

After lunch Marcos made his move.

'I have some urgent papers for you, Angela,' he said as they were all leaving the hotel. 'I'll bring them over to your car and we can discuss them before you go back home.'

Her blue eyes stared through him. 'Please give the papers to Raúl Jones. He's still down at the stockyards. I'm afraid I have another appointment.'

She said goodbye to the rest of the men and walked off, leaving Marcos with a hopeful smile frozen on his face. After that he gave up trying. Angela's coldness unnerved him because it was so relentless, so final. He couldn't understand why she treated him like this. What had happened at Los Alamos was over and done with. He didn't want it to keep poisoning their relationship. He wanted to tell her so; reassure her of his love. He couldn't reassure an iceberg that had snubbed him so brutally in public. The frustration of being unable to break through her glacial defences was killing him.

Marcos told himself not to be a fool. Sooner or later Angela would get over whatever was bothering her and would return to him. She had been upset when he went to see her at Los Alamos: that was understandable. The things she had said were caused by the strain of the moment. He decided to make one more attempt and phoned Los Alamos.

'Doña Angela's busy with accounts now,' announced Dominga glibly. 'She doesn't want to be disturbed.'

Marcos slammed down the receiver. Accounts be damned. If a woman was going to tell lies, the least she could do was use a bit of imagination.

Months dragged by and there was still no sign of the iceberg thawing.

Marcos stubbornly bolstered his flagging hopes with the thought that time was irrelevant in matters of love. He loved Angela passionately. She was his mind, his body and his heart. He couldn't live without her. He would wait for her to return to him, even if it took forever.

He did not know then just how long forever would be.

IV

The tragedy at Los Alamos held Laguna Grande's interest throughout the summer until it was replaced by the political upheavals of 1962. A military coup that ousted a constitutionally elected president in the name of democracy was meatier gossip than a man's death. Everyone knew *el loco* Morgan was crazy, but no one knew what the puppet president installed by the generals was like. Laguna Grande speculated, conjectured, argued. The winds of national chaos began to blow in earnest and local tragedy faded into legend.

V

Claudia learned about Jimmy Morgan from her mother. A few indifferent sentences tucked among a catalogue of complaints. Why were they still living in that horrible house? Why didn't she lose weight? Why didn't she do something about her hair? Isabel was pregnant again — of course she (heavily underscored) could afford another child. How was Claudia going to manage now that she had two children?

Jimmy Morgan died, wrote Gladys. *It was very unpleasant because he shot himself. An unstable man. I never understood why everyone liked him. We saw his wife in town on Thursday afternoon. She looks much older than her age, but then these* inglesas *let themselves go. A woman's appearance is so important. I'm enclosing the latest diet. You must lose weight! Morgan's wife was not at all friendly. In fact she hardly spoke to us, which is very ungrateful when you think of all we've done for them over the years. I never thought much of her, but she was really Mercedes's friend. Your stepfather is not well. After we returned from Laguna Grande on Thursday he acted very strangely. I think he may be about to have a stroke — or maybe a heart attack. He smokes too much and sleeps badly. Naturally I spend most of my time with him now . . .*

Claudia felt vaguely sorry for Jimmy Morgan because death was sad, but the incident no longer concerned her. Life was too cluttered and happy to worry about people who were no longer part of her world. Something was always going on at home. Aunt Lidia might be telling fortunes or Aunt Alba might hold a poetry reading. Little Albertito, aged two and a half, had an instinctive and devastating knack for getting into mischief. The cats bred kittens with the speed of rabbits, baby Gloria was teething, Luis was writing a novel.

'A satire denouncing the United States's enslavement of Latin America,' he explained proudly. 'I have a friend who promised to get it published in Cuba.'

Luis's friends were always dropping in for coffee or *maté*. At first most of their conversation was far above Claudia's head – long, convoluted discussions about dialectical materialism and proletarian revolution. Luis explained everything to her in ordinary, everyday terms. He was very good at that, Claudia told the aunts. Far more clever than most of the others, who wound themselves up sprouting pages of political theory without saying anything at all.

'Full of sound and fury,' murmured Alba. 'It signifies nothing, my dear.'

'But Luis does! He knows what he's talking about. Don't you think so?'

Alba waved a languid hand. 'I'm quite above all that. Poetry of the soul is all that matters. Communion with the celestial muses, with the immortal Sappho.'

'Well, I think Luis knows more than any of his friends,' insisted Claudia, plugging in the vacuum cleaner. 'Except for Father Rulo and Oscar, that it.'

'Religion is mere illusion, politics an intellectual fantasy,' proclaimed Sappho's spirit sister and sniffed the air hungrily. 'Oh, good! Lidia's making fresh *pesto* for the noodles . . .'

She drifted off towards the kitchen, followed by Albertito and half a dozen cats.

Father Rulo's real name was Patrick Boyle – a throwback to his paternal great-grandfather who had settled in Argentina at the turn of the century. 'Rulo' was an affectionate nickname on account of his ginger curls; to his superiors he was known as Father Boyle in public and a number of unclerical names in private.

He was, to put it mildly, an unwelcome thorn in their tradition-bound hides.

The Second Vatican Council reforms still lay a couple of years in the future, but initial shock waves were already battering the strongholds of Catholic tradition. Boyle's beliefs were not only well ahead of his Church's time, they were also far more radical. He belonged to a rising tide of young Third World priests who

363

insisted that the Church must go into the streets and fight for the poor. Spiritual comfort was not enough. The Church must be actively involved with the people, both in their material and their political needs.

'Patient suffering,' he cried from the pulpit, 'has run its course!'

Claudia liked Rulo Boyle. She was not so sure she liked Oscar.

Oscar Raskowitz had little use for religion, but shared Boyle's convictions about the rights of the people. He was an intense, sallow young man in his mid-twenties – an economics student gone sour. Harsh-tongued and bitterly resentful of success, wealth or anything else related to the so-called privileged classes. His parents owned a small business in downtown Buenos Aires; according to Luis the father was cantor in the local synagogue.

'Nice, harmless old folk, very bourgeois in their ways. Can't understand why Oscar's not interested in religion or the family business, for instance. Or why he doesn't settle down and marry a nice Jewish girl. Same with his sister Olga. They want her to marry a neighbour's son, but she's got her mind set on being a sociologist. Smart kid. Has good brains and the guts to use them.'

Olga came to the house with Oscar one warm October evening in 1963.

Aunt Lidia was holding what she called a 'horoscopic happening' to celebrate Argentina's new president. He was a relatively unknown, mild-mannered doctor from the provinces, who replaced the puppet president installed by the military eighteen months before. He entered the Casa Rosada on the tide of a bitterly contested general election; how long he would last there was anybody's guess. Aunt Lidia, effervescently optimistic, consulted her cards and predicted years of prosperity for the country.

'If the jackboots keep their feet out of our faces long enough,' sneered Oscar.

'They've promised to respect the will of the people,' drawled Luis. 'That's what the Walrus says, anyway.'

'Who's the Walrus?' asked Claudia, retrieving a cigarette stub from Gloria's inquisitive fingers.

They all laughed and someone draped a curtain fringe over his mouth like a moustache. 'Our commander general, head jackboot and leader of the blues.'

'Oh,' said Claudia. 'I thought *he* was one of the reds.'

Several voices immediately began to explain the difference between the blues and the reds – the two opposing factions of the

364

army which had been at each other's throats for the better part of two years. The blues claimed to favour democratic solutions, the reds threatened to install a military dictatorship that would crush the hated Peronists forever.

'The old boy still gives orders from Madrid,' remarked Luis. 'I wouldn't be surprised if he doesn't try and make a come-back one of these days.'

Another outburst as the party settled down to discuss Perón's chances with or without Perón. Olga Raskowitz strolled over to where Lidia was busily arranging her cards.

'Do you really believe in that stuff?' she asked, pointing to the painted cardboard figures.

'Oh, indeed. The cards speak the truth.' Lidia's plump face crinkled in a smile. 'Would you like me to tell your fortune?'

Olga shrugged. 'Why not?'

Lidia fanned out the pack face down. 'Pick seven, please.' She took the cards Olga handed her, laid them out like a cross and frowned. Her blue eyes studied the girl for a moment.

'Will you listen to some advice?' she said finally.

'What is it?'

'Marry. Settle down. Stay with your own people.'

Olga sneered. 'Is that what your cards say?'

'They counsel it.' The fortune-teller's short, plump finger tapped a card at the centre of the cross. 'Yourself.' She indicated the other cards, all of them swords. 'Trouble. At your head, at your feet, all around you. There is nothing to cut the streak. Take a card from the pack, please.' When Olga gave it to her she clucked disapprovingly and tossed it down. A king holding a club in his left hand. 'An affair of the heart – but not a fortunate one. Again I must warn you: stay with your own people.'

'Like hell I will!'

'No,' sighed Lidia sadly. 'You won't. It's in the cards.'

VI

Don Alfredo Castro gripped the carving knife in his right hand and darted a baleful brown eye around the lunch table.

'The trouble with this country is Communism,' he pronounced. 'Jews and Communists. The scourge of Humanity.

What we need is a strong military government to crush them. Peronists as well. Crush them all. That old sawbones we have for president's a well-meaning ass, but he's no good in the Casa Rosada.' The knife executed a series of flourishes at the roast. 'Politicians are soft these days. Look at Cuba. The whole Caribbean's a mess thanks to the bungling Americans . . .'

'The roast,' observed Fortunata tartly, 'is getting cold. I don't see why you insist on carving it at the table. Ridiculous! It's much more sensible to have the meat carved properly in the kitchen.'

Alfredo glared at her and began to carve. 'The meat's overdone again. Look at that!' He speared a limp brown slice and shook it. 'When are you going to fire that idiot of a cook and get someone decent? You'd think that in this house . . .'

His voice droned on, mixing politics and household complaints in a flat, pedantic monotone. Isabel sighed and stared at the food on her plate. Sunday lunches at her in-laws' townhouse. Dull dull dull. Overcooked meat, underdone vegetables, lumpy gravy. Roast beef, soggy potatoes, peas and carrots. Dry rice pudding for desert. The menu, like the conversation, never varied. She looked up and saw Elías frowning at her across the table. He wants me to smile and be polite to his mama. Stupid, sanctimonious cow. I loathe her. Sunday after Sunday, for the past four years.

'. . . and of course Perón's attempted comeback shows you how stupid he is,' Alfredo was saying. 'Good thing the Brazilian government forced his plane to turn back to Spain. If it were the Americans . . .'

Fortunata's nasal drawl cut across her husband's dreary speculation. 'When is your brother getting married, Isabel?'

'December tenth.'

'We know Ana Inés's family, of course. Very good Catholics.' Fortunata took a long sip of barley water. 'I have never heard a breath of scandal about them.'

Isabel's lip curled. 'I suppose we're the only ones you hear scandal about.'

'Don't be silly!' said Elías sharply, an eye on his mother. 'You know what Mama meant.'

'No, I don't.'

'What I mean, my dear,' explained Fortunata acidly, 'is that they lead moral, Catholic lives. No divorces, for instance. The number of couples separating these days is scandalous —

366

especially when you think that so many of them come from the very best families. And even more so considering that the Church *does not allow* divorce!'

'That's one of the few things we Lucianis haven't tried,' retorted Isabel and turned to Tiger, who was busily piling peas onto a potato mountain.

Elías scowled. He disliked it intensely when Isabel got on her high horse – something she did with increasing frequency these days. Elías did not like emotion. Feelings should be kept neat and tidy, like personal appearances. Passions were distortions of the senses. In his house everything was symmetrically placed and balanced; he wished his wife and children would conform to the pattern.

He intimated as much during the ride home after lunch. There was no reason for Isabel to snap back at his mother, who had made a perfectly harmless observation about Ana Inés's family. Mama was very kindhearted; it upset her when Isabel acted rudely.

'I'm sick and tired of hearing about morality,' said Isabel. 'Ana's a hell of a nice girl and far better than Miguel deserves – whether her family shares in the national divorce rate or not. Besides, it's none of your mother's business.'

'You know how Mama feels about divorce.'

'God, do I! I wonder what she would say if my father divorced Gladys.'

Elías nearly ran into the back of a bus. 'He wouldn't!'

'No, poor old Papa. He's so damned pigheaded about responsibility and family, it's pathetic.'

'I fail to see what's pathetic about responsibility and family.'

'Don't be so thick, Elías! Papa's in love with Angela Morgan.'

He stared at her in astonishment. 'Don't be ridiculous! Whatever put that idea into your head?'

Isabel opened her mouth and shut it again. She shouldn't have said that about Papa and Angela. Elías didn't understand. She wouldn't have said it if her mother-in-law hadn't been so goddamned priggish about moral Catholic lives. Fortunata Castro's views on morality were a growing source of irritation these days – but then so was everything else, including Elías.

Isabel reached for a cigarette. There was no point kidding herself. She was disenchanted with Elías. The things which had appealed to her during their courtship had soured and she could find nothing in him to replace them. She loved her home and she loved her children, but she was disenchanted with her husband. The worst thing was that she had a lifelong commitment to him: a commitment to responsibility and family. Like a bitter echo of her own thoughts she heard Angela Morgan's voice saying *it's not that simple* and remembered her father's hands clasped over the map of La Catalina. They loved each other. She had not wanted to understand then because she knew all about love . . . Isabel stubbed out her cigarette impatiently. She had been as bad as Fortunata Castro, passing judgement on other people's hearts. She hadn't known the first thing about love then, but now she understood her father's despair. Her own disenchantment had taught her that bitter lesson; a lifetime of loveless responsibility stretching down the years until 'death do us part'. Perhaps even then death had the last laugh. Jimmy Morgan was dead and Angela had faded from Papa's life altogether. He went through the motions of living, but every minute of his existence could only be hell. Was that what happened to love?

'I wish you wouldn't say things like that about your father,' said Elías. 'Especially in front of the children.'

Isabel switched on the radio. There was no point in arguing about love any longer.

VII

The following day Elías flew to Venezuela on a three-week business trip. Isabel left him at the airport and drove Tiger back to Barranco Rosales. Yvonne was sunbathing in the garden, her head wrapped in a purple towel. She grinned as Tiger took a running leap and landed on her bare stomach.

'Mind my hair!' as he made a grab for the towel. 'I've got a big date tonight.'

'Your hair's black,' announced Tiger in a puzzled voice. 'It was yellow before.'

Yvonne laughed. 'Woman-magic, you little devil. What's the trouble, Bela?' as the little devil raced off to inspect the garden. 'Had another fight with Elías?'

Isabel lit a cigarette. 'Elías doesn't fight, he freezes. Where are you going tonight?'

'Dining and dancing with a gorgeous *gringo*. A six-foot-four Texan with mountains of money and no brains. Glorious, old girl. He spends the whole time telling me how wonderfully beautiful I am. *Tu eres muy hermosa*,' mimicked Yvonne. 'Me! With my ugly mug!'

They laughed and then Isabel said, 'I've had a letter from Cristina.'

'So have I. I read it out loud at breakfast this morning. Uncle Marcos and la Glad were there.'

'You didn't!'

'Why the hell not? I'm fed up with not being able to talk about Cristina. She's happy, Lorenzo's making a name for himself, they've got a lovely little daughter – I don't see why Uncle has to be such a goddamned ass about the whole thing! Mind you,' Yvonne flicked a gold lighter at her cigarette, 'I was watching his face. He'd relent if weren't for la Glad. Stupid bitch. Sat there all puckered up like a sour lemon. So high and mighty she is and we musn't breathe a word about the Scandal . . . what's so funny?'

'Scandals. I gather the Lucianis are still in Fortunata's good books because we haven't tried the biggest scandal of all.'

'Divorce?' Yvonne yawned. 'It's up to you or Miguel, sweetie. I simply refuse to get married.' Her grey eyes narrowed against the sunlight. 'Here comes darling little Lalo.'

Eduardo, clumsy and awkward at twelve, shuffled down the garden path. He'd be much better looking if he stood up straight and didn't drag his feet, thought Isabel. I wish I could like him more. I wish Papa liked him. He doesn't like either of them – little Clara even less than Lalo. I don't think he's ever smiled at Clara since she was born. Insufferable brat, but she is his child.

Eduardo's hands and feet were outsized. He shuffled self-consciously and avoided looking at Yvonne. His hazel eyes darted a glance at Isabel and slid away again. He cleared his throat.

'Mama says Tiger can stay here for the day.'

Isabel's eyebrows climbed a couple of inches. 'I'm leaving him here whether she says so or not. Aunt Mercedes wants to take him to the zoo this afternoon.'

There was an embarrassed silence.

'Lalito,' purred Yvonne, smoothing tanning lotion over long legs, 'why aren't you in school today?'

369

Eduardo turned a dark, uncomfortable red. 'I have a cold,' he mumbled and slouched off towards the house.

'Gladys wants to keep darling Lalo chaste and virginal for his marriage bed,' chuckled Isabel. 'Don't steal her thunder, Yvo.'

She left Tiger happily munching biscuits and went back to the flat. The day stretched ahead much the same as every other day. The night would stretch ahead like any other night – except that she would be alone. Not that there was much difference between being alone in bed and being with Elías, reflected Isabel wryly. She had learnt that much on her wedding night.

Love had been a clinical performance, executed with fastidious detachment.

The minute it ended Elías leapt out of bed and fled into the bathroom. Isabel heard water running in the basin; it ran for what seemed like forever and after a while she began to shiver. This was certainly not what she had expected from her first full experience with lovemaking. Where was the passion she longed for? The ecstasy and tenderness? She tried to embrace Elías when he returned to bed, but he shrugged her away and turned his back. Two minutes later he was asleep.

The indication of what Elías was like had been there from the very beginning; if she hadn't been so blinded by rose-coloured fantasies of love, she would have seen them. The truth was that she had been infatuated with the romantic ideal of marriage. Her engagement had left no time for reality. There had been a whirlwind of parties, dances and shopping. The wedding gifts. Guest lists. Invitations. Her wedding dress. Plans for the honeymoon . . . It had been a time of exhilarating, glamorous excitement because Isabel Luciani was going to be married.

Only one person questioned the future and that was her father.

'Are you sure you want to marry Elías Castro?' he asked.

At the time the incident with Angela still lay between them. Isabel remembered that and Stefan Stervic's strong body pressing shamelessly against her own. She answered sharply, 'Of course I want to marry him!'

'I want you to be happy, Bela.'

'Don't you like Elías?'

Marcos's voice was even. 'So far he hasn't given me cause to dislike him. I just want you to be happy, that's all.'

'I am going to be very happy.'

Her father's silence had been eloquent enough, but Isabel ignored it. She was going to be very happy with Elías Castro.

VIII

Marcos passed through Buenos Aires on his way back from El Remanso and offered to take Tiger to La Catalina. Fortunata Castro doted on Tiger's younger sister Laura – at the age of two the spitting image of Elías – and claimed her for a fortnight's holiday in Mar del Plata. Isabel delivered her children to their respective grandparents and went for a drive through Palermo Park.

The morning was hot and sunny. She parked the car on a side street and stolled along, enjoying the physical pleasure of exercise and warm spring air. There were few people about. A stiffly starched nanny pushing a baby carriage, an elderly couple, a man reading the newspaper under a eucalyptus tree. An ice-cream vendor cycled by. Isabel bought a chocolate cone and wandered into the rose garden. She sat on a bench and watched the traffic flowing past the palm trees on the far side of the lake. The air was blue and very clear; the water gleamed like a dark green mirror. Everything around her seemed unreal and distant – a make-believe world which had nothing to do at all with the world she lived in. Footsteps came along the path. Isabel continued to daydream, inexplicably happy and at peace with herself.

The footsteps stopped and Stefan Stervic's voice drawled, 'Enjoying your ice cream?'

She looked up with a start and he grinned. 'Nice to be rich and loaf in the rose garden on a Wednesday morning. Winking at the pigeons and watching the world float by. Some people have all the luck.'

Isabel tossed the end of her cone at an inquisitive pigeon. 'What about yourself? You're in the rose garden on a Wednesday morning.'

'I'm still poor. I was taking a short cut to catch the bus home.' He sat down on the bench, legs extended and hands in his pockets. A shock of light brown hair fell across a pale, inquisitive eye. 'What have you been doing since I last saw you?'

'I married Elías Castro and I have two children.'

'Ambition in a nutshell. Will you have lunch with me?'

'Why should I?'

Stefan shrugged. 'Because it's Wednesday. Do you have a car or did you come to the rose garden in a gold-plated pumpkin?'

Banter and sarcasm. Isabel laughed because she missed them. 'I left the gold-plated pumpkin at home. The car's a Mercedes.'

'It would be, wouldn't it?'

'What about yourself?'

'I told you. I'm still poor.' He stared at the lake for a moment, then stood up and held out his hand. 'Come on, drive me home in your damned Mercedes and I'll cook lunch. We can buy some food on the way.'

She went with him because it was Wednesday. A blue and gold and green Wednesday in November.

IX

They brought freshly made ravioli and a bottle of wine. The flat was still threadbare, still cluttered with papers and books. Several sketches were pinned to the walls; one of them showed a house set in a forest clearing. Isabel studied it for a long time. It was a graceful house, designed with clean, flowing lines. A spacious house, with room to move around in and breathe and feel free. The perfect balance between arch and perpendicular . . . She smiled at the sketch and went into the kitchen. Stefan handed her a glass of wine.

'*Salud*,' he said, raising his own.

'You drew the house I want.'

The pale eyes were suddenly guarded. 'What of it?'

'Nothing. When you're famous you can build my house for me.'

Her careless, laughing irony stung Stefan to the quick. In the world of the mini-gods anyone could be bought for money, but fame was something else. It had its own wealth and its own code. Only the very best were chosen by those who could afford them. Isabel Castro would only settle for the biggest name in architecture to build her dream house.

Stefan thought bitterly of the care he had lavished on that particular drawing; of the nights he had lain awake staring at it and imagining how things would be if they were in the house together. Pipe dreams. If he told Isabel about them she would think him a crackpot – a besotted fool to dangle on a string like she probably dangled her husband and God only knew how many others as well. He was a fool. In the park he had thought he could handle Isabel Castro, but that was a mistake. You didn't handle a woman you wanted more than any other woman in the world; a woman you couldn't afford. You either took her or you told her to get the hell out of your life. Stefan slammed down his wine glass.

'Get out,' he said harshly.

'Why? What's the matter?'

He turned his back and began to scoop the ravioli back into their box. They would keep for tonight. Tomorrow as well, if he was careful.

'You haven't changed at all!' jeered Isabel. 'The last time I was here you acted like a lout and this time isn't any different!'

'Just get out!'

'Damn you, I'm leaving!'

'*Isabel!*'

He swung her roughly around, pinning her arms as she struggled to break loose from his grasp. The strap on her sundress broke; he tugged down a handful of bright green material and crushed his mouth against the soft, bronzed breasts swelling underneath. Isabel protested sharply. She wrenched a hand free and struck him hard. There was a puddle of water on the floor. Stefan's foot skidded and they went down heavily, still fighting each other. His voice rasped angry, frenzied words in his native tongue. She cried out again.

'Let me go!'

'*No!*'

He pulled up her dress with one hand; the other worked feverishly at his own clothes. His face was drawn with fury and excitement. He wanted to grind Isabel into the ground with his body; make her beg him to stop and when he did, hear her beg for more. She was wearing yellow lace panties. He tore them off and shoved his way past her furious attempts to resist, forcing her legs apart and driving his stiff, frustrated pride hard into another man's territory.

'I am going to make you forget Castro!' whispered Stefan savagely. 'I'm going to damn him forever!'

She tried to scratch his face. He laughed and began to kiss her, forcing his tongue violently between her tightly closed lips. The taste of his mouth excited Isabel in spite of her outrage. Not the tepid sensation she experienced with Elías's very proper kisses, but a hot, aching surge of sexual hunger. Her mind struggled to keep the flag of respectability flying, but her body had already kicked over the traces and was yielding eagerly to outrageous sensations of pleasure. She wanted to gallop with the hardness inside her, feel it swelling, feel it pushing deep within. She wanted more of it much more . . . Isabel arched herself against Stefan's strong thighs; her mouth formed frantic whispers.

'More . . . Stefan . . . I want you . . . more . . .'

'You like my prick, don't you?' he muttered against her lips. 'You like me to love you. Drive you crazy.' He thrust harder. 'Tell me you like it. I want to hear you say you like my prick inside you.'

'Oh God, yes!' she gasped. 'I never knew love could be like this. Make it last, Stefan . . . don't stop . . . make it last . . .'

He wrapped her legs around him and made it last as long as he could.

X

Later they lay close together under the rough blanket on the bed and shared a cigarette, savouring the cat-like contentment of physical satisfaction.

'They're going to wonder at home what I've been up to,' said Isabel. She chuckled softly and ran her foot along Stefan's bare leg. 'I took a good look at myself in the bathroom mirror. You're a brute.'

'You enjoyed it.' He watched a smoke ring curl lazily around the November sunshine filtering through the window. 'Why go home at all?'

'I have to at some point.'

'Is Elías coming back tonight?'

'No.'

Stefan laughed. 'Then what's your problem? Spend the night with me. There's a callbox on the corner. You can think up a good excuse.'

Isabel propped herself up on her elbow and studied him curiously. Less than an hour ago he had raped her on the kitchen floor. There was no blunter way of putting it. *You enjoyed it.* There was no way of disguising that either. Stefan Stervic was a passionate, violent man when aroused; what he wanted he took and damn the consequences. He had taken her and given her more sexual pleasure than she had ever imagined possible. Certainly far, far more than she had dreamt of in her romantic, gallant-prince dreams. She couldn't hate him for that. Perhaps she was in love with him. Perhaps she had been in love with Stefan all these years when she thought she was in love with a perfect marriage. Sacramental vows of fidelity. *With my body I honour you . . .* Fidelity had been slammed to hell on Stefan's kitchen floor. The strange thing was that she didn't feel guilty. Just ecstatic and slightly nervous about her new discovery, because love was a passionate miracle.

She smiled down into his pale eyes. 'Do you really want me to spend the night?'

'I wouldn't bother to ask if I didn't.'

Not a gallant answer. Isabel laughed.

'All right,' she said. 'Why not?'

Stefan pulled down the blanket and stroked the curve of her breasts; his lips touched the inside of her arm. 'I want to keep on making love to you,' he said. His left hand caressed her hip and belly with surprising tenderness. 'I want to smother you with love all night. Not just tonight. Whenever we can — daytime or night-time, it doesn't matter. I don't give a fucking damn about Castro.' He kissed a small mole on her breast. 'You're mine and I want you now, Isabel. Someday I'll be able to afford you permanently.'

She slid impatiently into his arms. Someday was far away. Her hunger for love needed Stefan now.

PART IV

1969–1974

*'I will make the sun go down at noon
And darken the earth in broad daylight.'*

(Amos 8:9)

CHAPTER TWENTY-EIGHT

I

A thin shaft of sunlight broke through winter clouds, warming the morning's brittle light. South of Chañarcito the wind had blown ragged blue patches in the sky; through the dark screen of *chañar* trees La Catalina emerged like a chequer-board of browns and yellows and dusty greens. Not far from the edge of the wood a half-rotted carcass had attracted a flock of buzzards. They circled lazily above death, weaving black patterns against the pale grey clouds.

Tiger watched the birds with a nine-year-old's avid curiosity. 'Are there buzzards on the moon, Grandfather?'

'There's nothing on the moon but rocks and dust. Don't you remember we saw it on television last week?'

'Oh, that.' Tiger shrugged. 'I meant the other side. Lalo says the Americans are going to build a secret city on the other side. Like New York. Then they'll control the world.'

Marcos grunted. The moon had turned out to be a wasteland. Despite ambitious space programmes and the imaginings of Eduardo's beloved science fiction authors the rest of the planets could not be much better. Eduardo ate, slept, breathed science fiction. UFOs, black holes and time warps. Hydroponic farming on Mars and solar winds.

No practicality in the boy at all.

Tiger shaded his eyes against the winter light. 'There's a car in the field, Grandfather.'

A light-brown car, barely distinguishable from its surroundings. Marcos frowned. There was a narrow road bordering La Catalina just beyond the field, but the car was definitely on this side of the fence. He gathered up his reins and flicked them impatiently.

'Come on, Tiger. Let's see what this is all about.'

They rode out of the wood at a slow canter; while they were still halfway across the field the car suddenly backed around and

379

headed for the gate. Marcos yelled and touched his horse's flank. The bay broke into a run, but by the time it reached the fence the car was gone.

'Who were they?' asked Tiger, galloping up.

'Someone who didn't want to give explanations. That's strange – no one uses this road these days. Whoever wanted to see me should have come the other way.'

'Maybe he wanted to go to the *puesto*.'

'You can't reach the *puesto* from here. There's only this one gate on the road and we keep it locked.' Marcos held up a thick chain and padlock. 'Someone's opened it. Come on, we'll talk to Fuentes at the *puesto* and see what he has to say.'

Fuentes, who had been at Chañarcito for six years, was a stout, florid man with thinning hair and prominent brown eyes. He looked blank when Marcos told him about the car and the open gate.

'Couldn't say who it was, *patrón*. I rode out there to check a fence yesterday and that gate was closed. Locked tight.'

'Someone's unlocked it.'

Fuentes's red cheeks turned a shade darker. 'Ain't no one got the key except yourself and Don Losa. We don't ever use that gate. The road don't go nowhere.'

'And that's all he knows,' Marcos told his grandson in disgust as they rode off. 'Old Benítez, who used to be at the *puesto*, would have turned the place upside down if he knew of anything suspicious. Not Fuentes. He does what he's paid to do and that's all.'

Tiger looked business-like. 'Why don't you fire him?'

'The man does his work all right – I can't fault him for that. He's just not interested in anything beyond his wages. No real feeling for La Catalina. There's too much of that around these days.' Marcos studied the wide expanse of fields stretching unchecked towards the horizon. 'This country's wealth lies in the land, boy. Our roots run right down into the earth. It's our blood, our food, our only hope for the future. Don't you ever forget that – no matter what anyone tells you.'

'Yes, Grandfather.'

'A man must love the land like he loves a woman – with his body, his mind and his heart. Do you understand that?'

'Sort of,' said Tiger doubtfully.

Marcos grinned and pointed to a windmill glinting across the field. 'You will one day. Come on, I'll race you.'

II

Pablo Losa looked puzzled when he heard about the mysterious car in the field. 'How did they get in?'

'Any chance of Fuentes fooling around with that gate?'

Losa sighed. 'There's always a chance, Don Marcos. Men don't work like they used to. No sense of duty, no loyalty to the *patrón*. It's a sign of the times, I guess. Maybe they were smugglers reconnoitering for an illegal airstrip. Pereda over at Cruz Blanca was telling me they've been having problems with smugglers recently. Planes bringing in cigarettes and whisky from Paraguay – they use an empty field or even the road if they're quick enough. A man like Fuentes would take a bribe to let someone into that field, no doubt about it.'

'How the hell did he open the gate?'

The mystery cropped up later that day during a conversation with the manager of El Ombú.

At the end of 1964 Roberto Gabán's heirs sold El Ombú to an American corporation. The sale had sparked a flurry of furious nationalist protests in Laguna Grande, but nothing ever came of them and in 1965 John Borden arrived as ranch manager.

Borden was a capable, good-natured man, who had adapted well to the local scene. In their four years at El Ombú both he and his wife had made many friends; now their stay was coming to an end. The American's blue eyes smiled ruefully at Marcos from behind large horn-rimmed glasses.

'I'm being transferred,' he said. 'The company's bringing in a new man. Len Sussler.' His voice soured slightly. 'One of our marketing experts.'

Marcos raised his eyebrows. 'Does he know anything about cattle?'

'Only what they look like on a plate – medium rare, with a baked potato and tossed salad.' Borden grinned. 'Len Sussler spent two weeks vacationing on a dude ranch in California and three summers in Acapulo. That makes him an expert on cattle and Latin America.'

Hearty sarcasm, but behind it lay a touch of genuine anger. For a man with all the qualifications that anger was fully justified.

Marcos shook his head. 'Your company's crazy.'

'That's the way it goes up at head office. One of these days I'll say screw the employee benefit plan and send them all to hell. Buy me a place in the Rockies and spend the rest of my life listening to the wind in the pines. Or go trout fishing.' Borden stared wistfully out of the window for a moment and then shrugged. 'We're being sent to Bangkok.'

'There are cattle ranches in Thailand?'

'Elephant farms, maybe. By the way, Sussler and his wife are coming out to El Ombú this week. Carol and I want to have an *asado* for them on Sunday – all our friends and the local brass from Laguna. We'd like you to come. Bring the whole family, kids and all.'

Marcos laughed. 'All seventeen of us?'

'The more the merrier. Angela Morgan's coming as well. Do her good to get away from Los Alamos and relax. Have some fun.' Borden stubbed out his cigarette and lit another one. 'Angela works too damned hard. She should find herself a husband to handle the ranch. Doesn't seem right for a good-looking woman like her to be saddled with all that responsibility.'

There was an awkward silence. Marcos stared glumly at the ashtray on his desk. Angela was still holding him at bay. Eight years and the iceberg had not thawed a single drop. If they met for business she was brisk and matter-of-fact; if they met on social occasions she treated him with cool, indifferent courtesy. He had long since abandoned any attempt to break the ice. It was too harrowing a task for his pride. His only consolation was that Angela had no other man in her life. He would have known immediately had there been one. Everyone in the Laguna Grande area liked Jimmy Morgan's widow; if there was a new husband in the offing the local gossips would be shouting it from the rooftops.

John Borden saw Marcos's expression and wondered if he had put his foot in it. He decided to change the subject.

'Did you hear about the trouble in Cardales this morning?' he asked. 'A gang tried to kidnap the Ford dealer. Stopped his car as he was driving to work. The man escaped, shot one of them. The bastards got away in a waiting car.'

Marcos looked up sharply. 'What make of car?'

'Don't know. Why?'

He told the American about the car in the field. 'That road used to be a short cut to Cardales until the floods washed part of it away in fifty-seven. I suppose a car could get through now.'

'If it's the same one, then something mighty queer's going on,' said John Borden uneasily. 'The Ford dealer swears those guys in Cardales were terrorists.'

III

Sixty miles southeast of La Catalina a light-brown car raced along a wide dirt road. Part of the road had been covered with a flimsy layer of asphalt, but this stretch running through yellow fields was untouched; at seventy miles an hour it made for uncomfortable travelling. Driver and passengers clenched their teeth against the rocking, jolting motion and kept their eyes trained on the road ahead. A man and a woman sat in the front seat, another man lay in the back. The car hit a rut, swerved sharply from side to side and jolted on. The man lying on the back seat groaned.

'Christ! Take it easy, will you?'

The woman was driving. She glanced at him briefly through the mirror and laughed. The man beside her began to gnaw on his thumb. A dark reddish stain covered the left side of his face.

'How were we supposed to know the bastard had a gun?' he complained. 'What's he need it for? He's a businessman.'

'Who's smart enough to take precautions,' sneered the woman. 'Idiots like you don't realize that. You think just because a man's a capitalist pig or works for the Americans he's a fool, but that's where you're wrong. These men aren't fools. That's why they must be eliminated.'

From the back seat came another groan. 'How much further, Olga?'

'How the hell should I know?' She threw a bitter, jeering glance at the man beside her. 'López here's the local expert.'

López flushed. 'It's not my fault things went wrong. That idiot in Cardales promised another car, but he never showed up. We're damned lucky we found an empty field and a lock I could pick. He,' jerking his head at the back seat, 'would've bled his guts out if I hadn't picked that lock. If I hadn't spotted that field we wouldn't have been able to patch him up. It's not my fault the contact let us down. That's the trouble with rustics – they're hot on words but no damned good when it comes to action.'

'You're so good, of course,' sneered Olga. 'Making sure it was Oscar who got shot.' She twisted the steering wheel violently to avoid a pothole. 'I wish that filthy swine had hit you instead of my brother!'

López muttered under his breath and glared at the road ahead. Women. Nothing but trouble. He had been against including Olga in the operation, but no one listened to his opinions these days. Not since people like Oscar Raskowitz and his sister had joined the Front. Long-haired intellectuals full of new ideas and new ways, bent on restructuring things to suit them.

López was not an intellectual. He like things to be simple. Burn cars, build barricades, throw a couple of petrol bombs and run. Tough, macho stuff. None of this airy-fairy cloak-and-dagger business, with combat cells, code names, secret contacts. He stared apprehensively at Olga as the car suddenly lost speed, sputtered several times and stopped.

'Now what?'

She pumped the accelerator furiously and switched on the ignition. The needle on the fuel gauge quivered below Empty and stayed there.

'Great bleeding bitch!' screamed López. 'We're stuck! Dry as a bone! What the hell are we going to do?'

Olga ignored him and climbed into the back of the car. Oscar lay sprawled on the seat, his head cushioned uncomfortably on a jacket. He opened his eyes as she bent over him; the makeshift bandage around his left thigh was wet and stained with blood.

'My leg's killing me.'

'Hang on,' she said shortly.

'We failed.'

Her thin hands worked deftly to staunch the blood. 'We won't fail next time.'

'There's someone coming,' announced López shrilly.

A blue Mercedes approached swiftly from the opposite direction. Olga stood in the middle of the road and motioned for it to stop. There were three people inside – a man, an auburn-haired woman and a little girl. The man rolled down the window and stuck his head out.

'Trouble?' he asked.

'I've run out of petrol. Is there a town near here?'

'Williams.' He gestured over his shoulder. 'About ten miles back.'

An attractive man in his early thirties. Dark, curly hair, dark, knowing eyes. The eyes studied Olga with approval and more than a hint of male challenge.

'I didn't realize the tank was so low,' she said, returning look for look.

The man grinned. 'Hop in and we'll give you a lift to the petrol station. There's one two miles this side of the town.'

'We're already late, Miguel,' protested the woman in the front seat. 'Your father's expecting us for tea.'

He scowled, but did not reply. Olga got into the car and leaned against white leather upholstery. The Mercedes turned smoothly and headed back down the road. No jolting, no jarring – just even, steady speed and the fragrant smells of luxury. A wealthy family, no doubt about that. The little girl was dressing an expensive doll. She stared at Olga with large, solemn eyes. The woman in front said something to her husband in a low voice.

'I forgot to buy cigarettes,' he said loudly.

She darted him an exasperated glance and began to fumble through her handbag. A pretty, well-groomed woman. The thick green mohair sweater she wore matched her woollen skirt – exclusive models that had never rubbed shoulders with mass production. A cluster of diamonds and emeralds sparkled on her left hand. Olga studied the stones for a long moment and then looked up. The man was watching her through the mirror.

'Have you come from far?'

'Far enough.'

No point in giving more details. She turned her head to look at the passing fields. Rich, well-groomed people arrived late for tea; other people struggled to survive. There was only one way to redress the balance.

By force of arms.

IV

Miguel Luciani rarely saw further than his own nose, but for a brief moment on a dusty road in the middle of the pampa, he glimpsed a foreign world. It was a strangely intriguing world, peopled by a mysterious dark girl, a light-brown car and two men. The men had taken pains to keep in the background, but he sensed their uneasiness all the same. Some trouble there, he thought and wondered what it could be. The mysterious dark girl fascinated Miguel. She was attractive in a hard, reckless way. A cool customer. Whatever the trouble might be, she was evidently in control. If he hadn't been driving his wife and daughter to La Catalina, he would have tried his luck with adventure.

If only he didn't have a wife.

If only Ana Inés hadn't told her parents he wanted to marry her. He hadn't had the faintest intention of doing so. He had kissed Ana Inés one night at a dance because she was very pretty; he had whispered the conventional nonsense a man whispers in the moonlight. That was all. Not a word about marriage. They hadn't even made love, but Ana Inés had been fool enough to believe in his kisses and ardent phrases. She had rushed all over town spreading the word that they were engaged. The next thing Miguel knew her father was demanding a formal statement of his intentions.

Their interview had been one of the most uncomfortable, exasperating moments of Miguel's life. He couldn't bluff his way out of the engagement without making a fool of himself; he had been paying too much attention to Ana Inés to begin with. In her parents' world a man who paid that kind of attention to their daughter had marriage on his mind. He was a responsible member of society. To deny such responsibility and survive the ensuing scandal unscathed required a nerve which Miguel did not possess. He might have attempted it if his own father hadn't been around, but by then Marcos Luciani, alerted by a delighted Mercedes via Ana Inés's mother, was very much in the picture and responsibility won the day.

There were too many 'ifs' in life, Miguel reflected grimly. If only he didn't have to spend a week at La Catalina. The family was bad enough to digest in small doses; seventeen of them under the same roof was too much to stomach. If his father hadn't summoned him to La Catalina, he could have spent more time with Monique.

Monique was petite, blonde and French. She had taken a very dim view of his absence.

'Your family means more than I do, *chéri*?'

'Of course not! Trouble is my old man wants to talk over business at the ranch and I can't get out of going.'

386

Monique had cocked a quizzical eyebrow. 'So you are still tied to Papa's apronstrings, eh?'

Too true, reflected Miguel glumly as he gazed around the living-room at La Catalina. The old man's king spider and this bloody ranch is his web. He traps us in it with family and responsibility, holds us like obedient little flies . . . Damn him! You can't be sure of a woman like Monique. Can't take your eyes off her for a second. She's bound to find someone else just to spite me. Damn them all!

'You look like a sour lemon,' drawled Isabel, coming over to the window. 'Another quarrel with Ana Inés?'

'Did Ana say so?'

She blew a smoke ring at him. 'Ana doesn't have to say anything. A blind man can see she's unhappy. I'd watch my step if I were you. Papa isn't blind.'

'It's none of his business!'

'He thinks it is. Ana's your wife and you're his son. A equals B, B equals C, C equals A. There's a formula in logic for that, isn't there? Don't hurt her, Miguel. Please.'

He drained his drink and sauntered over to the fireplace without bothering to reply.

If I were a painter I'd paint us in renaissance colours, mused Isabel wryly. Scarlets and blues and warm, glowing magenta. Vivid hues of prosperity and self-satisfaction. The contrast of the black-and-white hide on the floor, the silver bowl on the mantelpiece filled with eucalyptus leaves and creamy silk flowers. Firelight and the rough-woven russet curtains at the windows. Mellowness. Well-being. Magnificent setting for a magnificent farce.

Family portrait.

Papa sitting in that deep leather chair which has been his ever since I can remember. They belong together – weather-beaten, slightly worn around the edges but still holding up in spite of the years. Fifty-four for Papa . . . I wonder if Elías will look that well when he's fifty-four. Probably not. He is already started to go bald and he's not even thirty-five. Thank God Papa's not bald. Grey, but it suits him.

He's enjoying the family gathering. It's good for him.

Look at the way he's discussing politics with Elías and Gastón. Going at it hammer and tongs and getting a kick out of needling them both. Eduardo hovers in the background like an anxious puppy. Poor kid – he doesn't fit, no matter how hard he tries. He looks so ill-at-ease in this setting. An actor from another play dropped by mistake into the third act of this one without a script or stage instructions. He doesn't know what to do with his hands.

Gastón and María Marta – *they* belong. Damn them, they look so happy! Sitting side by side on the sofa, his arm around her. The perfect couple. Eight years of marriage and they're still in love. Damn damn damn! María Marta makes pregnancy look beautiful. I wish I did. True to tradition we breed like rabbits. Three children for them and another on the way. Four for us – no, not four. Three. Lies don't count, even when others believe them . . . oh, God! Mustn't think about that now.

Think of something else.

Miguel. He's too busy chasing other women to make a family. Four and a half years of marriage and there's only little Catalina to account for. Ana's so pretty and she looks so unhappy. Curled up in a chair by the bookshelves, pretending to read. She's not reading, she's waiting. He hasn't said a word to her all evening. I wonder what they quarrelled about this time. Damn Miguel! Ana's a fool for putting up with him. Why the hell should she? Because she's in love? Love's a sick joke!

Think about something else.

Gladys, for instance. She doesn't fit into the setting either. Too much make-up and her clothes are too new, too smart – even after all these years. Here we are all in jeans and bulky sweaters or tweeds like Mercedes, and there's Gladys in a silk dress and a cashmere cardigan that looks as though it still has the price-tag on it. Four-inch heels instead of loafers or boots. Blood-red nails. Gold and topaz earrings, gold brooch shaped like a horse's head, pearls. A gold mesh bracelet encrusted with topaz and diamonds – where the hell did she find something so revolting? Schwarzkopf, no doubt. He caters to the *nouveau riche*.

Half a bottle of Chanel No 5 on each earlobe.

Pathetic. Why do I feel so sorry for her?

Her hair's the wrong colour. It makes her look older. Shrewish. She should be fat and red-cheeked and hearty, married to the local butcher instead of trying so desperately to be Papa's wife. She can't sit still. She keeps fidgeting, looking at him. Willing him to pay attention to her.

It's like getting a stone wall to smile.

'Marcos,' said Gladys's shrill voice from the small, chintz-covered sofa near the window, 'have you spoken to Alberto Navone's friend in the ministry?'

Marcos continued discussing the economic situation.

'Marcos!' Gladys caught Isabel's eye, shook her head and tapped her ear. 'He's getting deaf,' she mouthed and raised her voice. 'Have you spoken to Alberto's friend?'

Marcos glanced up. 'I heard you the first time. No, I haven't.'

'When are you going to speak to him?'

'I'm not. There's no question of buying Eduardo out of his military service.'

Her voice scaled a bit higher. 'Surely you don't expect Lalito to be a conscript!'

Eduardo, as painfully shy and self-conscious at seventeen as he had been at twelve, blushed scarlet with embarrassment and avoided his father's eye.

'It's all right, Mama,' he muttered unhappily.

'It is *not* all right! I don't see why your father doesn't lift a finger to help you. There's no reason why you shouldn't be exempt.'

'Why should he?' snapped Marcos. 'I wasn't. Neither were Miguel or Gastón. Do the boy good. Should put some spine into him.'

Gastón, recalling his two miserable years in the navy, pulled a face. 'If Lalo has a chance to get out of it, why not?'

'Or at least find him a job as some colonel's chauffeur,' suggested Elías. 'All he'd have to do is drive the colonel's wife around all day.'

'Where did you do your military service?' drawled Miguel.

Elías flushed. 'As a matter of fact, I didn't. I was exempt.'

'Flat feet,' said Isabel and laughed.

'I quite agree with Marcos,' said Mercedes. 'Young men need the discipline of military training, especially these days.' She threaded a needle with green silk and pushed it through the rose on her embroidery. 'Eduardo's strong and healthy. There's no reason why he shouldn't do his military service like anyone else.'

Gladys bristled with indignation. Her apparent truce with Mercedes was a shaky one, mainly because Mercedes refused to play the game. This further proof of treachery only added fuel to smouldering fires.

'You say that,' she cried dramatically, 'because you have never had a son!'

'Nonsense!' blazed Mercedes and the family settled back to enjoy the row.

Isabel turned to the window again. The park was lost in darkness, a chilly moon glimmered fitfully between shreds of cloud. The last time she had seen the moon was from Stefan's flat. One interminable week ago. A winter moon framed between the naked arms of four cranes, the nakedness of their own bodies silhouetted in its bleak light. Stefan's voice, demanding the impossible.

'Will you leave Elías and come with me?'

'You know I can't'

'Because I'm not rich enough?'

There were other reasons as well. She had explained them carefully, anxious to make him understand.

'I have four children, Stefan. I love them very much. If I leave, I'll lose all my rights – including the right to my children. Elías would never agree to a separation and he'd make damned sure I never saw the children again. I can't hurt them like that.' Her voice trembled slightly. 'I can't hurt my father either. He thinks Elías and I are happily married. It's-it's hard to explain, but I don't want him to know the truth. He's had enough blows in that quarter. Can you understand what I mean?'

'For the time being,' he murmured and began to caress her body with a lover's secret knowledge of its moods and longings. She remembered everything he did and whispered as though he were caressing her now.

V

El Ombú lay twelve long miles northeast of Laguna Grande. By the time the party from La Catalina arrived for the *asado* on Sunday the yard in front of the sprawling blue stucco ranch house was packed with cars.

'Laguna's social event of the year,' remarked Gastón piloting his children around an outsized cactus plant. 'What's this new *gringo* like?'

Marcos grinned. 'Pure Walt Disney, according to Tadeo. He speaks a bastardized version of Mexican Spanish, including all the wrong words you don't use in mixed company.'

390

'Gladys,' laughed María Marta, 'cover your ears.'

Gladys fingered the silk scarf around her neck and clung to Marcos's arm. Even after all these years there were certain situations where she did not feel at ease, no matter how well she played the game. Laguna Grande was one of them. Marcos's friends tolerated her because she was his wife; they had little interest in her as an individual. People like Norma Mendes cut her dead, people like the mayor's wife smiled vaguely and called her Señora Luciani. Never Doña Gladys. The subtle omission was a galling reminder of her mother's warning that sow's ears did not make silk purses.

The Bordens, on the other hand, called her Gladys - but they were *gringos* and did not count.

The Bordens were determined to make a success of their *asado*. Every detail, from guitars strumming gaucho melodies in the background to the waiters in gaucho costume and the exhibition of folk dancing, had been planned with great care. It was not their fault if the Susslers made everything seem artificial, reflected Angela. They were an artificial couple – bigger than life and too plastic to be true. Len, intense and sharp-eyed, bristled with aggressive bonhomie. His execrable Spanish rattled blatantly through everyone else's conversation, offering opinions on every subject under the sun and arranging the world with slick, corporate zeal. Blonde, voluptuous Sally – miniskirted in fringed pink suede – applauded her husband's zeal and fluttered incredibly long blue eyelashes at the men.

'I hope they fall into her drink,' muttered Ana Inés sourly as she watched Miguel ogle the pink suede curves. 'She's too old to prance around in that ridiculous get-up.'

Isabel chuckled. 'Her husband keeps boasting about how much his house cost and his car and his new golf clubs. You should have seen Papa's face when Sussler asked him what our ranches were worth.'

They all laughed. María Marta turned to Angela, who had joined the group, and said with a friendly smile, 'How are you? We haven't seen you for a long time.'

'I hear you've done wonders with Los Alamos,' added Gastón. 'Tadeo Ortíz says you're turning the ranch around singlehanded.'

Angela smiled. 'Not quite, but it's getting there.'

Her reply was measured and polite: the sort of reply one made to acquaintances at a cocktail party. Isabel frowned. The whole situation was so damned stupid. Here was Angela being carefully polite and there was Papa across the patio pretending not to notice her. You'd think they were old enough to stop playing that kind of game, she told herself impatiently. What's the point in making each other so miserable? Exasperation edged her voice.

'You haven't been out at La Catalina for ages, Angela,' she said. 'Why don't you come over for lunch tomorrow?'

'I'd love to, but I'm going to be in Cardales all day,' replied Angela and left it at that.

She could count on the fingers of one hand the times she had visited La Catalina during the past eight years. Twice with Tadeo and Julia, once with the Bordens, once with Raúl Jones to discuss urgent business matters. That was all. Four visits in eight years and each one of them hell. Every time she drove through the white gate with its iron L proudly anchored by solid chains her heart climbed into her throat; every time she saw the sprawling white ranch house in its shelter of acacias and oleander bushes her eyes filled with bitter tears. The memories of the times she had travelled that same path alive with the excitement and tenderness of love were still raw, still painful. They still tore at her heart, even after the stern discipline of eight years.

The trouble was that Angela's heart refused to be disciplined. No matter how angry or disillusioned she might be with Marcos, love cried out from under the ashes and was resurrected in rebellious dreams. During the day she could stifle love with work, but one could not work twenty-four hours. In the darkness of her bedroom pride and anger no longer mattered. No one saw her tears. In a cold ghost-filled bed she could weep her heart out for what had once been; she could even trick herself into believing that love whenever possible was better than no love at all. There were times when the temptation to reach for the telephone and ring Marcos was so strong she could hardly bear it. Times when every inch of her body ached with the memory of their lovemaking. His voice echoed so loudly in her dreams that she would wake up with a start, uncertain whether she was at Los Alamos or back at El Remanso. In the end she took to sleeping with the light on because darkness was a hazardous refuge.

Fortunately cold-blooded reason governed daylight. Over breakfast Angela would tell herself not to be a fool and turn her thoughts to whatever problem was waiting to be tackled. There were enough problems on Los Alamos to keep her busy until the night; sometimes, if she was lucky, the problems were so exhausting they wore her out and she didn't dream.

It was a bitter, lonely struggle. As far as Los Alamos was concerned the struggle was paying off, but Angela Morgan was not sure she could say the same about the battle between cold-blooded reason and her heart.

VI

By half-past three Angela had had enough of guitars and grilled meat. She made her way back to the house, hoping to find a quiet spot for a siesta. Tadeo Ortíz snored gently in the chair by the living-room fire, Julia dozed with her head on his knee. Angela grinned at them and went into the library. No luck there. Miguel and Ana Inés broke off in the middle of an angry quarrel as soon as she opened the door; Ana's face was streaked with tears. Angela beat a hasty retreat and tried the small room John Borden used for a study.

Two upholstered easy chairs were drawn up in front of a small hearth; from their depths floated Sally Sussler's throaty drawl and Marcos's answering laughter. They both looked around as Angela came in and Sally smiled.

'Hi,' she said.

Definitely an unenthusiastic 'hi'. Her hand rested on Marcos's arm; the long fingers ringed with silver and turquoise closed on his sleeve in a gesture that spelt an unmistakable message for the intruder.

Get lost.

'Sorry,' said Angela and backed out, nearly slamming the door.

Stupid of her to imagine that Marcos would not be over-whelmed by Sally Sussler. The American oozed sex from every pore and knew how to use it as well. A man is a man is a man. Angela trudged across the prickly lawn and tried to think about something else, but her mind clung tenaciously to two easy chairs before a hearth. Long silver and turquoise fingers claiming possession. *I like to amuse myself with women, but love is something different . . .* 'Oh, triple blast and damnation!' muttered Angela and headed for a small pinewood on the far side of the lawn. Three minutes later Marcos caught up with her.

'Why did you go away?' he demanded.

Angela kept on walking. 'You were obviously enjoying yourself. I didn't want to interrupt anything.'

'Sally is an amusing woman.'

Sally. 'I'm sure she is.'

They reached the end of the wood. A long, empty field stretched on the other side, drab and colourless under the pale winter sun. Angela gripped a fence-post with both hands. She could feel Marcos's eyes boring into her.

'Why won't you let me near you?' he asked roughly.

She let a few seconds go by. 'What do you mean?'

'You know what I mean! You never answered my letters or my phone calls, you never want to see me alone. When we do meet you act as though I were a leper. Why? *It's been eight years, Angela!*' he exploded when she didn't reply. 'You've been treating me like dirt for eight goddamned years! What have I done to deserve it? I love you, I want to keep on loving you – for Christ's sake, look at me!'

Her fingers tightened around the fence-post. She continued to stare at the colourless expanse of grass and sky.

'What the hell do you think I'm made of?' shouted Marcos. 'Stone? I'm fed up with being shut out of your life like this! I want to know what's wrong, Angela! *Why won't you let me near you?*'

She turned and started to walk briskly back towards the house. Marcos strode beside her, his face congested with frustration and anger. He had been a fool to run after Angela, but he couldn't help himself. Eight years of hell was too long for any man to bear without knowing the reason why. He had to know what was wrong so he could set it right again. He couldn't take any more punishment. Marcos grabbed hold of Angela's arm and pulled her round. There could be only one terrible, incredible reason why. He had pushed that reason aside for eight years; he flung it out now in a harsh, tortured question.

'Is it because of Jimmy?'

'Let me go!' cried Angela sharply.

'*Is it?*' He shook her. 'You think I killed Jimmy, don't you?'

Angela raised her glance slowly and deliberately to his face. Eight years ago he had said *there's nothing between us.* Impatiently and without hesitation, as though he had meant every word. Love replaced by expediency; a love he had denied at the crucial, agonizing moment of truth. Cold-blooded reason reminded her of that denial now, dredging up the bitter dregs of disillusion and betrayal in case she should be tempted to forget.

Marcos turned white. He let go of her arm and repeated the question in a brittle, anguished voice.

'Do you think I killed Jimmy?'

Reason's revenge is a terrible thing. Angela Morgan locked her heart against anguish and walked off without replying, leaving her icy silence to speak for itself.

CHAPTER TWENTY-NINE

I

At the end of 1969 an armed group of terrorists kidnapped General Pedro Aramburu, one of the leaders of the revolution that toppled Perón.

They entered his flat in downtown Buenos Aires early one morning, seized him in front of his wife and small grandson, forced him downstairs and into a waiting car. By the time the alarm was raised the general and his captors had merged into the rush-hour traffic and were gone.

The kidnapping shocked Argentina. Whether one agreed with the general's views or not, he was a prominent member of the armed forces and a man to be reckoned with. To be dragged out of his flat in broad daylight and virtually made to vanish was clearly not the work of amateurs. Several years later Aramburu's months of captivity in the cellar of an abandoned farmhouse and his subsequent murder were described in gruesome detail in a militant newspaper, but by then the account was just one more fragment of a terrifying nightmare.

Olga Raskowitz thought the murder fully justified.

She had been a political activist ever since 1966, when a hard-fisted military government ousted the affable doctor and took over power in the name of democracy. In 1970 the hand holding the whip was a different one, but the uniform had not changed. A so-called National Reconciliation Plan meant nothing at all. As long as the jackboots trampled men's dignity and rights, as long as the Yankees stuffed their pockets with the wealth of the land – as long as the rich gathered for tea, Olga vowed she would continue to fight and hate.

The Front was the framework of her crusade. She learnt from the mistakes at Cardales and saw to it that the right people in the organization came to know of her existence. Soon they put her in charge of more ambitious assignments; hijacking a pay truck, kidnapping the manager of a small textile firm licensed by the Americans, ambushing an army convoy, robbing a provincial bank. The Front needed money. Olga Raskowitz was one of those who worked hardest to supply the need.

Her closest collaborators were her brother and Rulo Boyle.

The priest had been severely cautioned by his superiors about attacking the government from the pulpit. He was hauled over the coals several times by the diocesan bishop who in despair finally sent him to the cardinal's office in Buenos Aires.

Rulo Boyle had no intention of wasting his time listening to a mealy-mouthed lecture about his religious duties. The Church had little right to preach when it was allied to a state that jailed men for their political beliefs. He said as much, loudly and firmly to the tall, grey-haired priest interviewing him. The priest smiled faintly.

'What kind of a State should we be allied with?' he asked.

'One where every man has the right to express himself freely and to live with dignity.'

'Even if the right of expression includes bombs?'

'People use violence when they can't get what they want by other means.'

'And you believe the Church should use violence?'

Boyle hesitated. Pedro Arcos Arizu was on the cardinal's staff – an influential man. More intelligent than most of the priests who scuttled through episcopal headquarters. A man to be careful of. Rulo Boyle shifted uneasily in his seat.

'Is this a formal interview, father?'

'Not necessarily. You're free to say whatever you like, I'm here to listen.' Pedro removed his glasses and began to polish them. When he judged the silence to have gone on long enough he repeated, 'Do you believe the Church should use violence?'

'To fight for people's needs – yes. Christ himself said "I have not come to bring peace, but a sword."'

'Christ said many things,' remarked Pedro blandly. 'They can be interpreted in different ways and for different purposes.'

Boyle leaned forward, his blue eyes hard and searching. 'The Church must fight for the people!'

'But not be trapped into believing that people's needs are purely political. If the Church becomes bogged down in politics Her spiritual strength will be dangerously weakened. Men's bodies must be cared for, indeed – but their souls are far more important.'

There was no point discussing the issue any further, decided Boyle. Informally or otherwise, he would never make the Establishment understand. He returned to his church and spent the night pacing up and down the darkened aisles, debating what to do. The next day he wrote to his bishop, stating that for reasons of conscience he could no longer remain in the priesthood of a Church which refused to fight for the people. The bishop advised him to think things over, but the advice fell on deaf ears.

In May 1970 Rulo Boyle left the Church of Saint Lazarus on Cano Street and moved into Oscar Raskowitz's minute flat. The political man prevailed, but in his heart Boyle was still a priest.

II

Political uncertainty deepened.

The military government, which had been ruling by decree since 1966, kept a heavy hand on the reins – but the rumour mills continued to creak and clatter. In the event of a general election the Peronists would win, they said. Perón would return to Argentina and life would be as it was in the good old days. Anxious embassies of the ageing dictator's supporters shuttled between Buenos Aires and Madrid. Juan Gaspari went on one of them and reported back to Marcos that the general was in excellent health.

'As strong as an ox and raring to go! He's the only man who can keep this country together, *amigo*. It's about time the rest of you realized that.'

Ever-optimistic Gaspari. The useful clown had a foot in the ministries again – a cautious one to be sure, but if the rumours were true he would become a necessary fact of life once more. Marcos frowned at his cup of coffee.

'What's your damned general going to do about the Left?' he demanded impatiently. 'They've jumped on Perón's bandwagon – do you think he can control them if he returns?'

Gaspari waved the question aside. 'You have an obsession with the Left these days, Marcos! A handful of young idealists, that's all they are. The general knows how to deal with them.

Besides, it's not a question of Left or Right, but of Argentina and Argentines. You, me . . .' he swept a plump hand around the crowded café. 'All of us pulling together! If we don't unite now, we'll be eaten up by the *gringos*.'

'The maggots that riddle this country won't leave anything for them,' predicted Marcos glumly as he paid the bill.

III

Uncertainty worked its way deep into everyday life.

The Laguna Grande area was hit by a series of freak hailstorms and floods. Gale-force winds stripped off roofs and twisted the metal cross on top of the church. Two of Los Alamos's fields were under water; a number of other ranches, including La Juana and La Catalina, lost important harvests. A large section of the main road was washed away by floods, leaving an enormous crater. The provincial authorities promised to repair it, but several years later the crater was still there.

Bad weather, ruined crops, difficulties arising from the country's chaotic economic situation – as far as Marcos was concerned they were all welcome burdens.

The brief, bitter exchange with Angela at El Ombú had dealt a death-blow to his hopes of reconciliation. She believed him to be a murderer. No matter how monstrous the idea, no matter how much it shocked him there could be no other reason for her refusal to answer his question. It fitted in so well with her coldness, with her categorical rejection of everything between them.

What you want no longer matters.

Angela had said that the day he went to see her after Jimmy's death. At the time Marcos had been too upset himself to take in the true significance of those six words. He thought they had been prompted by emotional stress; he realized now with dismay that she had meant every single one of them.

Marcos Luciani no longer mattered. He was nothing.

It was no use trying to explain any more, Marcos told himself wearily. Angela's love for him was dead; all the explaining in the world wouldn't bring it back to life. Her icy silence had made that very clear.

He no longer meant anything to the woman he loved.

Partly from the need to redress his pride and partly from loneliness, Marcos turned briefly to Sally Sussler. She was a generous, uncomplicated woman who made no demands on his affections or loyalties. Good for a few laughs. A few laughs, he told himself glumly, was precisely what he needed right now.

Yet for all her generosity and uncomplicated nature Sally Sussler was no fool.

'You guys don't really like Len, do you?' she remarked one afternoon.

'Why do you say that?'

'I'm not stupid. I know we don't fit. Len doesn't see it, but I do. We stick out like sore thumbs.'

Marcos studied the yellow-and-orange striped awning ground El Ombú's swimming pool. In Roberto Gabán's day the only shade came from an acacia tree and the pool was always choked with leaves. The Bordens had chopped down the tree and installed a filtering system; the Susslers added the awning, an out-door bar and peacock-blue deck chairs. He wondered what kind of man Len Sussler must be to accept his frequent afternoon visits without comment – especially when he spent so much time with Sally. A wife like Sally was too attractive to be left on her own – but then Len Sussler had his own ideas about such things. He had other ideas as well which were not popular in Laguna Grande.

'Your husband does not understand our ways,' said Marcos after a moment's silence. 'We are cattlemen. We know our country and its problems. They are not easy to solve, but your husband has an answer for everything.'

'Meaning he doesn't know what he's talking about?' Sally smiled wryly and clasped her hands around her knees. 'Shall I tell you about Len? He grew up in the Bronx – that's in New York City. He's one of seven and none of the others ever did anything with their lives. His father ran off the night Len's youngest sister was born, his mother's an alcoholic. Len had the guts to break away. He sold newspapers, washed dishes, worked as a barman in cheap dives – anything that would pay the way. He put himself through college and went on to an MA in business administration. When I met him he was living in a grubby one-room apartment in the Puerto Rican section of New York. That's one step removed from Hell – but just barely.'

'Why are you telling me this?'

400

'I don't know. Maybe because everything Len Sussler earned he earned by sweating blood and I'm proud of him. Does that surprise you?'

Marcos leaned across the deck chair and kissed her. 'No.'

Dragonflies made long, darting swoops at the surface of the pool; beyond the yellow-and-orange awning the sky was dull green and sultry with storm. Sally fidgeted with the end of her towel.

'I would have liked children,' she said. 'We were going to have four kids, but then – well, it never seemed the right moment. Len's smart in his field and the promotions started coming faster than we could count them. The rat-race and all the social jazz that goes with it. Drinks and parties and weekends and golf. Living in Manhattan. You can't bring up kids properly in Manhattan. Of course now we could with our new house in the country, but the company transferred us here and anyway that part of our marriage isn't so hot these days.' She slanted a long, mocking look at Marcos from under the blue lashes. 'Story of my life. I'm five years older than Len, you know.'

'And a very beautiful woman. Len should take better care of you.'

'You damned latinos always say the right things, don't you?' Sally raised her glass. 'Here's to us – me married to a piece of corporation machinery and you trying to forget.'

Marcos suddenly became very interested in an ant floating in his drink. 'Forget what?'

'The English blonde – Angela, isn't that her name? The one who's so polite it's an insult. She can't stand me and you wife hates her guts. Two plus two makes four.'

'Not always.'

Sally Sussler's rich, warm laughter echoed across the heavy summer air. 'I may be beautiful, but I ain't dumb. Two plus two makes four – even in Argentina.'

IV

Alfredo Castro died of a heart attack in 1971.

He had travelled to the Iguazú Falls on a business trip; the next morning he was found dead in his hotel room. Fortunata, who had not accompanied him, was understandably shocked. She was even more shocked to learn that her husband had died in another woman's arms.

'A common tramp!' sobbed Fortunata, clutching her son's lapels and shaking him. 'Betraying me with a common tramp! How dare he!'

Elías, who had always suspected his father's dour virtue, made comforting noises and later informed Isabel that Fortunata could not be left alone.

'She has an army of servants in that ghastly townhouse and hordes of friends to look after her,' pointed out Isabel bluntly. 'If there's one thing your mother won't be it's alone.'

'I've sold the townhouse. A developer came to see me the other day about it. He's tearing it down and building a block of luxury flats. I bought one for Mama, but in the meantime she'll have to live with us.'

'For how long?'

'The developer says construction should be completed by September seventy-three.'

'*Two* years of your mother here? You must be joking!'

Elías bridled angrily. 'I don't see why you're so rude. Mother's always very kind and considerate to you. Besides she adores the children.'

'The only one of our children Fortunata cares about is Laura because she looks like you,' snapped Isabel. 'She couldn't give a damn for the other three.'

He muttered something unintelligible and retired behind the morning newspaper. Isabel crumbled a piece of toast and stared bleakly through the dining-room window. A broad, tree-lined avenue flowed north through the green spread of Palermo towards more buildings on the horizon. To the east the river shimmered copper under a clear winter sky; from where she sat she could just see the beginning of the port. A distorted view that had nothing to do with the one from Stefan's window.

If only I had the courage to leave Elías, she mused unhappily. If only we didn't have the children . . . No, that's not true. I love my children. I can't hurt them – oh, God! How difficult it all is. I don't even know if I'm using the children as an excuse. Why can't Stefan be wealthy? I couldn't live like he does, struggling for every peso, never knowing when the next one's coming in. He slaves away year after year, fighting for every contract – what kind of life is that? Stefan swears he'll get to the top, but when? When he's eighty? I want him at the top now, while we're both young and able to enjoy life. If he were at the top . . . I don't know! I just don't know what to do.

Elías folded the newspaper and reached for the toast. 'Mama will be moving in on Friday. Please see that the maids air the guest-room properly. And you'd better order some flowers. White camelias. Mama likes camelias.' He buttered his toast with neat, precise little movements – just enough and no more. 'We must be very kind to her. She's had a terrible shock . . . Why are you laughing?'

'Just think of the shock if your father had been found with a man,' chuckled Isabel and left the dining-room.

It was an unsatisfactory day. Ana Inés rang after lunch with a dreary list of complaints about Miguel, who had moved his family into Barranco Rosales because it made sponging off his father look more respectable. Mercedes was delighted to have them, but Gladys embarked on her own particular brand of warfare.

'She objects to having a few pieces of our furniture,' said Ana Inés. 'I want to do Catalina's room with the curtains and things from our flat, but Gladys won't hear of it. Or having my secretaire in the drawing-room. Not even our dinner service or our glasses at meals! All very nicely said, of course. She told your father last night it was such a shame for our things to get ruined.'

'What did Papa say?'

The telephone echoed a gusty sigh. 'You know how he is, Bela! He never pays any attention to what she says. The point is I don't want all our things in storage. I want to use them! I don't want to live at Barranco Rosales.'

'I don't see why the hell you moved there in the first place,' said Isabel.

'Miguel insisted our flat was too small,' replied her sister-in-law wearily. 'I'm pregnant again.'

No Stefan today.

He was working on the design for a new block of offices to be built in the port area – the most important contract he had ever been after. With the deadline for submitting projects only three weeks off everything else must be set aside. Even Isabel. She sighed and wandered into her daughters' bedroom.

Symmetry in keeping with Elías Castro's home.

Pale pink wallpaper, flowered curtains and matching bed spreads, thick pale pink carpeting. Twin beds. Twin desks side by side in front of the window. Even the plants on the balcony grew in neat, symmetrical tubs.

Isabel watched her daughters as they struggled with their homework. Ten-year-old Laura's wavy dark hair framed an uninteresting face; the hazel eyes and thin, fastidious features could only belong to Elías. Seven-year-old Elena's hair was light brown, her features strongly marked: a straight nose, generous mouth, high cheekbones. She looked up from her copybook and smiled at her mother out of very pale eyes.

'What's two times eight, Mama?'

Holy Virgin! thought Isabel, suddenly turning cold. He's there in every line of her. Elías must be blind!

Her only consolation was that Elías had never heard of Stefan Stervic.

V

The following weekend Marcos and Isabel took the girls to a Saturday afternoon performance of *Swan Lake* at the Colón.

It was one of the most enjoyable occasions either of them had spent for a long time. Laura and Elena chattered merrily all the way into town about Elena's ambitions to be a ballet dancer; by the time they arrived at the theatre both girls were so keyed up they could hardly wait for Marcos to lock the car.

'Hurry up, Grandfather!' squealed Elena, hopping up and down. 'We'll never get there!'

'It doesn't take us three quarters of an hour to walk three blocks,' he grinned, but let her pull him along just the same.

Elena perched spellbound on the edge of her seat through all four acts; when they left the theatre she pirouetted all the way back to the car. Marcos grinned.

'So we have a mini-Pavlova in the family, eh?' he remarked, winking at Isabel.

'Her ballet mistress says Elena has tremendous talent. Heaven only knows where she got it from.' Isabel linked her arm through Marcos's. 'Are you happy, Papa?'

'Very,' he replied. 'It was a nice afternoon.'

They walked a bit further in silence.

'Papa . . .'

'What is it, *ñatita*?'

Isabel laughed. 'You haven't called me that for a long time.' She squeezed his arm, her eyes suddenly bright with emotion. 'I didn't mean to be such a fool – all those years ago. I didn't understand. I do now. I just want to say I'm sorry for having said things that hurt you.'

She felt his eyes on her, very dark and questioning. After a moment he bent his head and kissed her cheek. 'Thank you, *ñatita*.' If Marcos had understood more than was intended, he did not show it.

Two minutes later they bumped into Stefan.

He was on his way back home from a business meeting. Marcos invited him to join them for tea with the girls. Isabel tried to behave normally, but her heart was pounding and the inside of her mouth felt like sandpaper.

'I want chocolate ice cream, Grandfather,' chirped Elena, tugging at Marcos's hand. 'Lots of it, with whipped cream and a cherry.'

Stefan stared at her for a very long time. He raised his eyes and looked at Isabel. His face was a mask, but she knew him well enough to sense astonishment and anger behind the pale, hard eyes. Her heart sank.

'I'd be delighted to join you,' said Stefan, still looking at Isabel. 'Are these your daughters?'

'I'm Elena and this is Laura,' said Elena boldly. 'I'm going to be a ballet dancer. Who are you?'

He smiled at her. 'My name's Stefan.'

'Come on, Grandfather!' insisted Laura. 'I'm hungry.'

Somehow Isabel made it through tea. The girls consumed tremendous quantities of ice cream and thoroughly enjoyed themselves. Stefan told Marcos about the new project he was designing. He never once looked at Isabel, but his eyes continually strayed to Elena. When tea was over he shook hands and hurried off. Isabel's knees trembled.

'Stervic's an intelligent man,' remarked Marcos. 'He'll get to the top. I like him.'

'Why don't you have dinner with us tonight, Papa?' asked Isabel as though Stefan Stervic were unimportant.

It was all she could trust herself to say.

They were sitting down at the dinner table when Stefan rang.

'For God's sake!' Isabel hissed into the telephone. 'Why are you ringing me at home?'

His voice crackled across the wires. 'I want to talk to you. Now.'

'I can't now! My father's having dinner with us.'

'If you don't come now, I'm coming over there,' he replied angrily. 'You can choose: tell me about my daughter here, or tell me in front of Castro and your father.'

'Stefan!' She had to sit down on the chair next to the telephone stand; her voice jerked out in frantic whispers. 'You're crazy! I don't know what you're talking about! *I can't come now*! I'll – I'll be there tomorrow morning. Ten o'clock! Stefan, please!'

There was a moment's silence. 'All right. If you're not here by ten o'clock I'm going over to your place!' he snapped and slammed down the receiver.

The next eleven hours were the worst Isabel had ever been through in all her life.

She drove to Stefan's flat the next morning in a panic; her careful make-up, expensive scent and new sealskin coat did little to hide the traces. Stefan stood by the window. He was haggard and unshaven; cigarette stubs littered the floor. His voice barely rose above a whisper. Perhaps that was what frightened Isabel the most.

'Why didn't you tell me about my daughter?' he demanded.

Isabel swallowed. 'I don't know what you're talking about!'

'Elena. She's my daughter, isn't she?'

'You're crazy!'

'Goddamn it, do you think I'm as stupid as that cuckold you married?' he cried savagely. 'I'm not blind! That girl is my daughter!'

'Stefan, for heaven's sake! You're imagining things! Just because Elena has light eyes . . . My-my grandmother had light eyes. Mama's mother. Elena l-looks like her!'

He picked up a photograph lying amongst the papers that littered the table and thrust it at her without saying a word. The photograph showed a young girl of about eleven dressed in a fluffy pink tutu with roses in her hair. The picture was slightly faded, but apart from the difference in ages the girl's resemblance to Elena was startling. Isabel's hand trembled.

'That's my youngest sister,' said Stefan tonelessly. 'She was two years younger than I am. She died of pneumonia when she was thirteen. Do you recognize the face?'

'It's a coincidence!'

He uttered a dry, bitter laugh. 'By God, you'd even lie in death's teeth, wouldn't you?' His hand closed roughly around her arm. 'I want to see Elena again.'

'No!'

He shook her. 'She is my daughter, isn't she?'

'No!'

'What if I show this photograph to Castro – what do you think he'd say?'

'Are you out of your mind?' shrilled Isabel, pulling away from him. 'Do you want to hurt Elena? She doesn't have anything to do with this . . . it's not her fault . . . good God, Stefan! Don't you understand what that kind of a scandal would do to the child? I won't allow it! I will not allow you to ruin my daughter's life!'

Stefan tossed the photograph on to the table. She was right. He didn't have a leg to stand on, except Elena's startling resemblance to someone who had died more than twenty years ago. Isabel would never admit he was the father. The rest of the family would close ranks as well – even Elías Castro. Far better to swallow a lie than publicly acknowledge being a cuckold. Nikos Kestri had been right. The mini-gods defended themselves tooth and nail. Damn their rich, stinking hides. He was going to break through that defence if it took him a lifetime. One day he was going to give Isabel a taste of her own medicine. Right now he was so angry he never wanted to see her again. Her expensive fragrance choked him.

'Get out of here,' said Stefan.

Isabel licked her lips. 'Please try and understand,' she pleaded. 'Don't you see it's the only way . . .'

'You've been tricking Castro for the past seven years and you've been tricking me – that's what I understand! You've got me by the balls because you know I can't give my daughter the kind of life she's used to! You know I won't hurt her, but you still want me to like the thought of Elena calling that goddamned whey-face "Daddy"!'

She struck back viciously, goaded by frustration and guilt. 'You've enjoyed screwing that whey-face's wife these past seven years, haven't you?'

407

'You bitch!' shouted Stefan and slapped her.

She screamed an incoherent insult and rushed from the flat. The clock of her car's dashboard read twenty-five past ten. Isabel stepped furiously on the accelerator, her eyes blinded by tears. The car shot away from the kerb, swerved to miss a bus and sped along the riverfront. The tears streamed down her face, her cheeks burned like fire. An eternity had passed since ten o'clock, but it had taken only twenty-five minutes for love to end.

VI

In the twelve years since her daughter's marriage Gladys had only set foot twice inside the aunts' house. Once at the wedding reception, the second time after her third grandson César was born. The birth had been a difficult one and Claudia was under the doctor's orders to rest. Gladys, struck by belated pangs of motherly duty, swooped down to take her other two grandchildren to Barranco Rosales for a fortnight; her son-in-law checked the swoop in mid-flight.

'My aunts are quite capable of looking after Albertito and Gloria,' said Luis, interrupting Gladys's indignant announcement of her intentions. 'So am I, for that matter. There's no reason for the children to leave home.'

Gladys glanced around the shabby living-room. 'I never see them.'

'You never bother to come.'

A tap gurgled and wheezed in the kitchen, reminding her of Quilmes. Cabales's flannel trousers and brown jersey were rumpled, his face pale and unshaven. He had spent the past two days and nights at Claudia's beside, sick with worry and fear. He was exhausted, but Gladys saw only what she wanted to see and no further.

'I think two weeks at Barranco Rosales would be very good for Albertito and Gloria,' she insisted.

'I don't. My children stay here.'

That exchange had taken place nearly eight years ago. There was another grandson now, but this time Gladys

408

limited herself to sending a pair of knitted booties from Harrods.

Every now and then she showed her motherly concern by sending a gift – mainly cast-offs from Clara, who at age twelve was growing like a weed. Clara was thin and leggy, her cousin Gloria decidedly chubby. Few of the clothes dutifully delivered by the Luciani chauffeur ever fitted. Claudia cut and added and stitched as best she could; when Luis protested angrily she laughed.

'Don't look a gift horse in the mouth. Mama thinks she's doing her duty and that makes her happy. I don't imagine much else does.'

VII

Miguel had no interest in Gladys's sense of duty or Claudia's growing family. He remembered his stepsister as the chubby, humourless Porky of their childhood – a brief, unimportant memory. Like Gladys, he rarely saw beyond the end of his nose; not having seen or spoken to Claudia for many years it never occurred to him that she might be anything more than what he remembered.

Their paths crossed again one rainy July evening in 1972.

Everything had gone wrong at the office that day. Marcos rang up from La Catalina and demanded to know why Miguel had not yet contacted their buyer in Uruguay; in the next breathe he began to lecture about family responsibilities. According to Mercedes, Ana Inés was very unhappy. Miguel's behaviour left a lot to be desired.

'Just because I came home late the other night!'

'Drunk,' crackled Marcos's voice at the other end of the line. 'Ana Inés is your wife and you are living in my house. I expect you to use discretion.'

Miguel had nearly hurled the telephone across the office. He was fed up with his father's expectations; on the other hand he didn't dare tell him he had neglected work because of a few drinks with Lucas. The drinks were Lucas's idea. He wanted money.

'Lend me a couple of thousand, old boy. I'm in a spot of need these days. Grandi went to Europe, damn him! I have to rent a place now and nothing's cheap.' Lucas rubbed a thin thumb and forefinger together. 'Just a couple of thousand. Five, maybe. Ten, if you've got it.'

It never occurred to Miguel to see beyond his uncle's shaking hands and gaunt, yellowish face.

At fifty-one Lucas was nearly penniless and struggling wearily to keep up with a world which no longer had any use for him. His dreams of fame and fortune had never materialized. Fabio Grandi had returned to Italy, Iván Torres ran a flourishing racket in Colombia. Neither one wanted Lucas Luciani hanging around their necks. In his heart of hearts he longed for Barranco Rosales and the old, familiar memories; he even dared dream that his nephew would take the hint and help pave the way for a reconciliation with Marcos. Miguel, with characteristic lack of imagination, gave Lucas a five-thousand peso note and began to complain about his own lot in life.

Home was just as bad as the office.

Mercedes lectured Miguel over tea. Ana Inés, still smouldering after the previous night's quarrel, refused to speak to him. His daughter Catalina, handed over by the ageless Miss Nelly, gave him a prim and very English kiss; the baby screamed the minute he touched her. Miguel stormed out of the nursery and went downstairs to the family living-room; half an hour later Gladys appeared with a brown paper parcel.

'I must get this to Claudia's,' she said irritably. 'I was going to send the chauffeur around, but he's driven Mercedes to a concert and they won't be back until late. Very thoughtless of her. She should have consulted me first.'

Miguel continued to leaf through his magazine.

'You wouldn't mind driving over to Claudia's with this, would you?' asked Gladys, shaking the parcel in front of him. 'It's Gloria's birthday next week. There's a nice little dress of Clara's she can wear.'

Anything to get out of the house, decided Miguel sourly. He took the parcel and wondered, not for the first time, why the hell he had let Ana Inés's parents pressurize him into marrying her.

VIII

The street lamp outside the aunts' house was dark. Miguel stumbled over several broken pieces of pavement, pushed open an iron gate and made his way gingerly through a mini-jungle. A cat slinked out from among the weeds and wound itself around his legs. He kicked the cat aside and pressed the doorbell; after what seemed like forever someone fumbled with the bolts and the door opened with a weary, reluctant groan.

'Luis, the door needs oiling again,' called the woman who held it open. She peered at Miguel, her face hidden by shadow. 'What can I do for you?'

'I'm looking for Claudia Cabales.'

'That's me.' She threw open the door so that the light from the passage shone down on her. A plump, smiling woman dressed in a faded blue skirt and voluminous purple sweater; her hair was cut very short, brushed back from a good-natured face. Miguel stared.

'You're Claudia? I'm Miguel Luciani. Your – well, you know.'

'Miguel?' Claudia pulled him across the threshold and slammed the door quickly as a little boy darted for the opening. 'Get away from here, Luisito! Come in, come in. Isn't this a nice surprise? Luis,' dragging Miguel into the living-room, 'look who's here. My stepbrother.'

There were half a dozen people in the room. A slight, spectacled man sitting on the floor got up and came over. He stared curiously and, Miguel thought, with a certain amount of hostility.

'Hello.' There was no offer of a handshake.

'I've brought a package from your mother,' said Miguel, handing the parcel to Claudia. 'Clothes or something like that.'

'The horse's mouth,' sneered a woman seated on a sofa at the far end of the room. 'Lace knickers and velvet vests.'

She was a thin, dark-haired young woman – attractive in a hungry, restless way. The jeans and black shirt she wore made her lean and angular; her leaness emphasized a pair of long, intensely black eyes. Miguel frowned, trying to recall why she looked familiar.

'Have some coffee,' said Claudia, thrusting him firmly towards the sofa. 'Sit over there beside Olga. Push the cats out of the way. Do you like milk and sugar? I've forgotten.'

'Black, thank you,' said Miguel and sat down.

A discussion had obviously been underway before he came in; it was just as obvious it would not continue until he left. Miguel sipped his coffee slowly. The room was warm and comfortable in spite of its shabbiness. Like Claudia. The thought surprised him. Porky had not done too badly for herself after all.

A ginger-haired man who shared an armchair with three cats cleared his throat. 'Mild weather we're having. Hope it holds.'

'Lousy weather,' snapped Olga and got to her feet. 'I'm off, *compañeros*. Too bad you don't agree with me, Luis. Any means justifies the end.'

'Not in this case,' replied Cabales unhappily. 'The dancers had nothing to do with the rest of it.'

'They let the wrong people back them.'

'But they were wonderful!' cried Claudia. 'We took the children to every single performance. The theatre was always packed, people even sat on the stage. Free entry so that anyone could go – that's the way it should be, don't you agree? Music and dancing and singing and plays – all those cultural things should be free for people to enjoy.'

'What do you think?' demanded Olga, turning suddenly on Miguel. 'Do you think the people should have free access to culture? Or is culture merely for the élite?'

'Don't embarrass him,' laughed the ginger-haired man.

'Shut up, Rulo! I want to know what he thinks.'

Miguel shrugged. 'There's nothing to keep people from enjoying culture in this country. Look at the queues for performances at the Colón . . .'

'But the people can't afford the stalls or the boxes. They have to crowd upstairs!'

'Upstairs,' drawled Miguel, momentarily irritated by her anger, 'is where the true music-lovers go. I've never been up there, but I'm told it's the only place where one can appreciate music – if you know anything about it, that is.'

Rulo Boyle grinned. 'We're having a theoretical discussion about the ballet dancers who died last October. Do you remember the case?'

412

'Their plane crashed into the river a few minutes after take-off and all ten were killed, including two of the Colón's leading dancers. They were sponsored by an American firm or something like that.'

'That's right,' nodded Boyle. 'The firm sponsored a series of free Sunday morning performances all during last winter. For argument's sake – suppose a bomb had been put on board that plane by people who believe the dancers were agents of what some call Yankee imperialism. Do you think it was justified?'

'Good God, no!'

Olga laughed angrily and put on a shabby sheepskin coat. 'The weather gets worse by the minute. I'm going home.'

'I'll give you a lift,' offered Miguel. 'It's raining outside.'

She stared at him for a moment and then drew back her lips in a thin, mocking grin. 'Why the hell not? Ring me tomorrow, Rulo. Same place.'

'You're wrong, you know,' murmured Luis as he accompanied Olga to the door. 'Their deaths can't be justified that easily.' He put his hand on her arm. 'Be careful, it's a dangerous game. Don't be so blinded you lose all sense of perspective.'

She shook him off impatiently and stepped into the shadowy garden; after a moment's hesitation Miguel followed.

IX

They said very little to each other as the Mercedes threaded its way through the evening traffic. Olga gave a downtown address; when the car drew up in front of it Miguel saw a café. The place was full of people, most of whom looked like university students.

'You're a student?'

'Sociology.'

Miguel grinned. 'My old man calls sociology the useless science.'

'What the hell does he know about it?'

'Not much, I guess. He's a cattleman.'

Olga studied him speculatively. 'And what are you?'

There was more than a hint of bitterness in Miguel's reply which he did not bother to disguise. 'I'm the cattleman's son.

413

Wait,' as she started to get out of the car. 'I don't know your last name.'

'Raskowitz. Olga Raskowitz.'

'Will you have a drink with me, Olga?'

'No.'

'Some other time?'

She gave him another hard, speculative look and got out of the car before Miguel could stop her.

He drove home in the same disgruntled mood, compounded by a nagging restlessness which seemed to have no definite origin. Ana Inés was watching television; she paid no attention when he came into the living-room. Miguel sighed. Some sort of reconciliation was clearly called for, if only to keep her from complaining again about his behaviour. He wandered around for a few minutes and finally produced an uninspired apology.

'Look, Ana – I'm sorry about our quarrel last night.'

On the television Othello ranted over Desdemona. Miguel switched off the Moor and sat down on the sofa. Ana Inés stared straight ahead, but her eyes were moist and her mouth trembled. He kissed it tentatively.

'Come on, Ana. Don't be so mean to me.' His voice coaxed, his kiss grew more insistent. 'I'm sorry. It won't happen again. Come on, give me a smile.'

She gave him a woeful, watery smile and put her arms around his neck. Mercedes, coming into the living-room ten minutes later, beat a hasty retreat and offered up a prayerful thanks for God's help in the reconciliation.

Much later Miguel lay awake in bed, listening to Ana Inés's gentle breathing and trying to remember where he had seen Olga Raskowitz before. There was something mysterious about her – an air of adventure, even danger. He liked that. She was an exciting woman. His last thought before dropping off to sleep was that he must see Olga Raskowitz again.

X

An American named George Blakely was kidnapped for a twenty million dollar ranson. His firm dug in its heels and refused to give into terrorists. The Front held a brief

council of war; the next day Olga received her instructions.

'The council wants to prod the *gringos* a bit,' she told her
group. 'A taste of what Blakely can expect if they don't pay up.'
Her long black eyes studied the faces around the table. 'We're to
do the prodding.'

'When?' asked a thin, nondescript man known as Zorro.

'Forty-eight hours before Blakely's deadline.'

'Where?'

Olga returned Zorro's glance evenly. 'You'll find out when
we get there.'

The less details were known the better. Zorro was a newcomer
to the group and still on probation; Olga thought he could be
trusted, but she was not sure about López. An unstable tough
who easily lost his head. Ever since Cardales she had mistrusted
him. Men like López must be kept on a short rein and not allowed
to think for themselves.

The other two were no problem. Olga filled in the details
after López and Zorro had left; when she finished Rulo Boyle
shook his head.

'Risky,' he remarked, filling his *maté* gourd and taking an
experimental suck on the metal straw. 'Do you know the area?'

'I've been finding out about it.'

Oscar Raskowitz scowled at his sister. 'From that rich bastard
who keeps bothering you — what's his name?'

She lit a cigarette and blew the smoke in his face. 'That's right.
From Miguel.'

He had haunted the café for days on end before she finally
agreed to a cup of coffee. They sat at a corner table tucked
between the toilets and the espresso machine. Miguel was
fascinated by the atmosphere. The cheap formica tables, the
grafitti on the walls, the bearded young men and intense-looking
girls heatedly discussing political philosophy — all formed part of
an exotic sub-culture that both intrigued and disconcerted him.
He felt out of place in his grey flannels and tailored blazer, as
though he were a ridiculously polished specimen on display. Olga
answered his questions with monosyllables and that was part of
the fascination as well. Her rudeness excited him because it was
a challenge. He came back the next day. And the day after that.

'Don't you have anything better to do with your time?'
mocked Olga.

415

'If I did I wouldn't be here.'

'I suppose you're so rich you can afford to be idle.'

Miguel shrugged. 'Will you have dinner with me tonight?'

'Why the hell should I?'

'Why not? I'd like to get to know you better.' He removed the cigarette from her mouth, took a puff, and stuck it between her lips again, all the while keeping his eyes fixed on hers.

She leaned back in her chair and studied him for a long time without replying. He couldn't read the expression in her eyes — speculation, maybe. Possibly more interest than she cared to let on. Miguel leaned across the table.

'How about it?' he murmured.

Olga Raskowitz was thinking of her instructions to prod the *gringos*. 'Operation Roast Pig' would take place in the Laguna Grande area. Miguel Luciani had done quite a bit of talking about himself during the past couple of days; among other things she had learned that he knew the Laguna Grande area very well. If handled properly he could give them some very useful information . . . She felt his knee pressing hers and gave him a faint, mocking smile.

'All right. I'll tell you the story of my life over a pizza.'

That night in a small, airless room above a laundry Miguel became Olga's infatuated lover.

XI

The road that led northeast out of Laguna Grande ran straight as an arrow for ten miles before curving sharply as it reached the entrance to El Ombú. There was a large eucalyptus grove just before the curve. A car concealed among the trees could not be easily spotted by anyone coming from the ranch; the dull green Ford blended into sunlight and shadow as though it were part of the grove itself.

The Ford had been waiting since before dawn.

'How do we know he'll come today?' López asked nervously gnawing on his thumb.

Olga ignored him, but Boyle thought it best to give some information. López jibbering questions was enough to try the patience of ten thousand saints.

416

'Monthly meeting of the local cattlemen's association,' he explained briefly. 'Our contact at the ranch says the *gringo*'s supposed to give a talk.'

'What if he's not alone?'

'That's just too bad, isn't it?' snapped Oscar. 'Shut up, López!'

'How can we trust the contact?' grumbled López, glaring at the back of Oscar's head. 'She may sell out to easy money, you know.'

Boyle shook his head. 'Not the Dove. She's been Sussler's secretary for the past three years and hates his guts.'

'Someone's coming,' warned Zorro. 'White estate wagon. That's him, isn't it?'

The white estate wagon sped down the road from El Ombú, jolted over the cattle-guard and headed towards Laguna Grande. Two minutes later the summer morning exploded in a shower of bullets and shattered glass.

CHAPTER THIRTY

I

The shooting of Len Sussler was in itself an isolated case. The Front needed money to finance its operations and US firms were a prime source of income. Their executives were targets for kidnapping, not murder. Sussler, who had the misfortune of being important, but not important enough, merely served as a grim reminder.

When US firms removed their executives to safer shores the burden of violence fell on the local men who took their place. Armed guards became as essential as daily bread, but even they were no guarantee against sudden death. More than one man was gunned down on his doorstep as he left for work, more than one car intercepted along the way. Wives were sent miniature coffins inscribed with their husband's name, bombs and bodies were routine news. As the seventies dragged on a bloody war between extremes claimed scores of lives every day, with the people of Argentina caught in its deadly crossfire.

II

The 1973 general elections placed yet another puppet in the Casa Rosada – this time a dentist devoted to Perón. One of the dentist's first acts was to declare a general amnesty for political prisoners. His intentions may have been honest, but the flood of men and women pouring through prison gates with roars of revenge brought little comfort to those who heard them.

In the winter of 1973 Juan Domingo Perón returned from exile.

His arrival, heralded as a day of national rejoicing, sparked off a raging gun battle between rival bands of supporters. The enthusiastic crowds that went to the airport to cheer their general's return were trapped in a storm of bullets. Juan Gaspari, a member of the official welcoming party, later told Marcos how he ran for his life when a frenzied mob clashed with soldiers and police on the runway.

'The general can handle it,' added Gaspari, mopping his brow. 'He's ordered an end to all violence, no matter where it comes from. His first priority, he claims, is to rebuild this country. What a man! Seventy-odd years and you wouldn't give him a day over sixty!'

Marcos shook his head. 'Perón's a has-been, Gaspari. He wooed the militant Left because it suited his purpose, but he won't be able to control them. They aren't scatterbrained idealists.' He stared uneasily at the picture of La Catalina on his desk. 'Sharp brains direct movements like the Front these days. A new mentality. Your general's too old for it.'

Juan Gaspari toyed with an ashtray; in the warm, golden lamplight his face looked older and surprisingly sad. 'I agree with you,' he said after a moment. 'There's a new mentality in this country and I don't think I like it very much. Perón will continue, yes, but things aren't the same.' His faint smile grew wistful. 'One almost wishes for the days of Artemio Mendes again, eh?'

By a cunning political sleight-of-hand Argentines suddenly found themselves faced with another general election within the space of a few months. The devoted dentist resigned and Perón was re-elected by the ever-hopeful majority. His third wife, saddled with the thankless task of living up to Evita's image, became vice-president.

Times had changed indeed.

III

The political storms barely touched Angela at Los Alamos; for the past twenty-two years there had always been some political upheaval or other going on in Argentina. Bombs and bodies and kidnappings were far removed from the problems of cattle and crops. She took note of them and turned her attention to matters more vital to her own existence.

The ranch was holding its own — some years better than others, but on the whole she felt satisfied. Raúl Jones, the manager, had turned out to be more than a godsend. He was intelligent, hard-working and honest; he raised no objections to receiving orders from a *patrona*. If he disagreed, he made his point tactfully and with a dry sense of humour which Angela found very refreshing. She often wished Jimmy could have had a Raúl Jones as his right hand; things would undoubtedly have gone better for him.

She found herself thinking frequently about Jimmy these days. It was almost as though his ghost had crept back to sit in his chair by the fire – a bit shamefacedly, perhaps, with the wry, boyish expression of guilt that used to settle on his ruddy features just before he admitted to mischief.

'I've made a hell-smashing balls-up of things again, angel, haven't I?'

That was the Jimmy Angela wanted to remember. One of her greatest sorrows would always be that they had not had a chance to forgive each other before he was gone forever.

At times it was difficult to believe that twenty-two years ago she had come out from England as Jimmy Morgan's bride; bright-eyed and eager for a new life in a new land, yet so damnably uncertain about so many important things. She was fifty-four now, physically fit and reasonably content with the life she had reconstructed for herself. She had many good friends and Los Alamos provided a different challenge almost every day. There were the children in Laguna Grande who needed her care and affection, and for the past three years she had been giving English lessons at the convent school. Small mercies, perhaps, but they were vitally necessary to counter the weeping wound that continued to tear her heart.

Her affair with Marcos had been dead for twelve years now, but the hungry memory of their love still haunted her dreams.

IV

Olga and her friends saw Perón's return to power as a sign of the Front's indisputable strength. It had added valuable votes to victory and the old man would be thankful. He was a useful figurehead who could be manoeuvred into putting the official seal on the Front's own plans.

Luis Cabales, however, was openly sceptical.

'Violence only breeds violence,' he broke in over Oscar's rousing defence of blood and fire. 'What this country needs is true social reform and a stable economy. We won't get them by killings and kidnappings.'

'Why the hell should the *gringos* and their lackeys suck this country dry!' exploded Oscar.

'I agree – but change the laws, don't kill people.' Luis whittled at his pencil with nervous, energetic strokes. 'The Front isn't a coherent political force. It never can be as long as its image is a bomb or a gun. People don't like bombs and guns. They don't trust them.'

'The Front fights for the people,' said Rulo Boyle.

Luis stared at the priest over his glasses. 'Does it?' he murmured after a moment. 'I wonder.'

'What does your fancy boyfriend think about all this, Olga?' sneered Oscar. 'Does he have any brains in that handsome head of his?'

She flicked the ash off her cigarette. 'He's got brains all right, but he hasn't learned to use them. He's been conditioned from birth not to think.' Her dark eyes followed a smoke-ring towards the ceiling; after a moment she laughed. 'He got drunk the other night. Poured out his heart as though I were his mother confessor. He told me he hates being "the cattleman's son". Said he's always wanted to break away, but never had the guts. Went on and on about his wife, about his old man; about how he wants to be free. I'm his freedom, he said. "When I'm with you I feel like another man. Alive . . ." He blubbered for hours.' Olga took a long, deliberate sip of coffee. 'The cattleman is worth a lot of money, *compañeros*.'

The three men stared at her. 'What do you mean?' demanded Oscar.

'I mean that this is our chance to make a big coup for the Front. Miguel's old man doesn't have guards or anything like that on the ranch; it should be easy to pick him up for a tidy little ransom.'

'Not easy if the man lives on his ranch all the time,' commented Boyle. 'Strangers stick out like sore thumbs in those places.'

Olga smiled unpleasantly. 'The cattleman has a son, *padre*. The son has a grudge. The son is, if you will forgive the expression, hornier than the devil for his little Olga. Put two and two together.'

Luis frowned uneasily. 'I'd be careful if I were you.'

'Stay out of this, Cabales,' interrupted Oscar. 'You're too soft. Just stick to your theories and leave us to the action. What are you suggesting, Olga? That we rope your boyfriend into the movement?'

'As a fall guy,' she said. 'He's too immature to be used politically – but he's the perfect patsy.'

Rulo Boyle looked sceptical. 'I don't know. How would we use him?'

Olga laughed again. 'Leave it to me, *padre*. Just leave the boyfriend to me.'

V

National culture flourished.

The intellectual movement surfaced from underground with a sigh of relief. A wealth of long-neglected folklore was thrust into the limelight and became fashionable. Argentina discovered her native talents; culture no longer had to be European to be acceptable.

For a brief, exhilarating period the country's natural heritage was stimulated to the full.

Gladys could not be expected to share in the new trends. She did not understand the new Peronism and thought folklore vulgar. She deplored Lalo's liking for it, especially after discovering him listening to records in Yvonne's bedroom. He might have been listening to Beethoven or Bach – the effect on his mother was just the same.

'Lalo darling! I must see you at once. It's important.'

Lalo darling scowled. 'Not now, Mama. Later.'

Gladys eyed Yvonne in alarm. Henna-red hair and frosted gold fingernails. Gold lamé pyjamas and glittering bangles practically up to her elbow. At thirty the woman was far too old to be making such an exhibition of herself. The shrill voice tightened.

'*Lalo!*'

He waved impatiently for her to be quiet and turned up the record player. Yvonne laughed. Clearly there was much more to Cousin Lalo than met the eye.

Dismayed by her son's unexpected defiance Gladys left the room in a cloud of injured motherhood. The door to Marcos's study was open: peering in she saw several unopened letters on his desk. She glanced through them suspiciously, remembering that other crumpled note written so many years ago. Even now she could not be certain the affair was over. Marcos was a difficult man to keep tabs on and she was beginning to grow weary of the game. It had not made much difference in their relationship. She stared at the letters, her face shadowed with sudden bitterness.

Gladys Gómez had everything she wanted, but Gladys Luciani was unbearably lonely.

The letter from Milan lay at the bottom of the pile. Gladys turned it over several times and then thrust it quickly into her pocket. The thin, reedy complaint of a *quena* drifted from Yvonne's room, punctuated by sounds of laughter. Gladys sped down the corridor and into the bathroom, locking the door behind her. She tore open the envelope with nervous fingers; inside there were two sheets of paper.

Her eyes fled angrily over the written lines.

Dear Papa,

One of us has to take the first step and I've finally found the courage to do so. Fourteen years is a long time. I want us to make up before more time goes by. Isabel tells me you are well, but working too hard as usual. Do you know you have a very beautiful granddaughter named Magdalena? She'll be twelve next month. She looks so much like Mama. I brought a picture of you and Mama with me – the one under the grape arbour at La Catalina. I often tell Magdalena about La Catalina and you and the years when we were all happy together.

No one knows I've written this letter – not even Isabel. I hope you answer it. We've said such terrible things to hurt each other in the past – hasn't the time come to forgive and forget? I know I want to more than anything in the world.

Love,
Cristina

The sheets of paper trembled. If Marcos read Cristina's letter he would relent. Gladys was as sure of that as she was of her own reflection in the mirror. He was growing old. A granddaughter named Magdalena would easily worm her way into his heart and replace Clara, who was his own child. *The years when we were all happy together*. Clever. A clever letter, written by a clever, calculating woman. Cristina knew what she was after.

Gladys tore the letter into tiny pieces, dropped them into an ashtray and struck a match. She watched the pieces curl around the edges and catch fire; when they were ashes she emptied everything into the toilet and flushed it. Then she washed her hands. Her reflection smiled back triumphantly from the mirror. Clever, clever Gladys to have nipped that danger in the bud.

Perhaps it was just as well she could not foresee the consequences of her cleverness.

VI

Miguel soon discovered that he did not have the upper hand with Olga. She moved in and out of his life as she pleased, and gave no explanations; when he angrily demanded one she mocked his infatuation. He slammed out of her place, vowing not to return. Two days later he was back again, banging on the door of the flat above the laundry.

'I can't live without you!'

She leered. 'Not even in your old man's golden cage? What's the matter – did the butler pour too much cream into your coffee or was the toast cold?'

'I don't give a fucking damn about all that! Olga . . .' He tried to pull her towards him. 'Olga, for Christ's sake – can't you understand I'm crazy about you? These past two days've been hell!'

She shoved him away and walked over to a table on the other side of the room. Two of its legs were uneven; the balance had been compensated by stacks of books. A small gas burner stood next to a coffee tin. Olga lit the burner, filled a battered saucepan from a tap in the basin by the window, and slammed it on to the flickering flame.

'You'll have to get used to life without me,' she said.

'What?'

'I'm leaving.'

'*Leaving*? Why? Where are you going?'

She dumped a few spoonfuls of coffee into two cracked mugs. 'None of your business.'

'You can't leave!' he exclaimed. 'I don't want you to go!'

Her long, dark eyes challenged him from across the room. 'What are you going to do about it? Not a damn thing. I could move across the street, but you wouldn't follow me.' She snatched the saucepan off the burner and filled the mugs. Her mouth twisted in a thin, mocking smile. 'You don't have the guts.'

'Olga!'

'You come here because it's different,' she continued bitterly, ignoring him. 'It's a novelty for you – like the café and my friends. We're strange creatures. You think we're exotic. Something you want to see from close-up and sniff at. We smell differently, don't we? Even the words we use are different. You don't understand half of them, but you like to think you do. You like to look and smell, but you're afraid to touch us. You might get your hands dirty.'

He stared at her. She was leaving and he didn't have the guts to follow. Olga pushed his mug over to the edge of the table.

'You don't give a peso's worth of shit for me,' she sneered. 'You're just like the rest of your class. Blood-sucking cowards.'

'If I weren't so crazy about you,' he rasped, 'I wouldn't have come back!'

'Prove it!'

Miguel took the mug of coffee. A neon sign across the street flashed into the room; in its intermittent red glow Olga's eyes gleamed like coals. He drank a few sips to moisten his throat; his heart was beating very fast.

'What do you want me to do?' he asked.

Olga shrugged. 'You'd be afraid.'

'I've got as much balls as the rest of your friends!' he countered angrily. 'You think I don't have any because I'm rich. You think I'm a fool because I don't stand up to my old man . . .' His voice rose sharply. 'Goddamit – I'm fed up with being taken for a fool by you or anyone else!'

She watched him from underneath the lashes of her dark eyes for a moment and then shrugged. 'Maybe you're not such a fool after all. Your old man really rubs you up the wrong way, doesn't he?'

'Yes!'

Olga reached for a cigarette. 'Rich, domineering bastard – I'd like to really make him sweat.' She smiled at Miguel for the first time. 'Be a good idea, wouldn't it? Make your old man sweat for a while. Give him a taste of his own medicine.'

He laughed shortly. 'Not a chance in hell.'

'Miguel . . .' It was one of the few times she called him by name. Her voice had a compelling urgency now he could not quite define. 'Men like your father only breed misery. Look at you – he's ruined your life. Do you know how many people there are in this country who suffer because of men like that? People who don't even have a miserable hole like this to live in? There's no reason for them to suffer – like there's no reason for you to be saddled with your old man for the rest of your life.' She waited a moment and then added harshly, 'I work with others to end that misery.'

There was a short silence.

'What are you trying to tell me?' Miguel asked finally.

Olga leaned forward. The top button of her shirt was open; she didn't wear a bra. 'I need your help,' she said, 'but I don't know if you can be trusted.'

Her small pointed breasts tantalized him. He slid his hand inside her shirt and began to fondle them, rubbing the nipples with eager fingers.

'You can trust me,' he muttered hoarsely. 'I've been a fool too long. I'm leaving with you.'

'We'll talk about that later,' she said. 'Will you help me now?'

'I'm going to make love to you now. Two days without you . . .' He began to unbutton her shirt. 'I thought I would go crazy . . . Olga . . .'

She pushed his hands away. 'That can wait. I want you to meet some friends of mine first.'

Had she been any other woman Miguel would have sent her to hell. She was Olga. He felt recklessly alive with her and equal to anything. Capable of even breaking away from responsibility and family and heritage. Olga stimulated him enough to defy the world – but she doubted him. If he didn't prove her wrong he would lose her, and his only chance for freedom.

VII

Olga's friends were very much on their guard. They crowded around a small table in a smoky café and watched Miguel with wary eyes while Olga explained that he would be helping them.

'He knows the project area like the back of his hand,' she said. 'It's just the information we need. Tell him about the project, Rulo.'

A ginger-haired man who looked vaguely familiar began to fold a paper napkin in small triangles. 'We want to raise social consciousness at grass-roots level,' he said after a moment. 'It's easy enough in the urban areas — factories and all that, you know. The rural areas are a problem, especially where there are large landowners. They don't like us preaching politics they don't agree with.'

Miguel grinned. 'You can say that again! My old man's been fighting politics on his ranch for years. He won't allow meetings or anything like that.'

'Sounds like a good place to begin with,' observed a dark man sitting next to Olga.

'What we want is to talk to the *peones*,' continued the man named Rulo. 'Nothing violent — no inciting to strikes or anything like that. Just talk to them about important social matters. It goes beyond politics, really — but people like your father wouldn't understand that.'

'If you want to talk to the *peones* on La Catalina without my old man catching you, your best bet's after Easter,' suggested Miguel. 'He's going down south for a couple of weeks. The manager's going to be away as well.' He gave them a conspiratorial wink. 'I'm supposed to be in charge.'

Olga and the others exchanged glances. 'When's this?'

'The old man's leaving on April eighteenth. I'm taking my family back to Buenos Aries, but I'll be back on the twenty-second. Let me have a day or so to organize things. How about the twenty-fourth? Does that suit your plans all right?'

'That should be all right,' agreed ginger-haired Rulo flatly.

'How the hell are we going to find this place?' asked his neighbour. 'We don't want to advertise ourselves.'

427

Miguel reached for his pen. 'No problem. Anyone have a piece of paper I can use?'

Someone shoved a blank sheet across the table. He began to sketch a map of La Catalina and the surrounding area. He felt buoyed up by a defiant sense of adventure and challenge. His pen drew inspiration from excitement and flowed. Trees with smiles, a cross-eyed gaucho on a bow-legged horse, the ranch house sprouting pot-bellied chimneys. Cattle dancing a tango. The crater in the main road with a whale spouting DANGER! and the meandering detour, studded with grinning skulls and crossbones. Witty little legends. On the bottom right-hand corner he drew a heart, glancing at Olga as he did so, and wrote in bold letters, 'The Cattleman's Kingdom. Enjoy it with me. Miguel, the Cattleman's Son.' The others watched in silence.

'You can't go wrong with this,' he grinned. 'If you come down the road from Cardales and enter by this gate,' marking it on the map with a dragon's head, 'no one'll see you. There's an abandoned *puesto* in that field. You can hold your meeting there. I'll make sure the gate's open.'

Olga took the map. 'You really know how to draw, eh? Clever boy.'

They began to ask questions. Miguel assured them not to worry. He would ring Olga on Easter Sunday and report any changes. He saw himself fully in command of the situation; his words, like his pen, flowed. He did not stop to think beyond the excitement of the moment. He began to dream of the future with Olga. Maybe he would become a cartoonist. Satirize the world he knew so well. Make a name for himself on his own. Why the hell not? Stuff responsibility and heritage up convention's ass. Be a man for once, instead of the cattleman's son.

In the exciting world of Olga's arms, anything was possible.

VIII

For the first time in her life Isabel was not enjoying the family Easter at La Catalina. She wanted to be alone. She didn't want to have to smile and make conversation and be Elías's wife. She wanted to be Isabel Luciani again: ten years old and mistress of her sunlit, golden-green world. She wanted to gallop across the pampa and let the wind cleanse her thoughts. Rid them of Stefan. She had not seen him again since their quarrel. He hadn't rung her up or even written, and she was certainly not going to take the first step. The days had accumulated into nearly two years. She wanted him out of her thoughts, but he continued to mock her. Even here at La Catalina.

'I was talking to Manolo San Martín the other day,' remarked Gastón. 'His father's bought land in that new beach resort at Los Pinos. According to Manolo the old man's going to build a fabulous villa. He contracted an architect no one's ever heard of to design it. A Yugoslav called Stefan Stervic.'

'Knowing old San Martín, he probably hired the man for peanuts,' said Elías.

Gastón squirted soda into his drink. 'Manolo says the guy's charging the earth. Nobody knows how he convinced the old boy to pay his price, except that the blueprints sound incredible. No one in Los Pinos is going to have a house like it.'

'He's probably very young and handsome and has wrapped Manolo's mother around his little finger,' chuckled María Marta. 'Or Manolo's sister. She's in-between husbands, isn't she?'

Isabel dropped her drink and could think of nothing better than to blame her husband, who was sitting beside her on the sofa and at that moment had been reaching for a bowl of cheese straws on the table in front of them.

'Watch what you're doing, Elías! You're so clumsy!'

He stared in astonishment. 'I never touched you!'

'Yes, you did,' she insisted. 'You jogged my elbow. Oh, stop fussing!' as he began to mop up the drink. 'Get me another one.' Her voice rose shrilly as Elías went across to the drinks tray and picked up a bottle. 'Not sweet vermouth, you know I hate it! Anyway I was having a gin and tonic.'

Elías frowned as he poured out the drink. Isabel was in one of her queer moods again; he wished she weren't so temperamental. Perhaps Isabel should see a psychoanalyst. Someone who would straighten her out and put an end to all these emotional fireworks. He decided to make inquiries as soon as they returned to Buenos Aires.

Yvonne arrived on Thursday in a bright pink Volkswagon decorated with orange butterflies. She was trying out a new look this month. Platinum ringlets, cobalt-blue eyeshadow, plum-purple mouth and nails. Gladys gave a shudder of disgust. Scarlet silk trousers and transparent blouses were not appropriate for Holy Week. Driving Lalo to the casino in Cardales and returning at four in the morning was even worse. Indecent and immoral, complained Gladys tearfully to Marcos.

'Yvonne may be outrageous, but at least she's amusing,' he countered irritably. 'Let Eduardo enjoy himself. It's about time that boy cut loose from your apronstrings.'

He ignored the rest of Gladys's tears and went in search of Tiger, who was waiting to go hunting. Perhaps it was significant that at the last minute he invited Lalo to come along as well.

Significant events often seem inconsequential at the time. If Gladys had not complained about Yvonne, Marcos might not have taken that first tentative step towards his younger son. If old Rosario's replacement had known how to cook codfish, chances are Isabel would not have turned up at Los Alamos on Good Friday.

Angela was pleased to see her. This particular Good Friday was dull and unseasonably cold. She felt strangely uneasy and on edge, plagued by whispering ghosts and the sorrowful reproaches of her heart. The warm, living sound of another voice made a welcome contrast to the empty echoes of silence.

'How pleasant your house looks!' exclaimed Isabel, glancing around the room. 'You've made changes – is that a new table?'

'Julia Ortíz's great-aunt left it to me. The birds on the mantelpiece were hers as well.' Angela removed a large ginger cat from its favourite cushion on the sofa. 'Will you have some tea?'

'Thanks, I need it! We have an impossible cook at La Catalina these days – some female Gladys took on without consulting Mercedes. Rosario'll be ninety next month and Papa can't keep her any longer. This one's called Zoila and she's simply appalling! The cod for lunch was so tough and salty no one could eat it. The cornmeal cakes were burnt, the salad hadn't been cleaned and by the time we reached dessert . . .' Isabel laughed. 'You know the Luciani clan at table! We like good food – especially Papa.'

'Oh, indeed,' grinned Angela. 'I'll never forget my first meal at La Catalina.'

'Papa ordered Gladys to fire Zoila. She complained no one else could do the cooking and he told her to go into the kitchen herself if she wasn't capable of hiring a proper cook. What a meal! Miguel's all keyed up about something – a woman, I suspect. He told Papa at least ten times not to worry about La Catalina while Papa and Pablo Losa are down south. I only hope he doesn't plan to have a dirty week on the ranch while they're gone. Gastón's eldest dropped an ice cube down Laura's neck, little Catalina choked on a fishbone. Yvonne and Uncle Pedro started to argue about religion. Elías joined in . . .' Isabel threw up her hands. 'Absolute chaos. Papa and Gladys were still squabbling over Zoila when I left. Lucky you! You don't have to put up with the Lucianis wholesale!'

Angela smiled faintly and refilled their cups. The fire crackled on the hearth, the ginger cat purred contentedly beside the log basket. Outside in the yard a row of dispirited poplars drooped in the gloomy mist. Isabel lit a cigarette and settled back against the sofa.

'Will you come to the *asado* on Easter Sunday?' she asked. 'Mercedes says she invited you, but you're not sure.'

'I'm not sure.'

Isabel studied the tip of her cigarette. 'It's because of Papa, isn't it?'

There was no reply.

'Why do you hate him so much?'

'I don't hate him, Isabel.'

'Then why do you stay away? We all notice it, you know. Even Elías. For years now you've been avoiding Papa like the plague.' Her voice hesitated a moment and then rushed on. 'You were in love with him once, weren't you? I remember that time we met . . . Stupid, priggish me! You were in love with him and he – he's miserable, Angela!'

Angela stared down at her hands. There were no rings on them now – not even Jimmy Morgan's plain gold band. It lay at the bottom of her jewel box, buried in memory.

'I loved your father very much,' she said after a moment. 'I still do, but too many things stand between us.'

'Gladys?'

'She's one of them, yes.'

Isabel tossed her cigarette into the fire and lit another one. 'I suppose we all make our own little hells, don't we?' she remarked. 'Society calls it being responsible and honouring commitments, the Church calls it holy matrimony.

431

It's a sacrament.' Her mouth twisted into a bitter smile. 'White veil and orange blossoms. Chained together by them until death does us part.'

She jumped up and went over to Lucía Claire's table. Her fingers picked up ornaments, put them down, fiddled with others. A minute ticked by and then she said with a sob in her voice, 'The priests have it all wrong, you know. God doesn't have to tax His imagination devising Hell; we do a better job and make it respectable into the bargain.'

'You're very unhappy, aren't you?' asked Angela gently.

Isabel fingered a small bronze horse. 'Yes,' she said. 'I'm in love with another man.'

'And he wants you to leave Elías?'

'He wanted me to, but I wouldn't. It's all over now.' Her eyes met Angela's. 'I'm my father's daughter. Damnable, isn't it? Please come to La Catalina on Sunday.'

Angela went to the Easter Sunday *asado*, but left before Marcos had a chance to talk to her. He wanted to explain about Jimmy; even if she didn't love him any more he had to clear up the matter. It wasn't a spur of the moment decision; he had been gathering courage for a long time. Had he been ten years younger he might have taken the bull by the horns sooner, but he would be sixty-one next month and the prospect of yet another rejection at this stage of his life filled him with considerable dread.

It occurred to Marcos when he saw Angela chatting after lunch with Mercedes that this might be a good time to speak his piece. Five minutes in his study — that was all he needed. Five minutes to tell Angela the truth. She could do what she liked after that; all he wanted was to get everything off his chest. He made his plans carefully, but it wasn't until nearly an hour later that he was able to leave his guests and by then Angela was gone.

Marcos panicked. A precious opportunity had slipped away; the way matters stood now he certainly wouldn't get another chance for five minutes alone with Angela. He swallowed his pride, rushed into his study and began to write her a panic-stricken letter. A few minutes later Pablo Losa called him to the telephone.

IX

Gladys had been keeping a sharp eye on Marcos all afternoon. He was never alone with Angela Morgan, but that didn't mean anything. They could still be meeting secretly. Her attention was momentarily distracted by domestic details; when she looked around again both Marcos and Angela had disappeared. Gladys hurried back to the house. If there was still anything going on between them, she would catch them at it red-handed. Her eyes blazed with indignation as she thought of the scene. That pale, insipid *gringa* kissing her husband, doing things no decent woman would do in some dark, secret corner of the house. Not in a bedroom because someone might come in. Marcos's study was the safest place . . . Gladys tiptoed over to the study door, opened it carefully and peered in. No one was there, but an unfinished letter lay on the desk.

By this time Gladys Luciani had developed a fixation with her husband's letters. She hurried over and scanned the few lines scrawled in Marcos's bold, untidy handwriting.

Angela, you must know how much I love you. Please let me . . .

Gladys read the words several times, her face pinched and grey. This letter she could not burn.

X

Miguel made a phone call to Olga.

'Everything's OK for the twenty-fourth,' he said. 'The old man's leaving on the eighteenth. He'll be back in two weeks. I'm taking my family home tomorrow. I'll see you at the flat on Tuesday . . .'

'I have to visit my grandmother,' she interrupted.

'How long will you be away?'

'I don't know.'

'Olga . . .'

'Call me at the end of the week,' she said and rang off.

XI

On Thursday 18 April Marcos Luciani drove to Buenos Aires with his wife and youngest daughter. They left La Catalina at half-past eight, a good hour behind schedule because Gladys had mislaid her reading glasses. The glasses eventually turned up under a sofa cushion, where Marcos suspected her of hiding them on purpose. There had been a series of similar little incidents over the past four days – petty, irritating tricks which served to remind him continually of Gladys's presence.

The car turned left at the main gate and headed south. Gladys complained that Marcos was driving too fast. He ignored her. Eight miles further on, the road detoured along a narrow track; Gladys continued to complain. Lalo was the subject now. Her sharp, high voice rattled on, listing his virtues and his father's sins of omission. Marcos countered angrily. In the back seat Clara stared out of the window and listened to her parents' quarrel. Her face was white and her hands clenched into fists, but no one bothered to notice.

'I don't care what you say. Eduardo's starting work at the office next week,' snapped Marcos. 'He's a man, not a baby. I won't have my son coddled like a girl.'

'As if you ever cared for your son!' hissed Gladys furiously. 'As if you ever cared! You hate them both – Lalo and Clara! I'm not blind, you know. I'm not a fool! I know you're carrying on with Morgan's widow. If they were her children you'd care, but they're mine! *They are mine!*'

'Don't I know it!'

She rushed on, too wound up now to be careful of words. 'No one's going to push my children out! No one, do you hear? Certainly not that daughter of yours and her gigolo husband! She thinks she's so clever, writing about your granddaughter . . .'

Marcos turned his head to stare at her, his eyes blazing. 'My *granddaughter*? What the hell are you talking about? Who wrote what?'

Gladys could have bitten off her tongue. She twisted the rings on her fingers. 'Don't drive so fast.'

'Answer me!'

'You know what I'm talking about!' she retorted, taking refuge in confusion. 'You read letters.'

'Cristina must have written. You've been going through my mail, is that it? When did she write? What did you do with her letter? Read it?' Marcos took one hand off the steering wheel and shook Gladys. 'God damn you – did you read my daughter's letter? Have you kept it from me?'

'What if I did? I'm your wife, aren't I? I've got a right to know what's going on!'

'You stupid woman,' said Marcos between clenched teeth. 'I'll never forgive you for this!'

'I'm the one who should do the forgiving! You and that stupid, insipid *inglesa*! I've seen the way you look at her. I know you two meet behind my back . . .'

'What of it?' he shouted. 'If I weren't chained to you I'd marry Angela right now. *Right now*!'

'Why did you marry me?' shrieked Gladys. 'Why?'

He slowed down to make room for a car approaching from the rear. 'Because your brother tricked me into taking the cheap way out, that's why. Christ, what a fool I was! I'm sick to death of you . . .'

The car started to pass, swerved sharply and forced Marcos on to the grass. He cursed and banged his hand on the horn. The car stopped, blocking the road. Four men jumped out. They raced over and wrenched open his door before he realized what was happening. Gladys screamed. Marcos felt himself being dragged across the seat. A hand slapped a cloth over his nose and mouth; he struggled furiously, choking on sweet, sickening wetness. Gladys screamed again and he heard shots.

After that, nothing.

CHAPTER THIRTY-ONE

I

Nearly an hour later Raúl Jones, Los Alamos's manager, passed the car on his way into Laguna Grande.

The windscreen was smashed, the right side riddled with bullet holes. Gladys's lifeless body lay sprawled the length of the front seat. Her face was streaked with blood, her eyes stared blankly at the roof. Several curious flies, unperturbed by death, clustered near the corner of her mouth. Jones reached forward to brush them off; his hands were shaking.

Something moved in the back of the car. He took a deep breath and peered over the seat. Clara sat on the floor, rigid with terror; when she saw him she began to scream.

II

Pablo Losa's call to the Buenos Aires office interrupted a meeting between Gastón, Miguel and Jorge Robles, the office manager. Miguel took it. His face changed colour. The hand holding the receiver began to shake, his other hand clutched the desk top so hard the fingers turned white. Gastón and Robles stared at him in alarm.

'What's happened?' demanded Gastón. 'What's wrong, Miguel?'

The receiver dropped on to the desk. He backed away from it and stammered in a strangled voice, 'It's Papa. He's – he's been kidnapped.'

Jorges Robles dropped the file he had been looking through. The papers scattered on the floor, but no one noticed.

'My God!' whispered Gastón. 'When? What happened? How did Losa find out? Say something, won't you?'

436

as Miguel continued to stare at the receiver. '*What happened?*'

Miguel looked up very slowly. His eyes were dead. He licked his lips and made words. They sounded horrible.

'J-Jones from Los Alamos found the car. About tw-twelve miles from La Catalina. Gladys . . .' His voice stuck. He licked his lips again. 'Gladys – dead. M-murdered. Papa gone. Clara's alive . . . in shock . . .' He buried his face in his hands. 'Oh, Jesus!'

After what seemed like forever he heard Gastón's voice.

'Any idea who kidnapped Marcos? Did Losa say?'

Miguel shook his head. He had to find Olga – but Olga had not returned to the flat. He didn't know where her grandmother lived. The meeting planned for the twenty-fourth would have to be called off . . . With a sudden, chilling echo of memory he heard her mocking voice. *Be a good idea, wouldn't it? Make your old man sweat for a while.* He remembered her friends' questions. He had supplied a great deal of information that night. Now that he thought about it, no one had seemed too interested in his suggestions for holding a clandestine meeting. They had wanted details about his father. What time did he normally leave the ranch when he went to Buenos Aires? What car did he drive? Was there much traffic on the detour? And the map – the clever cartoon map he had drawn to impress Olga. 'Clever boy,' she had said . . . Miguel stared through Gastón and Robles, his mouth trembling.

He had proved himself, all right. Clever boy. He would have to continue being clever until the bitter end.

III

To be murdered on a dusty road in the middle of nowhere was an undignified way to die. Gladys would have undoubtedly expected a grandiose burial to redress the balance and ease the frustrations of her soul. Her husband's family, however, had other things to worry about.

Gladys Luciani's funeral was spartan and strictly private.

A hasty mass in the cemetery chapel, a silent procession between rows of marble angels, a few moments of uncomfortable silence before the coffin was lowered into the family vault. Lalo, looking pale and frightened, helped a stone-faced Clara light candles on the tiny altar overpowered by a stained-glass Resurrection. Claudia clung to Luis and sobbed, 'poor Mama, poor Mama.' *Rest in peace. Miserere.* A chilly wind shook the cypresses and scattered withered petals along the narrow cemetery lanes. *Poor Mama.* The rest of the family drifted away, embarrassed by a grief they did not share.

Celestina did not go to her daughter's funeral. Juan told her Gladys had been badly injured in an accident, but she knew he was lying. Her sallow, wrinkled face was expressionless as she held out the evening paper.

'It says here she was shot. WEALTHY CATTLEMAN KIDNAPPED, WIFE SHOT DEAD. That's the headlines. I may be old, but I can still read.'

Gaspari swallowed. 'It's a terrible thing. I didn't want you to know how it happened.'

Celestina got up and shuffled over to the stove. He watched her reach for the kettle, light the gas, take down the battered blue tin of *maté*. Her chin quivered and she clutched the kitchen counter. Gaspari put his arms around her awkwardly.

'I'm here, Mama.'

'Gladys was my daughter,' said Celestina Gaspari heavily. 'She may have been a fool, but she was my daughter. She didn't deserve to die like that.'

IV

The national press gave the Luciani kidnapping front-page treatment for three days and then moved it discreetly to the back. *No word of missing cattleman.* Politics, Vietnam, economic shock waves from the rise in world oil prices . . . Routine copy reasserted itself in banner headlines while *no word* languished between the comic strips and the daily horoscope. After another week it disappeared from the public eye altogether.

V

On the first of May Gastón received a phone call; an hour later he drove to Barranco Rosales for a meeting with Miguel and Elías. A balding, energetic man in civilian clothes went with him. The man's name was Enrique Hartridge and he was a commander in the security forces.

The kidnappers had made contact.

'They want ten million dollars for Marcos,' said Gastón. 'We have two weeks to pay it.'

Elías stared. '*Ten million dollars*? In two weeks' time? They're crazy!'

Miguel looked sick. 'They're crazy,' he echoed in a loud voice.

'No doubt about that,' agreed Hartridge, 'but they mean business, señores.'

Gastón leaned his head on his hands and stared down at the photograph of La Catalina on Marcos's desk. 'Two weeks – or they'll kill him,' he repeated unsteadily. '"Like a dog" were the man's words. "We'll shoot Luciani like a dog".'

Enrique Hartridge blew a smoke-ring and watched it disappear over Miguel's head. 'There's another problem,' he remarked almost cheerfully. 'Once you pay the ransom they may kill Luciani anyway. There's a very strong chance of that, señores. A very strong chance.'

VI

A core of light stabbed the rim of darkness. La Catalina's early morning sun, perhaps, shining though a chink in the bedroom shutters. Marcos stirred uneasily. He must have overslept again. The light moved and a woman's voice said, 'He's coming around.' A man replied and she laughed. Harsh, discordant laughter without mirth or soul to it. Somewhere beyond the core of light a door shut and then there was silence.

Marcos opened his eyes. A young man with ginger hair and very blue eyes sat next to a wooden table; there was a gun on the table and a tray of coffee. The man poured out a cup from a chipped enamel pot and brought it over to the bed.

'Better drink this. Don't burn yourself.'

The coffee was hot and bitter. Marcos managed to force most of it down; when he lay back on the bed his head was swimming.

'Feel like some exercise?' asked the man. 'A couple of minutes back and forth across the room. Take it slowly.'

He obeyed reluctantly, still dazed from a sleep which seemed to have no beginning. His legs felt like cotton, the floorboards were rough and splintered under his bare feet. After several shaky steps Marcos groped for the bed and sat down. His watch was gone.

'What day is it?'

The ginger-haired man grinned. 'Saturday.'

'Saturday what?'

'Just Saturday.'

Marcos glanced around the room. Four brown walls, a narrow bed. A chair and battered table. The inevitable light bulb hanging from a frayed cord. The words LIBERATION FRONT had been sprayed with red paint on the far wall; below them someone had printed a political slogan in crooked letters. The only window in the room was boarded over.

'I'd like a cigarette,' he said thickly.

His guard lit one and placed it on the edge of the table. Marcos took the cigarette and smoked slowly, staring at the slogan on the wall. Thoughts came and went in brief snatches of memory. He chased them impatiently, aware of the blue eyes watching him over the muzzle of the gun.

'Where am I?' he demanded after a moment.

'Somewhere.'

'What do you want with me?'

'Ten million dollars. Think you're worth it?'

The door opened and a man wearing battle fatigues came in. He glared at the guard. 'You're wanted downstairs.' His eyes darted nervously at the prisoner. 'I'm not having him on the loose while I'm here.'

'You can shoot, can't you?' jeered the ginger-haired man, but he shoved Marcos down on to the bed and clamped an iron shackle around his right ankle. 'Don't talk to López,' he warned in a low voice. 'The man's trigger-happy. Loses his head.'

'Shut up, holy boy!' growled López.

'You're a priest?' asked Marcos in astonishment.
'What of it?'
'You look too intelligent for this sort of nonsense.'
The reluctant priest flushed. 'You wouldn't understand!'
'I don't want to,' replied Marcos wearily and turned his face to the wall.

VII

There were three guards. Boyle the priest, trigger-happy López and a taciturn chain-smoker they called Zorro. Of the three Marcos preferred Boyle. The priest seemed friendly enough despite his gun; he appeared to be obsessed with the need to explain why he had joined the Front.

'You're wasting your time with me,' interrupted Marcos wryly. 'I'm old-fashioned. I don't believe religion and politics should mix. The Church's mission is purely spiritual.'

'The Church has the moral obligation to fight for people's right to live with dignity!'

'Every political party claims to do that in one way or another. The right to live with dignity is one of the most hackneyed slogans around.'

Boyle frowned. 'You think I'm a fool, don't you?'

'A misguided idealist. You've entrusted your dreams to criminals.'

'Maybe because it's the only way.'

Marcos shook his head. 'It never was and never will be, no matter which side the criminals are on. The Front cons idealists like yourself into believing violence is the only way. You're the useful fools who do its dirty work. How much ransom money has gone into helping people 'live with dignity' or bettering the lot of the poor? Not a peso's worth – and you know it, Boyle. The money the Front extorts purchases death. It pays for hideaways abroad; it probably helps fund operations in other countries. There are no charitable ideals behind operations like the Front. No true patriots. It's dreamers like yourself who make their crimes possible.'

'You're bound to think like that! You're rich, you've never had to fight for anything. You don't know what it's like to be poor!'

'Show me concrete proof that I'm wrong,' replied Marcos.

He could not help liking Rulo Boyle – but López was another matter.

López did not argue political ideology; he boasted. About the bombs he had planted, the cars he had burnt, the men he had killed. The women as well. He stood over Marcos, his face glistening with sweat, and told him exactly how he had killed Gladys. How her screams got on his nerves. The pleasure it gave him to pull the trigger and the way her body twitched as the bullets hit it. Like a puppet with broken strings.

'You filthy bastard!' yelled Marcos and lunged at him.

The iron around his ankle brought him up short, but he managed to get his hands around López's throat. The guard stumbled backwards and fell to the floor, dragging him off the bed. Marcos tightened his grip. It took three men to pull him off the choking guard; after that they kept him handcuffed and heavily drugged.

Olga was taking no more chances.

VIII

The kidnappers contacted Gastón three days before the deadline. This time a woman rang. He asked for more time; she took so long to reply that at first he thought the communication had been cut off. He said 'hello!' several times, his voice jarring nervously across the silence. The woman laughed.

'Five minutes more, *compañero*. That's all you get,' she jeered.

Hartridge and Miguel saw Gastón go white.

'They won't give us more time,' he said, hanging up the receiver. 'The woman says someone will ring up at midday on the fifteenth with the final instructions. I'm to make the delivery alone. If they suspect the security forces have been alerted they'll kill Marcos – and me.'

Miguel appeared to shrink inside his clothes. 'You spoke with a woman?' he asked, trying to sound natural.

'If you can call her that. I'd rather deal with the man.'

'What we need,' remarked Enrique Hartridge, blowing a pale blue smoke-ring at the ceiling, 'is a miracle. Just one little miracle,

442

señores. Something that will tell us where they're holding Luciani. It could be anywhere in the country – what I want to know is where. The rest is a question of coordinating strategy.'

Miguel excused himself and left the study. He didn't want to think about miracles or strategies or what would happen when they found his father. What the hell was he going to do? Hartridge wanted the kidnappers alive. He wanted to make them talk. If they talked – *Christ – if they talked*! Miguel paced up and down in the garden. There was no excitement now, no thrill of adventure or danger. He was trapped in a cage of his own making. Olga's making as well. She had goaded him. Mocked him for not having the guts to follow her . . . He turned with a start as little Catalina's voice echoed behind him.

'Will you take Inesita and me to the zoo, Daddy? Mama's got a headache.'

Ana Inés had a headache because they had quarrelled that morning – he couldn't even remember what about. Miguel glanced down at his two daughters with desperate eyes. Inesita beamed happily and chirped with a two-year-old's sunny determination, 'Monkeys, Daddy!'

He took his daughters to the zoo. He bought them popcorn and balloons. He stood with them in front of the monkey cages and made himself laugh. He rode with them on the merry-go-round. The music wound in and out of his thoughts like a tinny, mocking refrain. *Prove yourself clever boy prove yourself.* They went to see the lions.

'Daddy,' asked Catalina, 'why did the bad men take Grandfather away?'

Miguel stared at the two lion cubs sparring. 'Because they're bad men, Cata.'

'Will we find Grandfather?'

'Yes.' His voice made a harsh, jarring sound. 'Of course we'll find him. Let's go see the elephants.'

He took the girls back home. Mercedes was praying with Ana Inés and Yvonne before a painting of the Virgin on the upstairs landing. Miguel didn't want to pray. He wanted to find Olga.

Ring me at the end of the week, she had said. That had been over three weeks ago. The day before the kidnapping. He had rung, but there had been no answer. He had gone around to the flat above the laundry, but there had been no sign of her. He went back now. Perhaps a miracle . . . The woman who owned the flat had a face like a fish and eyes like ice. The ice-eyes drilled into Miguel.

'Olga Raskowitz? She's cleared out.'

'Do you know where she went?' he demanded.

The woman's mouth opened and closed with a snap. 'No.'

There would be no miracle; he was certain of that. Olga had never cared about him; she only wanted to pick his brains. Details of other conversations kept returning. He remembered one in particular about the American at El Ombú. What was his name? Sussler. He had told Olga quite a bit about Sussler; had made witty jokes about the man's Spanish and his blonde, curvaceous wife. The plastic *gringos*. Olga had laughed – and Sussler was dead.

Miguel drove back to Barranco Rosales. He went into the library and poured himself a stiff drink. There was a bowl of white chrysanthemums on the massive desk. He stared bitterly at the flowers. He had given Olga more than just physical love; he had trusted her with the intimate secrets of his heart. Maybe he had been drunk at the time, but the things he had told her were still important. Things he had never told anyone else. He had been fool enough to bare his soul and Olga Raskowitz had used his secrets to trap him. That was the bitterest truth of all.

IX

Stefan Stervic spent several hours that morning inspecting a possible site for a plastics factory in the suburb of San Justo. There was not much of interest in the neighbourhood. Empty lots, old houses, a derelict warehouse. He walked thoughtfully back to his car. The factory was well worth a draft project, mainly because the owner was a wealthy Lebanese. Stervic stared idly at a house across the street. Depressing-looking place. Windows boarded over and rubble strewn all over the front yard. He continued to think about the plastics factory. Two men came from around the back of the house – or they might have been coming from the warehouse a bit further on, it was difficult to tell. They hurried by the car and turned the corner. One of the men had a dark red stain on the left side of his face. Stervic noticed it, but paid little attention. His mind was busy with architectural details.

444

He decided to have lunch at a neighbourhood restaurant before heading back to town. While he waited for his steak, he glanced through the paper. The world continued to be in a mess and the missing cattleman had not been found. Stefan frowned at the small headline on the back page. Marcos Luciani's kidnapping had shocked him, partly because they were acquaintances, partly because of Isabel. Even after two years he had not forgotten her. He was still angry, still hurt – but he could not forget her. Ironically, his career had taken off the day of their quarrel. An afternoon interview had resulted in a large contract and an invitation to an important business reception. More contracts had followed, business led to social contacts. Stefan Stervic was fast becoming a name to reckon with in the world of architecture. He scaled quickly and he scaled high.

Stefan began to eat his steak. There was nothing he could do about Marcos Luciani's kidnapping or about Isabel. He poured himself another glass of wine. It was then that he became aware of the two men at the next table. One was thin and cadaverous-looking, the other had a dark red stain on the left side of his face. The restaurant was noisy, but their voices reached Stefan very clearly. He listened with increasing astonishment to their conversation.

'I tell you we can't trust a fool like that!' hissed the man with the stain. 'After all, it's his old man. What if he blabs to the police?'

His thin friend laughed. 'What's he going to tell 'em? That he gave Olga all the info about Luciani . . .'

'Ssshht!' shushed the other one. 'You crazy or something? No names!'

The thin man belched. 'Stop worrying, López. The cattleman's son won't talk. He doesn't even know where she is.' He took a long, noisy sip of wine. 'The bitch's got guts, even if she does use long words. Mind you, if it were me I would've already blown the bastard's head off.'

'I don't like it,' repeated the one called López. 'Too risky. Can't expect the son to twiddle his fingers and wait for Daddy to drop down from the clouds, can we?'

'From what Olga says the son's a gutless cock who's only good for one thing – and it ain't thinking, mate,' observed his friend with a laugh. He reached for his wallet; a folded piece of paper fell unnoticed from his pocket to the floor. 'Come

445

on, we'd better get back to the house before the Jew starts squawking.'

Stefan waited until they had left and then retrieved the paper. It turned out to be a map of Marcos Luciani's ranch La Catalina and the surrounding area. It was a cartoon map, sketched with clever, diabolical humour; someone had pencilled in 8:50 above a spot on one of the roads. He sat staring at the map for several minutes, unable to believe his eyes. *The Cattleman's Kingdom. Enjoy it with me. Miguel, the Cattleman's Son.* The heart in the corner had been twisted into an obscenity by another hand.

Stefan made a harsh, angry noise in his throat. He remembered the look of failure on Marcos Luciani's face as he bent over a bloodied, battered Miguel on that winter night so many years ago. He remembered his own father, gunned down in cold blood. Two isolated incidents that were connected by a very personal logic. He had seen his father murdered because of political beliefs; he was not going to stand by and let another man's father die for the same senseless reason. He would not let another man die for any reason if he could help it, but in this case his determination carried even greater urgency. Isabel's face surfaced through his thoughts. That alone was reason enough.

X

Miguel was still sitting alone in the library when the butler paused just inside the doorway and gave a discreet cough.

'A gentleman to see you, Señor Miguel. Architect Stervic. He says it's urgent.'

The name meant nothing. The man entering the library meant nothing. A pair of hard, pale eyes studied Miguel with disconcerting intentness. He returned the look uneasily.

'What can I do for you?'

Stefan Stervic held out a piece of paper. 'You can read this.'

The words on the map leapt out boldly. Miguel swallowed. His eyes stared at the heart in the corner; his face seemed to have aged twenty years.

'Where did you find this?'

Stefan told him. He repeated the conversation between the thin man and the man called López word for word. When he

446

finished speaking there was such complete silence they could hear the church bells chiming down the street.

'There's no mistaking the intention of that map,' continued Stefan after a moment. 'There's no mistaking who drew it, either.' His voice grated harshly. 'The cattleman's son.'

Miguel moistened his lips. 'It wasn't for that reason! Good God, do you think I would . . . I didn't know! She said . . . Oh Christ!' He buried his face in his hands. 'I swear by my children I didn't know.'

'That's what Judas said – *I didn't know.*' The mimicry was bitter.

Miguel brought his hands down from his face and ran one hand through his hair. 'What the hell's it to you?'

'I saw my father shot because he refused to be a pawn,' replied Stefan slowly. 'You don't forget things like that. It's none of my business why you're mixed up in this, but by God I'll make it my business to get Marcos Luciani away from those bastards – alive!' He pointed to the map. 'If you're worth a drop of your father's blood, you'll act on that now. Undo what you've done.'

'What have you done, Miguel?' demanded Isabel from the doorway.

Even her mouth lacked colour. It moved stiffly, repeating the question as she came into the library and shut the door. She made no sign of having noticed Stefan; her eyes were riveted on the paper in Miguel's hand.

'What's that?'

She grabbed the map before he could stop her. He snatched it back again, but Isabel had seen enough.

'Dear Holy Virgin!' she whispered in horror. 'What have you done?'

'It's not what you think,' rasped Miguel. 'I swear it's not what you think, Bela!'

'Those numbers – it's marked La Lomita under them. That's where the . . . where Papa's car was found. You drew that map! I recognize your writing. The gaucho and – the cows dancing. You're always drawing them.' She turned to Stervic, her eyes brimming with tears; he was no more than a face. 'He drew one for T-Tiger's birthday. The cows and the house with those ch-chimneys. Miguelomania, we call it. A f-family joke – God in Heaven!' she screamed, throwing herself at Miguel. '*How could you do something like this!*'

447

He fought her off while Stervic watched in silence. 'Shut up! You'll bring everyone in here!'

'Let them come! If Papa dies – you filthy traitor . . .'

'Damn you, be quiet!' shouted Miguel and rushed from the room.

Isabel sank into the nearest chair and buried her face in her hands. A door slammed upstairs. The house shuddered briefly and then settled down again into uneasy, waiting silence.

'I'll never forgive him for this!' she sobbed. 'God rot his soul in Hell – I'll never forgive him!'

'The less people who know about it the better,' warned Stefan quietly.

She looked up with a start at the sound of his voice. He walked over to the bar and poured them both a drink. No social ceremonies, no excuses. A cool, practical gesture that brought things strangely back into perspective.

'Your father's life depends on Miguel's conscience,' he said. 'Your brother's rattled, Isabel. He's up to his neck and he's a frightened man. If he feels threatened further he may do something we'll all regret.' He held out the drink. 'How much of our conversation did you hear?'

Her eyes didn't leave his face. 'About your father.'

Stefan hesitated. She looked too thin and too pale; her dark eyes were too bright. The questions they asked were painful; he could not thrust himself to answer them. Instead he said dryly, 'There's more to it than that,' and gave a brief account of the conversation in the restaurant, omitting the harsher details.

Isabel got up and walked over to the window. The drink was a strong one; she gulped half of it down with a shudder and fingered a tassel on the curtains. They were made of heavy, wine-coloured velvet. A moth had nibbled a minute hole into one of the thick folds.

'What you must think of us!' she said bitterly. 'The wealthy, upper-crust Lucianis! We can't even keep the rot out of our own house.'

There was no answer.

'I hear you're doing very well for yourself.' She rattled the ice in her glass. 'Designing expensive summer villas for retired racing kings.'

'I'm doing all right.'

'Stefan . . .'

He cut in quickly. 'How's my daughter?'

Isabel closed her eyes. His words sounded so flat; they revealed nothing of the effort it cost him to say them.

'Very well. Growing.' She forced herself to look around. 'You had better tell my cousin Gastón. He's in charge of the family now that Papa . . . Tell him what you like about Miguel.'

'My concern is helping your father. Miguel's old enough to pull his own chestnuts out of the fire.' Stefan took a business card from his wallet and handed it to her. 'Tell your cousin he can reach me at this number. I'll be waiting for his call.'

They said goodbye coolly, like well-bred strangers who had never kissed or made love or watched the moon rising above the river. Perhaps it was best that way after all.

XI

The house in San Justo was a two-storey building at the end of a narrow walk flanked by untidy orange trees. The roof was gabled and a wide porch with ornate ironwork ran the length of the front. A headless stone angel lay across the walk, its grotesque form swollen by lonely shadows. Once the house had been a family home of some importance; now it stood silent, shrouded in sinister secrecy. A soulless place, without any hint of life behind the planks nailed across its many windows.

A drunk wandered along the pavement, paused to relieve himself by a lamp-post and stumbled on. Three men sat in a parked car a few yards from the narrow walk; other cars waited nearby. In the first car Miguel lit a cigarette.

'Put that out!' hissed Hartridge from the back seat.

Miguel stubbed out the cigarette and began to fidget with the keys in the ignition. His mouth felt like sawdust, his stomach knotted itself in his throat. He wished Stefan Stervic would stop watching him.

Judas.

The 'cattleman's kingdom' crackled softly in Miguel's pocket. After the scene in the library he had locked himself in his father's study and rifled through the desk. In the bottom drawer he had discovered a stack of road maps. He had taken one of the Laguna Grande area, torn off the section roughly corresponding to the map he had drawn and copied the kidnappers' notes on it. His hand shook, but he had managed to produce a credible forgery. He had even crumpled the map and stepped on it for greater effect. It was the sort of thing that happened in the adventure stories he used to read as a boy – but it was no adventure now. He felt withered and numb. Sickened by the conversation Stervic had repeated, even more sickened by the realization that events were beyond his control. He could continue being clever and faking innocence, but for how much longer? A day at the most, if he was lucky.

Miguel stared blankly through the windscreen. He tried to think coherently, but all he could think about was Hartridge's confident 'We'll get the bastards alive, señores. We'll make them talk.' *Christ, what am I going to do?* Keep on being clever and stop them from talking. Ram his fear and frustration and disillusion down Olga's throat. Choke her on the 'cattleman's kingdom'. His lungs craved for a smoke. The road map had been a good blind. No one suspected anything. He had told Servic's story about finding it in the restaurant convincingly to Gastón and Hartridge without going into dangerous details; the architect had corroborated his half truth and had made no remark on the substitution of maps.

Miguel turned his head uneasily. The pale, hard eyes watching him showed no mercy. Stefan Stervic would not betray the cattleman's son, but he demanded redress. At any price. Miguel swallowed and looked away again; after a moment Stervic returned to his vigil of the deserted house.

'You're sure this is the place?' whispered Hartridge without moving his lips.

Stefan nodded. 'Here's one of them now.'

A man came around the side of the house, keeping to the shadows. Once or twice he glanced over his shoulder as he hurried down the walk; a shabby leather shopping bag dangled from his right hand. The car parked in the shadow of a plane tree did not spell danger until he came abreast of it; then there was barely time for a brief, strangled cry before Hartridge's hand closed over his mouth.

XII

In the dreary space that had once been a living-room Oscar Raskowitz looked up from the gun he was cleaning.

'What was that?'

'Cat,' said Boyle.

The minutes ticked by.

'What the hell's keeping López?' muttered Raskowitz impatiently. 'All he had to get was a package of *maté* and some bread, not buy out the goddamned *almacén*.'

Boyle grinned. 'Maybe he went to that fancy delicatessen on the avenue. He's been complaining about your cooking lately.'

'I don't trust López.'

'Relax. Look at me, I'm not nervous.'

'You've been muttering your god-damned prayers. I heard you.'

Half an hour came and went. Raskowitz wondered with increasing irritation about López.

XIII

He would not have been comforted to know that López stood spreadeagled against a wall in a nearby alley. A gun was jammed into the small of his back and another one pressed against his right temple. Four men crowded around him, others waited in the shadows. A torch flashed in his eyes.

'How many in the house?' whispered a voice.

López sneered.

'Which room is Luciani in?'

He laughed. The questions had been going on for quite some time.

The voice hissed softly. 'Take him back to the car and soften him up a bit.'

López began to sweat. He knew all about the softening-up game. Not one of the group waiting for their bread and *maté*

451

was worth it. He made a sick little noise in his throat and began to stammer.

'There's four. Luciani's upstairs.'

The gun prodded the small of his back. 'How do we get in?'

López told them.

XIV

Raskowitz gave up complaining and went to sleep on a broken-down sofa. The room was cold and damp; rats scrabbled nervously behind the woodwork. He dreamt he was in his father's house. The beautiful seven-branched candlestick Grandfather Samuel had brought over from Israel stood in the middle of the dining-room table. The flames from the candles were red, like blood. His mother's face swam through them; she was weeping.

'What have you done, Oscar? What have you done?'

Raskowitz muttered uneasily and opened his eyes. The paraffin lamp on the floor spluttered. He turned up the wick and lay back again, watching long yellow shadows dance along the walls.

What have you done?

In the kitchen Zorro gave the pipes under the sink a savage kick; they hiccoughed and a gush of rusty water streamed from the open tap. He filled the kettle and slammed it on to the only gas ring that worked. Waiting was the worst bit. He didn't mind the danger or the risks, but waiting got on his nerves. He sat down at the kitchen table and began to roll a cigarette. His mind was blank. There was no one to ask him what he had done.

Rulo Boyle leaned against the basin in the upstairs bathroom and prayed. It was the only place he could do so without any of the others mocking his devotions. He prayed for courage because he was too restless to pray for anything else. The words raised whispering echoes of fear in the silence. *Lord have mercy. Lord have mercy.*

It wasn't what he had meant to pray at all.

He washed his hands several times and went out into the narrow corridor. A room to his right, one to his left. At the far end the stairway and the 'cell' where they kept Luciani. Next to it a door and another corridor. The house was a maze of doors and corridors; at the end of this one a long, narrow stairway plunged straight down into a cellar.

Boyle went into the 'cell'. Olga sat on the edge of the chair, her gun trained on the bed. He glanced at their prisoner and shook his head. Not good. Not good at all. Luciani's colour was bad and he breathed with difficulty. Sometimes, when struggling to wake from his drugged stupor, he talked. Rambling phrases, names, private ghosts . . . Boyle smiled grimly. In the fight for people's dignity a man's secret sins were of little consequence, but he pitied them just the same.

'Luciani doesn't look too good,' he remarked. 'We'd better ease up on the drugs.'

Olga hunched a thin shoulder. 'It won't make any difference one way or the other.'

'Meaning?'

'He's as good as dead. When they hand over the money we'll send him back – in a fruit crate.'

It was the tone of her voice. Impersonal and matter-of-fact, as though discussing the weather. Boyle swallowed. Ten million dollars bought Marcos Luciani a cheap coffin made from a fruit crate. What did it buy them? The figure on the bed stirred, showing the whites of its eyes.

'No one ordered us to kill him,' said Boyle slowly.

'So he was trying to escape. What's the matter – your holy boy's conscience bothering you?'

He was about to reply when Zorro yelled.

XV

Hartridge's plan hinged on surprise.

López was to knock on the back door as usual; when it opened Hartridge and his men would rush through. Four would tackle downstairs, three would reach the first floor and capture the guard. There was a chance he might shoot Marcos Luciani before they made it, but the risk had to be taken. Surprise was vital. There could be no hesitations. Hartridge wanted the kidnappers alive, he wanted their prisoner released – he wanted the operation over and done with as quickly as possible.

Later Enrique Hartridge maintained the plan would have worked – if Miguel hadn't interfered.

Miguel had to prevent the kidnappers from talking. He had to ram the cattleman's kingdom down Olga's throat. He had to be clever and save his own skin. He insisted on joining the assault group instead of waiting with Stervic in the car.

'It's my responsibility to help free my father!' he whispered wildly.

Hartridge tried to argue him out of it; Stefan Stervic said nothing. Miguel grew frantic; in the end Hartridge agreed because time was running out. He ordered Miguel to stay at the back and keep out of firing range. Then, deploying five of his men to cover the front of the house, he led the rest around the back.

'Now!' hissed Hartridge, giving López a shove forward.

The kidnapper licked his lips and tapped on the door. They heard a chair being pushed back; after a moment a voice growled softly, 'Who is it?'

'López. Open up.'

The door opened wide enough to show a thin man silhouetted against the dim light.

'What the hell took you so long?' grunted Zorro. 'The Jew thought you'd run out on us.'

He stepped back to let López through and Miguel charged past like a madman.

Zorro yelled and hurled a lamp after him. The lamp hit the floor and exploded in a sheet of white flame. Oscar ran towards the kitchen, saw Hartridge's men and raced for the stairs. The lamp in the front room rocked unsteadily on its base and toppled over. A fiery river licked the sofa and spread across the dry, wooden floor. Boyle opened the 'cell' door a crack and closed it quickly.

'What's going on?' barked Olga.

'Security forces. We've got to get out of here! For God's sake, forget Luciani!' he rasped, grabbing her as she moved towards the bed. 'Let them have him! The cellar's our only chance!'

'Not alive!' she panted, struggling to break lose. 'They won't have him alive!'

And then Miguel appeared.

He burst through the door, pale and dishevelled, too distraught to be aware of his surroundings. All he could see was Olga. Her mocking dark eyes and the mouth that had kissed him for betrayal, not for love. The mouth laughed at him now and Miguel forgot to be clever. He lunged at Olga, shaking the map in her face.

'Why?' he sobbed. 'Why did you trick me?'

She spat in his face.

On the bed Marcos groaned and opened his eyes. Spectres grappled in a nightmare of smoke and shadows. Two men and a woman, he thought. One of the men looked like Miguel – but perhaps it was part of the nightmare as well. Marcos started to cough. Smoke filled his nostrils and crowded into his lungs. He called to Miguel for help, but his nightmare voice was too feeble. The spectres continued to battle. He began to slide into darkness again – a frightening, unreal sensation of being carried along by invisible hands. A voice that sounded like Boyle's whispered in his ear.

'Get yourself down the stairs! Hurry!'

The hands pushed him urgently and were gone. He tottered forward, groping blindly for the light flickering beyond the edge of darkness. A woman's face and a gun appeared over a railing; the spectre that was Miguel leapt out of the smoking shadows behind her.

'*Olga*!'

She laughed. The sound of her laughter and his son's voice followed Marcos as he fell through a wall of fire. They were to remain with him for a very long time.

CHAPTER THIRTY-TWO

I

The assault on the house in San Justo did not take more than seven minutes.

It was long enough for Zorro and Oscar Raskowitz to die, for Marcos Luciani to plunge headlong down the stairs, for Hartridge's men to drag him from under blazing timbers and out of the burning building. Then the flames found a stack of ammunition boxes in an alcove next to the kitchen. The blast ripped a gaping hole in the front; a second blast all but demolished the first floor. The next morning the firemen sifting through the wreckage uncovered the map of the cattleman's kingdom. Only the edges had been scorched; the rest was miraculously intact and marked in a bold hand.

The Cattleman's Kingdom. Enjoy it with me. Miguel, the Cattleman's Son.

When confronted with the map López declared that it had been drawn by Luciani's son for Olga Raskowitz. The man was crazy about her, López added in disgust. Everyone knew that.

'Did he belong to your group?' demanded Hartridge.

López rolled his eyes. 'He drew the map, didn't he? It was his idea. He gave us all the info. Those fancy touches – he told the Raskowitz woman they were a family joke.'

The ice-eyed landlady confirmed that a man looking like Miguel Luciani had frequently visited Olga. Pressed by eager reporters she coloured her account with a series of improbable but suitably sinister details which soon found their way into the popular press. CATTLEMAN'S SON MEMBER OF TERRORIST GANG. Someone remembered the shooting at El Ombú. Questioned again by Hartridge, López admitted that his group had carried out the attack. He didn't know who had given Olga Raskowitz her instructions, but he did know that the cattleman's son had supplied her with details about the area. The headlines

456

blazed with excitement. MIGUEL LUCIANI MASTERMINDS KID-NAPPING IN LAGUNA GRANDE AREA. SON OF LOCAL RANCHER LEADS DOUBLE LIFE. THE FRONT'S RICH RECRUITS.

The Front, which had never heard of Miguel Luciani, quickly washed its hands of the Raskowitz fiasco and remained silent. The telephone at Barranco Rosales did not stop ringing.

II

Cristina arrived in Buenos Aires the day after her father's rescue. Isabel and Gastón met her at the airport; on the way back they told her about Miguel.

'We don't know why he joined the Front,' said Gastón. 'He never showed any interest in politics – and certainly not in any terrorist movement. I can't understand it.' His voice faltered. 'Miguel had everything he wanted.'

Perhaps not, reflected Cristina sadly. Perhaps he didn't want the life that was planned for him. I didn't and I eloped. Perhaps Miguel didn't have the courage to break away. She suddenly remembered as if it were yesterday the old chapel in Milan and Miguel coming up to her while Papa and Lorenzo exchanged insults in front of the altar. *Hang on to your piano-playing husband, little sister. You're the only one of us who has any guts* . . . Cristina brushed away bitter tears.

'And Papa?' she asked. 'How badly hurt is he?'

'Badly burned and his right hip's broken,' replied Isabel unsteadily. 'The terrorists kept him drugged for weeks, Cristina! Chained to a bed and drugged. The man the security forces caught boasted about it.' Her eyes blazed. 'They treated Papa like an animal!'

'We don't know if he'll make it,' added Gastón. 'All we can do is hope and pray.'

III

For days Marcos drifted uneasily through a shadowy no-man's land between life and death. Voices made hollow echoes inside

457

faceless blurs, hands touched him, he felt pain. A white-robed nun kept constant vigil on the threshold of his shadows; whenever he opened his eyes her whiteness loomed over him like an impassive, immaculate wall. Sometimes the wall prayed. He could hear rosary beads clicking like relentless drops of water on his pain. Click, click . . . Hands touched him again and the beads receded into silence.

Sometimes the whiteness looked like Angela.

He tried to tell her about Jimmy, struggling for the words in her own language because then she would understand. The words echoed very clearly in his ears; it seemed strange that she could not hear them. Perhaps he wasn't talking to Angela after all. Perhaps the whiteness that clicked Hail Marys and touched his pain was Death.

He sobbed in terror because he was afraid of dying, but no one heard him.

IV

The family practically lived in the waiting room at the hospital. Angela came down from Los Alamos to be with them. She sat unnaturally still on a chair in the corner and stared at the floor with dull, unseeing eyes. No one seemed to know what to do. They made desultory small talk to wile away the time, but their minds hovered around the motionless figure lying behind a closed door halfway down the corridor. Mercedes's rosary beads clicked endlessly. The hands on the large wall clock above the lift ticked off minutes and hours with monotonous precision.

Tiger perched on the edge of his chair and watched the clock with agonized eyes. Another minute went by. Grandfather was still alive. Every time the minute-hand moved he expected someone to come and tell them Grandfather had died. His dark eyes filled with tears. He gulped them back because men of thirteen didn't cry in public, and shifted his gaze from the clock to the window. Rain streaked the panes; a sorry wind soughed around the corner of the building. Tiger shivered. He felt very much alone and afraid.

At some point during the afternoon a voluminous nun in

antiseptic white bustled into the waiting room and looked around the tense, questioning faces.

'Señora Morgan?' She smiled with depressing reassurance as Angela started up nervously from her chair. 'Would you like to come with me? He's calling for you . . .'

'Why her?' Clara's voice grated sharply. 'She's not family! I want to see him. He's my father. *I want to see him*!'

The family chorused in embarrassment. 'Sit down, Clara!'

'No!' She rushed over to the door and tugged at the nun's arm. 'He's my father! I was with him . . . I heard . . .' Her voice rose hysterically as Angela pushed past. 'I know about you two! I heard what he said to my mother . . .'

'Shut up!' cried Isabel and slapped her.

Clara dropped on to the edge of a chair and began to rock, moaning and hugging her thin body. The rest of the family looked away; after a moment small talk broke out again. The clock crept towards five and the lift doors opened to disgorge a crowd of anxious visitors. A warm fragrance of flowers and perfume and cigarette smoke briefly masked the sterile smell of hospital. Clara's whispers made a dreary counterpoint to the uneasy hum of conversation.

'I hope he dies . . . I hope he dies . . .'

Tiger stared at her in angry astonishment. 'How can you want Grandfather to die?'

She turned her back and began to tear at her nails. Tiger continued to stare. Clara wanted Grandfather to die. It was monstrous. He couldn't understand her hatred, but he would never forget what she had whispered.

V

Angela sat on a wooden bench in the hospital chapel and stared at St Anthony.

Prayer was difficult because she could not remember any set formula for despair, and ad-libbing to God seemed like a waste of time. God had more important things to do than to listen to the confusion of a woman's heart. What could she tell Him? Thank you, God – now that Gladys is dead everything will be A OK Jack? Trite blasphemy – and anyway, Gladys was not really

459

dead. She haunted her husband with unforgiving, relentless fury. She twisted a knife into his conscience, reminding him of their last, bitter quarrel and of the death that had come in the midst of his anger. Isabel said that Clara had repeated the quarrel word for word . . . Angela closed her eyes.

Gladys was not the only ghost.

Marcos's letter had reached her on the Tuesday after Easter. She had read it through several times and put it in a desk drawer. There would be plenty of time to think about an answer. All he wanted was a chance to see her. She told herself that there was no harm in giving him that chance – but the demon that remembered denial and moments of truth kept putting off the reply until it was too late.

What the hell did moments of truth matter when Marcos was so close to death that his own brother-in-law had administered Extreme Unction? She wanted him to live – but perhaps that was blasphemy as well.

A hand touched her shoulder very gently.

'Will you come with me a minute?' asked Pedro in a low voice.

Angela rose quickly and followed him, her throat tight and dry with sudden fear. They walked in silence down a short corridor, passed through swinging doors and came to a window overlooking a small walled garden. Rain fell dismally on a white marble Virgin; beyond the wall a tall line of buildings cut uneven edges against an indifferent sky. Angela stared at them and waited.

'I've just come from seeing Marcos,' said Pedro, offering her a cigarette. He lit his own slowly, deliberately nursing the flame. 'He is very distressed in his mind. He seems to think for some reason that you believe he shot your husband.'

Angela swallowed.

'Do you?'

'Of course I don't!' she cried. 'Marcos tried to take the gun, but Jimmy turned it on himself and pulled the trigger. I – I saw it happen from the window.'

'Does he know that?'

She watched the rain splashing off the Virgin's marble mantle. 'He once asked me if I – if I thought he had killed Jimmy. I didn't answer him.' Her voice shook. 'Do you want to know why?'

There was a pause before Pedro asked gently, 'Do you want to tell me, Angela?'

Somehow it was easier to talk to Pedro than to God.

VI

One small detail about the Luciani case bothered Enrique Hartridge. At the time it had slipped through his fingers; later other cases claimed his attention and it was not until several months afterwards that he called on Stefan Stervic.

The minute flat by the docks belonged to yesterday. Hartridge glanced around a spacious living-room on the top floor of a new fourteen-storey building. Black leather upholstery and stark white walls. A pen-and-ink nude hung above the sofa, there were startling touches of scarlet in the carpet and curtains. A picture window took up the entire east wall. Palermo Park lay below; beyond it the river stretched like a silver sheet towards the horizon. Hartridge grinned.

'Do pretty well for yourself, eh?'

'I designed the building,' replied Stefan dryly. 'This is part of my contract.' He handed the commander a drink. 'What did you want to see me about?'

'That map Miguel Luciani gave me. Where did you find it?'

'Where he told you. In the restaurant.'

'What about the other one? The one he signed. Listen, Stervic,' when there was no reply, 'Miguel Luciani's dead. We know he was mixed up with the Front. What I want to know is why there were two maps.'

'How the hell should I know?'

'You're sure about the one he gave you?'

'That's right.'

Hartridge pulled out a cigar, inspected it thoughtfully between his fingers. 'We found a cellar under the ruins,' he said after a moment. 'A tunnel leading from it surfaces about a hundred yards away in an old warehouse.'

Stefan Stervic's pause was a fraction of a second too long. 'No one could have left that house alive,' he said. 'You yourself barely got out in time. The place was blazing like Hell. Besides – your men found bodies all over the place afterwards, didn't they? Luciani's cousin told me all that was left of him was his watch.'

461

Hartridge struck a match. 'Why do you think a man like Miguel Luciani would join the Front?'

Stervic shrugged but did not reply.

'Did you know him well?'

'No.'

'Know his father?'

'We met several times.'

They eyed each other for a long moment and then Hartridge gave a dissatisfied grunt. 'Tough on the family. I hear Marcos Luciani's been flown to hospital in the States.'

VII

Marcos's doctors had recommended the move because he was not responding well to treatment. To make matters worse there was the publicity surrounding the case; once he returned home from hospital it would be impossible to keep him isolated. The doctors warned the family that Marcos was neither physically nor emotionally strong enough to stand the strain. Several months away from everything should give his body and mind a chance to recover; by the time he returned, the 'cattleman's son' would no longer be news.

Mercedes and Cristina went with him; at the last minute they convinced Ana Inés to go as well. Isabel offered to take care of the girls while she was gone.

'Ana Inés's parents want her to move in with them,' she told Angela. 'Ana won't leave Barranco Rosales. She's quite stubborn on that point. She doesn't think it's right to take the girls away from Papa, especially when he – when he doesn't have much else worth remembering about Miguel. Besides, Mercedes will need help. Yvonne's not much use when it comes to running a house and Clara . . .' Her voice tightened. 'Well, you know all about Clara.'

'Yes,' replied Angela wearily. 'I know about Clara.'

Isabel glanced around the family living-room. Her eyes lit on the *Four Seasons at Play* and she smiled faintly.

'Strange, isn't it? So many things have happened to all of us since Papa gave those figurines to Mama – yet they remain the same. All the upheavals and changes, all the sorrows – nothing

462

has affected them. They continue to be as beautiful and graceful as they were when Mama placed them on the mantelpiece. I suppose there's a moral in that somewhere.'

They both gazed at the white porcelain figurines dancing in the lamplight.

'I don't think Ana Inés was surprised about Miguel,' said Isabel slowly. 'She loved him and she's shattered – but deep in her heart I don't think she's really surprised. Perhaps because he had already destroyed all her illusions.'

'Perhaps,' agreed Angela.

VIII

In June 1974 Perón, politically embarrassed by the wave of violence, disowned the militant Left in a raging speech delivered from the balcony of the Casa Rosada. It was a raw winter afternoon and the ageing dictator caught a chill.

Three weeks later he was dead.

Perón's death left a vacuum of political uncertainty. His third wife was no Evita and his followers were bitterly divided amongst themselves. Three-digit inflation continued to fuel economic nightmares, violence from both the Left and the Right fuelled fear.

It was a time of darkness for Argentina – and its shadows were very long.

IX

Marcos spent five months recovering in the States; when he was strong enough to travel the chief surgeon of the hospital suggested a period of convalescence in the Caribbean.

'My wife and I own a place on the island of St Lucia,' he told Mercedes. 'Modern bungalow with all the conveniences, private beach, no noisy neighbours. We want you to stay there as long as is necessary, Miss Luciani.'

Mercedes smiled wanly. 'You are very kind.'

'Plenty of warm sunshine, fresh air and good food,' grinned the surgeon. 'I want all of you to relax and try to forget what happened. Those are doctor's orders.'

They spent six weeks relaxing in the sun and watching the changing hues of a limpid, turquoise sea. They tried to forget. They talked about local customs and people, the number of fishing boats out that morning, or what Ana Inés should buy for the girls. Only once did Marcos break the pattern, and that was when he and Cristina were sitting alone together on the beach.

'I never received your letter,' he said abruptly. 'I would have answered it at once.'

She reached over and squeezed his hand. 'It doesn't matter now. Will you come to Milan soon? You have a beautiful granddaughter. She's longing to meet you.'

'Yes,' he said after a moment. 'I'll come to Milan.' Another moment went by. 'You're happy, aren't you?'

Cristina met her father's eyes. 'I'm very happy with Lorenzo, Papa. I don't regret marrying him and if I had to do it over again I would – in the same way.'

Marcos sighed. 'I suppose you would,' he said wryly and began to talk about fishing boats.

The day he began to complain about the food the three women knew it was time to go home.

X

Rain had fallen all night and most of the morning, but by early afternoon the sky above La Catalina was a clear cobalt blue. The car swerved to avoid a large puddle, bounced on to the grass and careered to a jolting holt in front of the main gate. Tiger revved the engine and winked at his grandfather.

'Not bad, eh? I've been practising all winter.'

'Mind the fence post,' laughed Isabel from the back seat. 'Last time you dented a fender your father had hysterics.'

Tiger dismissed his father's hysterics with a lofty grin and began to open the door. Marcos stopped him.

'I'll get the gate,' he said. 'I want to walk in the park a while.'

Isabel bit her lip. How did one handle Papa these days? The doctor had said he must take things easy. He needed plenty of rest and no emotional stress. A gradual return to normal activity – the more gradual the better. It was very sound medical advice, but try convincing Marcos Luciani of that. The week since his return to Argentina had been a stubborn tug-of-war between medical caution and his bitter impatience; in the end the doctor grudgingly capitulated because Marcos Luciani was driving everyone mad.

'Do you really think you should walk right now?' asked Isabel. 'You're not supposed to overdo things and it's been a long ride.'

'That's because you wouldn't let me drive on the highway,' broke in Tiger indignantly. 'We would've made it in half the time if I'd done that.'

'Nonsense. Papa,' as Marcos climbed stiffly out of the car, 'please come on with us to the house. Lie down for a while and after tea we'll go for a walk.' Her smile coaxed. 'I have a surprise for you – a very nice one.'

He managed to return the smile because she sounded so much in earnest. 'Your surprise can keep for half an hour, can't it?'

He was so pathetically stubborn. Isabel looked quickly away from the bleak, scarred face and swallowed a sudden lump in her throat. 'At least use your crutches,' she pleaded. 'Just to keep the strain off your hip.'

Marcos drew himself up. 'I don't need crutches.'

'But the doctor . . .'

'Stop nagging, Bela.' His dark eyes glinted briefly at his grandson with a trace of lost humour. 'Try not to knock down all the trees on the way, Tiger. They take a long time to grow.'

He limped off before there were any more arguments. In half an hour he would be caught up in La Catalina's familiar rhythm once again – but not now. Now he needed to be alone with the trees and the dark, pungent smell of moist earth. He needed to fill his eyes with a billowing sea of blue lucerne, a herd of grazing cattle, a windmill flashing in the sunlight. Overwhelm mind and sight and senses with memories that were good. Memories that held neither bitterness nor guilt, nor the sour taste of failure and fear. Clouds drifted in shreds across the sky. He needed to see them as well and the long, sweeping fields that stretched into the horizon. He needed to know that the land and the sky were still there – that as long as they continued to be there he would find a reason for living. Marcos scooped up a handful of earth and pressed it like a talisman between unsteady fingers.

A man must love the land like he loves a woman – with his body and mind and heart.

He looked up, half blinded by tears, and saw Angela coming between the trees towards him.

She stopped several yards away, caught in a web of sunlight and shadow. Her uncertain smile spanned the years and stirred wistful memories of dreams within dreams. Marcos sighed wearily.

'Isabel doesn't think you should be left alone,' said Angela. 'I volunteered to come and keep an eye on you.'

'I must tell you something.'

'Marcos, please . . .'

'Let me finish,' he interrupted. 'It doesn't matter if you don't want to hear, I must say it. I did not kill Jimmy. You may hate me for other reasons, but for God's sake – not that one!'

The anguish in his voice shook Angela more than the sight of his scars. Her heart cried out to love him, but the love she gave now must be gentle and compassionate – a refuge from bitter ghosts and wounds of the soul. Her voice echoed softly through the silence.

'I don't hate you.'

'Do you believe me?'

'Yes.'

Marcos stared at her, trying to read past the light in her eyes. Some day there might be a new beginning, perhaps not. He didn't know. It wasn't important just now. Even the many other things he wanted to tell her could wait. A gust of wind tossed the branches overhead, turning blue-grey leaves to silver in the sunshine. He hesitated for a moment and then held out his hand.

'I want to walk in the park a while. Will you keep me company, *gringuita*?'

'For as long as you want me to.'

He laughed unsteadily. 'That may be a long time. I walk slowly now.'

Angela came forward and took his hand firmly in her own. Her grasp was warm and strong.

'I have all the time in the world,' she said. 'We'll walk slowly together.'